The Neanderthal Within

Historical Context Edition

The Neanderthal Within

Historical Context Edition

by

Robert Mitchell

Seacrest Literary Press

Corvallis, Oregon

ISBN: 979-8-9940116-2-1

This book is a work of historical fiction, supported by nonfiction research essays. The narrative is fictional; however, the interspersed essays are based on current scientific research, archaeological evidence, and scholarly interpretation. Some analytical sections include reasonable reconstructions and the author's interpretations where definitive evidence is limited. Every effort has been made to present the nonfiction material accurately.

First Edition

Published by Seacrest Literary Press
Corvallis, Oregon, USA

Cover design by Robert Mitchell

Printed in the United States of America

Table of Contents

Preface

This expanded edition of *The Neanderthal Within* is divided into twenty-five story-chapters and six *Historical Context* essays. Each essay provides the most up to date scientific understanding of the time, culture, and evolutionary backdrop of the events and characters in the chapters that follow the essay.

These reflective context pages are meant to provide the reader with scientifically accurate information about the world in which the story unfolds. They are not part of the story itself.

The Neanderthal Within is a story that begins at the point where science and imagination meet—a story that seeks to transform archaeological discovery into living human experience.

Forty thousand years ago, two human lineages lived side by side in southern Europe and western Asia. *Homo neanderthalensis*—the Neanderthals—had thrived in Europe for hundreds of thousands of years. Then, beginning about 65,000 years ago, *Homo sapiens*, who had evolved in Africa, began slowly migrating northward into Neanderthal lands. For a time, the two species met, mingled, and left traces of themselves in one another's bloodlines.

Those meetings marked a turning point in the story of humankind. They took place at a time when one lineage—*Homo sapiens*—was better adapted to survive the challenges presented by a changing climate, while the other—the Neanderthals—struggled against forces that would soon find them teetering on extinction.

DNA evidence now confirms what many scientists long suspected: Neanderthals and *Homo sapiens* interbred. Their encounters—likely complex, intimate, and filled with the full range of human emotions—left genetic traces that remain with us today. More than ninety-nine percent of people living now carry small but unmistakable fragments of Neanderthal DNA—living proof that such interbreeding occurred and resulted in the birth of many mixed-lineage children. Through those children, the Neanderthal lineage did not vanish entirely, but endures as a faint genetic legacy within nearly all modern humans.

This novel imagines one of those encounters—an unlikely friendship that tested the boundaries that had been set by tradition and by instinctive caution.

The Neanderthal Within is the story of a Neanderthal woman and a *Homo sapiens* man—both young and curious, and each brave enough to step beyond the limits of their clans. They lived in a time ruled by custom and driven by the need to survive. Choices had to be made, and in those choices, human emotions inevitably played their part.

From their joining comes the possibility of a child—equal parts Neanderthal and *Homo sapiens*. Until modern biological discoveries, such a union between two distinct human lineages would have seemed almost unthinkable—the possibility of a shared genetic inheritance between two separate human types.

The child in the story is fictional, but the interbreeding between Neanderthals and *Homo sapiens* is not. Our DNA reveals that mixed-lineage children once lived in Ice Age Europe. Though their lives were often brief and difficult, enough survived for their legacy to endure—a legacy now woven into the genetic threads of who we are.

The Neanderthal Within is not a definitive account, nor does it reconstruct scientific certainties. What it offers instead is an imaginative lens: a way to feel closer to those moments when two distinct peoples came face to face and chose to support and learn from each other in the larger story of survival.

To imagine today how they might have lived 40,000 years ago is to honor both Neanderthals and *Homo sapiens*. The story reminds us that curiosity, courage, and care for one another are not inventions of modern times, but ancient companions of the human spirit.

By imagining the lives behind the fossils and the data, we glimpse what evidence alone cannot show—what it may have felt like to stand at the threshold between two human lineages, not knowing that one was nearing its end and the other just beginning to ascend.

Even though each lineage was uncertain about both the present and the future, they faced their fates with courage and determination.

Neanderthals may have vanished as a people, but nature found a way for their legacy to endure. Fragments of their DNA remain within the human genome—the complete set of genetic material in each living person.

As a result, traces of Neanderthal lives are not found only in fossils in the earth, but within the cells of each of us.

The Neanderthal Within honors this legacy. It tells of Ahna and Rynn—two fictional lives whose crossing of paths feels both destined and compelling, revealing a rare moment in the shared past of two human lineages who came together and changed what it meant to be human.

Note for Readers:
Section dividers (✵ ✵ ✵ ✵ ✵ ✵) indicate the conclusion of a group of story chapters or a historical context essay, and signal a natural pause before the book continues.

Characters in the Novel

The following list is provided for quick reference.

Neanderthals

Ahna – adolescent woman, intelligent and thoughtful
Goma – man elder, leader of the clan
Marga – woman elder, friend to Ahna
Tov – man elder, quiet, says very little
Enu – man elder, skilled maker of stone tools
Yaya – woman elder, keeper of the clan's stories
Vahra – woman, clan's healer
Akran – Ahna's brother
Ghar – man hunter, Ahna's cousin
Bren – woman elder, friend of Ahna
Zarn – man, hunter
Yana – young woman

Homo sapiens

Rynn – adolescent man, curious and a born leader
Marek – oldest man elder, clan leader, nearing death
Omak – second-oldest man elder
Terah – woman elder, Rynn's aunt
Duma – man elder, highly respected by all
Tamik – adolescent man, Rynn's same-age friend
Lauq – man hunter, known for his courage
Lurea – clan's healer
Banek – man, skilled hunt leader
Plen – man elder, quiet, deliberate in speech
Daul – man hunter, courageous and loyal
Torg – outspoken man hunter, forceful in manner
Yana – young woman

Historical Context I

First Encounters

"We are the product of millions of ancestors who adapted, endured, and imagined."
—source uncertain, often attributed to Carl Sagan

The Existence of Human Lineages

By 40,000 years ago, two main human lineages lived in overlapping regions of Europe and western Asia: *Homo sapiens* and *Homo neanderthalensis*—commonly referred to as Neanderthals. They were not simply different tribes or cultures; they were two closely related types of human beings.

Scientific Naming Conventions

In keeping with widely accepted rules of biological nomenclature, *Homo sapiens* is written with the genus name *Homo* capitalized and the species name *sapiens* in lowercase.

Additionally, scientific names of all recognized species are written in italics to maintain consistency, clarity, and international standardization across scientific disciplines and publications. This convention—followed throughout this book—reflects the universal system of classification used in biology to accurately identify living and extinct species across time, geography, and evolutionary history.

A Note on Denisovans

A third, much smaller lineage, Denisovans (*Homo denisova*), lived in northern and eastern Asia during the same period. Many scientists consider them a subspecies or close sister group to Neanderthals.

Today, Melanesians—people from island regions in the southwestern Pacific Ocean—along with Aboriginal Australians and some populations in Southeast Asia, especially Papua New Guinea and the Philippines, carry the highest known Denisovan ancestry, roughly 3–6% of their DNA. East and South Asian populations carry smaller traces, usually 0.1–0.5%.

The total Denisovan population appears to have been small, and there is no evidence of their presence in Ice Age Europe. For this reason, Denisovans play no role in this volume and are not discussed further.

The Human Story, Divided and Shared

Today, the presence of Neanderthal DNA in modern humans is proof that Neanderthals and *Homo sapiens* were capable of interbreeding and having fertile offspring. The discovery of the interbreeding of the two lineages has led many scientists today to consider Neanderthals and *Homo sapiens* a single species that simply exhibited regional variation. Others, however, regard Neanderthals as a unique species, distinct from *Homo sapiens*, that evolved along a separate but closely related path.

Evidence indicates that *Homo sapiens* and Neanderthals evolved from a common ancestor—*Homo heidelbergensis*— a tall and resilient species that itself evolved in Africa roughly 700,000 to 800,000 years ago.

By about 450,000 years ago, *Homo heidelbergensis* had separated into two branches, one spread throughout Europe and one spread throughout Africa.

The European branch slowly began evolving into Neanderthals—a powerfully built human lineage that adapted to the cold Ice Age temperatures of what is now Europe and Western Asia.

During the tens of thousands of years that followed, the African branch of *Homo heidelbergensis* slowly evolved along its own path, eventually giving rise to *Homo sapiens* by about 325,000 years ago—a taller, lighter human lineage that adapted to warmer climates in the southern continent.

As evolution continued on both continents, each lineage developed traits best suited to its own environment. Anatomical, behavioral, and genetic differences became so pronounced that neither Neanderthals nor *Homo sapiens* would regard *Homo heidelbergensis* as a potential mate.

Indeed, there is no evidence that either human lineage ever interbred with *Homo heidelbergensis*, though the presence on Earth of all three overlapped for roughly 100,000 years before *Homo heidelbergensis* went extinct.

Neanderthals inhabited Europe for about 400,000 years before *Homo sapiens* began migrating from Africa 60,000 years ago. By 40,000 years ago, the populations of the two lineages in Europe—Neanderthals and *Homo sapiens*—may have been comparable in size, with estimates suggesting on the order of fifty thousand individuals each.

DNA evidence from modern humans confirms that *Homo sapiens* and Neanderthals did interbreed, even though many scientists still regard the two as distinct species. These lineages are now understood as closely related branches of the same human family tree, sharing sufficient genetic compatibility to produce fertile offspring. Most people alive today outside of sub-Saharan Africa carry traces of Neanderthal DNA—small but unmistakable signatures of a shared past. These fragments persist within our genetic code and stand as living evidence that such interbreeding occurred, likely within the full range of human experience, including cooperation, emotional attachment, conflict, and daily survival.

Different Physical Characteristics

Although Neanderthals and *Homo sapiens* shared a common ancestor, each lineage evolved on a different continent and faced different environmental pressures.

In the colder climates of Ice Age Europe, Neanderthals developed compact, muscular bodies that conserved heat, broad noses that warmed frigid air, and strong bones suited to the physical demands of hunting large Ice Age animals. Their world consisted of dense forests and caves, bitter winters, and the ever-present need to hunt and stay warm.

The light skin of Neanderthals likely aided vitamin D production in low sunlight, while their large chests and powerful lungs supported endurance in the cold. These features, refined over hundreds of thousands of years, enabled Neanderthals to become highly specialized for survival in harsh glacial environments across Ice Age Europe. They evolved, in every sense, to become remarkably resilient survivors shaped by cold, scarcity, and long winters.

By contrast, *Homo sapiens* evolved in the warmer, more varied environments of Africa. Their taller, leaner bodies dissipated heat efficiently, and their darker skin protected them from intense sunlight. A more flexible diet and a wider range of habitats encouraged adaptability, complex tool use, long-distance travel, and cooperation.

As they migrated to southern Europe from Africa, *Homo sapiens*, rather than physically evolving for colder climates, relied on behavioral adaptation, planning, and innovation—traits that allowed them to inhabit the homelands of their cold-adapted cousins and eventually to adapt to the full range of the planet's environments.

Skeletal remains show that 40,000 years ago, *Homo sapiens* men averaged about 5'6" and 150 pounds, and women about 5'2" and 125 pounds—slightly shorter and lighter than modern humans, but more muscular, hardier, and better adapted to cold, Ice Age life than modern *Homo sapiens*.

Neanderthal men averaged about 5'5" and 178 pounds, and women about 5'1" and 150 pounds—shorter, heavier, and more powerfully built than early *Homo sapiens*.

Broad shoulders, thick ribcages, and heavily built limbs gave Neanderthals a compact form ideal for conserving heat and generating power—a near perfect adaptation to Europe's cold, harsh Ice Age climate at that time.

After *Homo sapiens* began migrating from Africa to Europe 60,000 years ago, the two human lineages lived side by side for 25,000 years, and at times they met—until Neanderthals became extinct around 35,000 years ago. Many novels, including *The Neanderthal Within*, envision evidence-based encounters between the two lineages.

Different Tongues, Shared Meaning

One of the earliest barriers between *Homo sapiens* and Neanderthals would likely have been communication.

Both lineages had large brains—Neanderthals, in fact, had slightly larger average brain volume than *Homo sapiens*. Today, scientists believe that both lineages might have developed rich—but different—languages.

There is evidence that both Neanderthals and *Homo sapiens* possessed the FOXP2 gene—a gene known to be critical to speech and language—giving both groups the capacity for spoken language.

Homo sapiens had a modern larynx and a descended voice box, allowing for full-range vowel and consonant sounds needed for complex language, storytelling, and abstract thought. Their vocal tract supported syntax and varied intonation essential for nuanced communication.

Scientists believe that when *Homo sapiens* reached southern Europe after migrating from Africa, they brought with them a complex language that supported long-range hunting strategies and coordinated group movement— techniques that relied on coordination and reasonably accurate verbal communication.

Neanderthals likely communicated verbally as well, but evidence suggest that Neanderthal conversations might have relied as much on gestures and facial expressions as on spoken words. Neanderthal communication was likely shaped by the close-range hunting skills they developed to enable stealth, where silent cooperation was essential for safety and success.

The words that Neanderthals did use on a daily basis were likely few and carefully chosen. Talking may have carried deep emotional weight—words used not for idle chatter, but to convey meaning and exchange essential information.

Now imagine two adolescents—one from each lineage—meeting for the first time. One might have said a word whose meaning left the other confused. The other might have crouched slightly, signaling friendliness rather than threat. Hands could lift, a head tilt, breathing slow to show peace. A single friendly gesture may have become the first communication between Neanderthals and *Homo sapiens*.

Today, gestures, more than words, are often used to communicate between people who don't speak the same language—and between people and pets. A baby reacts warmly to a smile, more so than to words. A dog may know a pointed finger, but not spoken words.

In gestures and simple sounds, Neanderthals and *Homo sapiens* could "speak"—at least a little—to one another, even during a first meeting. And it is very believable that within a short time of meeting, the two lineages would be able to communicate both in gestures and verbally.

Fiction and the Problem of Language

As the author of *The Neanderthal Within*, I faced a question that authors of similar novels have faced: How should a story of two human lineages represent communication?

Historically, two adolescents in the Ice Age—a young Neanderthal woman and a young *Homo sapiens* man— would almost certainly not have shared a common spoken language, especially at their first meeting.

Words attempted during a first meeting would likely not have been understood, but gestures might have eased the way. We know that over time, members of the two lineages managed to communicate well enough to live together, raise children, share knowledge, and survive.

For the sake of storytelling, I decided, as most other authors have, that after a brief introduction, all characters would speak a shared, simplified language—a common compromise in situations where communication between individuals would likely need time to evolve.

This does not imply that the two lineages could quickly develop a shared language. Rather, it is a narrative device used by most authors to help readers enter the world of the characters and imagine what might have happened, while minimizing disruption to the flow of the story.

Authors who imagine and write about the encounters between Neanderthals and *Homo sapiens* are not attempting to reconstruct precise communication. Rather, they seek to convey the emotional and social realities of lives past. Their goal is to help readers imagine those vanished worlds in ways that feel human, immediate, and meaningful.

What the Science Suggests

The real-world evidence behind such a meeting is both sparse and tantalizing. Here's what the evidence tells us:

- Populations of both Neanderthals and *Homo sapiens* coexisted in southern Europe during the final 5,000 years of Neanderthal existence—40,000 to 35,000 years ago.

- The two lineages interbred, and most people today carry between 1% and 3% Neanderthal DNA. Less than a fraction of 1% of humans—a minority with ancestry in sub-Saharan Africa, where Neanderthals and mixed-lineage adults didn't travel—carry no Neanderthal DNA.

- Neither Neanderthals nor *Homo sapiens* were brutish or mindless. Both human lineages buried their dead, cared for their sick and injured, and made tools. Archaeological sites show evidence of healed fractures and of elderly Neanderthals and *Homo sapiens* who lived far past the years of hunting, clear proof that others looked after them with deliberate, sustained care.

- Both Neanderthals and *Homo sapiens* may have used pigments such as red ochre, worn ornaments, and etched marks onto stones and cave walls. Many researchers view these traces as symbolic behavior, suggesting that both groups could think abstractly— perhaps even creating early forms of art that carried meaning within their communities.

- Neanderthals often hunted in dense forests, close-range, using strength, hand axes, and thrusting knives and spears. *Homo sapiens* more often hunted in open areas using spears and atlatls—spear throwers. Both *Homo sapiens* and Neanderthals hunted through coordinated group strategies.

- Groups of both lineages were small and vulnerable. The average size of a group (band) of Neanderthals was from 10 to 20 individuals; a group of *Homo sapiens* usually numbered 25 to 50. In such small and fragile communities, a single injury, a failed hunt, or a disease could tip the balance toward survival or collapse. A single meeting between two adolescents might not have happened often, but any meeting could be deeply consequential.

We can never know exactly how a young *Homo sapiens* man and a young Neanderthal woman might have spoken to one another on first meeting. But we know that many such couples found a way to communicate, to have and raise a child, and that such mixed-lineage unions ensured that Neanderthal DNA lived on, long after the Neanderthal lineage ceased to exist.

A Meeting of Two Worlds

The setting of many Ice Age novels—40,000 years ago— was a pivotal era in human history. Neanderthals still occupied much of western and central Europe, while *Homo sapiens* had already spread across much of the continent, with additional groups continuing to arrive in waves from

Africa. While the population of Neanderthals was slowly decreasing, the population of *Homo sapiens* was rapidly increasing. The climate was cold, vegetation was shifting, and mammoth and bison herds were roaming the steppes.

Over the thousands of years during which they lived near one another, genetic evidence confirms that *Homo sapiens* and Neanderthals did interbreed. Yet during the roughly twenty-five thousand years when they shared regions of what is now Europe, members of each lineage looked physically distinct enough to regard one another with a wary mix of curiosity and caution.

To the characters in Ice Age novels, the contrast between the two lineages may have seemed striking. What they perceived, though, were the differences between two distinct human groups, not the regional physical variations seen among Homo sapiens today.

Forty thousand years ago, at the time of *The Neanderthal Within* and similar novels, the "foreignness" of another person lay not in skin color or hair texture, but in shared, group characteristics: slope of the forehead, breadth of the chest, deeper timbre of a voice. The wide range of physical variation seen today within our single species of modern humans had not yet evolved.

The Origins of Human Diversity

Many people who read about Neanderthals and *Homo sapiens* living side by side for thousands of years wonder if the physical differences between these two human lineages have anything to do with the diversity we see today.

Were the differences between those two lineages—body shape, facial structure, bone strength, and adaptation to cold—somehow the beginnings of the variations now seen among modern peoples? Did differences in appearance between Neanderthals and *Homo sapiens* give rise to the later differences we see now: skin color, eye shape, hair texture, and other features that are characteristic of today's many ethnic groups?

The answer to all these questions is an unequivocal no. The contrasts between human lineages belong to an earlier chapter of evolution. The observable and genetic diversity we see in *Homo sapiens* today emerged much later, long after Neanderthals—and Denisovans—had vanished from the human story.

Between 35,000 years ago and today, only *Homo sapiens* remained. At that time—the time of the disappearance of Neanderthals and Denisovans—*Homo sapiens* all looked pretty much the same wherever they lived. Their features reflected a common ancestry and a long evolution in Africa rather than regional variations. For a time, our species was remarkably uniform, descended from shared African roots and united by more similarities than distinctions.

But as groups of modern humans (*Homo sapiens*) spread across the continents, climate, sunlight, and diet began to shape them in new and lasting ways. Over thousands of generations, those gradual environmental pressures slowly produced the range of skin tones, body forms, and facial features that are characteristic of the rich diversity of humankind today.

The Long Birth of Diversity

The earliest visual differences among modern humans first began to appear after groups became isolated in distinct environments over the next few thousand years, gradually adapting to the varied climates they encountered.

When *Homo sapiens* first entered Europe and northern Asia, they retained the dark skin of their African ancestors. Gradually, as sunlight weakened at higher latitudes, mutations reducing melanin began to spread. This allowed more ultraviolet light to reach the skin and produce vitamin D—vital in regions where winter could last most of the year.

Genetic studies suggest that the light skin tones of Europeans did not become widespread until between 20,000 and 10,000 years ago, near the end of the last Ice Age —long after the last Neanderthals had disappeared.

In contrast, groups who remained closer to the equator —across Africa, India, and southern Asia—retained their protective dark pigmentation.

What Neanderthals and *Homo sapiens* Never Saw

If we could step back 40,000 years into the Ice Age, we would not see the full range of human physical diversity visible today. Populations of early *Homo sapiens* were more physically uniform, with features adapted primarily to the warmer, high-sunlight environments of Africa. The wide variety of eye colors, hair textures, and skin tones familiar to us today developed gradually over tens of thousands of years as *Homo sapiens* spread into varied environments.

The scattered clans of migrating *Homo sapiens* who lived among Neanderthals could not have imagined the variety that was to follow. They lived before humans had spread to every corner of Earth and long before nations had formed.

When the Neanderthals disappeared about 35,000 years ago, a single lineage—a single species—remained: *Homo sapiens*.

Almost uniform in appearance, *Homo sapiens* carried within their genes the potential for every variation of skin, eye, hair, and body shape that would one day develop as modern humans spread across every inhabitable continent, eventually reaching the most remote corners of the globe.

Across the Land Bridge and Beyond

Between 23,000 and 16,000 years ago, small groups of *Homo sapiens* crossed the Bering land bridge from Siberia into North America, following herds and seasonal migrations across the vast, frozen tundra. They reached South America by around 14,000 years ago, moving gradually through river valleys, scattered forests, and open grasslands.

Over time, adaptation to local climates—desert plains, high mountains, and tropical forests—gradually shaped the characteristic copper and bronze tones of Native American peoples found throughout North and South America, reflecting long environmental adaptations.

All of this remarkable diversity, though vast and deeply rooted, unfolded within the last twenty thousand years—a mere blink in the long span of evolutionary time.

The Continuum of Humanity

As has been discussed, most visible differences among people today developed within the last 20,000 years. Genetically, humans around the world—no matter where they live—are about 99.9 percent the same. Even though many populations carry small inherited fragments of Neanderthal DNA, modern humans remain remarkably alike, sharing virtually all of their genetic material with one another.

We are all descendants of African ancestors, many of whom migrated north 60,000 years ago. Some of those ancestors arrived in southern Europe and met and interbred with Neanderthals, and those unions left a small but lasting imprint on our—*Homo sapiens*—DNA.

With the extinction of all other human lineages except *Homo sapiens*, a new kind of diversity began—one marked not only by mixed ancestral genes but also by emerging regional variations in skin color, facial features, and body shape unknown in the time of the Neanderthals.

Chapter One

R ynn stepped lightly through the underbrush, his bare toes finding the patches of moss between scattered leaves and cold stones. The late sun threaded through the trees in golden beams and caught the edges of his shaggy dark hair and the lines of his lean frame. A sharp breath of wind moved the branches above, carrying with it the scent of something—not a familiar animal, not an impending storm. Something else—new, enticing.

He paused. Listened.

The forest was full of noise, followed by moments of eerie silence, the way it often was. Creaking wood. The faint humming of insects. The occasional rustle of things unseen. But now there was something more, and Rynn felt it—not something heard, something perceived through other senses, including a tingling down his spine.

He was fifteen summers, strong and sure-footed, but still learning to tread between boldness and danger. The tracks of a roe deer had led him to the riverbank, where they vanished. Although crossing was beyond his usual wandering, he drew a deep breath and waded across at a shallow place near a bend of the river—answering the call of the forest across the river he had never dared enter.

He saw her before he understood what he was seeing.

At first, she looked like a shadow bent over something on the ground—thick shoulders, tangled reddish-brown hair, wide fingers brushing the leaves aside. She was crouched by a small tree, not far from the water, one foot planted firm, one hand resting on her bent knee. Then she moved—and Rynn stopped breathing for a few moments.

She turned her head and her eyes met his.

He found her pleasant to look at, but she was not a familiar sight and surely not one of his people.

Her eyes widened. She froze, just as he did. They stared across a space of maybe thirty paces, each too surprised to move. Rynn did not raise his spear. She did not run.

The girl—if that is what she was—had a broad, low brow, powerful limbs, and a nose that struck him as wide. Her body was young but heavy with muscle, her chest broad. Her face displayed a calm unlike anything he had seen before—neither fear nor confusion, but an unreadable stillness. She watched him as he watched her: not predator, not prey. She must be one of the *others* he'd heard about— the different type of people living in the forest.

Then slowly—so slowly she seemed to move like the swaying of a stout tree in a strong wind—she lowered her eyes, raised her palms, and turned them toward him.

Rynn had no words. Not because he could not speak, but because something deep inside told him to wait.

He crouched, lowering his spear until its tip touched the ground. He mirrored her movement, opening his hands. His heart thudded as if it wanted to break away from him.

They stayed there, facing each other across the small clearing on her side of the river. Ahna had only just stepped from the edge of the forest, where the trees pressed close. Nearby, her clan's camp lay hidden within the trees.

The space between them was strewn with ferns, fallen branches, and drifting leaves caught in a restless wind.

To each, the other was neither child nor adult, but something in between, and something different.

The nearby forest stayed quiet except for the wind.

Ahna looked to the side, toward a tree where the bark had been peeled away. She picked up something from the ground—a bit of bark, a stick, or maybe a mushroom cap—then glanced back at Rynn. Her expression was unreadable. She turned it over in her fingers, then placed it on a flat rock on the ground and stood.

Her rising was slow, careful. She looked at him once more. Then, with a single backward glance, she slipped into the trees and vanished.

Rynn remained frozen, the image of her burned into him—not just her face, but the whole moment: the stillness, the stir in his emotions.

He exhaled a long, thin stream of air that he had held in his lungs.

Back at the camp that night, Rynn said nothing.

He sat by the fire and warmed a strip of dried meat and then chewed it without thinking about its taste. Around him, the others talked.

His friend Tamik sharpened a spearhead.

Rynn's mother braided sinew.

A woman elder hummed a chant under her breath as she rubbed crushed roots on a child's skin to ease a rash.

As he ate, Rynn's eyes strayed to the tree line across the river, just about as far as he could see from the shelters. Out there, beyond where the firelight ended, the forest waited—dark, close enough to be inviting, but a little unsettling.

He could not explain what had happened earlier on the far side of the river. Now he was not even sure he had seen what he thought he had seen. Yet something told him she was real. Not a dream. Not a spirit. A girl—different in her looks, unfamiliar in her ways.

He remembered the way she had not been afraid—not of him, not of being seen. There had been no panic, no alarm. Just that look. Cautious, but calm.

She showed no fear. Did she think she understood him, somehow, without knowing anything about him?

The next day, Rynn rose early. Before the sun could be seen above the horizon, he took a strip of smoked fish, tucked a small flint knife into his belt, and slipped away from the camp, saying only that he wanted to check a trapline.

No one stopped him. Being young, he often wandered and sought adventure. But he was old enough to be aware of danger and to be trusted not to take unnecessary risks.

His feet found the same mossy trail as before, and he passed the grove where birch trees grew thin. He walked until he saw the clearing on the far side of the river—he found it empty now.

He waited and an unfamiliar longing settled over him.

As he waited, the wind shifted once. A squirrel chattered. Nothing else. No one came.

She was not there.

He crossed the river and crouched by the same tree where she had been. The ground had been disturbed. Her handprint—or maybe the trace of her foot.

Then he heard a soft footfall behind him.

He turned.

She was standing at the edge of the forest, partly shadowed by pine and birch trees, watching him.

He was taken by surprise—but this time, he did not freeze.

He rose, slowly, arms loose at his sides. She watched him. Neither smiled, not yet.

He took a single step forward, then another.

At first, she did not move. Then she took several steps forward and did the unexpected—she held out her hand, palm flat. A stone lay in it.

Rynn stepped forward carefully, uncertain. She knelt and set the stone on a mossy log between them, then backed away again.

A gift?

He moved to the log and picked up the stone. It was a smooth river stone. Remarkable because it came from her.

He looked up to thank her—and she was watching his face, as if searching for something in his expression.

"I…" he began, then stopped.

She tilted her head.

He tapped his chest. "Rynn."

She narrowed her eyes and tried to imitate the sound he had made: "Rynn."

He smiled.

She tapped her own chest. "Ahna."

"Ahna," he echoed.

And now they were no longer strangers.

She crouched again, mimicking him, their knees nearly level with the moss between them. They stared, eyes alert but no longer wide with tension. The air between them had changed and was no longer charged with alarm, but now was alive with anticipation, perhaps hope.

Rynn turned the stone over in his hand. It was ordinary —smooth, cool. It might have come fresh from the river, or she might have used it to press hide flat, or to grind seeds. Its use did not matter. She had given it to him.

He looked around. Nearby, a small patch of wild mint clung to a decaying branch. He carefully pinched off a sprig. With two fingers, he held it out.

Ahna watched him. He leaned forward and set it on the log where she had placed the stone before. Then he backed away, mirroring her earlier motion.

Her hand moved slowly toward the sprig. She sniffed it. Crushed a leaf between her fingers. The scent spread.

Ahna's eyes shifted toward a distant ridge. She seemed to know the land in a way that was not just memory. It was as if she could feel the hills and rivers without needing to see them.

Rynn felt an odd tug in his chest—a wish to understand the land the way that she might.

Did she think of hills and rivers as hers, or did the land and its forests belong to everyone—or to no one?

A pinkish-brown jay cried sharply overhead, then went quiet. The forest held its breath, and so did they.

This was the first time Rynn had ever been on this side of the river. Now he was here, close to the dangers of the forest, with someone not of his own clan—his own kind. And she felt no urge to fill the silence, as his people did. The quiet was not empty, but not what he was used to.

Her eyes flicked to his, and for a moment she smiled.

Not a full smile, not the grinning kind children in his clan made. Just the barest curve of recognition. The kind that hinted, "I see what you are thinking."

A dragonfly drifted through the space between them, its wings catching the light like shards of river ice.

Rynn watched it hover, dart, and then vanish into the shadows.

The air was cool here, layered with the scents of damp moss and old bark. As they sat there, the river meandered over the rocky-bottom shallows near the bend—a winding ribbon of water murmuring softly.

Rynn wondered if Ahna followed that sound when she came here. Did she have places she liked to go, the way he did?

She rose to her feet and stepped into the trees. But this time, she did not vanish. She stood beneath a crooked pine and looked back at him, as if she were waiting for him to follow, still not moving away.

He rose and started toward her, slowly.

They walked together—half apart, yet not turning away —through a low glade where the ground dipped and small birds darted between limbs of nearby trees.

They did not speak—not yet.

After walking a short distance, Ahna stopped. She crouched beside a fallen tree and pulled something from a hollow rot in the trunk: a long bone, smooth and bleached. It was not fresh. Not dangerous. She held it lightly, as if it were a toy or a tool.

Rynn shook his head, signaling confusion.

She tapped a nearby rock with the bone. Once. Then twice. A rhythm.

He knelt, curious.

She tapped again. Then gestured to him.

He looked around, then picked up a dry stick and tapped back. Two beats. Pause. One beat. She answered: one. One. Two.

He grinned. It was a game. Or maybe just a sharing, a way of getting to know one another.

The sound echoed in the surrounding forest, fading into the trees and undergrowth.

They continued for a time, tapping bone and stick in rhythm against stone, inventing and sharing patterns of sound. Beneath the bark of the fallen tree, they uncovered a beetle, then paused to watch a bird glide across the sky.

Rynn twisted plant fibers to make her a length of twine. Ahna sniffed the strands and laughed when they frayed apart in her fingers. Then, with a single slow pull of her nail, she showed him how bark could be stripped clean.

They did all this without using many words other than the most important words—their names.

The sun began to lower in the sky, its angle turning the forest a shimmering green again. Shadows stretched, and the warmth faded.

Ahna looked at the darkening forest behind her, then back at Rynn. Her body shifted slightly—he could tell she was about to leave.

He stood. "Ahna," he said, his voice low.

She nodded.

He tapped his chest to remind her. "Rynn."

She gave the smallest nod of her head. Then, crouching, she drew a mark in the dirt with her finger—two short lines crossing. Then she looked at him, pointing at the symbol, then back at herself.

Was it her sign? Her mark?

He knelt and made his own mark beside hers—a curved line like the bend of a river, the sign his father once taught him to mark a trail. It meant "return."

They looked at their two marks, side by side in the dirt. They would vanish with the next rain, but for now, they meant something.

She stood, and so did he.

Then—just before she stepped back into the trees—she reached down, picked up the mint sprig he had given her, and tucked it behind her ear.

She smiled lightly as she disappeared into the trees.

Rynn smiled a goodbye and watched her go.

He did not mention her when he returned to camp.

Other members of his clan were tending to a small fire, cooking fish caught from the river. His ten-summers-old cousin asked if he had seen a tiger. He shook his head.

He held the smooth stone in his hand beneath the folds of his primitive tunic.

He turned it over slowly as the stars began to show.

That night, lying on a bed of fur and woven reeds, he did not sleep. He thought of the tap-tap-tap of the bone on the rock, the lines drawn in the dirt, the glint of red in her hair when the light hit it just so.

He did not know much about her, only that she was unlike anyone he had ever known.

But he knew this: She had looked at him in a strange way, not just with her eyes, but with something deeper.

And he had seen something in her.

Not a stranger.

Not an enemy—maybe a friend.

But, for now, just someone.

* * *

The next day he left camp very early and returned to the clearing across the river, hoping to see her again.

The morning sun would rise into a high, cloudless sky, the kind that would paint everything in warm hues and cast shadows even at midday.

Rynn crouched beside a patch of soft soil, running his finger around the rim of a hoof print. "Roe deer," he said aloud, not because anyone was near enough to hear, but because the act of naming felt like giving meaning to the wildness in this land—pulling it slightly closer.

A low whistle cut the air behind him. Not an insect. Not a bird. Maybe…

He turned.

Ahna stood several paces back, knees slightly bent, her lips pursed and chest rising slowly. She whistled again— this time in two short bursts followed by a low, throaty click…click…click.

Rynn raised an eyebrow, and decided to try his words.

"A bird?" he asked.

She tilted her head. "No," she said. "Owl calling fox away from nest. Protect babies."

She smiled faintly and then, with great seriousness, made the call again.

He could not help himself. He tried to mimic her.

His first attempt caused Rynn himself to laugh—too high-pitched, too wet.

Ahna's expression did not change, but something in her eyes moved, like the slow advance of a cloud across water. "You sound like a frog."

"Better than a fox that has been stepped on," he said.

She laughed very gently.

The sun warmed the back of his neck as he stepped closer. "Alright," he said. "Teach me. Owl first."

Ahna crouched low, motioning for him to sit. "Owl is short wind. Like this."

She inhaled through her nose, puffed her cheeks slightly, and gave a low "hoo" followed by a pause, then a shorter "hoo-hoo."

Rynn attempted it.

His first try startled a small lizard from under a nearby rock. His second try sounded worse than his first.

Ahna looked at him and smiled again. "Less throat. More chest. Pretend your breath is deep water, not surface wind."

He tried again. This time the sound was gentler, more rounded. A nearby jay chirped in irritation.

Ahna nodded. "Better. You learn like child. No shame."

He gave her a side glance.

"Child has open ears," she said.

Rynn mimicked the call again and again—each one closer to the original. After several attempts, they fell into rhythm—she would call, and he would answer, and sometimes the two would overlap in imperfect harmony.

They sat together, shoulder to shoulder, facing a patch of blue sky above the forest, while several birds flew overhead.

"Do those birds talk to each other?" Rynn asked.

Ahna did not answer immediately. She plucked a blade of grass and split it between her fingers.

"Yes," she said. "With sounds that carry meaning: want, warning, pain. Many animals do this."

Rynn nodded. "Once, there was a wolf that stayed near our camp. It seemed to know when someone was sad."

She turned her head slightly. "A wolf that stayed?"

He paused. "Not like the others. It did not keep away. It came close. Slept near our fire sometimes."

Ahna considered this. "A wolf that chooses people."

"Yes."

"A very strange wolf."

"Yes," Rynn said, smiling.

Ahna picked up a smooth stone and rolled it in her palm. "Once I watched a crow pretending to be hurt. It dragged its wing, calling out. Then, when a fox came close, it flew away and laughed."

"Laughed?"

"Yes. Not a noise. A feeling. It rose into the trees and dropped something on the fox's head."

Rynn chuckled. "That is not laughter. That is mischief."

She nodded. "Laughter and mischief can be close."

They fell quiet again. A breeze moved through the tall grass, and somewhere in the distance, the call of a wood pigeon rose—a slow, thoughtful sound.

Both of them turned toward it instinctively.

"I want to know what they are saying," Rynn said.

"You do know," Ahna said. "You just forgot."

He looked at her, puzzled.

"Maybe you forgot how to listen to meaning," she added.

They watched the tree line. No bird appeared.

Ahna stood. "Now you teach me."

"Teach you what?" Rynn asked.

"Something that your people say. A word or sound."

He rubbed his chin. "We have many words and sounds. Many words are sounds without much meaning."

"Then teach me one that has meaning—that matters."

He thought a moment, then said, "We have a word—*friend*. It means someone you trust. Someone who stays."

She tried it carefully. "Frr…end."

He nodded. "Yes. That is right."

Her eyes searched his. "Who do you say it to?"

"To those you do not want to lose," he answered. "When I say *friend,* it means you are close to me."

She tilted her head, considering. "My people do not use words for that. We show it by giving food. Sometimes by sharing silence."

Rynn smiled faintly. "We like the sound of words. We believe that sound carries meaning."

Again she repeated it, this time more sure. "Friend."

"Yes," he said softly. "You are."

For a while they stood without speaking, the word hanging between them. Then Ahna cupped her hands and gave the owl call, sharp and rising.

Rynn answered, steadier than before. The sound carried into the trees, and even Ahna blinked at him in surprise.

A long pause—and then an owl answered back.

Ahna looked at him. "Now you are the strange wolf."

"Maybe," he said. "But I would rather be a wolf that stays."

For a few moments, they stood in the sunlight, two young people practicing the ancient art of connection—in mimicry, in curiosity, and in the strange, laughter-tinged dance of allowing oneself to be known.

And then, as if it were the most natural thing, she turned and walked toward the darkening trees. Her voice was quiet, but the new word was strong as she spoke.

"Friend."

Chapter Two

Three days later, Rynn slipped out of camp at first light. The sky was a dull sheet of gray, the drizzle steady, soft but relentless.

The clan was slow to stir in weather like this. Fires smoldered low, and damp wood coughed smoke.

A few hunters tightened cloaks around their shoulders, muttering about the morning hunt. Rynn kept his eyes down as he walked past them, but he could feel the glance of one, then another.

A boy, about twelve summers of age, turned his head and watched Rynn with quiet interest. The boy's curiosity had him asking questions in his mind. *What hunter leaves without other hunters or a bundle of traps? What hunter walks into a drizzle carrying only a spear and a pouch?*

Rynn ignored the boy. Still, as he left camp alone with his secret, he felt tightness in his stomach. He told himself he was not breaking rules—not really. He had not been forbidden by an elder from leaving. And yet he knew well that if anyone guessed where he planned to go, or why, hard questions would likely turn to anger.

He stepped beyond the ring of shelters and let the camp fade behind him. The air outside was cool and fresh—full of the smell of rain-washed earth. He drew a breath deep into his chest and set his feet toward the river.

The ground sloped gently, and the grass underfoot was slick with drizzle. Patches of bare ground indicated a trail where many, including himself, had walked to the river from their camp. As everyone knew, the river was not to be crossed, and until recently no one had crossed—until Rynn.

Marek, the respected clan leader, had warned the clan of the dangers lurking on the other side of the river.

Heeding Marek's warning, Rynn's clan stayed on one side of the river, while Ahna's stayed on the other—where rumored dangers waited for anyone who dared to cross.

The river itself was not deep near the bend, and spread out wide. Rain dimpled its surface, sending small ripples outward. Rocks broke the surface here and there, slick and shining. The water slid around them, weaving threads of pale current over the pebbles lining much of the bottom.

Rynn paused at the bank. He bent, dipped his hand, and tasted the water—cold, fresh. For a moment he stared at the opposite bank, where trees pressed close and the forest loomed shadowy and foreboding.

Somewhere within those shadows, Ahna might be waiting—or she might not. He could not predict what she would do. He would feel uncertain until he saw her.

As he stepped into the river, the water first covered his ankles, then his shins. Small stones shifted underfoot, so he spread his toes for balance, moving slowly. Each step sent ripples outward. The drizzle blurred the surface, softening everything to silver and gray.

Halfway across, he paused and looked back. His camp was little more than wisps of smoke from damp fires, rising above the shapes of low shelters—veiled in mist and made small by distance.

He wondered if anyone watched him cross the river. If so, they would only see a distant figure wading where no one in his clan had reason to go.

As he waded farther, his heart thudded harder. He quickened his pace as his hide leggings soaked through, until he reached the far bank.

The forest greeted him with silence.

Rain pattered against leaves, filling the air with scent: pine, wet soil, decaying wood. The ground of much of the clearing was rocky, uneven, and littered with old branches and pine needles. Each step pressed softly through mud and small stones. The forest was close, trunks dark with rain, branches dripping steadily. He felt uncomfortable here, more closed in than he was used to.

Rynn hesitated and listened. No birds were singing. No voices were carrying from either camp. He stood still as the drizzle grew heavier and rain water ran down his cheek.

Then he began to walk again.

He did not follow a trail, but he knew what to look for. The signs of her passing were subtle: a fern crushed, its frond bent low; the faint print of a heel pressed into softened soil; moss rubbed smoother where a hand had caught balance against a tree. She had been here, and she now walked with confidence, as if she expected him to follow—and he suspected she knew he would.

Rynn crouched once to study a footprint. Her stride was longer than his, her foot broader, toes splayed. She moved without hesitation, sure of the land beneath her. His people were hunters of the plains, of open ground with scattered foliage, their steps trained for unbound movement. She seemed to feel at home in the shadows, in enclosed spaces of forest, in places where walking was difficult.

He studied the signs and pushed deeper. The forest canopy thickened overhead, catching most of the drizzle. Droplets gathered heavy at the tips of branches before falling with sudden splashes onto his head and shoulders. His cloak grew heavier, clinging damp to his skin. He adjusted it and pressed on.

He thought, not for the first time, of the risk. *If his people followed, if they discovered where he went and why, what then?* He imagined his uncle's scowl, the sharp questions, the accusations. "You waste your time with them," he would say. "They are not us. They are dangerous. They are *others.*"

But as he walked, the pull of curiosity overcame the grip of fear. Each step away from camp felt like a step into something larger than himself. With her, he imagined things he could not name—ways of living and thinking that felt unfamiliar, but called to him in his sleep.

The drizzle deepened into rain, steady now. Water ran down the trunks of trees in thin lines, dripping from the bark into shallow pools. The ground softened, sucking at his feet. He slowed, scanning for signs again, and saw them: a broken branch dangling on a tree, a smear of mud on a stone. She had passed here, not long ago.

A crow called harshly in the distance. The sound echoed through the wet trees, then faded. Rynn's heartbeat slowly increased. Crows often foretold of danger in his people's stories. In hers, he did not know.

He pressed on, his breath misting in the cool air. He tried to imagine what she thought of him—if she thought of him at all—when they were apart.

To her, he might seem too young, too loud, too eager in his curiosity. And yet, when close to him, she showed no urgency to leave. Nor did she show fear. In fact, she seemed to welcome his presence. That meant something.

The trees opened slightly, and he saw her.

Ahna stood twenty paces ahead, half-shrouded by mist and branches. Her stride was steady, her cloak heavy with damp mist, its fur trim darkened by rain. Her reddish-brown hair hung in wet strands against her back. She did not look back, but lifted her hand—not high, not in greeting, but low, motioning him to follow.

Rynn's heartbeat steadied at that small motion. She had expected him and waited for him to catch up. Without words, she welcomed him into her shadowed world.

He followed, bare feet squishing in the softened earth. The forest slowly closed behind them, swallowing the open ground, the river, and the camp he had left behind.

They moved in silence, Ahna ahead, Rynn close behind. Her stride never faltered, though branches clawed at her cloak and left beads of water glistening in her hair. She walked like someone who trusted the land completely, as though the forest made way for her steps.

Rynn's own steps were less sure. He pushed a damp bough aside, shook the water from his sleeve, and pressed on. He did not ask where she was leading him. He trusted her and, besides, he liked not knowing.

At last, she pushed through a curtain of moss and ducked beneath a rocky overhang. The ground there was dry, the air still. The drizzle had stopped, leaving the fresh scent of damp leaves and soil.

"Good place," she said without turning.

Rynn moved under the overhang, grateful to be free of dripping branches. He shook the wet from his sleeves, then looked around.

The space was little more than a hollow carved by time and weather, but it was enough to keep them dry. "Very dry," he said with a smile. "You come here often?"

"When storms come. When I want to be alone." She dropped to her knees, unwrapping a leather bundle. "You want to see how I make a fire?"

Rynn nodded. "I always want to see fire."

She laid out her tools on a flat stone: a sharp-edged flint, a golden-brown lump of pyrite, a soft, spongy fungus half-crumbling with age, and a bundle of dried bark shavings and grass.

"Fungus from an old tree," she explained. "Used to make an ember hot. Then it holds the heat of the ember."

Rynn crouched beside her, watching. Her hands were thick-fingered but moved with patience. No rush. No wasted motion.

"Do you carry embers from camp?" he asked.

"Sometimes," she said. "But sometimes the embers grow cold. Then I must start again."

He nodded. His people carried embers in bark wrappings, swaddled like sleeping creatures. But when they failed, they had their own ways of starting new.

She picked up the flint and pyrite.

Crk! Crk!

A spray of sparks flashed, tiny stars against the dimness. They danced over the fungus and died. She struck again, harder. Crk! Crk! A sharper sound, and this time a faint wisp of smoke lifted.

She bent close, lips pursed, and breathed one long, steady breath.

The fungus caught the spark and smoldered, burning without flame. Its heat fed the ember, which soon glowed— spreading like blood beneath skin.

She calmly tucked it into her bundle of grass and bark. Another breath. Another. The ember brightened. Thin flames curled upward as the grass and bark ignited. She added a twig, then another.

Fire!

Rynn watched closely, entranced. She made no show of it, no grin of triumph. Just steady work, as though fire were not a marvel but an old companion.

"Your turn," she said.

He blinked. "Now?"

"You show me your way."

He grinned. "My way is more complicated. More... parts."

From his pouch he unwrapped his bow drill: a curved stick strung with sinew cord, a spindle polished smooth from use, and a hearth board with a shallow notch.

Ahna narrowed her eyes at the contraption. "That? You hunt with that?"

He laughed. "No. Just for making fire. Watch."

He looped the cord around the spindle, pressed the spindle into the notch of the hearth board, and steadied it with a stone socket. Then he began sawing the bow back and forth. The spindle spun rapidly, biting into the wood.

At first it was only motion and sound—creak, scrape, hiss. His arm ached, his palm pressed firm against the socket stone.

Then smoke began to rise, thin at first, then thicker. The smell of scorched wood filled the hollow.

He tapped the blackened dust into his tinder bundle, lifted it in his hands, and blew gently. Once. Twice. . .

Flame!

Two fires now burned between them, small but alive.

Ahna reached out, touched the bow. "Strange tool."

"It took me many moons to learn," Rynn admitted. "My hands got sore. But now I can do it even in wind."

She tapped her flint. "No cord. No wood. Just stone and spark."

"Yours is faster," he said. "Mine is quieter."

She tilted her head. "You circle, I strike."

Rynn arched a brow. "How so?"

"You use trick. Rope, bow, many things. Like a dance."

"And you?" he asked.

She grinned, just slightly. "I strike hard. Sparks come. We say, 'Hit tree till fruit falls.'"

He laughed aloud, the sound echoing off the rocks in the overhang. It felt good to laugh, especially here as they warmed themselves with two fires.

They tended their flames in silence for a while, each feeding twigs and dried moss, watching the flames grow.

Then Ahna asked softly, "What is fire—in the stories of your people?"

Rynn hesitated, then said, "Some think it came from the sky—a gift of lightning. Or, a raven stole it from the sun."

Her brow furrowed. "Fire… from a bird?"

"Yes. A raven. It carried fire in its beak and dropped it after getting burned. That is why its feathers are black."

Ahna considered. "We say fire sleeps under stone. You wake it when you strike the stone. Like waking an animal. If you are not kind, it bites."

"I like your story better," he admitted.

She replied, "Fire is the same, but the path is different."

"Like you and me," Rynn said quietly.

For a long while, they listened to the crackle of flame. Rain tapped softly in the nearby forest.

"When I was little," Ahna said, "I thought fire had a face. Always looking at me. Always hungry."

Rynn smiled faintly. "I used to be afraid of it. I thought it would chase me at night, like a wild thing."

"It is wild," she said. "But we tame it—for a short time."

He shifted an ember toward her flame. "Maybe we should feed the fire as one, together."

They fed twigs between the two fires until the flames joined, the one combined blaze rising higher and brighter than either fire had on its own.

"Do you sit with your people like this?" he asked.

She shook her head. "Not like this. Sit with clan, yes. But not like this."

"Me neither," he murmured. "Not with someone... different."

She turned, eyes searching his. "I see you as the different one."

Rynn studied her. Her brow was heavier, her voice rounder, her scent more of pine and earth. But her eyes—curious, steady, lit with thought—were not so different at all. "In some ways we are different from one another, yes. In some ways, no."

After a long pause, she touched her chest, then his. "You made a fire. I made a fire. We share the same heat."

He looked at the flame. "And we share the same light."

The words settled between them.

Ahna leaned back slightly, her gaze on the flames. "In my clan," she said, "fire belongs to mothers. They guard it. Men bring wood, women keep the flame. If the flame dies, women strike stones until it returns."

Rynn thought for a moment. "With us, it is a woman elder who keeps the fire. She says the fire is a child. We feed it, clothe it with wood, and let it sleep under ashes."

Ahna's lips quirked in thought. "Yes, a hungry child."

"Or a thief," Rynn added. "It steals wood, it steals air, and if you are careless, it steals life."

Her eyes narrowed with amusement. "Like a wild animal."

They laughed softly, their voices mingling with the hiss of the light breeze blowing through the wet trees.

Not far away, a crow cried harshly and its call echoed through the forest. Rynn glanced toward the sound, then back at Ahna.

"What do your people say of crows?" he asked.

"That they follow death," she said simply. "Always near when something is about to end."

"My people say that crows often warn of fire," Rynn said. "Their black feathers are made dark from smoke, and their sharp voices warn if flames are growing wild."

Ahna considered for a moment. "Maybe both are true"

The rain thickened briefly, then softened again. The flames crackled steady, throwing shifting light into the shadows.

The hollow seemed smaller now, the forest drawn closer by shadows playing in the dimming light.

For a time, they sat in silence, each lost in thought. Two small fires between them had merged into a single brighter flame that belonged to neither alone—but to both.

They sat together, the fire steady. The drizzle had softened into mist, but neither stirred to leave.

Rynn reached into his pouch and unwrapped a small bundle. Inside lay roots, knobby and pale, their skins flecked with soil. "For eating," he said, holding them out.

Ahna raised an eyebrow. "Your digging?"

"My digging," he confirmed.

She took them, turning one over in her hand. "Good. Fire makes them sweet."

She set them on a flat stone near the flame, turning them now and then. The skins blistered, split, released a faint hiss of steam. The scent grew rich and earthy, curling upward with the smoke. Rynn felt hunger rise.

When the roots split at the touch, Ahna cracked one open, its insides soft and steaming, and handed Rynn half. Her thick fingers brushed his hand. Neither pulled back quickly—but neither mentioned it.

Rynn ate slowly. The warmth filled his mouth, spread through his chest, easing the chill of the damp air. He thought of meals at camp—noisy, hurried, crowded around the hearth. Here it was quiet, broken only by the popping and hissing of wet wood, and the nearby dripping of rain.

Ahna chewed thoughtfully. "When I was little," she said at last, "I made fire alone. Then I hid in the woods. My mother found me and struck my ear and called me foolish. She said I would burn myself or burn the forest."

She paused, poking the fire with a stick.

"Later, she told my father about what I had done. He laughed and said, 'The girl has courage.'"

Rynn swallowed. "My uncle taught me fire. He said I was too weak for hunting, so I must learn it. I proved him wrong. I learned both. But fire came slower."

"Learning fire is slow," she said. "But it stays."

For a while they ate in silence. In the nearby forest, mist curled through the trees. The caw of a crow echoed again, faint but sharp.

Rynn added sticks to the fire. "What do your people do around fire?" he asked.

"Tell stories," she said simply. "At night, always stories. Elders tell, children listen. Sometimes we sing. Fire is our center. Without it, we are often like shadows."

He nodded. "The same for us. On long hunts, we carry it with us. At night, it holds us together. My uncle said the fire is the heart of the clan. If it dies, the heart of the clan grows weak."

Ahna tilted her head. "Maybe we are not so different."

"Maybe not," he agreed.

The roots were finished, skins charred and crisp. They ate the last of them, licking soot from their fingers. Rynn wiped his hands on his cloak. He felt oddly full, though he had eaten little.

The fire snapped, throwing sparks. Rynn's voice broke the quiet. "Do members of your clan sing to fire?"

She frowned. "Sing to fire?"

He hummed softly, low in his throat. A tune rose—a chant sung on long nights, when hunters returned weary and children drifted to sleep. It was a song of rhythm and tone, and had been passed down through generations.

Ahna listened, her head tilted. After a moment, she began tapping her palm lightly against her knee, matching the beat. Then she added her own sound—a deep, wordless tone that rose and fell like the moan of wind through trees.

Their voices braided together, rough and imperfect, yet something in the weaving felt whole. The flame seemed to answer, shadows leaping into the dim light.

When the song faded, quiet returned. They sat for awhile without talking, each studying the fire.

Ahna spoke first. "My mother sang like that. No words, only humming. She said words belong only to the day."

Rynn nodded slowly. "Members of my clan say that fire listens closely at night. Words please it, and please it most of all when they are given as song."

She looked at him. "Same fire, different ways."

He smiled faintly. "Like us."

A long pause settled. The rain had thinned to the faintest mist, barely more than breath against the forest canopy. Still, neither moved to leave.

At last, Ahna reached into her bundle, pulled out a small strip of dried meat. She tore it in half, offered him a piece. "Better with roots," she said.

He accepted it. The meat was tough, salty, but the gesture warmed him.

They chewed in silence.

Rynn found himself studying the way her eyes reflected the firelight, steady and calm, as if the flames bent to her gaze. He shook the thought away. This was not the time for such wondering.

Instead, he asked, "Do your people speak of what happens if fire is gone?"

Her expression grew sober. "We say that when fire dies, night grows teeth. Cold creeps in, and we are no longer people. Only animals."

He nodded slowly. "My people say that fire makes us more than beasts. Without it, we crawl in dark."

"Then, we will let fire be our bond," she said.

He met her eyes, then looked back at the flame. "Yes."

The fire crackled, burning low now. Together, they crouched near the flames, adding twigs, coaxing it back to life. Their hands moved together in an unspoken rhythm, moving as one.

Outside, a branch snapped in the forest. Both stiffened, eyes meeting. They waited, listening. Only the drip of water followed. Whatever had moved was gone.

Ahna's shoulders eased. "The forest always watches," she murmured.

Rynn nodded. "So does my camp."

The words hung heavy.

They both knew they had to leave soon. The more time spent together, the greater the chance of discovery—from his people or maybe hers. Yet neither moved. The fire had become more than warmth; it had become a bridge.

At last, Ahna took the lead. "This place is warm—and outside waits cold. But we must go."

Rynn sighed. "Yes."

She nodded, though her eyes stayed on the flame a few moments longer. Then she began to gather her tools and wrap them in hide. Rynn did the same with his bow drill.

When the fire had burned to embers, he drew the glowing coals together. She added a few sticks, coaxing them back to flame. Together, they made one small fire again.

"Better this way," she said softly.

"One flame," he agreed.

After the fire went out, they rose. At the mouth of the hollow, mist drifted through the trees. The crow called again, distant, its cry sharp and thin.

Ahna touched her chest, then his. "Same heat."

Rynn met her eyes. "Same light."

For a moment, neither moved. Then she turned and slowly walked into the shadows of the forest.

Rynn stayed a few moments longer, watching smoke from the dying embers curl upward into the mist. He felt the pull of his camp: the familiar weight of obligation, and the newer weight of suspicion. Ahead, away from the overhang, lay the damp forest and the river he must cross.

He drew his cloak tight and began the walk back. Each step sank into the wet forest floor.

The drizzle returned, soft but steady, beading on his hair and lashes. Yet beneath the damp, he carried warmth —not from his cloak, not from the roots in his belly, but from the memory of the fire they had made together.

As he neared the river, Rynn paused to look back again. The forest stood quiet, unreadable, keeping its secrets. Somewhere within, Ahna was moving, perhaps already back with her people and tending to her duties.

He stepped into the water, the current tugging gently at his legs, stones shifting beneath his feet. The cold on his legs jolted him, and he splashed his way across the river.

When he reached the far bank, he began to laugh. He felt good. The drizzle had almost stopped, and the open ground had softened into fields of shallow puddles.

Ahead lay his camp, small figures moving in the gray distance, smoke drifting upward from several fires. He already knew what lay ahead—voices that would call to him, questions that would be asked, and daily duties that never changed.

He walked toward the camp carrying a warmth no fire could give—an ember of another kind glowing deep within.

For now, it was his alone.

Chapter Three

Rynn still felt her eyes lingering on him even now, a day after they had parted—eyes unlike any he had ever known, searching yet unafraid.

Tonight's fire crackled with a low, steady rhythm, the kind that lulled some into sleep, while others lay awake as they watched flames dance above the embers.

Rynn sat near the edge of the circle, close enough to feel the warmth on his knees but far enough that his presence would go unnoticed. After returning from his wanderings yesterday, he had kept silent, especially about where he had been or whom he had seen—wanderings that had stirred a change he carried quietly within.

He was not alone in sensing change.

"It is no trick of the shadows," said Omak, the second-oldest elder who was acting as clan leader during Marek's infirmity. Omak had been a great hunter and now, as he aged, his voice had become low and grainy. "They walk upright like us, but something is off. Their arms, their posture. And the way they move. Like boulders on legs."

"They seldom speak," another elder muttered. "And when they do, it is hard to know their meaning. More whistles, more clicks. None of the sing-song patterns we often use. Just low noises—sometimes grunts, sometimes nothing."

Rynn felt his spine straighten. His chest tightened.

He knew exactly what ones they were talking about.

"She looks almost like us," he wanted to shout. "Just a little different. Stronger maybe. But she saw me and then spoke to me, and she did not run." But he said nothing. He stayed quiet, letting the words play in his thoughts like smoke playing in the fire.

"They have been watching the mammoth herds," Omak continued. "They do not use spears the way we do. They rush in, get too close, and surround their prey. Too risky. Too dangerous. I saw four of them kill a young bison using only stones and short sticks. Brave—but foolish."

"Foolish," muttered Terah—Rynn's aunt—herself a clan elder. "Only people with no sense would fight that close. One misstep and you are under hoof or horn."

"And if they are that foolish," another said, "what else might they do? If they get hungry… desperate?"

A silence followed—a silence Rynn was not used to. Not just the missing words, but the absence of clear meaning.

"They are not like us," Terah cautioned. "That is what we need to remember."

Rynn's thoughts spun in place. Not like us. The girl—Ahna—had been different, yes. But dangerous? Foolish? He had not seen that. He had seen eyes full of wonder, not malice, not fear, not foolishness. A way of standing that spoke of strength, not threat. And above all, he had seen her curiosity match his own.

He slipped away from the fire as the elders moved on to other matters: food supplies, weather, and shelter.

By the time the stars were overhead, Rynn had walked back to the river and now sat near the bank, across the water from the clearing where he had first seen her.

The nearby tree canopy of birch had begun to whisper the promise of autumn—leaves loosening their grip in slow surrender. Not far away, the pine and fir trees saw there needles darkening, with only older needles dropping to the ground with the approaching colder weather.

As he sat near the river, Rynn let his fingers trail in the water and tried to conjure her face. It was not difficult.

She would come back. He was sure of it. But he could not wait without doing something.

The way she said words was different—that was true, but words had never been the only way to communicate. More important were facial expressions and hand gestures.

Whatever barrier stood between them, it had openings. And through those openings, meaning and intent had passed between them.

The next day, Rynn rose early—well before the first hunt would begin and well before the food gatherers had starting weaving baskets for today's foraging.

He moved like a shadow along the northern trail, the one that led to the rock ledge overlooking the river and the eastern woods. He had seen her go in that direction.

He carried a single short spear and a pouch with a few smooth stones he had found by the edge of the water—round, palm-sized, and comforting in their weight.

One of them was striped with white.

He would give that stone to her if he saw her again.

Unfortunately, that would not be today—nor the next.

Each morning for three days, he returned to the same place, watching the trees. Sometimes he left a gift in plain sight—a stone, a carving, a piece of dried meat wrapped in bark. Each time he returned, the gift was gone.

Then, on the fourth morning, she was there.

Standing still, on the far side of the river. Watching him.

She did not move forward, so once again he crossed the river. Once next to her, he reached into his pouch, took out the striped stone, and held it out in both hands.

She looked closely. A long pause.

Then she reached into the pouch she was carrying and pulled out something wrapped in hide—pieces of cooked hare—and placed it atop the flat rock between them.

An exchange. Her way of giving and receiving.

He nodded. She nodded in reply.

Rynn picked up the meat she had placed on the rock, and he left the striped stone he was holding.

Ahna picked up the striped stone, turned, and once again retreated into the forest.

* * *

To Rynn, Ahna was becoming even more of a mystery.

Later, back at camp, Rynn said little. He knew better than to mention her. Even Tamik, a friend his own age, would not understand. He might be frightened or tell the elders. And the elders might forbid any such contact. They might set strict boundaries along the river. Just to be safe.

But Rynn did not want safety. Not from Ahna.

He wanted the truth of her. He wanted to understand what her life was like, why her people hunted differently, what stories her eyes carried, what played in her thoughts. He wanted to know if her people feared his the way his feared hers, and to understand her moments of silence.

More than anything, though, he wanted to spend more time with her—to better understand her effect on him.

He began making drawings in the dirt by the river—simple shapes at first: sun, moon, river, trees. Then two figures, one taller, one broader, facing each other. A stick figure with thick arms and a wide stance. And one thinner and taller with long legs. Ahna and Rynn.

One evening, when he returned to his drawings, he saw that she had scratched her own marks next to his. Not the same shapes. Hers were angled, tighter, more deliberate. Maybe they were not drawings at all—maybe they were something else. A code? A story?

What message, if any, had she left him?

That night in camp, as the campfire danced in front of him, and the elders spoke of the danger of the *others*, Rynn stared into the embers and became even more convinced that it was best not to mention his meeting with Ahna.

Certainly for now, and maybe not ever.

He was involved in a mystery he barely understood, and he was not ready to share it.

Rynn crouched with his knees drawn up, close enough for the fire's warmth to reach him, but far enough from other clan members to be left alone.

The elders were talking again. Not loud. Not like they did when there was a recent kill to celebrate or stories to tell. This was the low murmur of ongoing concern. They were talking about the *others* across the river.

"They do not look like us," said Duma, eyes narrowed.

Omak, normally quiet about such things, had a couple of things to add. "Their chests are very broad, and necks very short. The arms—longer than ours, I think. Or maybe it just looks that way because of the way they stand."

"Posture like a bear on hind legs," muttered Banek, rubbing his calloused hands over old knees. "It is not just shape, it is movement. I watched one yesterday from the rise near the burnt cedar. Watched it bring down an injured wild goat. Did not throw a spear. Did not even use a trap. It just walked up and crushed its head with a rock."

A grunt passed through the four elders sitting there.

Rynn pretended to rub his foot, listening intently. They were talking about *them* again. The *others*. The ones who lived across the river. The ones who did not belong.

Rynn heard comments from the elders, but not all bad.

"They are reckless," said one.

"They seem very brave," said another.

"Brave or not, they may be a threat," Duma concluded.

Rynn's hands curled around his ankles. The girl—Ahna, as she had called herself—was not reckless and did not pose a threat. She was brave and a bit curious, perhaps a little cautious. She had not looked frightened. Just… alert.

Rynn felt like a puzzle she was trying to understand. She taught him some things, and he taught her too.

"They speak in a different way," said Duma, the elder who knew more sounds than most birds. "They use words than are unlike any I have heard. Many sound like noise."

"No rhythm to it," Banek added. "No repetition. No call and response. How do they pass on anything that way? How do they teach the children?"

"They may not teach by talking," said Terah, an elder who is considered quite wise. "Maybe they just show. Maybe they do not *think* like we do."

A long silence followed.

Rynn felt his skin prickle.

Not think like we do!

What other way is there to think?

Omak offered more. "The point is, we do not know what they are, and even Marek, when he spoke of them, advised caution."

Rynn swallowed hard.

Omak continued, "Maybe they are something between people and animals. We need to be careful. Keep the little ones close. Tell the hunters to watch their flanks. And if anyone sees them again, do not approach. Return. Report."

Rynn took a deep breath. He had already *approached*. He had stood a few paces from Ahna, and looked into her eyes.

And now, sitting in the red light of the fire—surrounded by those who had raised him, taught him, fed him, and cared for him when he was sick—he understood things about his people that made him uncomfortable in ways he had never felt before. Now, he had secrets he might never be able to share with them.

Later that night, lying on soft hides placed atop woven reeds, he listened to the sounds beyond his shelter.

The wind stirred the distant canopy and brought with it the soft hiss of pine needles brushing each other. The sound had once comforted him. Now it whispered doubts.

Not like us.

Not people.

Dangerous.

And yet... her face, so close to his in the forest light. The way her eyes had followed his hands. The way her brow had furrowed when he smiled.

There had been recognition.

Maybe not of a common past—but of being.

The next morning, before smoke rose from the first fire, Rynn slipped out of the camp. His heart fluttered in his chest—not from the early chill. He was ignoring clan rules, taking a risk he was not supposed to take. A risk that felt a little like betrayal.

He followed the path to the river, stopping where it faced the ridge below which the canopy opened. This spot, near the bend of the river, was where he had first seen Ahna. He did not know where her camp was, exactly. But he remembered where she had walked into the trees, close to where the sun rose each morning over the mountain.

He did not expect to see her that day. He even thought that she might have decided never to see him again.

He waited until the sun stood high above the mountain before leaving, and planned to return the next morning.

Which he did... on several mornings.

Each morning, he returned to the same place and walked along the edge of the river. Sometimes he circled, slowly, marking nearby trees with stones to remember his route. Thinking about her gift to him, Rynn left a single piece of smoked deer meat wrapped in birch bark and set it on a flat stone that marked their first meeting place.

The next morning, the deer meat was gone.

At first, he was not sure that Ahna had taken it. Could have been a fox, or a hungry raccoon.

But a new stone sat in place of the meat. Shaped smooth by the river. Darker than those he had seen before.

Now he knew for sure. She had left a reply.

After he returned to camp, Rynn was quieter than usual. He took on chores without asking: repairing spears and fetching water—and said very little while doing so.

But his eyes stayed watchful. Listening to the talk.

The elders were still worried. A small hunting party had returned from the north with news of strange footprints— heavy and wide. They had found bones from a recent kill of a small hare—stripped of meat, but no tools nearby. No tracks of a hunting party.

"Beasts, not men," someone said.

"They leave no signs of planning," Omak said. "No pits, no markers. Just kill and vanish."

Rynn bit the inside of his cheek. The girl was not like that. She did not act without planning. Had she not taught him and learned from him?

On the following day, as he knelt near the river and traced patterns in the wet sand, she appeared.

Not with noise. Not with motion.

He had looked up, and she was simply there.

Standing across the water, near a maple tree whose branches had begun to turn orange.

Her posture was the same—shoulders slightly forward, arms loose but alert.

She crossed the river and came to where he sat and looked at his drawings in the sand.

Then at him.

At first, Rynn did not move.

Then, he reached slowly into his pouch, pulled out another striped stone, and placed it in the sand.

As he did so, he saw her eyes narrow slightly. She stepped forward. Slowly. Deliberately.

Then she crouched, picked up a thin twig, scratched something into the dirt beside her feet, and looked up.

Not a shape Rynn recognized. Just lines—crossing, curving. It meant something to her. He knew that much.

Then he crouched and copied the lines into his own patch of dirt. As best he could. They were not perfect.

When he looked up, she was watching.

And then—just slightly—she smiled.

Or something close to it.

Rynn knew Ahna could talk. He had talked with her. But, she did not speak often. Meeting without using words seemed fine with her. This was different from the noisy meetings of people in his clan.

She did not stay long. Pointing to herself and then toward the forest, she crossed the river and was gone.

Later that evening, Rynn sat near the fire again, but the talk was of weather now. Smoke could be seen in the west, a sign of lightning fires in the hills. He nodded along, but he was not listening. His mind was near the river. With her.

He did not know what he was doing. Did not know what any of it meant.

But he had crossed a line.

And for now, he could not tell anyone.

He hoped he would see her again. He would learn. He would make sense of it.

Even if no one else believed him.

Even if they said she was not like them.

He knew better.

She was… a little different. Yes.

Like a different kind of star.

* * *

To Ahna, Rynn's movements played in her memory long after they parted: strange, smooth, like a river flowing gently over small pebbles. Strength did not lead him.

Rynn was not designed, as she was, for strength, nor did he seem designed for quiet movement. She could move through the undergrowth as easily as water finds its way downhill—regardless of what was in the way. She could overpower beasts that were her people's source of food.

She knew the forest was alive around her, and she could listen to its many voices—twigs snapping under deer hooves in the distance, crows calling from high nests, a single branch creaking in the breeze. She heard it all, while he did not seem to notice the forest speak.

But what she kept thinking about—what she couldn't push from her mind—was the pull she felt toward him.

The *tall one*. Long legs, narrow arms, smooth face. Eyes always full of something unspoken.

Rynn.

She was not sure the word he spoke was his name. But she used it in her mind—a private sound he had uttered, like wind finding its way through narrow rock. To her, it meant *thin but full of light*.

They had met again today, first across the river, and then on the same side. He had given her another stone, marked and striped, like the back of a beetle. He had copied her marks into the dirt. Clumsily. But with care.

She had watched his hands—long, quick, almost delicate. So different from her own hands—strong and powerful fingers useful for building shelters, killing game, and stripping meat from bone. His hands reminded her of river reeds—flexible, sensitive to current. Hers were strong branches.

When he crouched, he folded at the knees like a young antelope. Neat, balanced. She moved more from the hips, a wider sway, her center lower. Her people were closer to the ground, their weight settled.

And yet… he moved with awareness. With care.

He did not smell like her people either. Not just the smoke and oil and blood they all carried, but something else. Something sharp. His skin was cooler when he had stood near her that first day. She had felt it across the air. A kind of cool radiance. She did not know what to make of it.

His face was smooth. No ridge above the eyes—and his eyes seemed more open. He looked surprised all the time.

And when he looked at her, he did not hide it.

Among her people, you did not stare. You glanced, then turned away, unless you were challenging or grieving. But he looked directly into her eyes, into her face. Like trying to see what was behind it.

And he had smiled.

But how he smiled was the strangest thing.

Teeth, shown deliberately. Not in threat. Not in hunger. In an emotion without shape in her understanding. Her people did not show teeth that way. Not unless they were about to bite. . . or giving a warning.

She had felt something twist inside when he did it.

Not fear.

Something else.

Curiosity, yes. But deeper. Something she did not have a word for.

That night, curled on a bed of dry moss beneath a hid covering, Ahna listened to her uncle Goma speaking to the clan elders by the fire.

"The *tall ones* are not like us," he said. "Long bones, narrow skulls. Their voices are high, like birds. Their only weapons fly from far away. They do not touch the animals the way we do. They throw things at them."

Laughter.

"They are clever," said Marga, a loved and respected woman elder. "But they are weak. They are not shaped to climb trees or crawl in caves. And their bones break easily.

I saw one stumble while running on uneven ground. Their heads are too high above their feet."

Ahna said nothing. She turned toward the opening flap of her shelter, eyes open. She thought to herself: *Weak?*

She had seen strength in him—not of body, but of attention. He watched like a hunter as if what he saw in each moment mattered.

She did not know if she believed what the elders said. Maybe they were right. Maybe his kind were fragile—quick to wound, slow to fight up close. But she and Rynn had crossed a boundary that neither clan approved of. He had stood still when she emerged, and neither had run.

Or thrown a stone—or barked a sound.

He had opened his hands, and she had opened hers.

She would continue to meet him, but not mention it.

And she would keep watching, learning.

She knew he was not like her, but he was something special, and she wanted to find out more.

The next day, when she saw him at their meeting place by the river, her thoughts and feelings were mixed.

Ahna's eyes fixated on him for a moment, weighing something for which she had no word. Then she turned and looked into the shadows between the trees, the place she would soon return. But her feet did not move.

In that stillness, she felt a quiet change—small as the shift of light across a stone, yet enough to notice.

Ahna did not see Rynn now as the same person she had first seen in the clearing. Something in the way he stood, in the way his hands rested at his sides, seemed different.

The wind stirred, and the scent of mint reached her again. Thinking of Rynn, she placed a mint sprig behind her ear—she had continued to wear one ever since the day he had first given her one. She looked at him, but she did not smile. She also did not turn away.

Rynn smiled, his hands resting loosely by his sides.

Ahna stood just beyond his reach, her eyes holding his for a moment longer than before. The air between them felt different now—like the forest after rain, heavy and close.

She glanced upward, following the slow arc of a hawk circling high above the trees. She noticed that Rynn had followed her gaze. They watched together, in silence, as the bird turned, then rose, its wings steady against the wind.

Ahna crouched, picked up a fallen feather—grey and tipped in black—and rolled the quill between her fingers. She stepped forward and placed it on a flat rock lying between them. No words. No gesture demanding thanks. Just a small offering, like the hare before.

She watched as Rynn studied the feather. He touched it once, then lifted it carefully and slid it into his tunic.

From somewhere deep in the forest came the low, rising call of the owl again. Ahna turned her head toward the sound, and this time she knew Rynn understood without asking—she was listening for meaning.

The hawk wheeled once more overhead, and for a moment, they both stood as if the movement of the hawk and the call of the owl were meant for them.

Chapter Four

Many days after last meeting Ahna in the clearing near the river, Rynn returned, hoping to see her again. To his joy, she was there, but she looked different now. Smudges of red ocher streaked her cheeks, and coarse fibers of twine hung from her belt. When he stepped into view, she looked at him, pointed toward the trees, and waited.

Rynn felt a bit awkward and uncertain.

He hesitated.

Rynn knew that he was not supposed to venture to the far side of the river. He knew that the elders would never approve of him following Ahna into the dense forest. But she waited patiently, and there was something in her eyes —the quiet promise of safety and invitation.

He crossed the river and followed.

They walked in silence, weaving among pines, firs, and birches. Ahna moved silently, like a cat artfully stalking its prey—avoiding dry leaves and branches and slipping past thorn brush. She kept her head slightly askew as if listening to something the trees were saying.

Rynn did his best to follow quietly, though his footfalls were heavier than hers. She glanced back a few times to check on him—not impatiently, but thoughtfully.

After a long walk, they reached a high ridge where craggy rocks jutted out like an ancient skeleton of stone. Below it, a narrow gorge stretched out in both directions. The air smelled sharp, alive with pine resin, fresh blood, and something else—something more primal.

She motioned for Rynn to crouch.

Down below, across the gorge, four figures knelt behind a low screen of branches and rocks. The hunters he saw were her kind—the ones his people called the *others*.

Even at this distance, Rynn could see difference—thick chests, muscular limbs, low-to-the-ground stance. Their faces were painted the color of the ground. Weapons were held in the shadows. They were waiting.

Ahna did not move closer. She had brought Rynn to this place to observe how her people hunted. That was all. She stayed beside him, silent, eyes fixed on the hunters.

Then he saw it, not long after he smelled it: a carcass—a young ibex—spread on the ground like an offering, soaked in its own blood.

The carcass was absolutely still. Nothing moved.

The silence was ominous. The kind of silence that spoke of things destined to happen. Even the wind seemed to pause. Rynn's pulse began to rise.

Then, not far from the hunters, the deep grass shivered.

A flash of golden fur. A tail.

The saber-toothed cat rose from the grass and moved forward without sound. Rynn had never seen one before, and it was everything he had imagined and more—grace wrapped in muscle, looming death on padded feet.

Its head was massive, its bone-and-enamel fangs shaped to embody the cat's imposing power and lethal beauty in the way it would impale its wary prey—each movement toward the bloody ibex carcass now deliberate, silent, inevitable.

Ahna tensed beside him, but her breathing never changed.

Across the gorge, the Neanderthals waited, unmoving.

The cat paused and looked up, smelling the air.

Rynn held his breath. *Had it spotted them? Had it picked up an unfriendly scent?*

Then it moved forward.

A soft grunt—a signal.

Three spears arced through the air. One struck the cat's shoulder. The second grazed its back. The third clattered uselessly against stone.

The fourth had not yet been thrown.

The cat shrieked—a scream that shattered the stillness. Then it leapt, claws tearing for the rocks above.

That is when the last spear flew.

The flint head sliced into the cat's body just below its ribs. The shaft quivered as the beast fell, its scream turning to a wet gurgle. Blood frothed from its jaws.

The hunters below erupted into motion. The closest spear-bearer fell as the flailing cat slashed his arm. The three others surged forward, now meeting the animal with axes and shouts and bare, brutal force.

A stone axe cracked against its neck.

More blood. More rage. More strikes by stone axes.

The cat twisted, snarled, tried to lunge—but finally, fell.

The silence afterward was more profound than before. It had the smell of victory, the smell of death.

Rynn realized that he had not moved.

Beside him, Ahna exhaled softly.

He looked at her, unsure of what he was supposed to say—or even think.

She met his eyes and raised her chin slightly, not in pride, but in statement.

This is who we are.

She did not speak, but the message was clear. Her people did not run from danger. They met it head-on, face to face, with strength and trust in one another.

Their way did not depend on hurling weapons from a safe distance, avoiding direct contact with living prey, and celebrating the hunt afterward—having taken little risk. Their way was to meet the prey close in; their stories were carved in blood, and their victories measured in scars.

Rynn swallowed hard.

The cat's body was already being prepared. Its fur would provide warmth, and its flesh would provide food. Its death, though somber, was not a spectacle—it was a necessity, a reminder that hunters demand respect.

The injured hunter was attended to, his arm tightly wrapped to stop the bleeding. Vahra, the clan's healer, would tend him further once they returned to camp.

Rynn thought of his own people—spears thrown from cover, traps set in advance, pits dug. The goal was to kill from afar, move in quickly, and avoid risk.

Was it cowardice? No. Just a different way to hunt. His people had mastered distance. Ahna's people had mastered closeness. Two peoples. Two ways.

And yet, the two ways could not help but speak to each other—to teach each other.

She had brought him here not to scare him, but to teach him.

To show that her people were not beasts. They were brave. They were hunters, just as his people were—two peoples seeking the same things: food, shelter, survival. They hunted the same beasts.

That night, when Rynn lay under the stars, in his own shelter again, he could not sleep for a long while.

The image of the struggling cat haunted him—but not in terror... in awe.

And he envisioned Ahna at the hunt, unmoving at his side, her eyes steady even as death unfolded before her.

He had seen something that had spoken to him, but not in words—in thought, and he would not forget it.

* * *

At dawn the next morning in the Neanderthal camp, a summons came for Ahna.

A boy no older than nine summers, still not fully awake, padded over to Ahna's shelter and spoke her name quietly in the gray light of early morning. No need for elaboration. She already knew why she was being called. The elders of the clan were not happy.

She stepped into the cool morning air. Her hands were steady, but her stomach felt heavy, like uncooked root.

66

The fire circle where decisions were made was sacred ground—not because of any mark on the soil, but because of what it meant. Disputes were not shouted here. Truths were not dressed in pride or panic. The elders gathered at first light when something unsettled the balance. And this morning, Ahna was the imbalance.

She entered without hesitation.

Five of the eight elders in the clan were present: Marga, the oldest woman—Ahna's friend—with white streaks in her hair; Goma, Ahna's uncle, now seated not as kin but as clan leader; Tov, whose silence spoke more than words; Enu, the stone tool maker; and Yaya, the story keeper.

They said nothing at first. A space beside the fire had been left open. Ahna crossed to her place quietly.

Marga was the one to speak. "We are told you brought one of the *tall ones* to watch the hunt."

Ahna nodded. "I did."

Tov grunted softly. It might have meant approval. It might have meant she had better say more.

Marga waited, her eyes never blinking.

"He is young," Ahna continued. "And, yes, he is from the *tall ones*. Long-limbed. Not having a greatly muscled chest. I met him by the river many days ago. We do not speak many words. But we... understood."

"Understood what?" asked Enu.

"That we are not enemies," Ahna said. "That we are just different in some ways."

Goma folded his arms. "You brought him to watch the hunt."

67

"I did," she said. "Not to take part. To watch from a distance. I wanted him to know what we can do."

"You showed him our methods?" Yaya asked, her voice not angry, just surprised. "He watched the great cat die?"

"Yes."

Tov leaned forward. "And what did he do?"

"Nothing," Ahna said. "He watched. Quietly. No fear, but no joy either. He did not run. He saw us kill what we had to kill. He saw us risk our lives. I wanted him to understand that our ways are not… less."

"Less! Less than what?" Enu asked.

"Than their ways," said Ahna.

Ahna looked down at the ground for a moment. "They use distance. They throw. They stay far away from danger. We do not. We meet it bravely. They may think their way is the better way—the only way—but they are wrong."

Goma spoke in a measured tone. "And you wanted him to see that ours is a way, too?"

"Yes."

The fire popped.

Yaya asked, "And what did you see, Ahna? In him?"

She hesitated, then said, "Kindness and strength. Not weakness. A kind of… softness, maybe. But not fear. He listens. He looks into you—like he wants to understand. And I think he sees deeply."

"And if you are wrong?" Tov asked. "If his people come with spears?"

"The two clans have long lived apart, and—despite nearness to each other—spears have never been needed."

Enu shook his head slowly. "Our way has always been that the two clans avoid contact. It is dangerous to open your heart before you know if the hand reaching toward it holds a gift or a blade. Marek has warned of the danger."

"I did not open my heart," Ahna said. "I only showed him the ways of the hunt."

The circle went quiet.

Marga finally spoke. "You have not broken law. In fact, it's possible that what you shared may be of benefit."

"That is my hope," Ahna said. "The two clans may have much to learn from one another."

Marga nodded once, slowly. "Then it is you who must carry the burden of what comes from this sharing."

"I will."

Goma exhaled and looked away, toward the hills.

Yaya touched her necklace—two worn teeth from a lynx killed many moons past. "If he returns, will you see him?"

"Yes," Ahna said.

Tov nodded and grunted again. This time, it sounded like agreement.

They dismissed her with no gesture, no verdict. That was their way. Nothing was settled. Only set aside for now.

As she left, the fire popped behind her, and what she had done did feel like a burden—but for now, she was willing to carry it. Rynn seemed worth the risk.

She had said only what she believed to be true.

For now, she knew that the memory of watching the hunt with Rynn would stay with her—the cries of the great cat, the scent of its blood, the moment its struggle ended.

Even now, walking away from the fire circle, she could still hear the cat's scream and see its final struggle, both alive in her mind as though the dying creature had asked her to remember.

Even as she walked in the open spaces between the trees, she could also imagine Rynn watching the great cat struggle—his eyes locked on the fight as if each moment carried a meaning he was still trying to understand.

She wondered how he would remember it. Would he think of her people as less than reckless? Would he see the way their courage and strength bound them together?

Before she reached her shelter, a few clan members were gathered around a low fire talking about the hunt. Word of the kill had spread fast, especially after the injured hunter, Toran, was attended by Vahra, the clan healer.

At the evening meal, the clan would enjoy meat from the kill. Yet, their voices at tonight's fire would carry a sharpened pitch of hunger and of concern for Toran.

That morning, Goma, crouching near the fire as well, saw Ahna passing by and asked, "The hunt you showed him... will he tell it truthfully?"

"I think so," Ahna answered.

Goma's gaze was hopeful. "Then perhaps his people will come to believe that peace is better than fighting."

Later than evening, in the *Homo sapiens* camp, Rynn was sitting on a log, staring into the embers of a dying fire. Other clan members had gone to their shelters.

He stayed, warming himself, tracing the scene again in his mind—the *others* rushing forward the moment death hung in the balance for both the injured hunter and the great cat. And Ahna, beside him, had not even flinched.

He felt a pull to see her again, but he knew the risk. Her people were likely very upset, and his people would not understand. Yet, as he lay down and covered himself in hides, he kept thoughts of her close.

In the dark, each of Rynn's thoughts returned to the same truth: There was something in her that called to him —not in words, something deeper than words, something he could not name.

That night, sleep did not come easily to either of them.

For Ahna, the forest around her camp seemed more alive than usual. Every crack of branch, every shuffle of small paws in the leaf litter seemed to draw her eyes toward the darkness. She pictured the ridge where they had crouched, the gorge yawning below, and she wondered if Rynn was awake as well, his gaze turned toward the same shadows.

She took up her bone-handled knife and began carving at a length of antler, not to make a tool but for the comfort of working something into shape. The scraping sound was steady, like the slow settling of freshly turned soil.

Shapes emerged—lines, curves, something almost like the arc of a leaping cat. She ran her thumb along the carved ridges and felt an imprint of the hunt in her fingertips.

Across the river, Rynn turned in his hides and opened his eyes to the faint glow of embers. Unable to sleep, he rose and walked outside. A figure moved near the edge of his people's camp—a hunter on watch, scanning the tree line.

Rynn imagined explaining what he had seen: the closeness of the fight—and especially the unity in the rush toward the great cat. He could not forget the bravery of these hunters—Ahna's people.

In his mind he could hear the scoffs of his own people if he were to tell what he saw. He could imagine the warnings he would hear about getting too close to the *others*.

Not wanting to sleep, he walked over to the edge of the water where moonlight struck the slow current. He knelt and let the cold soak into his hands. For a long moment, he simply watched the river gently move past, wondering if, in its journey, it flowed past the place she fetched water.

On the other side of the river, Ahna left her half-carved antler beside the fire and walked toward the sound of water. The air was colder here and she felt it deeply in her lungs. She crouched at the bank, letting the chilly water seep through her fingers until they ached.

Neither knew that they were less than three hundred paces apart, divided only by the darkness and the current.

The night was silent except for the murmur of water and the faint call of a night bird.

And though they could not see each other, Ahna and Rynn both looked across the darkness as if some part of each sensed the nearness of the other—an unspoken pull, fragile and stubborn, somewhat like the first thread in a new weaving.

When Ahna had left the elders late that morning, the fire had burned brightly behind her, and the sense of what she had done rested lightly on her shoulders—noticeable, but not crushing..

She had spoken only what was true.

And somewhere, across the river, and close to the camp of the *tall ones* she hoped he was thinking of her.

Ahna stepped into the pale light, her breath drifting faintly in the cool air. The camp of her people was quiet now, with thin curls of smoke rising from dying fires.

A pair of young hunters, returning from a late hunt, passed by, their arms full of small game. One of them—Zarn, whose eyes always narrowed at her—slowed his pace just enough to glance at her. It was not a friendly glance. His mouth tightened, but he said nothing, disappearing into the trees. The other hunter gave a small nod, not approval exactly, but something less cold.

Ahna stayed near the edge of the river. The scent of wet soil rose from the ground. She crouched by the bank, letting her fingers trail in the water. Her reflection wavered in the ripples, hair loose around her shoulders. She thought of Rynn's face as the great cat had emerged, the way he had not shown fear, though she wondered if his people might have. That mattered to her.

A soft step behind her made her turn. It was Vestra, a young member of the clan, carrying a bundle of drying reeds. "You went before the elders?" She asked quietly.

"I did," Ahna replied.

"They say you brought a *tall one* to the hunt."

"Yes, I did."

Vestra's brow furrowed, but her voice held no anger. "Some say it was foolish."

"Some," Ahna said, dipping her hand in again and watching the ripples. "And some do not."

Vestra crouched beside her. "I think it was brave. If they are ever to know us, they must see us as we are."

She shifted the bundle. "Will he see you again?"

"I hope so."

When Vestra left, Ahna stayed by the water. She thought of Enu's words—*the gift or the blade*—and smiled inwardly, knowing which Rynn would choose.

While Ahna was sitting near the water on the far side of the river, Rynn was relaxing near the water not far from his clan's camp. They could not see one another, but each imagined feeling the other's presence.

Earlier in the evening, Rynn had performed his usual chores—repairing spear shafts and checking the edge of flint blades—before entering his shelter for the night. While working, his hands had slowed more than once, his eyes drifting toward the tree line.

Now, as he sat near the water, he replayed the hunt in his mind, the smell of the cat's blood hot in the air. He had not spoken of it to other members of the clan; they would wonder why he had been near her people at all. But he could not shake the image of Ahna staying so still beside him, as if her breath was part of the breath of the forest.

After returning to his shelter, Rynn took small strips of sinew from his pouch. He began to braid them, fingers working automatically, as he sat outside looking at the stars. Into the weave he set three tiny beads of bone. He thought of leaving it where Ahna might find it. Not a gift for trading, but a sign that he had understood her gift of the hunt to him, and that he would remember.

A little later, Ahna returned to her shelter. Looking at the sky, she did not envision seeing Rynn again soon.

She let her mind wander through the day's events. The gorge where the hunt had taken place would be empty now, the scent of the cat long gone, but the blood-soaked ground would hold the memory of the hunt, Toran's injury, and the great cat's death.

She tried to imagine how Rynn might tell the story.

Would he speak of the spears striking true?

Of the one who had fallen injured?

Would he tell how they moved together, no one hanging back?

Her mind wandered further.

Could the two clans ever share the meaning of the hunt?

She smiled at the thought. Many would call it impossible. Yet impossible things often found a way.

A raven glided overhead, its cry sharp. In her people's stories, ravens watched both the living and the dead, and she took its passing as a sign of regard, not warning.

As the night air cooled and the smoke thinned, the stars grew brighter. Ahna remained outside her shelter, and Rynn outside his. Though apart, both lay awake beneath the same sky, wondering when they would meet again— and hoping it would be soon.

Historical Context II
Life Within Each Clan

"The past is never dead. It is not even past."
—William Faulkner

Survival and Strategy

Though often portrayed as competitors, Neanderthals and *Homo sapiens*—according to recent evidence—not only came into contact with one another, but in some regions, they may have hunted the same animals, drawn water from the same rivers, and constructed similar shelters from the same harsh winters.

How they adapted to survive reveals as much about their lives as do the traits they shared. Their strategies for enduring the brutal demands of Ice Age life reflect two paths shaped by distinct evolutionary pressures—and perhaps by different ways of seeing the world. Nowhere were these differences more evident than in how they hunted, a task demanding both ingenuity and courage.

Dangers of the Hunt

Hunting was both a necessity and a peril for Neanderthals and *Homo sapiens* alike. Among their most formidable prey was the woolly mammoth (*Mammuthus primigenius*)—the only mammoth roaming Ice Age Europe 40,000 years ago.

A full-grown mammoth could weigh six tons or more, stand over three meters at the shoulder, and move with startling speed, capable of charging at more than twenty miles per hour. Pursuing such a creature was one of the most dangerous undertakings imaginable, a life-and-death gamble against six tons of tusks, muscle, and rage.

One misstep, one mistimed thrust, or one misjudged retreat could mean instant death. Hunters who fell beneath a mammoth's feet or tusks were crushed or gored beyond recognition. The danger was not theoretical: fractured bones, crushed ribs, and embedded spear points found in both Neanderthal and early *Homo sapiens* skeletons testify to the physical toll of hunting mammoths and other large animals.

A single mammoth could feed a group for weeks, but the risk-to-reward ratio was extreme. To survive, both Neanderthals and *Homo sapiens* had to develop methods that balanced courage with caution—using their differing physical and technological strengths to reduce exposure to the animal's lethal power.

Neanderthal Tactics: Strength and Proximity

Neanderthals relied on close-range, high-risk techniques. Their heavy thrusting spears, designed to be driven deep into flesh by sheer force, required hunters to approach within a few meters of the animal. This demanded exceptional strength and coordination.

Anatomical evidence shows that Neanderthals were built for such work: short, broad bodies with powerful chests and limbs ideal for generating the torque and leverage needed in hand-to-hand combat with large prey. Their dense bones and robust musculature acted as natural armor against falls and impacts, though no body could withstand a direct strike from a mammoth's tusk or trunk.

To minimize danger, Neanderthals likely chose terrain that restricted the animal's movement—closely-spaced trees, mud flats, snowdrifts, or narrow valleys—and attacked from multiple sides. Some evidence from kill sites suggests that, whenever possible, they used pits or natural obstacles to immobilize a mammoth's legs before closing in. Even so, the risk remained staggering. A single failed thrust or a sudden turn by the animal could kill one or more hunters instantly.

Homo sapiens Strategies: Distance and Coordination

When *Homo sapiens* arrived in Europe, they faced the same formidable prey but brought different solutions to the hunt. Rather than relying on sheer strength and a close-range attack strategy, they kept their distance—using weapons that allowed them to strike from afar, and relying on both coordination and planning to turn caution into advantage.

Their lighter body build was compensated by invention —spears that could be thrown by hand or by atlatls (spear throwers) that extended the hunter's reach and throwing speed. These weapons allowed attacks from safer distances, reducing the number of direct confrontations.

Homo sapiens also developed complex communication, both verbal and symbolic, allowing them to plan for coordinated multi-phase hunts: driving animals toward ambush points, separating individuals from herds, and timing attacks with precision.

By maintaining distance, *Homo sapiens* improved their chances of survival. They could wound a mammoth many times from a safe distance, then follow the blood trail until the animal weakened. Their campsites show evidence of strategic butchering and meat transport, implying that they sometimes killed an animal far from camp and carried selected parts back—a practice that reflects a more deliberate and logistical approach to hunting.

Protective Adaptations and Social Insurance

For both lineages, protection during the hunt was not limited to weaponry. It was also social. Hunters rarely acted alone; groups operated as units, with designated attackers, distractors, and observers. Injured hunters were often cared for afterward—archaeological remains show that both Neanderthals and *Homo sapiens* tended to individuals who survived crippling injuries, suggesting communal protection and recovery systems.

Physical adaptations also played a role in risk mitigation. Neanderthals' heavy musculature and thick bones reduced fracture severity, while *Homo sapiens* relied on speed, agility, and foresight to avoid direct engagement. In both lineages, experience mattered: older hunters with scarred bones likely served as strategists and teachers, ensuring that younger members learned how to approach danger methodically rather than recklessly.

Summary of a Mammoth Kill

To kill a mammoth 40,000 years ago was to gamble with death. Neanderthals met that danger head-on, relying on raw strength, proximity, and precise coordination within the attack zone. *Homo sapiens*, by contrast, sought safety in distance—using projectiles, cooperative planning, and communication to strike from afar.

For both lineages, the hunt was an act of extreme peril, demanding courage, intelligence, and cohesion. Those who survived earned not only meat but stature within their group—the respect reserved for those who had faced the Ice Age's most formidable challenge.

The contrast between these two hunting styles reveals more than technical difference; it reflects two ways of thinking. Neanderthals were masters of the immediate, with exceptional working memory and spatial awareness, able to react swiftly to shifting circumstances. *Homo sapiens*, on the other hand, were planners and foreseers—inclined toward strategy, abstraction, and long-term vision. When the two kinds of hunters finally observed each other, each would have seen not just another method of survival, but another kind of mind at work.

Two Ways of Adapting

The Neanderthal skeleton tells a story of strength. Their grip strength may have exceeded that of today's elite athletes. They could haul prey, lift wounded comrades, and wield heavy stone tools with precision and power.

But strength alone wasn't their only asset. The brains of Neanderthals seemed especially adapted to process spatial and physical information. They could memorize complex landscapes and navigate them with ease. Their strength, endurance, and terrain memory were all part of a robust survival strategy finely tuned to Ice Age Europe.

Homo sapiens, on the other hand, seem to have invested more cognitive energy into social coordination. Their tools were more standardized, often made far from where they were used—suggesting trade or organized transport. Their camps show evidence of planning, such as food storage, specialized work areas, and predictable daily routines. This suggests a different kind of intelligence—one that excelled at long-term planning, communication, and cooperative problem-solving.

Evidence suggests that Neanderthals thrived in the present moment—they were there, bodily and powerfully. *Homo sapiens* were likely more adapt at planning for a changing future.

When a Neanderthal and a *Homo sapiens* hunted side by side, each would have learned from the other, and each would have increased the survival odds of the other.

Burial 40,000 Years Ago: Death and Meaning

Around 40,000 years ago, both Neanderthals and early *Homo sapiens* lived across southern Europe and western Asia. Their world was cold, unpredictable, and often perilous. Life expectancy was short, injury common, and death a constant presence. Yet evidence from sites scattered across Europe and the Near East suggests that when death came, it was not met with indifference. Each lineage treated its dead with care—both in practical and symbolic ways—and in doing so, left behind some of the earliest signs of emotional and spiritual depth in human history.

The Origins of Burial Behavior

Intentional burial is among the clearest indicators of complex thinking and social structure. It requires planning, cooperation, and a degree of emotional investment. Simple disposal of corpses to avoid scavengers is a practical act; deliberate burial, often accompanied by body positioning, grave goods, or pigment, implies a different motivation—one involving remembrance or belief in continuity beyond death.

The earliest known burials predate 40,000 years ago. Both *Homo sapiens* and Neanderthals had already been burying their dead for tens of millennia. What makes the period around 40,000 years ago remarkable is that both lineages were present simultaneously, sometimes in overlapping territories, and each displayed distinct but comparable approaches to caring for their dead.

Neanderthal Burials: Simplicity and Care

The archaeological record for Neanderthal burial is modest but compelling. More than thirty potential Neanderthal burials have been identified across Europe and the Middle East, dating from roughly 100,000 to 40,000 years ago. Among the best-known examples are La Chapelle-aux-

Saints in France, Shanidar Cave in Iraq, and La Ferrassie in southwestern France.

At La Chapelle-aux-Saints, excavators in the early twentieth century uncovered the nearly complete skeleton of an elderly male Neanderthal placed in a shallow pit, flexed on his side, and partially surrounded by stone debris. The grave showed signs of intentional excavation and backfilling. At Shanidar, several individuals were interred in distinct depressions within the cave floor, one of which—"Shanidar IV"—was famously found with pollen traces once thought to indicate that flowers had been placed with the body. Later analyses suggest that the pollen may have entered the grave naturally, yet the evidence still points to careful placement of the corpse and possible repeated visits to the burial area.

The key characteristics of Neanderthal burials include:

- A deliberate pit or depression, dug or adapted to receive the body.
- The flexed position of the corpse, often lying on one side with limbs drawn toward the chest.
- Occasional presence of animal bones or tools, though not clearly as grave goods.
- Evidence of care for the injured or aged, suggesting emotional attachment within small social groups.

While the simplicity of these graves might reflect limited material culture, the consistent pattern of deliberate burial indicates more than pragmatic disposal. It suggests recognition of death—and perhaps a sense of loss or continuity that transcended mere survival.

Homo sapiens Burials: Ritual and Symbolism

When *Homo sapiens* appeared in Europe around 40,000 years ago, their burials quickly began to show greater elaboration.

Sites such as Sungir (Russia), Dolní Věstonice and Predmostí (Czech Republic), and Kostenki (Russia) reveal burials marked by ornamentation, pigment, and personal artifacts.

At Sungir, two children and an adult male were interred with extraordinary care about 34,000 years ago. The man's body was covered in thousands of ivory beads sewn into clothing and accompanied by spears made from straightened mammoth tusks.

The children's graves contained similar adornments, including fox teeth and ivory disks. Such treatment required immense labor, implying not only affection but also status and possibly belief in an afterlife where such possessions would matter.

At Dolní Věstonice, a triple burial of two young men and a woman was discovered, all lying close together and dusted with red ochre, a mineral pigment widely used in Upper Paleolithic rituals. Ochre is found in burials across Africa, the Levant, and Europe, symbolizing blood, life, or transformation. Its repeated use across vast distances and cultures hints at a shared conceptual framework about death and renewal.

The hallmarks of *Homo sapiens* burials from this era include:

- Use of pigment, especially red ochre

- Ornamentation with beads, animal teeth, ivory, or shells
- Extended or formal positioning of the body, often supine rather than flexed
- Occasional grave markers or structures, suggesting community participation

These practices display both grief and imagination. Burial became an act of storytelling—a way to link the dead to myths, ancestors, or cosmological ideas that were forming alongside symbolic art and ritual behavior.

Comparing the Two Traditions

The burial practices of Neanderthals and *Homo sapiens* reflect overlapping but distinct mental worlds.

Neanderthals buried their dead in a way that suggests compassion and familiarity—a desire to protect the body from scavengers, to preserve the dignity of the deceased, and perhaps to comfort the living. There is little evidence for symbolic elaboration, but ample evidence for emotional investment.

By contrast, *Homo sapiens* burials reveal an emerging symbolic consciousness—a worldview in which death required explanation or ritual response. The presence of ochre, ornaments, and deliberate arrangement suggests not only remembrance but belief in transformation—that something of the person survived beyond the physical body, something akin to spiritual beliefs today.

Still, the boundary between practical and symbolic is not absolute. Neanderthals, too, cared for the injured, buried their dead, and may have revisited graves. Such gestures speak of attachment and grief, even without the structure of a formal ritual.

In the end, both lineages appear to have recognized death as more than a simple ending. Each responded to loss through care and remembrance—Neanderthals through gestures grounded in familiarity and closeness, *Homo sapiens* through symbolic acts that hinted at belief in something beyond life itself. Together, they mark the beginnings of humanity's long effort to understand what it means to die, and what it means to endure.

The Emotional and Cognitive Dimensions

Burial offers a rare window into emotion and cognition among Ice Age peoples. To dig a grave is to act with foresight; to place a body carefully is to acknowledge individuality; to include pigments or objects is to invest the moment with symbolism. These are deeply human traits, whether or not accompanied by spoken theology.

Neanderthal care for the old and infirm—individuals who could not have survived without community support —shows that empathy and social responsibility were integral to their lives. Burial continued this pattern: the dead were not abandoned but incorporated into the ground and into the shared landscape of memory.

For *Homo sapiens*, burial may have served additional psychological functions. The living confronted mortality by embedding it in ritual—turning the chaos of death into ordered ceremony. Through color, ornament, and ritual burial, these early humans began to transform fear of the unknown into meaning. Many anthropologists view these behaviors as early expressions of abstract thought and symbolic reasoning—precursors to art, myth, and religion.

The Role of Place and Memory

Burial sites were often reused or revisited, implying a sense of continuity between generations. In both lineages, caves and rock shelters—natural places of protection and echo—were favored locations.

For Neanderthals, repeated use of the same cave chambers, such as at Shanidar, suggests that memory was spatially anchored; the dead rested within the same landscapes the living inhabited.

For *Homo sapiens*, burial sometimes extended to open-air camps and structured dwellings, with graves placed close to or even into living spaces. At Dolní Věstonice, burials, hearths, and art objects coexisted within the same site, indicating that life and death shared a common setting. This blending of daily life and remembrance shows that death was not viewed as complete separation or as exile. Rather, death was seen as a kind of transformation within the community that remained.

Possible Beliefs and Symbolic Thought

What did these Ice Age people believe about death? Archaeology cannot answer directly, but patterns suggest at least rudimentary spiritual awareness. The covering of bodies, use of red pigment, inclusion of personal items, and care for children's remains all point toward a belief that the dead retained significance beyond their physical decay.

For Neanderthals, this may have taken the form of ancestral memory—the idea that the deceased continued to influence the group, perhaps through remembered stories or lingering presence. For *Homo sapiens*, the combination of art, ornamentation, and burial points toward an emerging concept of the soul or a nonphysical essence. Expressing death through ritual or intuition, both lineages recognized death as a passage rather than an end.

Burial as Social Expression

Burial practices also reflected social identity and hierarchy. Among *Homo sapiens*, differences in burial preparation and the items left in a grave suggest that some individuals—perhaps elders, skilled hunters, or spiritual figures—were honored more elaborately, their resting places marked with objects that carried meaning for the living. The presence of ornaments and tools might symbolize particular skills, achievements, or status, tying the individual to customs the group valued.

Neanderthals, in contrast, show less evidence of differential treatment; most burials appear similar and suggest more egalitarian social structures—less emphasis on individual status. Yet the consistent presence of care and placement indicates that every life mattered deeply within the group, regardless of rank, and that the act of burial itself held profound communal significance for those who performed it.

Continuity and Legacy

Between 40,000 and 35,000 years ago, as Neanderthals began to disappear, their approach to death—humble, intimate, centered on care—had already entered the shared human inheritance. *Homo sapiens* added to that foundation, bringing color, ornaments, and stories to the act of burial. These traditions mark the dawn of symbolic behavior—the recognition that both life and death hold meaning.

From these early graves came a line of thought that would shape every culture to follow: the belief that the dead remain with us in some way and the living are bound to honor them. Whether through a simple placement in the earth or an elaborate interment, burial reflected more than mortality—it marked humanity's awakening to continuity in the face of loss.

Chapter Five

Rynn crouched beside the bank of the river, near the place he had crossed for the first time. As he crouched, he placed a smooth stone on a piece of bark he had been flattening all morning. He had brought several stones, each carefully selected for its color or markings—pale spirals, dark flecks, and veins of white that reminded of lightning ripping through the night sky. He did not know if she would understand why he brought them. He only knew that it felt important to him.

The flattened bark also held a length of sinew twisted into a circle, a new braid of grass, and a few sprigs of sage he had dried near the hearth. He did not know their words for gifts or greetings, but he hoped she would understand his meaning.

He felt her watching him even when she was not there.

She had changed his level of awareness.

Since the hunt, after seeing her people face death close up, Rynn had not been able to close his eyes without an image of the great cat's snarl, the splattering of blood, and the haunting memory of the screams. But more than the cat, he remembered the steadiness in her. Ahna, in the face of all that had happened, had not flinched.

She had invited him to witness her truth—something to be seen, not explained, revealed in the courage of hunters as they faced death head-on without hesitation. That was the essence of her truth: Death is always near, and it must be faced without flinching.

He tightened the final knot in the sinew bracelet and slowly stood, the sun catching in his hair. His fingers smelled of sage and yarrow. The air was heavy with pine.

It was time to return.

Back at camp, things had changed—slightly, subtly. Not in the open and not in words shouted across the fires, but in exchanged glances and silences that followed his arrival.

His childhood friend Tamik stopped joking so easily with him and often seemed to avoid contact.

Others—men older than himself—watched him without expression. They said nothing when he passed, but their silence felt unnatural and unfamiliar.

He had gone off on his own too often and for too long.

That morning, before he left for the river, his aging mother stopped him.

"Your feet are always outside the ring of shelters," she said. "Are you tracking something?"

Rynn did not answer right away.

"Just walking," he said.

She studied him. Her eyes were not unkind, but sharp. "Some walks are longer than others. And some are watched."

Rynn nodded and stepped past her, heart thudding.

He understood this as a caution.

Another hint of concern came when he returned from the river that evening and found Omak standing near the fire, speaking in low tones to several other elders.

He overheard Omak speak in a grave voice. "Elan saw him north of the bend of the river again. Always slipping off alone. Elan is not the only one who has noticed."

"What does he do?" someone asked Omak.

Omak looked at Rynn who acted as if he had not heard Omak talking.

"Elan says he enters the forest across the water, and often is not alone. He goes across and then disappears. Comes back carrying unusual scents. Not like the prey we hunt. Like something that shouldn't be touched."

"Or someone," another voice muttered.

Rynn overheard a lot, but not all, of what was said as he walked to the fire. He sat if he had overheard nothing.

They did not ask him anything directly.

But the silence closed around him, and he felt like a trapped insect sinking into sap.

Later that night, his friend Tamik approached him.

They walked together at the edge of camp, just as the firelight was dying to a glow.

"I saw her," Tamik said quietly. "The girl. The thick one with the short neck. I saw you two."

Rynn did not answer, and he picked up a pinecone and curled his fingers around it.

"She is not like us," Tamik added.

"No," Rynn said. "She is not."

"Then why?"

Rynn turned toward him. "Because she is there, and I am drawn to her."

Tamik frowned. "Like wolves to one another."

"She is not a wolf."

"She is one of the *others*—the different ones."

Rynn looked away. "And you have already decided what that means."

"It is not my place to decide. The elders have decided. Marek has warned the clan about dangers nearby."

Rynn stood. "Then do not follow me. There is no need."

But Tamik was not finished. "Out of concern for you, I told Omak what I saw. He'll speak to the council."

Rynn closed his eyes.

The storm had started.

The next morning, Rynn did not go to the river. He stayed in camp, fetching water and gutting fish, doing everything asked without question.

He thought it might help—but it did not.

By midday, Omak called for him.

The meeting was not for everyone. But, four elders sat in the shelter beside the storage cave—Omak, Terah, Duma, and Plen, who rarely spoke but missed nothing.

They asked Rynn to sit.

He sat.

Omak made the first comment. "You have been seen."

Rynn said nothing.

"With one of them," Terah added. "The girl from across the river. The girl of heavy shoulders and strong hands."

"She has a name," Rynn said softly.

"What is it?" Duma asked.

Rynn hesitated. Then he said, "Ahna."

Plen stirred. "That is a sound from their mouths, not ours."

"She told you this?" Terah said.

"Yes," Rynn replied. "The first word she spoke to me." Silence followed.

Omak spoke up. "What do you want from her?"

Rynn looked into Omak's eyes. "To understand."

"Understand what?"

"Why we fear them."

Omak's face twisted. "Because they are not like us."

"They do not act like beasts," Rynn said. "They hunt. They mourn. They care for their injured. They face death."

"Like wolves," Duma muttered.

Rynn's jaw clenched. "Wolves do not make fire."

Terah sighed. "It does not matter if they make fire or carry children on their backs. They are not us. We are not the same. They may be a danger to our people. It is not wise to tangle the roots of two trees."

"She is not a tree," Rynn said, his voice sharp. "She is alive and not afraid. I saw her when death was near."

Plen finally spoke. "Do you intend to see her again?"

"Yes."

Omak's face hardened. "Do you no longer want to walk as one of us?"

For a moment, Rynn's heart forgot its rhythm.

Before Rynn could answer, Terah raised a hand. "Let us not rush to judge."

Duma looked at her, surprised. "He walks with another clan—a clan very much unlike us."

"He walks alone for now," she said. "But not in hate. He is young. He seeks meaning. Let us not break him for that."

Omak shook his head. "Meaning is found here. In *our* clan. Not in the company of the *others*."

"Ahna is not a danger," Rynn said quietly. "There is friendship in her eyes. And she has new ways of seeing."

The elders fell silent again.

At last, Terah said, "Then we will watch. You will not be judged, yet. But your actions may put the clan at risk."

Omak dismissed him, spitting into the dust as he did so and saying, "Softness can be a curse."

Rynn rose after being dismissed and left the gathering.

He did not stop walking until the river was close. He hoped she would be there, and he felt no guilt.

He brought no gift, just himself.

Reaching the river, he saw her waiting.

As if she had known.

She stood across the water, her eyes scanning him. No smile this time. Just stillness. Her face was unreadable, but not cold.

He held up both hands. Empty.

Then, he slowly lowered himself onto the river stones.

She did the same.

They crouched, looking at one another, neither crossing the river, as the light grew dim.

Finally, she pointed to her chest, then to his.

Two beings.

Then she made a wide circle with her hands, drawing it in the air.

Then pointed again, from her to him.

All that holds us.

Rynn nodded.

He placed his hand to his own chest.

Then touched the ground.

Then touched it again.

She nodded.

Then rose.

So did he.

He did not know when they would speak again—or if there would even be an *again*.

But for now, he knew this: They were both choosing. Not running. Not hiding.

Choosing.

That night, Ahna sat in her own camp in silence.

No one questioned her. Not yet.

But the looks had changed.

Zarn saw her first. He said nothing, but his eyes spoke of disapproval.

Her uncle Goma met her with a small nod. She sat near him by the fire, not close, but not wide apart.

"You saw him again?" he asked.

"I did."

"I fear he brings danger," Goma added.

"No," Ahna said. "He brings change."

Goma stared into the fire for a long time, and then said, "Change can be more dangerous than death."

Ahna did not answer.

As she slept that night, her dreams were of Rynn.

The next morning, Rynn rose early and began to prepare again—this time not a gift, but words.

He would speak again, this time to the whole clan.

Not to ask for forgiveness—to ask for understanding.

Somewhere inside his being, he believed that seeing her mattered, not just to him but to them all.

Meeting Ahna had changed the way he thought about the *others*—the clan so feared across the river.

The elders chose the place where the entire clan would gather to hear Rynn speak—a level clearing marked by the Gathering Stones, a ring of twelve pale rocks set upright long ago, standing apart from the camp and used only for matters of shared importance.

Unlike the smoke-warmed fire circle used by Ahna's clan, the Gathering Stones bore no fire at its center. Light and sky and ancestors were the witnesses here.

Each new speech was an offering to those who had stood and spoken before and was meant for the entire clan.

It was not a place of punishment nor of judgment. But words offered here could shape a future within the clan.

Rynn stood ready, his hands empty, his heart loud in his chest. The sun had passed its peak. Shadows were starting to stretch long.

Omak was already there, seated on a low stone, arms folded. Rynn's aunt Terah was seated next to Omak, and several steps away, Duma was seated next to Plen.

Rynn stood alone, hands at his sides.

All members of the clan were invited to attend as observers. No one was required to be there, but word had traveled of the young man who walked alone with the young woman with strong shoulders and strange brow—one of the *others*, a woman now facing judgment without even being present.

Rynn's aging mother positioned herself far behind the main group of onlookers, her lips tight.

Tamik arrived last. He did not speak but stood only three steps from Rynn.

When the elders were ready, Omak rose.

"Rynn, son of beloved Rellan—who died during the Great Storm—walks with concern among us and wishes to speak," he said. "He has been seen where we do not go. With one we do not know. He has not hidden it and now chooses to explain his actions to the clan."

Omak turned to Rynn. "Say what you will."

Rynn stepped forward. The space between the stones felt large. His own voice surprised him with its steadiness.

"You all know," he began, "that I have crossed the river. You know I have seen someone there."

He paused. The silence from all in attendance was attentive and unbroken.

"She is not like us," Rynn continued. "Her arms are thick. Her jaw is wide. She says much with her hands and her arms. Her breath smells of yarrow and sage. But she watches as we watch. She feels as we feel."

Someone shifted in the circle. A cough from the onlookers. The rustle of movement against hides.

"I saw her clan kill a great cat," Rynn said. "I saw a hunter torn open. I saw another hunter, close enough to touch the beast, split the cat's neck with a stone axe. They do not often throw from far. They meet danger head-on. They bleed for their lives. And they survive."

Omak grunted, loud enough to be heard.

Rynn turned toward him. "You say they are beasts. But I have seen beasts. I have hunted beasts. Beasts do not bury their dead with red soil. Beasts do not leave their marks on the walls of caves. Beasts do not kneel beside a stranger and offer a gift without fear."

Murmurs now. Some faint, some loud enough to hear a few words. Some agreement, some disapproval.

Rynn pressed on. "You say they might be beasts, not like us. A danger. But have you stood with them? Have you seen them? How they hold each other? How they find meaning in their marks? How they color their faces?"

He walked slowly around the ring, meeting the eyes of everyone who looked at him.

"We think our way is the only way to hunt. We think distance is wisdom. We strike from afar. We do not invite danger. This is what keeps us alive. But what if there is another way—one that meets danger face-to-face?"

He stopped before the largest of the stones, the one etched with the oldest marks—the spiral for time, the cross for death, the crescent for vision.

"She made no threat. She brought no weapon. She could have vanished the first day. But she stayed. She watched me. And I watched her."

The wind shifted. Clouds began to gather in the western sky. There was murmuring among members of the clan.

"Maybe I am wrong," Rynn said. "Maybe she is unlike other members of her clan. Maybe others are not like her. Maybe they will turn on us. I do not know."

He turned, slowly facing them all as he continued.

"But I do know this: I will not be the first to throw a stone or raise a spear."

No one spoke for a minute.

Then, Rynn added. "I will meet her again. I will keep meeting her. Not to betray any of you. But to learn about her way of life."

He stepped back.

Finished.

Omak rose slowly. The tendons in his neck stood out as he lifted himself. His voice was sharp.

"You speak well, young man. But words alone do not keep a clan alive. We listen, and we remember—but it is living that proves a speaker true."

"True," Rynn said. "But fear does not feed a clan, nor does it teach them how to endure."

The older Omak stepped toward him. For a moment, everyone tensed.

But Omak only looked into his face, then nodded once.

"You speak what you believe. That is something."

He turned to the other elders. "Let it be known that Rynn walks along the edge."

That was the phrase. The edge. Not inside. Not exiled. Watched. A hushed murmur ran through the onlookers.

Terah raised her voice. "None shall harm him. None shall stop him. But he is responsible for the path he shapes."

And that was that.

The Gathering Stones meeting emptied slowly. Three elders shook their heads and talked among themselves. Two left in silence. The onlookers slowly dispersed.

Tamik delayed leaving. When Rynn turned, he was there.

"You meant it?" Tamik asked.

"Yes."

"Even if the clan turns on you?"

"I am already outside."

Tamik hesitated. "Not to me."

Rynn said nothing.

Then Tamik added, "If anything goes wrong—if her people move toward us—I will support you."

Rynn nodded.

Then he turned back toward the river.

The line between the life he had known and the one he was entering had never been thinner.

And he was still challenging it.

The path to the river felt different that evening. The air felt heavy—not like when a storm is coming, but like when unexpected change is about to happen.

A jay shrieked somewhere across the water.

Rynn moved without hurry, but every step drew him further from the voices of his own people and closer to the stillness he had come to expect near the water.

When he reached the bend where the river widened and the current slowed, he stopped. He gazed at the ground.

A roe deer had crossed here recently—the fresh slots of its hooves pressed into the mud, still holding a sheen of water. He crouched, touching one print, thinking of how her feet had stood in this same river, how her eyes had searched him without fear.

He straightened and stepped into the shallows, letting the cold water flow over his calves and feet. Across the way, the bank rose steep and shadowed near the trees.

A shape moved there—low at first, then rising.

It was Ahna.

No gift in her hands. Her hair caught the last rim of sunlight. They stood facing each other with the river between, the sound of water the only speech.

Rynn felt the small bundle in his pouch—the sinew bracelet he had carefully made for Ahna. Slowly, he drew it out and held it in his open palm, letting her see it.

She moved to the edge of the river, and her gaze locked on the bracelet. Without taking her eyes from his, she bent and picked up a stone—dark, smooth, wet with river water —and held it the same way.

For a breath, they stayed like that, each holding something small, but symbolically chosen.

Then she lowered the stone, placing it on a small rock on a cleared space of ground. Watching her, Rynn stepped out of the water and placed the bracelet on a flat rock.

They then stepped back in unison, as though some wordless accord had been made.

Rynn turned toward his camp, the sky behind him deepening to blue. She faded into the shadowed trees.

Neither knew what tomorrow would bring, but both understood that the ground between them—like the gifts they had set down—now carried a deeper meaning.

Chapter Six

The path Ahna followed was one she had not taken in many summers. The forest had shifted since then— trees fallen, moss spread thick over rocks like green blankets, and the scent of age-heavy soil stronger than she remembered. But she knew the turns, the rises and falls, the pattern of light breaking through the canopy. She had walked it often after the death of her cousin, sometimes alone, sometimes with her mother, once with her uncle. Never with anyone from the *tall ones*. Never with Rynn.

She glanced back. He was just behind her, stepping carefully, alert but not afraid. His footfalls were quieter now than they had been the first time they met. She had taught him how to read the mood of the forest, and how to walk it lightly. When to hurry and when to pause.

"Not far now," she said, slowing her pace.

Rynn nodded but said nothing. The air had taken on a certain stillness. Not silence—there were always birds and the occasional rustle of leaves—but a kind of hush in the trees. As if the forest knew where they were going.

Soon they reached a clearing. At the center of it stood a wide, flat rock, partly sunken, rimmed with lichen. Around it, a semicircle of rounded stones standing waist high, each one etched with small lines, not drawings as Rynn might know them, but patterns—some carved deep, others scratched shallow, like memory fading with time.

"This is where my father was put in the ground," Ahna said, her voice steady but low.

Rynn looked around slowly. "Your father is here?"

She nodded. "And many others. All from our clan. This place is hold ones who return to the ground."

Rynn stepped toward the largest stone and touched it lightly. The surface was cool, and beneath the lichen, he felt grooves of carving. "Did you make these marks?"

"My uncle made those for my father. My mother and I made some too, later, when I was old enough to know how. My father died a few summers after I was born."

She walked to the edge of the stone in the center and knelt beside it, brushing off a layer of leaves. "He died in the cold season. Fell into a crevice hunting boar. They lashed his body with sinew and strips of hide and carried him home. His face remained unharmed. That mattered.

Rynn listened, sensing the gravity of the moment, but also the strange comfort that seemed to come from Ahna's voice. She was not weeping. She was remembering.

"My mother helped prepare his body," Ahna continued. "She placed ocher on his cheeks and shoulders—red is the color of living things. Then she combed his hair. I helped by putting a throwing stone in his hand."

"A weapon?" Rynn asked gently.

"No. A smooth stone. For remembrance. We all had one as children." She turned to look at him. "We formed him in a tight shape, knees to chest. Like we are born to mothers. And this helps return the dead."

Rynn nodded slowly. "We do that too, and we leave things for the journey of their spirit."

She wanted to know more. "What else do your people do for the dead?"

He took a deep breath and crouched beside her. "We dig a hole deep in the ground. My sister was buried like that. They put feathers around her head and a bead necklace across her chest. My father said it was to guide her if she took a sky journey."

"A sky journey?" Ahna asked, her brow furrowed.

"Yes. Some say the life spirit leaves the body and rises. The stars are the lights of the life spirits who came before. They watch us."

Ahna looked up briefly, narrowing her eyes at the branches that obscured the midday sun. "We are told the spirit joins the ground. It goes where the roots go. That is why we do not build fires on graves."

Rynn thought for a moment. "So your dead go into the ground, and ours into the sky."

"Not always," she said. "Some in my clan say there is a shadow world that lasts a short time—here but unseen. Some who die walk beside us for a little while. That is why we leave food—in case it is needed by those who stay with us before returning to the ground in another form."

"We leave food, too," Rynn said with a faint smile. "Especially for the ones who lived very long lives. Dried meat, berries. A bowl of water. Once, my uncle left honey."

They sat in silence for a while, the only sound the occasional hum of insects and the chirp of a squirrel darting up a nearby trunk.

"What do you believe happens after?" Ahna asked, turning to face him directly.

Rynn looked down and then toward the stone before answering. "I do not know. When I was younger, I liked the stories. The idea of a life spirit flying up. But now…" He paused. "Now I think… maybe the body returns to the ground around us, becoming dirt or stones. But the life spirit—what made them laugh, or dream—that part does not stay. It becomes something else."

"A bird?" she asked.

He smiled faintly. "A star, I think."

"And maybe you see them at night?" Ahna asked.

"Maybe," Rynn replied softly.

Ahna sat back and looked at the stone circle around them. "I do not think the dead speak to me. But I feel them. Not in words. Just… warmth. Or a hush. Like now."

He nodded. "Like the dead know we are here."

"Yes." She pressed her palm to the stone. "I think all that is around us remembers. Not names, maybe. But touch. Tears. Footsteps. I think memory is in everything."

Rynn reached into his pouch and pulled out a small polished shell—spiraled, pale pink, worn smooth by time. "We sometimes bury things like this. Small, beautiful things. We say they help the life spirit remember joy."

She studied the shell with curiosity. "We sometimes bury things… for the living to remember—not the dead."

"Maybe both ways help," he said, offering her the shell.

Ahna hesitated, then took it gently and placed it beside the central stone. "Then I will leave this shell in honor of my father. He liked to chase water bugs when he was a boy. I will have the happy memory of leaving it with him."

Rynn watched as she pressed her fingers into the soft soil into which she placed the shell, not to bury it deep, but to nestle it in place.

"Do you believe you'll see him again?" he asked.

She looked at him, her eyes not sad but thoughtful. "No. But I think that parts of him—the way he looked when happy, the way he loved me—those are not gone. They live in my memory—how I move, how I watch the sky, how I wait to speak, how I listen to the ground.

"Memory holds what is gone and gives it back in ways we may not always see."

Rynn listened, feeling the truth in her words, though his own heart shaped the thought differently. To him, the life spirit did not stay in just memory and the ground around them, but moved freely to take a place among the stars. Perhaps both were true, he wondered—memory and the ground keeping some things close, the sky receiving part of the essence of life that sought to move freely.

Rynn did not speak right away. He watched a single leaf fall from a branch overhead and spiral to the ground. "I think I believe much of that, too—that we carry part of our dead with us wherever we go."

"Important memories," she said.

"Yes," he added, "we honor by not forgetting."

They sat in stillness for a while longer, until Ahna stood and said, "We should return. My uncle will worry."

Rynn stood too, brushing dirt from his hands. "Thank you for bringing me here."

"You are the only one I have brought," she said, then paused. "You honor my memories."

He grinned. "And you honor mine."

They turned to leave, but Ahna stopped one last time. She did not kneel or bow. She simply placed her hand on the upright stone and whispered something—not for Rynn to hear, not even for her father to hear, but perhaps for herself and for the trees and the soil.

Then she turned and led the way back.

They walked slowly at first, neither in a hurry. The air was warmer now, and beams of afternoon light shone through the trees in golden streams.

The forest, having kept its respectful hush during their visit, seemed to exhale: birdsong resumed, the distant call of a hawk echoed faintly, and the undergrowth shook where a fox or badger might be threading its way unseen.

Rynn kept glancing at Ahna. She was not speaking, but her shoulders had relaxed and her breathing had calmed. Her fingers brushed the bark of trees as they passed, as if reacquainting herself with the living after visiting the land of the dead.

Finally, he said, "You seemed different there."

She looked at him sideways. "In what way?"

He nodded. "Not like you were afraid. But like you were... looking at something."

Ahna considered. "Memory—a shadow beside me."

He nodded and asked, "Do you go there often?"

"Not often now ," she said. "Many summers after my father died, I would go there once each moon and sit. I would remember how he sounded when he teased me, and how he danced when trying to stay awake."

Rynn smiled. "My sister, Jara, used to hum when she was nervous. A tiny sound, like a bee stuck in her chest."

"How old was Jara?"

"Younger—by many summers. She died two summers ago."

Ahna walked a few more paces before asking, "Do you miss her a lot?"

"Yes. But I used to think missing meant pain," Rynn said. "But now it feels warm and close. Always with me. I do not look for her, but I know she is there."

She nodded. "We are taught not to cry after death. The elders say it slows the spirit's return to the ground."

Rynn raised an eyebrow. "We are told that crying helps keep the spirit from feeling forgotten."

They both laughed softly.

"Strange," Ahna said. "But maybe both are true. Maybe the spirits you speak of are like people—some want to be remembered, others want to be released."

"I like that," Rynn said. "Death is not the same for all."

A silence passed between them, gentle and unhurried.

Then Ahna asked, "Why did you bring the shell?"

Rynn looked down at the forest floor, watching his step over a root. "I found it near the river a few days ago.

Thought it was beautiful. I was going to give it to you at a time that seemed right.

"The burial site seemed a good time. Then, when you created a memory by leaving the shell at your father's resting place, it made me happy."

Ahna's fingers grazed the leather cord at her neck. She lifted it slightly to show a small, worn tooth tied to it. "I thought about leaving this today, too," she said. "It was his. He lost it not long before his death. My mother kept it and later gave it to me. I want to keep it with me."

"I think he would understand."

"I think so too," she said.

They walked on, the terrain beginning to slope down.

"Today," Ahna said slowly, "felt like mixing water from two rivers."

"How do you mean?"

"You brought your way. I brought mine. They met. And it did not feel wrong."

Rynn smiled at the image. "They do not need to become one river. Just share the same path."

Ahna looked thoughtful, her gaze tracing the dark soil at their feet. "Do you think our clans could ever share a burial space?"

Rynn hesitated. "You mean—a member of my clan buried beside one of yours?"

She nodded slowly. "Yes."

The question lingered between them, fragile and unsettling. He sensed she wasn't speaking of death, but of what might one day be possible—the moment when their people could stand is the same resting place and grieve as one.

Rynn's face grew serious. "Maybe. If the people stop being afraid. If they stop thinking one way is better."

"Or that one is less," she added.

He nodded. "We might have to make a new kind of burial place."

"Maybe a circle," she suggested. "Half of your stones, half of mine."

"A shell in one hand. A red stone in the other."

They smiled at the thought.

After a short time, Ahna said, "The elders say we return to the ground, to the roots of trees, to the animals in the forest. Some say we start by becoming like fallen leaves joining the soil."

"And my elders say we are up there," Rynn shrugged, pointing to the sky.

As he looked at the sky, he said, "Strange, though, even the stars fall sometimes. I saw one streak across the sky and my aunt said it was a spirit racing home."

Ahna grinned. "A strange thought."

They both laughed.

"You know," Rynn said, "I did not expect to learn so much today."

"Why did you decide to join me?"

"I hoped I would learn more about you and your people. But I also learned more about myself."

She glanced at him with curiosity. "What did you learn about yourself?"

He hesitated, then said, "That my grief is much like your grief. Even though we have different names for it."

Ahna's face looked understanding. She reached out and touched his arm briefly—both a gesture of comfort and a gesture usually reserved for kinship—offered by one who understood that words rarely carry all that is meant.

Ahead, the trees thinned, and the sounds of fires in the camp reached them—wood cracking, voices laughing, the winding down of daily activity.

"We are getting close," Ahna said.

Rynn sighed, not in sadness, but with a feeling that something sacred had ended.

"I am glad you showed me," he said.

"I am glad you came," she replied. "Next time, I will take you to the place where I go when I do not want to think of anything at all."

He raised an eyebrow. "And where is that?"

She smiled. "You'll see."

They walked on together—two young people, two peoples, bound not by ancestry but by attraction and a growing curiosity. The path behind them held the imprint of new memory, and the trail ahead held a promise: The journey was no longer one they walked alone.

When Ahna returned to her camp, the air was different.

The smoke from the cook fires carried no scent of meat. The laughter of the children was hushed. Eyes followed her, then looked away. Not in fear—she knew what fear looked like. This was unsettling—suspicion layered over uncertainty. And beneath that, an edge of quiet anger.

Goma waited for her near the shelter, arms crossed over his chest.

"You were gone long," he said.

"Yes."

He did not ask where. He did not really want to know.

Zarn stepped forward from the shadows of the tool cave. "The young *tall one*?" he asked.

She nodded.

"You keep returning to him," he said.

"And he returns to me."

"You let him see too much."

"I showed him our truth."

Goma raised a hand, silencing them both. "Enough. Ahna will speak. Not in corners. In the circle."

By midday, the fire circle filled with clan members— men marked by old hunts and half-healed scars, older women with faces etched by wind and smoke, young hunters with restless hands, and those who sat apart, watchful in their silence.

Ahna stepped into the center, close to the fire. She stood without fear, without defiance, without shame.

"I have seen Rynn again," she said. "And I have shared and I have learned."

No one interrupted.

"I have shown him who we are. Our hunts. Our silence. Our strength. And he has not run. He does not come with spears or shouts. He comes with open ears."

A few murmurs. Someone got up and walked away. One of the women spat into the fire.

Zarn stood. "What if he comes back with others? With traps and arrows and fire?"

Ahna replied. "We must know what they are. Not what we fear they might be."

Yaya shook her head. "And how do we know?"

Ahna turned slowly in a circle, meeting the eyes of those who dared look back. "We meet. Not in secret. Not in hiding. Not one to one. Clan to clan. Elders to elders."

Silence followed. Somewhere a child coughed.

Goma narrowed his eyes. "You want us to stand before them?"

"I want us to stand with them."

"On open ground?" Zarn asked.

"Yes. With open ears and gifts," replied Ahna.

Gasps and mutters passed through the circle.

"Gifts?" Yaya asked. "Like we are the smaller ones? The ones seeking approval?"

"No," Ahna said. "Like we are equals. Not a lower form. Not a higher form. Not ghosts. Like we are proud of who we are, and we accept them for who they are."

Goma said nothing. Then he turned to the oldest woman, Marga, who had spoken very little about the *tall ones*.

Her eyes were clouded with age, but she still heard all.

She raised one crooked finger and pointed at Ahna.

Then slowly nodded.

It was enough.

If the elders of the clan of the *tall ones* agreed, the elders of Ahna's clan would meet and exchange gifts.

A meeting would be set for two sunrises from now, at the flat stones near the river—halfway between the two camps—where the elders from each clan would gather. Each clan would bring a gift: something that showed their way of life, their meaning, their peace.

Ahna left the circle that evening with her heart steady.

She walked through the forest under a moon the color of newly cleaned bone.

The trees whispered, and her feet remembered the path without effort.

When she reached the river, Rynn was already there.

He looked up from where he was arranging something on a flat rock—smooth pebbles in a spiral, a piece of bark with markings.

His face lit up when he saw her. It faded slightly when he noticed her expression.

She crossed the river and knelt across from him, and said, "I have something important to share—and I want to share it in my way."

She touched her chest, then held up two fingers.

Two people.

Then she swept her hand wide to indicate a larger group. A circle.

Then, carefully, she touched her temple and made the shape of a spiral in the air—the old sign for elders, for memory, for decision-makers.

Rynn sensed her meaning and nodded.

Ahna mimed walking, and then pointed to a flat stone, and back to him. Back and forth.

She placed two stones on the ground. Then added a small dried leaf next to each. A gift beside a being.

Rynn's eyes widened.

"You mean…" he whispered, more to himself than to her. "Our elders? Meeting? Bringing gifts?"

She nodded, pleased at his understanding.

He stared at the stones. Then at her.

Then, slowly, he reached into his pouch and pulled out a sinew necklace he had made days ago. He placed it gently next to one of her stones.

She smiled.

He mimed a question with his hands: When?

She raised two fingers.

"Two nights must pass," she said.

"The meeting will be in two sunrises," he said.

She nodded.

"I will take this to my elders," Rynn said, steady but cautious. "They must hear it from me—that your people wish to meet, to speak together. If they agree, the clans will face one another not as hunters, but as peaceful elders."

They sat without words as the wind rustled the trees, and the river went on speaking its endless language.

They were participating in something that neither could be sure would work for either clan.

Chapter Seven

The elders of Rynn's clan had agreed to meet with the elders of the clan of the *others*—a meeting that many believed might upset the fragile peace between the two peoples. The morning of the meeting dawned windless, the sky layered in gray. Fires burned low, words were few, and even the elders of each clan seemed unsure whether they had chosen wisely.

The flat stones near the river had been chosen carefully as the meeting place. Neither clan claimed the land, though both used it. The river itself lay between the forest in the northeast near the ridges—home of the *others*, Ahna's people—and the open meadows on the southwest side of the river—home of the *tall ones*, Rynn's people.

Rynn, accompanied by four *Homo sapiens* elders and several other members of the clan, arrived first. He bore a strip of tanned hide painted with two joined circles—a bold gesture of peace: separate clans, peacefully existing side by side. To Rynn, the circles were a vision of what could be, a message of hope.

Omak, Terah, Duma, and Marek—the lead elder who was now very frail and limited in his ability to participate —walked with careful steps, each carrying a token of their life: a flint blade smoothed from use, a pouch of dried berries, a strand of shells strung on sinew, and a shaped spearhead made for long throws.

They waited next to the flat stones near the west side of the river.

Then, elders of Ahna's clan—the Neanderthals—came.

Goma led them. Yaya walked beside him, her face painted in red ocher. Behind them came Tov, eyes alert, and two others—Marga, oldest woman of their clan, and Enu, the stone tool maker.

Ahna followed with several others members of her clan. They walked behind, hands empty but hearts hopeful.

The Neanderthals carried their own gifts: a heavy hammer-stone, its surface worn smooth by many summers of tool making, a strip of smoked elk bound in birchbark, a small carved bear, and a flat stone decorated with a red handprint.

After crossing the river, they stopped at the edge of the meeting place.

For a moment, no one moved.

Then Rynn stepped forward, holding his decorated hide out with both hands so that Ahna's people could see it.

He crouched and placed it on the stone near the center of the circle where the meeting would take place.

Omak stepped forward next. He laid the flint blade beside the hide.

Then Yaya placed a carved bear near the flint blade.

Each gift was placed in order—no words yet, only nods and gentle sounds of objects being carefully laid down.

The two groups remained standing, facing one another.

Two clans.

Two stories.

One chance to come together.

Ahna moved to the center and held up both hands, fingers spread.

Then she pointed to Goma. To Yaya. To Omak, Terah, and Enu.

Then back to herself. And to Rynn.

She made circles with her arms, and then touched her chest with both hands.

Her message was clear: *family*.

Then, to make sure she was understood, she put her meaning into words. "Family."

Omak repeated Ahna's word. "Family."

Terah then rose to speak. She hoped to be understood, speaking slowly, clearly, with gestures.

"We live where the wind is strong," she said, pointing to the windswept grasslands behind her. "We hunt the herds. We teach our young."

She drew a shape of two figures beside a child.

From Ahna's clan, Yaya rose and replied.

"Trees," she said in her own way, and pointed to the forest across the river. She made a shelter shape with her hands, then mimed holding a child to her breast.

Omak took a step forward. He mimed throwing a spear —long arc, far distance.

Goma responded by miming holding a short spear, stepping forward, and striking close.

Then they both looked at one another—and nodded.

Different ways to hunt—both ways successful.

Different ways to live—but neither a threat to the other.

The clans were silent as they looked at one another. They still stood apart, with gifts laid out between them.

The *Homo sapiens* elders studied the *others* with quiet fascination—their powerful chests, shortened limbs, and deep-set eyes beneath heavy brows. They noted the thick hair, the breadth of shoulder, the compact strength that spoke of lives hardened by rough ground and the needs of the hunt. Yet beneath that ruggedness they noticed hints of unhurried stillness, careful eyes, a quiet measuring that seemed to belong to people seeking their own kind of trust.

At the same time, the Neanderthal elders studied the *tall ones*. Their bodies were longer, their movements lighter —as if built for movement over long distance rather than short-distance endurance—faces narrower and angular.

Smoke drifted between them, carrying the mixed scents of wood fire and damp soil. The *tall ones* stood patiently, with restraint that the *others* recognized. But between them remained that marks either possible kinship or conflict.

Each group waited, uncertain how to begin. A murmur ran through the observers behind them—soft, uneasy, like wind through dry grass. One of the elders shifted his weight, another glanced toward the forest, as if measuring the way back. Yet no one stepped away. For the first time, they stood close enough to see one another's breath in the cool air, and to wonder whether the distance between them was smaller than they had believed

At last, one of the *Homo sapiens* elders lifted a hand and tapped the haft of his spear, then gestured toward the forest beyond. A Neanderthal elder mirrored the motion, his deep-set eyes following the line of trees. The gesture was clear enough: *We hunt the same beasts.*

Rynn stepped between them, lifting the shell strand and laying it beside the bear carving.

He touched one, then the other, and linked them with his hands.

Tov, the quietest member of Ahna's clan, rose to speak. He tapped his chest, then pointed at Yaya—the clan's story keeper—and at Zarn—one of the clan's hunters.

He spread his arms wide.

"People," he said as he pointed. "Not beasts. People."

Omak nodded, slowly. "People."

The word sounded different in his mouth—but the meaning was clear.

We are all people.

Omak's words settled over them as the day drifted forward and the clouds thinned.

They spoke little at first. But, as they learned to speak to each other, they made sounds—repetitions as words and gestures were shared. Ahna and Rynn helped when they could, repeating each other's words.

At first, words were few and clumsy, but gestures filled the gaps. One Homo sapiens elder knelt to draw the outline of a roe deer in the dirt, marking tracks with quick strokes. Another pointed to the sky, miming the sweep of birds that signaled the coming herds. A Neanderthal elder showed, with careful pantomime, how his people drove animals into narrow ravines where spears waited. In answer, a *Homo sapiens* elder spread his arms wide, describing a circle —their way of driving prey into the open before chasing them down.

They laughed once—when Terah mimed running from a cave bear, and Yaya mimed hitting it with a stone.

Even Enu, a Neanderthal elder, smiled.

Then there were nods, grunts, and another burst of laughter when an elder's attempt at mimicking a bellowing aurochs turned more comical than fierce.

The tension eased by a small measure. They were beginning to seem less like strangers and more like people who shared the same land and sources of food—and were slowly learning to share language.

When the sun had passed its highest point, they placed their hands, one by one, on the center stone.

Not all at once—one after the other.

The warmth of each new palm joined the warmth of the one it covered.

Then they turned and left, each clan returning home.

No promises had been made. But when one elder had broken a strip of dried meat in two and laid half upon the ground between them, and the other had bent to take it, the worry of spears no longer felt so pressing.

Such simple acts of sharing had led to something important happening at the meeting of the two clans.

The old hesitancy had paused and the possibility of a new alliance had begun to form.

Ahna and Rynn stayed long after the elders departed.

They sat by the river again, not speaking, just watching the water.

"People," Rynn said softly, repeating Omak's word.

Ahna nodded, then said it too. "People."

Their mouths made the word differently.

But the meaning landed in the same place.

Later, Ahna and Rynn each returned to their own camp.

In the *Homo sapiens* camp, the mood was divided. Some said little. Others, as usual, said too much.

Rynn sat around the fire with the elders, who chattered and seemed quite relieved. He watched the way Omak was gesturing and the way Terah kept glancing toward the treetops. Even Enu seemed relaxed.

As the elders sat warming themselves, clan members who had stayed in camp gathered quickly. Many had been anxiously waiting and made no effort to hide it.

Omak raised his hand for silence. He stood before the gathered clan and gave a single nod.

"We met," he said. "All is well."

That was all.

Terah added more. "They brought gifts. They listened."

Whispers passed through the crowd.

Someone asked, "What do they want?"

"Nothing," Omak answered. "Only to live."

"To live near us?" another voice said.

"They live as we live," Terah said. "They are not beasts. They speak. They raise children. They bury their dead."

"But they are different," said one of the clan's hunters.

"Yes," Terah said. "As morning is different from afternoon."

The words were surprising.

Not everyone nodded.

But no one argued.

That night, the fire's flames reached higher than usual. No one sang. But a few stories were told. Not of monsters. Not of war. Just of the meeting.

Rynn sat beside his mother, crippled by old age and nearing death. When he handed her a pebble he had found near the river—a small one with a red streak like fire—she took it, smiled, and held it in her lap.

Across the river, deep in the forest, the Neanderthals had also returned in silence.

Goma sat near the opening of one of the larger shelters, the bear carving beside him, his gaze fixed on the fire.

Yaya hummed while grinding herbs, a bright little melody that carried her contentment into the air.

Ahna sat nearby, listening to the questions that drifted between the elders.

"They stood like reeds," someone said. "Tall, but soft."

"They brought food with no fat," Yaya said, wrinkling her nose at the dried berries.

"They smell of ash and char," another offered.

"They speak too much," grumbled the hunter Zarn. "But they watch like we do."

Marga spoke last. "Their skin is thin. But their eyes are strong."

That quieted the circle.

Later, as the fire dimmed, Ahna helped a child tie sinew for a slingshot. Her fingers moved smoothly, but her mind kept replaying the gesture Goma had made—how he had touched his chest, then touched the elder of the *tall ones*, then himself again.

An ancient sign that each clan used to mean "same."

That night, the wind returned.

It moved through both camps, stirring hides, rattling leaves. It cooled both clans equally, never blowing ever so slightly more toward one clan than the other.

Back in camp, the Neanderthal elders gathered in a small cave, often used as a shelter.

The cave was cool with the scent of old ash and damp soil. A low fire crackled in its center, casting flickers of orange light across the faces of the elders who sat in a circle —their massive brows furrowed in thought, their noses pulling in the scent of smoke-laced air.

A few days earlier, Enu, one of the younger elders, broad-chested and showing only a trace of gray in his beard, had ventured out to scout the *Homo sapiens* camp.

"They talk," he said. "They talk all the time."

Bren, a friend of Ahna's, rubbed her thumb over the handle of a stone tool made long ago by her deceased sister. "Do you think," she asked quietly, "that this noise—this jabber of the *tall ones*—blinds them?"

"Yes," Marga said, likely so. "To many things. The sound of a snowflake landing on a dry leaf. The way birds grow quiet when the a big cat prowls. The sound of moss sighing before the rain. They may not know these things."

"And I think they might not hear the welcoming voices that give greeting," Enu added. "The song of trees when the sun returns. The sigh of soil waking in the morning. The heartbeat of a cave when you lie upon its belly."

"They think the world must be explained," Marga said. "We think the world must be felt."

There was a reverent hush. Outside, beyond the mouth of the cave, night began its descent. The last glimmer of twilight gave way to the deeper blue that heralded the stars.

Somewhere far off, a wolf howled—not in hunger, but in longing, in loneliness for a mate. The elders tilted their heads in unison, like trees bending to the same breeze.

"They have a longing also," Enu said. "A longing to be heard—perhaps because they do not know how to hear."

"They speak their stories out loud," Marga said. "We carry ours in our bones, our memories, our tools."

Yaya added. "They believe that things will vanish if words are not used constantly."

Marga looked at Yaya. "And we believe that nothing vanishes. It only changes form."

Then, gazing into the dark just beyond the firelight, Marga said, "It is as if they are afraid of the silence—when the ground speaks the loudest. Do they fear what they might hear? Do they not want to listen? Do they wish to drown out the voice of the soil, the trees, the stones?"

There were nods, slow and heavy. Marga lifted her head to speak. Her hair was bone-white, braided with feathers—strands of age that endured like roots of an ancient tree.

Her voice came low and steady. Her eyes narrowed, and she nodded solemnly. "Perhaps they are running from the land's complaints: the dry river bed, the sick animal, the broken pattern of seasons. If they talked less, they too might hear the land weeping."

"And if they do not listen," Enu added, "if they speak louder and louder to keep the land quiet—then they will become her enemies. The land will not forget that."

There was a silence then—a shared silence, as if they all were watching the same invisible wind lightly brush across the ground.

The fire spoke in its own way—popping like snapping twigs. In response, Enu had more to say. "I have watched them, too. They do not sit long in silence. Their mouths move like they are hungry for their own voices. Even their children talk over each other. The old ones speak of the stars, the leaves, the shape of a tool, the color of meat. Yet, as their words spill out, I am not sure that their listening grows."

Enu frowned, running a thick finger along the line of his jaw. "Do they not hear the ground?" he asked. "Do they not feel the beat beneath their feet, or smell the cold before it arrives? Do they not notice the hush before animals flee?"

"They are clever," Marga said carefully. "Their hands are quick. Their eyes are sharp. They are like the fox—always moving, always alert. But I think they do not listen as we do—to the things that speak without words."

"Because they never stop using their own words" Tov grumbled.

"They speak like birds chirping at dawn," muttered Goma, whose ears had always been keen and who prided himself on hearing the change in a wind's direction before the trees bent to it. "But not with meaning. Only with sound that fills the air."

"They speak over nature like a man ignoring his wounded mother," Enu added. "And yet they expect her to go on feeding them."

"We must not be like them," said Marga softly. "No matter how close our clans draw, no matter how much we share. Never forget how to listen."

Silence again. This time, deeper. The flames dimmed, the wood nearly spent. Only the embers remained, like the hearts of ancestors watching from the coals.

Enu stood slowly. "Still," he said, "they are not without gifts. They move fast. Their eyes are quick. Their thoughts sharp... but strange."

"We must not mock what we do not yet understand," Goma said gently. "But we must guard what we know and do understand."

Enu gave a low grunt of agreement. "Let them have their jabber. We will keep the silence."

"And in that silence," Marga said, standing last, "we will hear what they miss."

The fire gave a final snap and folded into itself. The elders turned to the opening in the shelter, where the moon was climbing the horizon. One by one, they stepped into the dark, their feet pressing soft circles into the ground. The wind greeted them like an old friend.

A reverent hush settled. Twilight thinned into a deeper blue, the stars beginning to show. Somewhere far off, a wolf howled, again in longing. The elders turned to listen, like a stand of trees bending to the same breeze.

Enu's voice broke the silence, low but steady. "What we hold as true must be guarded. What we do not yet know must be met with open hearts."

Around them, the night grew calm enough that even its silence could be heard.

Chapter Eight

The young boy, Ahna's brother Akran had been fading for days.

Ahna became her brother's sole caregiver after her mother died of old age two summers ago.

At first, Akran's symptoms were subtle—so subtle that Ahna had convinced herself she was imagining it. The boy still laughed, still followed the others when they wandered toward the river, still picked berries with small, berry-stained fingers.

But his steps had slowed.

When the other children burst into a run, Akran trailed behind, head looking upward as if listening to something no one else could hear.

To members of the clan, Akran was known by a gesture: two fingers touched lightly to the brow and then opened to the sky. This simple gesture meant *sky-looking*.

He had been curious from birth, his questions most often answered only with glances and with palms open in honesty, indicating either confusion or not-knowing.

Now, as the summer wore into its waning days, Akron's curiosity dimmed.

Ahna noticed his quiet in the evenings. Around the fire, when children doubled over in laughter, *Sky-Looking*, as he was nick-named, sat without expression. He traced patterns in the dirt with a stick, his eyes half-closed.

Once, when the hunters returned with a young boar, several children shrieked with excitement, crowding close to see the tusks. Akran simply leaned against Ahna's arm and asked, in his unassuming way, if the boar dreamed about running before it had died.

The question played in Ahna's thoughts for a long time. Other children asked questions about hunting, but this was different. It was as if Akron had begun to step away from daily life, turning his thoughts somewhere else.

A few days later, his breathing grew shallow. He tired quickly, curling against the hides before the sun slipped down. He sipped water but left food untouched.

Ahna crushed berries into a paste and pressed it against her brother's lips, but he swallowed only once, reluctantly, and turned his face away.

Memories tugged at Ahna as she sat beside him. She remembered him darting after a firefly one spring night, his body vanishing as he ran into the shadows of the trees.

She had been frantic, calling after him and following the glow until she found him crouched at the base of an oak, staring upward in awe.

When Ahna scolded him gently with a frown, Akran had only laughed, showing a gap where his front tooth had once been. He could have easily found his way back by the shapes of the trees, he explained. He knew the trees.

That memory ached now, shadowed against the frailty of the child who could no longer rise without help.

Two more days passed and Akran did not improve, On the advice of the healer, Vahra, Ahna carried warm stones from the fire and laid them against Akran's belly and palms, hoping the heat would call him back. She stroked his brow and hummed softly, not a song, just a low sound to steady her own breath. She wept sometimes, but quietly because Sky-Looking had always been startled by loud emotion. A raised voice, even in play, had made him flinch. So Ahna kept her sorrow gentle, no sharper than the wind against grass.

Each time she held him, the boy seemed lighter in Ahna's arms, as though he was leaving piece by piece. His skin grew pale, his eyes drifting half-shut even when the camp stirred with noise around them. Once, he roused enough to lift his fingers and mimic his own gesture—brow to sky. Then his hand fell, too heavy to hold.

Clan members came and went, leaving gifts of food, herbs, or feathers beside his sleeping place. Some knelt to brush his hair. Others pressed foreheads briefly to his. But they did not stay long.

Vahra brought a mixture of herbs, rubbed some along his limbs and chest, and made a bitter-root potion for him to drink each evening before sleep. During the next three days, there was no improvement.

It was Ahna who kept watch through the slow-moving days, who listened to the ragged pattern of breath, who bore the weight of knowing that the child she held was slipping beyond reach.

And still, she hoped.

Ahna whispered in her thoughts that tomorrow the boy might wake hungry, might ask again for wild plums or laugh at the play of foxes across the ridge. Tomorrow, he might find his feet and return to taking part in laughter around the evening fire.

But even as she whispered, she felt the truth settling inside her—inevitable as the last breath of a wounded creature too tired to flee. The child's path was curving away, and no strength of arms could turn it back.

It happened near dawn, when the mist curled low over the valley and the light was still more shadow than day.

Ahna had not closed her eyes during the night. She had sat cross-legged beside her brother, her palms resting over the boy's hands, warming them with heated stones when they cooled.

The fire behind her had fallen to embers, but she had not fed it. Flames felt wrong in that stillness. They would crackle and flare, demanding attention when she had little left to give.

She wanted only to hear the slow rhythm of Akran's breath and to feel the slow beating of his heart.

Akran's chest rose and fell faintly—so faintly that Ahna gently moved her hands in the same up and down pattern, hoping that feeling her presence would strengthen him. Each time she moved her face close to his, she heard a whisper of air moving. In response, she willed her own lungs to match the rhythm of his breath.

But then, in the gray between night and morning, there was no rise, no fall. No breath. Only stillness.

Ahna did not cry out. She leaned forward and pressed her forehead gently to Akran's, closing his eyes. She stayed there until the warmth between them faded, until her own tears wet her brother's cool skin. She let them fall silently, letting grief move through her without making a sound.

After her breath steadied, she nodded to those waiting.

Relatives and friends from the clan had been keeping watch close by. They had stayed close enough to see her shelter but far enough away to give Ahna the space her grief required. When they saw her hand signal—fingers spread, palm turned down, then lowered once—they came.

They came without talking.

They did not wash his body. Dirt still clung to Akron's knees—marks of play from days ago. Under his fingernails were flakes of ocher, from when he had helped smear a sun symbol on the cave wall. No one tried to scrub these things away. His life was not meant to be erased as he returned to the ground.

Akran was still Akran.

One by one, each Neanderthal stepped into the shelter, pausing before crossing the threshold as a sign of both love and respect. They did not chant nor make other sounds. They simply carried smooth stones, river-worn and warmed by the fire.

These were not offerings in the way *Homo sapiens* made offerings. No food for his life spirit. No trinkets to guide his path into another life.

These stones were for *remembering*, each one chosen for both its beauty and for the weight of memory it carried.

An elder placed a rounded stone the size of Akran's palm by the child's feet. She said, with a slow curl of her lips, that it matched the boy's belly-laugh, the way it filled the camp and rolled outward.

Another elder brought a jagged stone, sharp on one side, smooth on the other, saying nothing—but all who knew Akran remembered the storms of his tantrums.

Another brought a red-speckled stone—the color of Akron's favorite berry that often stained his lips—and laid it gently next to his shoulder.

A young hunter stepped up, his shoulders broad, hair tied with a strip of sinew. He crouched low, placed a stone beside the body, and set a sliver of red ocher on the child's chest. The pigment was on his fingers, and he drew a faint line across the small stone eye that was sitting next to Akran's head. The gesture was brief, but full of meaning: Akran had been seen and would continue to be seen.

Another hunter came, bringing a blue stone and a strip of birch bark curling at the edges. He placed the bark across Akran's legs, then pressed his own forehead to the ground before placing the stone down and stepping back.

A mother followed, carrying dried flowers bound with twine, their petals faded but still fragrant. She laid them near the child's temple, where their scent might freshen the air beside Akran's head.

Ahna smiled. Each stone and object added another layer of the uniting with the ground. The child would return to the soil and become part of the life that stirred in roots, stones, and breath around them.

When Ahna's friend Bren approached, holding a pine bough fresh with resin, she paused longer than the others. She knew Akran well and loved him as she had loved her own brother before his death five summers ago. She bent low, brushed her lips against the child's cheek, then laid the bough across his legs. The green needles would release their sharp, clean smell during many, many days—long after most flowers had wilted.

As the stones gathered around his small body, the nest of Akran's memory was taking shape.

Objects from his life were placed around him. A bone smoothed by river water. A handful of lavender clay, cool and soft, pressed against the grasses. A feather from a crow, black and iridescent, placed above his head. Each object was chosen not only for beauty but for connection—for the way it carried his laughter, his curiosity, his quick steps in the forest.

The elder, Marga, stepped forward last. She placed her palm flat against the child's chest and left it there, still and steady, as though she could lend Akran her own heartbeat for a few moments. This was her way of helping weave the child back into the ground.

A crow cawed far off.

Then, with a slow exhale, Marga lifted her hand.

That was the signal. The moment of parting.

The group stepped back.

No members of Rynn's clan had joined them. Not yet. Ahna had asked Rynn and others to join the gathering at the burial site near the birches after she signaled them.

Rynn had seen the smoke earlier that morning, a thin column of pine-smoke drifting against the pale sky. Ahna had told him that a pine smoke signal meant death had arrived—and Ahna would send a second signal to let him know that burial was about to begin.

At Ahna's request he had shared this with members of his clan. The first smoke would be a signal to wait, to give space. The second would be an invitation to the burial.

After the stones had been laid, several elders lifted Akran gently—as one lifts a loved child.

Four pairs of arms steadied him, with Ahna walking close beside, her hand lightly touching Akran's shoulder. The burial site was nearby—a short climb to an open area below a rock outcrop.

Ahna sent a second smoke signal to Rynn, inviting the the mourners in his clan to come to the place of burial.

The burial site was private, below an overhanging rock formation and guarded by numerous nearby birch and ash.

After Rynn saw the signal, the Homo sapiens came quietly, gathering at the edge of the clearing. Rynn led, Omak and Tamik at his side, a small group that included Terah, Duma, and several others. They did not step forward or take part, only watched as the Neanderthals prepared to lay the child into the ground.

Waiting had not been easy. Among the Homo sapiens clan, when a life ended, the body was washed quickly, dressed in clean hide, and prepared for burial. Words were often spoken so that the dead might know they were remembered. Delay in freeing the life spirit felt unnatural.

They were about to witness an unfamiliar ceremony.

Rynn felt a sudden sadness. He remembered seeing Akron when he was well, and seeing him during his illness. During one visit to Ahna not long ago, Rynn had watched Akron follow fireflies in the dark—a favorite activity—moving unafraid among the shadows of the trees, his laughter carrying through the leaves. He had thought then how bold Akran was, how certain his steps.

To see Akron gone to silence filled Rynn with a sorrow he had not expected.

The place where Akran would rest was not like a resting place known to Rynn's clan. It looked more like a type of protected nest, the kind foxes build from leaves and tufts of wool. The resting place had been hollowed out and looked like a shallow bowl—an unfamiliar shape in which to place a recently departed. The surface on which Akron would rest was covered with grasses pressed flat and flowers crushed to release their scent, both lying over a thin layer of ash spread to soften the ground.

The carriers lowered Akran carefully, facing his closed eyes toward the morning sunlight. His hands and arms were folded across his chest and his knees drawn up. Cradled in his arms was the carved stone Ahna had shaped many days earlier—an open eye, unblinking. Not magic, not a charm—just a reminder that Akran's memory traveled with them, steady as the carved stone.

Ahna crouched near Akran's resting place. From her pouch she drew tufts of soft eagle down. She scattered them around the body, as if giving him one more dream.

Now, elders of Ahna's clan prepared for the final covering—the oldest and most important part of the ritual. No one gave instructions, but all knew what to do. One by one, they brought what they had gathered: a bone from a deer Akran had once watched at the bank of the river, a strip of bark curled like a sleeping fist, a handful of clay— the soft purple of lavender blossoms.

As this part of the ceremony ended, a light covering of dirt was laid over the nest.

Then, as a final step, Ahna laid a pine bough, fragrant with resin, gently on top.

Then came stillness.

No words. No chants. The mourners sat in a half-circle around Akran's resting place and did not speak.

Time slowly passed, and the wind shifted, carrying the hum of insects. A hawk wheeled above and vanished again. Some mourners wept, but quietly, their shoulders shaking, their throats closed against sound.

When Ahna finally rose, her knees stiff, the sun had set and darkness would soon be upon them.

Her brother was gone, but not lost.

The burial nest in which Akran was now at home was more than a place. It was a memory ground, chosen long ago by the elders for moments such as this.

The Neanderthals did not set apart the dead from the living with walls of stone or deep holes piled with dirt.

The birches leaned inward, pale trunks streaked with lichen. Their leaves flickered silver as the air shifted, casting light and shade across the group gathered below.

At the edge of the burial ground, grasses grew long and bent, lying almost flat. A patch of heather bloomed purple in late summer's stubborn hold, and somewhere close by, bees worked quietly among the flowers.

Later that evening, from where he stood, Rynn felt a strange pull—an urge to sit beside her, to share the silence. But something in him held back. This was not his place, not yet. He would mourn in his own way when the time came. Tonight, it was the Ahna's vigil.

As he slowly made his way back to his own shelter, birches whispered in the evening wind. Ahna remained with Akran for awhile longer, a lone figure keeping watch as darkness gathered.

Later that night, as the first stars pricked the sky, a small voice broke the hush inside the *Homo sapiens* camp.

"Rynn?"

It was Luna, a friend of Jara's from childhood—a friend long before Jara had died. She curled against Rynn's side, her face pale in the glow of the fire's last embers, drawing quiet strength from the warmth at her shoulder. Her voice was tentative, edged with worry.

"Yes, little one?" Rynn murmured, brushing a curl from her forehead.

"Will Akran's spirit find its way?" Luna asked.

The question hung between the girl's innocence and her worry. Rynn searched for words that would honor Luna's concern without brushing it aside. He knew children often listened more closely than adults imagined.

"What makes you ask that?" he said softly.

"I heard that they did not wash him," Luna whispered. "They did not put him deep in the ground. They did not speak words. They just… covered him with a few things and then dirt. And then they sat. Like they were waiting."

Rynn drew her close, exhaling softly as he chose his words carefully. "Yes," he said. "They prepared the body… in their way. And at the burial site they were listening, not using words as we do. That is their way."

"Is that what Akran wanted?" Luna pressed.

Rynn rocked her gently, his own eyes fixed on the fire. "Yes, I think so. There are many paths to the same place," he whispered. "And many kinds of love. They placed things over him very carefully, not for his use, but for the memories of those who still live. Then they sat with him for a very long time time. Those are also signs of love."

Luna was quiet, her breath slowing. "It feels… different. Was it sad."

Rynn kissed her forehead. "Yes, it was very sad."

Luna listened as a night owl called into the dark. Luna, soothed, returned to her shelter and drifted into sleep.

And some distance away at the burial place—the glade beneath the birches, Ahna's brother's rested quietly, joined to the ground, to the air, and to all who had known him.

Night pressed gently over both camps, laying shadows across the ground until the glow of their fires was the only light. Smoke drifted upward in slow spirals, carrying the faint scent of pine. Beyond the ridge, birch, pine, and fir trees whispered in the evening wind, and somewhere in the valley, a fox barked once, sharp and lonely.

The air had cooled. The valley shadows grew long, stretching toward the river. Starlight settled over the birch leaves, giving them a faint, silvery sheen.

Ahna remained at the edge of Akran's resting place, eyes vigilant, her body unmoving. She would not light a fire tonight. The moment said to Ahna that the fading light of Akran's day should be honored by the darkness of night as the ground welcomed the child back into its keeping.

Tomorrow there might be fire, or chants, or words spoken as a *remembering*. But tonight, there was only stillness, and the quiet truth that love—however it was shown—is enough.

Historical Context III

Care and Compassion

"To know a species, we must understand not only how it lived, but how it imagined its life."
—Ian Tattersall

Caring for the Injured

In the harsh Ice Age world of 40,000 years ago, survival depended not only on strength and skill but also on the care given to a sick or injured member of the clan. Both Neanderthals and *Homo sapiens* lived in small groups in which the loss of a single hunter, toolmaker, or mate could mean the difference between life and death for all.

Within this context, care for the injured was not merely an act of compassion, it was an adaptive necessity. The archaeological record shows that both lineages—when caring for the injured—acted out of genuine empathy, focused on short-term healing, and remained committed to long-term adjustment and reintegration within the clan.

Evidence of Healing

Fossilized bones dating to about 40,000 years ago reveal clear evidence of personal care. Many Neanderthal remains bear healed fractures and other marks of recovery, showing that some individuals lived months or even years beyond injuries that would otherwise have been fatal.

One of the most famous examples is a man given the name Shanidar 1, discovered in Iraq's Zagros Mountains. His bones reveal a crushed left eye socket that likely left him blind, a withered right arm ending in a healed amputation below the elbow, and damage to his right leg and foot. These injuries had healed long before he died, meaning he lived for years with his physical limitations.

To endure such trauma in the harsh Ice Age world, he must have received devoted care during recovery. Others must have provide him food, sheltered and protected him from cold and predators and included him in their daily lives. His survival into old age shows that his companions valued him greatly.

Shanidar 1 provides evidence that Neanderthals were empathetic and caring—a lineage that valued individuals for more than their immediate usefulness to the clan.

Other Neanderthal finds echo the same theme. The La Chapelle-aux-Saints skeleton in France belonged to an older male who suffered from severe arthritis, tooth loss, and bone degeneration, yet lived long enough for the disease to progress slowly. Someone must have chewed his food or prepared it soft enough to swallow. When buried, the body was placed in a pit with care, the limbs arranged in a deliberate order—a gesture suggesting reverence for life and respect for age.

Among early *Homo sapiens*, comparable patterns appear. Cro-Magnon skeletons of Europe and the Skhul and Qafzeh remains in the Levant show healed fractures and deformed knitting of bones that testify to long-term survival.

One individual from Skhul V had a serious head injury but lived with healed skull bones to adulthood.

Another, from Dolní Věstonice in Moravia, suffered from a congenital condition that fused the joints of his legs, rendering him immobile. Yet he was buried with shell beads and ornaments, a sign that his people valued him despite his disability.

The Nature of Care

The type of care required in common injuries would have been both practical and emotional. A fractured limb, for example, demands immobilization, rest, and protection from infection, while a deep cut might require cleaning, steady pressure, and repeated attention.

Though Neanderthals lacked splints in the modern sense, they could bind a limb with strips of hide, fiber, or flexible wood. Mosses and plant fibers could have been used as padding.

Evidence from Shanidar Cave includes traces of medicinal plants—yarrow, groundsel, and ephedra—whose properties suggest they were known as healing herbs. Whether they were placed intentionally or accidentally remains debated, yet the coincidence is telling.

Pain relief was likely achieved through natural means: poultices made from aromatic herbs, the numbing effects of cold, and possibly the analgesic qualities of willow bark, which contains salicylic acid—a main ingredient in aspirin.

Smoke and firelight may also have been used to induce calm during treatment, much as they played roles in rituals and storytelling.

Emotional support was no less vital. To survive after losing an arm or breaking ribs required reassurance, food sharing, and patience from others. Both species lived intimately—sleeping, eating, and working within meters of one another. Compassion would have been expressed through touch, gesture, and presence long before language could name it.

Division of Labor and Inclusion

Injured individuals could not hunt or travel as effectively, but this did not mean they became useless. Among hunter-gatherers, elders and the disabled often served as teachers, storytellers, and keepers of memory.

The elderly La Chapelle Neanderthal, for instance, might have instructed the young in toolmaking or animal behavior. Ethnographic parallels among modern hunter-gatherers show that knowledge transmission is as crucial to survival as hunting skill itself.

Although Neanderthal groups appear to have been small—perhaps ten to twenty individuals—they seem to have been tightly bonded. Every person mattered. If a hunter was injured by a charging bison or falling rock, others would have carried him home, using poles or hides as stretchers. Once there, fires provided warmth, hides insulated the wounded from the cold ground, and the clan's healer offered whatever comfort and aid possible.

The camp would have shifted rhythm to accommodate the injured hunter: fewer long-distance hunts, more local gathering, more time around the hearth.

Homo sapiens groups, often larger and more mobile, may have had a formal division of labor, with older members specializing in tool maintenance, food preparation, or child care when unable to hunt.

Archaeological evidence from Upper Paleolithic sites shows designated working areas—suggesting that not all group members were equally mobile, and that social structure allowed for specialized tasks

Shared Humanity in the Face of Pain

To care for another's wound is to recognize oneself in their suffering. This psychological leap—the ability to imagine another's pain—marks a profound step in the evolution of empathy. Neuroscientists call it "theory of mind": the awareness that others have feelings and experiences like one's own. Both Neanderthals and early modern humans show evidence of this capacity, not only in care for the injured but also in burial rites, ornamentation, and symbolic art.

The social cost of care was considerable. Each wounded member required food, protection, and attention that might otherwise go to the healthy. Yet both species repeatedly made that investment. In evolutionary terms, such behavior strengthens group cohesion and increases survival odds. Compassion, in this sense, became adaptive —a biological advantage.

How the Injured Were Treated

Forty thousand years ago, an injured hunter—whether carried to camp or returning under his own strength—would have undergone procedures we can still identify today.

The wound would first be cleaned—perhaps with cold water from a nearby stream. Bleeding might be stanched with moss, clay, or pressure from hides. If infection set in, herbal washes or smoke from aromatic plants could serve as antiseptics. Bones were probably set by aligning the limb so that pain lessened, and then binding it firmly.

Food rich in fat and protein—marrow, liver, brain—would help recovery. Rest and warmth would do the rest. Those who survived such trauma bore the marks visibly, their healed bones thickened by callus and their gait altered by pain. Yet these survivors also bore something less tangible: the respect of their peers. A scar, a missing limb, or a limp became not a sign of weakness but of endurance —a living record of what the group had overcome together. The injured often returned to roles suited to their abilities: tending the fire, preparing hides, crafting tools, or watching children. These contributions, though less visible than the hunt, sustained the continuity of daily life.

The Archaeology of Compassion

The evidence for such care continues to grow. At the site of Shanidar Cave, recent excavations have revealed that several Neanderthals were deliberately buried in proximity, their remains partially wrapped or positioned with attention. Shanidar Z, a female Neanderthal discovered in 2018, had a crushed rib cage and spinal injury that likely caused chronic pain—yet she lived long enough for healing to begin. Around her bones, researchers found traces of pollen and sediment suggesting flowers had been placed near the body, reigniting debate about how Neanderthals buried their dead—in symbolic or commemorative ways.

Similar findings at El Sidrón in Spain include a young Neanderthal male with jaw trauma that healed unevenly, meaning he lived months, perhaps years, after the injury. Another individual shows a rib fracture that healed cleanly, suggesting long-term protection during recovery. In a species that faced daily peril, such evidence points to a consistent pattern of care—cooperation rooted in herbal knowledge, empathy, and the understanding that an injured companion remained part of the group.

For *Homo sapiens*, buried artifacts tell a parallel story. The child's skeleton from Qafzeh 11 in Israel, dating to about 90,000 years ago, was found with deer antlers laid across the chest—an intentional act of adornment or offering. Another early burial from Skhul Cave includes a *Homo sapiens* male interred with a boar's jaw, hinting at symbolic gestures toward the dead and shared memory. The Dolní Věstonice burial of a woman with severe joint deformities, as noted earlier, suggests social inclusion despite physical limitation.

In both species, we see a fundamental truth emerging: to be human—whether Neanderthal or *Homo sapiens*—was to belong to your group, even when seriously injured.

Knowledge of the Body

How did these early people understand injury? They would have recognized cause and effect: a fall breaks bone, a wound festers if not cleaned, a chill worsens pain. Experience accumulated over generations would have guided their responses. They observed that warmth eased stiffness, that herbs soothed, that time could knit bone. Such empirical learning formed the foundation of prehistoric medicine.

The environment provided abundant resources. From birch trees, both species could extract tar used for hafting tools—yet the same resin, warmed and applied, may have served as a protective covering for wounds or irritated skin. Pine sap and beeswax offered similar antiseptic and sealing qualities. The bitter taste of willow or poplar bark, known to dull pain, could have been discovered through trial or simple observation. Fat rendered from animals, mixed with powdered herbs, might have created rudimentary salves used in moments of crisis.

Their understanding was tactile rather than theoretical. They did not name infections or bacteria, but they sensed what fostered healing. They saw how a wound covered with clean moss healed better than one left open, how a broken limb needed stillness, how fever eased when a person rested near warmth and the steady presence of others nearby.

Such knowledge, passed through demonstration rather than speech, was practical science at its earliest and most practical beginnings.

Social Bonds and Survival

The survival of an injured person required more than medicine—it demanded time, food, and the group's shared endurance. In a small band, every choice carried weight. Carrying a wounded hunter meant fewer spears ready for predators and fewer hands to gather wood or forage. Yet they did it. The logic was both emotional and strategic: each life preserved meant knowledge retained, alliances strengthened, and morale sustained.

Archaeological models suggest Neanderthals lived in extended family groups. Kinship, reinforced by lifelong familiarity, made altruism likely. Emotional bonds would have run deep; the death of one member was a shared wound.

Among *Homo sapiens*, whose networks extended across groups, cooperative care may have stretched even further —reciprocal support between families, shared food during hardship, the long memory of those who had once been helped.

Compassion thus evolved within the same pressures that honed toolmaking and language. A group that abandoned its wounded might gain short-term speed, but it lost something essential: trust. Without trust, coordinated hunting and shared childrearing—pillars of human success —would falter and leave the group exposed to every hardship.

Care for the injured, therefore, was not only sentimental but strategic, a cornerstone of social resilience and a defining strength of early human communities.

The Hearth as Hospital

If the hunt was the arena of danger, the hearth was the refuge of recovery. Archaeological sites show that both Neanderthals and *Homo sapiens* maintained organized living spaces with central fires, sleeping areas, and zones for tool work. Around the hearth, the injured would rest—warm, observed, and integrated into daily life.

Companions could feed them cooked marrow or softened tubers. Firelight allowed night-time vigilance; smoke deterred insects; the rhythmic work of others reassured the convalescent that life continued.

Caregiving also served as education. Younger members watching an elder treat a wound would learn the gestures of cleaning, binding, and comforting. Compassion, in this sense, was a taught skill—a cultural inheritance.

Long-Term Disabilities

Some injuries healed imperfectly, leaving visible disabilities: fused joints, chronic infections, or missing limbs. Yet even these individuals were valued. The endurance of Shanidar 1 or La Chapelle-aux-Saints shows that long-term disability was compatible with survival.

Within a cooperative system, the injured could still contribute. A one-armed Neanderthal might specialize in flake preparation or in teaching children how to track. A lame hunter might tend the fire, shape spears, or maintain order in camp.

Such inclusiveness contrasts sharply with the image of "brutish" Neanderthals once popular in 19th- and early

20th-century depictions. Far from being ruled by instinct alone, they demonstrate an ethical awareness akin to modern human sympathy. Their care for sick and injured clan members perhaps reveals the earliest glimmer of moral consciousness.

Ritual and Meaning

The line between medical care and spiritual practice was likely indistinct. Pain and recovery may have carried symbolic meaning—signs of endurance, favor, or transformation. Ethnographic parallels among traditional societies show that injuries often become woven into stories of courage or divine testing. A healed hunter might have been regarded as possessing special insight or protection.

In this light, burial of the injured dead—laid carefully, sometimes with tools or ornaments—may have expressed gratitude or continuity rather than mere disposal. Whether or not they believed in an afterlife, both Neanderthals and *Homo sapiens* acted as if life deserved acknowledgment and a final, deliberate gesture of respect even in death's quiet aftermath.

Such acts reaffirmed group identity: we remember, therefore we belong.

The Evolutionary Value of Compassion

From an evolutionary standpoint, compassion carried measurable benefits. Groups that cared for the wounded maintained higher survival rates during lean periods.

Injured individuals, once recovered, could continue to contribute, teach, and reproduce.

Moreover, acts of care reinforced emotional bonds, enhancing cooperation in hunts and defense. In evolutionary anthropology, this is known as "costly signaling": by expending energy on the vulnerable, a group demonstrates strength and cohesion.

Scientific models suggest that empathy co-evolved with the expansion of the prefrontal cortex and mirror neuron systems—structures shared by both Neanderthals and modern humans. This neurological capacity made compassion not only possible but rewarding. Helping another would have triggered the same hormonal responses—oxytocin, endorphins—that bind parents to infants and mates to one another. In this way, evolution sculpted kindness into survival strategy.

The Shared Legacy

By 40,000 years ago, Europe and western Asia hosted both lineages, sometimes overlapping, sometimes interbreeding. Their tools differed, but their hearts may not have. The fossil record hints at a common understanding—that to heal the wounded was to preserve the whole. Whether around a Neanderthal hearth or a *Homo sapiens* campsite, the scene was likely similar—a circle of faces lit by firelight, a wounded companion tended with care, the night watch shared by all.

From those small acts of tending grew the long human story of medicine and morality. The first healers were not shamans with chants, but ordinary people who refused to leave another behind. Their legacy endures not only in our genes but in our instincts—the impulse to comfort, to bandage, to wait beside the suffering.

When we look upon Shanidar's shattered skull or La Chapelle's arthritic bones, we glimpse more than anatomy; we glimpse ourselves. The impulse that once guided the hand of a Neanderthal or a *Homo sapiens* to lift a fallen comrade now guides ours across millennia. In that gesture lies the oldest truth of all: Survival, at its deepest level, has never been about the strongest alone—but about those who cared enough to keep one another alive.

Chapter Nine

T he morning mist was gray and still as six *Homo sapiens* crouched in the foliage on the near side of the river, their breaths visible in the cold air. The low mist hung over the water surface as the eyes of the hunters fixed on distant shapes—a small herd of woolly rhinoceroses, five in all— moving slowly across an small area of open grassland bounded by trees to the north. An adult male and three adult females were accompanied by a young calf trailing behind.

The hunters were not the only ones watching.

Not far away and downwind were four Neanderthals huddled together: the elders Goma and Marga, along with Tov, a sharp-eyed tracker, and Ahna's cousin Ghar, who had once brought down a cave bear with a single blow from a hafted flint hammer.

This was the first time Neanderthals had been invited by *Homo sapiens* elders to observe a hunt. And it was not without risk.

The plan had been explained the night before through gestures, simple words, and a demonstration with stick figures. It was an imaginative plan, using a less-dangerous approach than the tactics favored by Neanderthals.

Hunting in open terrain, as would be done here, was not a familiar practice for Neanderthals, whose methods relied on close-in, strength-driven kills—often involving the use of pits.

The *Homo sapiens'* plan, by contrast, was an unfolding map of movement, distance, timing, and deception.

Ahna and Rynn were also nearby—by choice—tasked not with hunting but with observing and, if needed, to assist in any way that would be helpful.

The target had been chosen: the second-largest female rhinoceros, marked by a falter in her stride—an awkward, limping motion as she walked.

Patience was a key strategy.

From southeast of the herd, a trio of hunters broke into a trot, brandishing fire-hardened spears tipped with flint. They shouted and whooped, driving the herd to the north —toward a narrowing through the trees where the other group of three hunters lay hidden.

The rhinoceroses responded in bursts of instinct. Dust rose. The matriarch bellowed. The herd turned west.

All except one—the limping female who, in the rush of the moment, stumbled, and continued moving north toward the narrowing through the trees.

The hunt leader, Banek, closed from the southeast and watched the limping female carve an uneven path in her panic. He turned toward the young Tamik and mimed the erratic pattern—the zigzag steps and the stumbling.

Banek called out the old warning, his tone carrying the weight of many hunts. "Death follows her."

Three other hunters, crouched in the trees to the north, rose as the limping rhinoceros came their way. They waved their arms as they gave chase. As the distance narrowed, the hunters hurled their spears—flint-tipped shafts cutting through the air toward the heaving rhinoceros.

The limping female thundered into the narrow opening in the trees, her sides heaving, her breath issuing in clouds. The hunters behind her kept their distance, running in long, measured strides. They did not rush. They hunted with both thought and patience. Their goal was to outlast the fury of this beast.

Leading the group of three hunters in the trees was Lauq. As the rhinoceros approached their position, Lauq steadied his breathing and raised his spear. He had seen the herd scatter and this lone animal run toward them—slow and limping. Lauq and his two companions rose from concealment, and each held a spear poised to strike.

The plan was unfolding just as Banek had envisioned. The wounded beast, left behind as the rest of the herd turned westward, lumbered north where three more hunters waited—their spears angled and ready.

In the next few moments the rhinoceros met the hunters head-on, and its instinct twisted to panic just as the final assault by the hunters began.

Spears flew, with Tamik throwing first. His spear cut a clean arc through the air and struck deep into the shoulder of the rhinoceros. The animal grunted, slightly staggering from the blow. Duma's followed, glancing along the thick hide before biting into flesh. Banek's throw struck lower, near the ribs, opening a wound that spilled dark blood across the animal's flank.

The rhinoceros bellowed, its cry echoing across the clearing—a sound that stilled birds in the reeds. It spun, wild-eyed, pain thickening into rage. The air filled with the smell of fresh blood.

Lauq motioned to the others, urging them forward. They fanned out, careful to keep a wide berth. Distance was safety; they knew it well. Their clan was not built for close combat against such power. Their gift was reach—the art of throwing a weapon of death before danger got close.

The wounded beast, trapped between hunters in front and behind, refused to fall. It wheeled toward Lauq. In that instant, he shifted his stance, feeling the weight of the spear settle in his grip, exhaled once, and hurled it—straight and true—high behind the shoulder.

For a heartbeat, it seemed the rhinoceros would buckle. But the wound only deepened its fury. It lowered its head and charged directly at Lauq.

"Back!" Banek shouted, but the warning could not prevent what followed. As Lauq leapt aside, he reached for another spear as he moved. But, the beast bore down with astonishing speed, its horn gouging at the ground as it charged.

Lauq hurled his second spear at near point-blank range; it buried itself in the thick neck. The impact staggered the rhinoceros—but didn't stop it.

The horn caught Lauq as he twisted away, tearing through his midsection, shearing flesh and muscle in a single dreadful motion as it tore a gaping hole below Lauq's ribs.

As he was flung backward, Lauq's cry could barely be heard above the screaming anguish of the fatally wounded rhinoceros as it still refused to fall.

Lauq, gasping for breath, collapsed onto the ground where he had tried to stand, blood and tissue—dark and heavy—streaming from his wound and soaking into the soil beneath him. The smell was metallic and hot.

The rhinoceros stumbled now, its strength ebbing. The remaining hunters pressed the advantage, moving as one. Tamik's next spear struck deep behind the shoulder; Goma's next pierced the beast's lung; Banek came last, his throw burying deep in the soft tissue below the ribs. At last, the beast staggered, exhaled in a long, ragged breath, and fell to its knees. One final shudder ran through its massive frame before it toppled onto its side.

After initial shouts of joy, silence spread among the hunters as they saw the seriousness of Lauq's injuries. Only the wind, unaware of the heartbreak of this moment, moved as usual, blowing cool air around the fallen beast.

Banek and Tamil reached Lauq first. They knelt beside him, pressing hides against the wound, but the blood kept coming. Lauq's eyes were open, unfocused, following the drifting clouds above.

"You did well," Banek said softly.

Lauq blinked once, his lips forming a faint, trembling smile. His gaze drifted toward the fallen rhinoceros—a creature of ancient power brought down by human hands.

The other hunters gathered in a loose circle around Lauq, their faces streaked with sweat. None spoke. They all knew, having often seen the face of death, how narrow the distance was between triumph and loss.

The hunt was over, yet the spears still quivered in the beast's flesh, the sunlight reflecting off wet, darkened shafts slick with blood. Within minutes, buzzing bloated flies were swarming over the blood-soaked earth, thick clouds converging around Lauq and the dying rhinoceros.

Lauq groaned, his body arched, and the bleeding slowed a little as his midsection was covered in hide that was tightened around him.

And then Banek spoke with authority.

"No time to waste," he said, calmly but frankly. "We need to get him back to camp. Now."

Banek reached into his pouch, pulled out a tightly wound bundle of fibers, and began wrapping Lauq's midsection even tighter. Terah stepped beside him with a pouch of pungent-smelling moss and slid it under the hides covering the wound. Lauq groaned and Rynn, having moved in to help, held his shoulders to stop him from thrashing about.

Then, a stretcher was made.

Two of the younger hunters stripped branches from a pair of saplings, cutting them to arm's length and laying crosspieces of green wood between. Over this, they stretched a hide, tying the whole thing together with strips of sinew pulled from a pouch that carried supplies meant for repairing spear bindings.

They lifted Lauq gently, but he cried out at each movement. They laid him on the hide.

Four hunters took the poles on their shoulders, each adjusting his grip for balance. The fifth walked beside him, hands still pressed to the cloth in the wound, muttering encouragement.

At first, it seemed possible. The bleeding had slowed, and Lauq's breathing was rough but steady. But after only a short distance, Lauq's skin paled and his lips turned the color of ash as more blood escaped his body. The hides over his midsection could no longer contain the pulsing blood or the darker fluids leaking from the wound as both seeped through the gaps in the tightly-drawn coverings.

Terah tried again to pack the wound with fresh moss, its fibrous texture having an ability to absorb and hold blood and other fluids. Even though she pushed the moss deep into the wound and pressed her palm tightly against it, the blood loss was so great that Lauq's eyes lost focus.

The stretcher bearers quickened their pace, each step jarring the frame.

The hunter near Lauq's head called to him again and again, keeping his voice low but urgent. "We are close. The healer is waiting. Water is waiting."

But Lauq's gaze rolled toward the clouds, unseeing.

A few moments later, his chest lifted once more in a strained rise—and then did not rise again.

The hunters carrying the stretcher felt the change—a subtle slackness, the settling and stillness of a body when the fight inside is over.

No one spoke for several steps. Then the man pressing on the wound lifted his hand away. Blood no longer pulsed. He wiped his palm on the hide he wore and shook his head once.

They carried Lauq the rest of the way in silence, the only sound was the soft creak of the sinew tying the stretcher together and the shifting of poles.

By the time they reached camp, the fire was already lit, the healer Lurea waiting with hot stones, water, and bundles of dried yarrow.

Seeing Lauq and the expressions of the hunters, Lurea did not reach for her medicines right away. Instead, she knelt beside Lauq. She touched her fingertips to his neck, listened to his chest, and felt along each wrist. Finding no throbbing anywhere, she placed her hand gently on Lauq's forehead and gently closed his eyes.

The stretcher was moved to be near the edge of the fire. Someone fetched a clean fur to cover him. The elders would decide soon where in the burial grounds his body should be laid to rest.

Lurea's movements slowed, changed in quality—from urgent and searching to deliberate and ceremonial. She asked for water, and a young woman, Mira, brought a full bladder.

Mira knelt as she poured water over Lurea's hands. With her hands washed, Lurea began washing Lauq as a first step in preparation for burial.

She first washed around the wound. Not for him—he would not feel pain now—but for those who felt close to him. Dried blood was wiped away with soft moss, the edges of the torn flesh pressed together so it would not gape in the sight of others. The legging had been torn away and in its place she bound a clean strip of hide.

For now, the only work left was to sit by him, let the fire warm the air above his still form, and speak his name so the night would carry it.

The stretcher would rest where they had set it down, the light of the fire would lick across the curve of Lauq's cheek, shadowing the deep lines at the corners of his eyes.

Pieces of his hunting spear were placed beside him— not as a weapon now, but as a sign that he had been a provider, a risk-taker.

In the silence that followed Lauq's death, those who prepared him for burial did not rush, but worked with the quiet steadiness their fallen clan member deserved.

Two men fetched a pouch of ocher from the storage pit. Lurea dipped her fingers into the fine red powder and rubbed it into the skin along Lauq's forehead, down the bridge of his nose, and across his chest in a wide band.

A boy, no more than twelve summers, appeared with a bundle wrapped in hide—Lauq's personal items. Inside were a small flint scraper, a carved bone whistle, and a braided cord of sinew.

Each object had meaning and might have use to Lauq's life spirit. The scraper, because Lauq had made it himself from stone. The whistle, because he had used it to call his son back from the rows of bushes during the berry season. The cord, because his mate had woven it for him.

These were placed beside his body, one by one. Not all tools of a hunter were buried with him—many would be passed on to others—but these were the ones that carried his spirit's mark and might be useful in Lauq's journey.

The burial grounds had been chosen long ago—a piece of land on which all hunters who died during a hunt were buried: a low rise at the edge of camp, looking toward the river and the mammoth plains beyond. From there, the sound of the herds could sometimes be heard on still nights. It was close enough for his spirit, if it so chose, to remain for a time among the living, far enough that his spirit would not be trapped within the noise of the camp.

To complete the preparation of Lauq for burial, the stretcher was carried inside Lurea's shelter. Lurea walked in front, holding a small burning branch..

The next morning broke gray and cold, the mist lying low along the edges of camp. The air smelled of damp soil and woodsmoke, heavy with the silence that comes when words feel too loud.

Lauq's body lay inside the shelter, wrapped in a hide that had been cleaned and softened during the night. A new spear rested along one side, his pouch on the other, the flap open to reveal the flint scraper, the small carved bone amulet, and a length of twisted sinew. A shallow bowl of dried berries had been placed at his feet.

The elders came to honor him.

Omak knelt beside him, dipping fingers into a bowl of red ocher and brushing the powder across his brow, his cheeks, and the backs of his hands. Terah scattered sprigs of green pine over his chest, the resin's sharp scent rising in the cool air. They spoke his name—not in wails, but in a steady, rhythmic murmur, as though setting it into the air where it would not be forgotten.

Rynn stood among the elders, his face solemn. He watched as Plen placed a piece of clean hide over Lauq's head and pinned the edges with small wooden pegs.

Four elders lifted Lauq to take him for burial.

Ahna and Rynn followed, their steps quiet on the damp ground. She had not been asked to come, but she was welcome, and she understood that to witness the burial of Lauq was an honor for her—and a show of her respect.

They walked to the low rise beyond the camp, where the graves of deceased hunters lay marked by stones and the occasional weathered spear. The ground here was soft from many summers of previous digging, and now a new grave needed to be dug.

Three members of the clan prepared a round deep pit, digging with digging sticks and flat shoulder blade bones —digging deep enough to keep the scavengers out.

Ahna watched each movement, noting how the burial space was shaped to hold the body in a curled position, as though resting before birth. Her people often laid their dead in a similar way, though they sometimes left them in rock shelters rather than buried deeply in open ground.

The pit was readied and the stretcher lowered. The hide-wrapped body was moved gently into place, the spear and pouch tucked against him. The bowl of berries was placed beside his head, and a final handful of ocher was scattered over Lauq's body. The clean hides were unpinned from the stretcher poles and served as Lauq's final wrap.

A hush followed. The elders stepped back, making space for other clan members to grieve up close.

One by one, the mourners came forward. A shell bead was placed on Lauq's chest above his folded arms. A handful of river stones was placed near his feet.

Many words were spoken in praise of Lauq, and every voice—bright, sorrowed, eager to honor him—carried the same truth: he had lived fully among them.

Rynn stood near the edge of the burial hole, laying his hand briefly on the ground and saying a few words too low for Ahna to catch. She understood the meaning without needing to know the exact sounds.

She stepped forward after him, crouching at the edge of the grave. Her fingers hovered over the body below before she touched the ground with a single, light press. In her own way of expressing her feelings, she thought of a short phrase: *The ground takes you back, the wind carries you on.*

Rynn's eyes caught hers. He did not speak, but there was a recognition—an understanding that the feelings and the words, though different, were born of the same human sorrow.

After mourners placed things Lauq might need on his journey on top of the body, the hole was filled with dirt, and the ground was patted down firmly, a layer of stones laid across it to keep scavengers away.

A small fire was kindled beside the grave, the smoke drifting in a thin column toward the pale sky. A fire branch was thrust into the ground at the head of the grave, its smoke curling upward in the still air.

The mourners stood there for a while, the cold pressing in, until one by one they turned back toward camp. Ahna stayed a few moments longer with Rynn, looking at the fresh mound. She thought of the rhinoceros herd and imagined the moment Lauq had fallen, a reminder of the danger every hunter carried into every hunt.

Then she turned to follow the others, walking beside Rynn in silence, the two of them united in grief by the death of the brave Lauq.

There would be meat tonight from the rhinoceros, and the clan could look forward to many more meals in the days ahead. But the absence of Lauq's voice would be felt next to every fire from that night forward.

Ahna did not leave for her camp at once, but sat with Rynn beside the fire near his shelter. The coals glowed low, their light catching the damp hide stretched behind them, the reflections shifting each time the wind stirred the camp.

Rynn sat still, his spear resting on the ground beside him. For a long time neither spoke, the quiet saying it all.

As they sat there in each other's company, many voices drifted in from the center of camp—low, murmured tones as Lauq's many friends mourned his passing.

At last, Ahna spoke, her voice soft with the weight of what she believed. "He met her horn on the path she could not change." She did not say Lauq's name, nor the prey's— too close, too soon for naming, as was her people's way when death was fresh.

Rynn nodded, gaze fixed on the fire. "He was very fast. Brave. A great hunter who will be missed."

He let out a breath. "We tell ourselves we know every danger, and we do what we can to avoid it. But it can still take us by surprise."

"I think Lauq will back in some way. Not as before. Perhaps as a tree… or a fox," said Ahna, smiling gently.

Rynn smiled also, though there was no joy in it. "We think Lauq's life spirit goes to another place. Away from here. But sometimes I feel the same way you do. That he may soon join the earth in some way, somewhere nearby."

The crack of a log shifting in the fire filled the pause.

"It is hard," Ahna said finally. "To watch. To see life leave. I know the hunt is a danger. My people hunt the great deer, the bison, the rhinoceros, the mammoth. And sometimes the hunt takes one of us—and every loss is painful."

Rynn's voice was gentle. "Lauq knew the danger. We all do. And he will be honored. His name will be spoken at the hunt-fire every season, so we do not forget. That is how we make the loss smaller—by knowing something better awaits him and by keeping him with us in the telling."

Ahna nodded slowly. "We tell stories too. Around the fire. We speak of those who are gone so that the young will honor them—and remember the shape of courage."

They sat in silence, the firelight flickering across their faces, bathing them in light and shadow. Beyond the camp drifted the faint sound and scent of the rhinoceros herd, moving slowly through the hunting grounds.

The hunt would feed the clan for many days, yet it had taken one life in return, and the scent of mingled blood still drifted across the hunting ground—a quiet reminder that nature gives and takes in the same breath.

In the days that followed, Rynn worked beside the others, skinning the great rhinoceros and carving away slabs of dark, heavy meat. The hides were stripped, the fat rendered, the bones cracked for marrow.

Across the river, Ahna tended to her own people, but her thoughts often drifted to the hunters and to Rynn. Both felt the loss of Lauq, and though a river divided them, the memory of the hunt—and the life it had taken—bound them in a quiet, growing kinship, strong as sinew, steady as firelight in the dark.

Chapter Ten

The fire had burned down to embers by the time Rynn was called into Marek's shelter. Smoke rose slowly, curling in thin gray wisps that veiled the already dim light.

Around the fire were several clan elders—men and women whose voices had carried judgment and instruction for as long as he could remember. Tonight, though, they were hushed as Rynn entered the shelter. Their eyes met his, solemn rather than reproachful, as if the gathering was for a purpose he did not yet fully understand.

On a bed of furs in the center lay Marek, the lead elder whose failing health had limited his activities for much of the past two summers. In his absence, Omak, the second-oldest elder, had often taken the leadership role.

Once, Marek's broad shoulders and commanding voice had marked him as a leader who drew the attention and respect of all. But in recent days his strength had ebbed swiftly, his chest rising with effort and his skin drawn thinner over bone. The change was sudden enough that even the elders who knew him best felt the looming nearness of death.

When Marek's eyes found Rynn, a glimmer stirred within, alive and intent, and he said, "Come closer."

Rynn obeyed, moving quietly across the earthen floor until he was beside the dying man. He dropped into a crouch, his legs folding beneath him, suddenly aware of how young he must seem among these watchers. He lowered his head, not knowing what to expect.

Marek slowly lifted his hand, letting it hover a moment before placing it on Rynn's arm. The touch was dry, frail, yet the grip held surprising insistence.

"You must listen," Marek whispered, his voice thin but edged with urgency. "Hear me, and carry what I say."

Rynn swallowed. "I will listen."

The elders exchanged looks, but none interrupted. They knew that whatever words Marek meant to speak belonged only to the dying man and the youth he had chosen.

Then, at Marek's request, the elders left the shelter, and Rynn was alone with the dying man.

For as long as Rynn could remember, Marek had been a figure of reverence. He had been the one who taught boys how to read the shadows of trees to find deer paths, how to read signs in the sky and smell the air to tell if rain would come. He had often sat at the center of a gathering and judged quarrels with steady calm.

Any time members of the clan grew angry, Marek had smiled gently, letting silence cool tempers. He had been patient with children, sharp with hunters, and unyielding in matters of the clan's survival.

When his health had started to decline, Marek asked Omak to act as clan leader, and Marek willingly started taking less of a role in all clan activities.

Until recently, Rynn had believed Marek would live forever, but death's approach was undeniable now. His strength was gone, and the once-steadfast elder, long a fixture of the clan, was nearing his end.

"You will someday lead, but now you are too young," Marek said after a long pause. "The elders told me nothing when I was your age. They left me with little preparation. I will not leave you that way."

Rynn's heart slowly gained beats. He did not know what preparation Marek spoke of, only that a solemn hush seemed to fill the shelter at the sound of his words.

"What do you want me to know?"

Marek's lips parted in a thin smile that had a look closer to grief than mirth. "That is what I must decide—how much, and how clearly. It is hard to open old wounds when the flesh has begun to fail."

He closed his eyes, breathing raggedly. For a moment, Rynn feared Marek had spent his last strength in those words. But the grip on his arm remained, tightening slightly, and when the elder opened his eyes, Rynn saw determination in them, steady and unyielding.

"Rynn," Marek said, "you will lead one day. Not yet— there are older heads, stronger arms. But the others will see in you what I have seen: patience, listening, the courage to wait before speaking.

"When my bones are ash and my voice is dust, you will still be here. And when the burden falls to you, you must have more than stories of hunts and fires. You must know truths, even the kind men hide."

Rynn shifted uneasily. He wanted to protest—he was not an elder, not a leader—but the words would not leave his mouth. Marek's gaze pinned him where he crouched. It was not a request. It was as if Marek wanted to leave him something—perhaps something important.

The fire popped, briefly sending sparks toward the roof of the shelter. Outside, a child laughed, then was hushed quickly. At that moment, all activity outside the shelter seemed distant to Rynn, as though he and Marek were sealed in a space apart from everything else.

"I will tell you a story," Marek said at last, voice rasping. "It is my story, though none here know it. None ever have. I thought I would carry it into the dark with me. But that would be wrong. A truth, even an unwelcome one, must be passed forward."

Rynn nodded, though he felt the knot in his stomach twist tighter. He had never seen Marek falter, never heard him speak with such shadow in his tone. Whatever the story was, it would not be easy to hear.

"Lean closer," Marek whispered. His breath was hot and sour against Rynn's cheek. "There are things you must learn about the *others*—things I once thought I understood. Things I believed would bind us, and things that taught me despair. You must know these things, because one day our clan will look to you for answers. And if you are not aware of what is true, you may guide them without direction."

Rynn lowered his head until his ear hovered near Marek's lips. The elder's hand trembled against his arm, frail yet gripping with authority.

"Tonight," Marek said, closing his eyes, "I will speak of what I buried long ago."

Then, before he began, the fire drew down to embers as the flames dimmed, as though the shelter itself waited with Rynn for Marek's story to begin.

Marek's breath rattled in his chest as he began speaking again, as if his body rebelled at the effort. Yet, when the words came, they carried the clearness of a memory long sharpened by silence.

"I was not much older than you are now," he began. "The clan was smaller then, though it felt large to me. We moved often—after big game, after roots and berries—always chasing what would keep us alive. My tasks were simple: carry meat, fetch wood, guard the edges of camp at night. But I burned for more. I wanted to prove myself, to step where the hunters were to cautious to go, to test myself against the wild—perhaps as you do now."

Rynn pictured the Marek of that earlier time: lean, eager, carrying the restlessness of youth in every stride. It was hard to imagine the dying elder as anything but frail, but the voice—low, steady—breathed life into the young man he had been.

"One morning, before the sun was up, I left the camp alone," Marek continued. "That was forbidden, but rules are easily forgotten when the blood is young. I followed the river north, where the mist hung low and the banks were soft with mud. I tracked deer prints, thinking if I returned with news of the herd, the hunters would see me as one of them."

His eyes grew distant, as though he still saw the river in front of him. "I was quiet, stepping where the reeds bent, when I caught a sound that was not a deer, more like a sound of stone striking stone. The rhythm of it told me it was not an accident. Someone was shaping a tool."

Rynn's breath caught. He knew where the story pointed, though Marek had not yet spoken the words.

"I crept forward," Marek said, "and there she was. Across the shallows. One of the *others*. She was the first of their kind I had ever seen so close—no animals between us, no fear or anger in the air.

"She sat on a fallen tree, chipping at a flint stone, her hands steady, her face calm as winter stone. Her hair was dark and thick, and her shoulders were broad. She looked like us—but not. Her body was wider, her brow heavier, and her jaw was square, not pointed.

Our people always said, "If you meet one while alone, you flee. But, showing my youth, I foolishly stayed."

The fire flickered against Marek's face, drawing shadows deep into his wrinkles as he slowly continued.

"She saw me. Her eyes lifted, and in them was no fear. No anger. Only a long gaze, curious, as though she too wondered if she should stay or run. I raised my hand— open, empty. She did not move. Then she did something I will never forget. She lifted the flint she had been shaping, set it aside, and showed me her hands. Empty."

Rynn shifted his position. Except for Marek's voice, the the shelter was silent. The other elders remained outside, letting the dim glow within belong to the two of them.

"I left, not knowing what to think or to feel. But I found myself wanting to see her again," Marek whispered.

"Days passed, and I returned. Again and again, to the same place by the river. She was there as if she knew I would come. We did not speak until we learned each other's words. At first, we learned to talk with hand gestures, with looks, with small offerings. I gave her a strip of dried meat once. She gave me a shell polished by water, bright as the moon. We were like children, testing the edge of fire with bare fingers, waiting to see if it burned."

He closed his eyes, the memory pulling at him like a tide. "I knew it was wrong. If my people had found me, they would have driven me out. If hers had come, they might have killed me. But youth cares little for danger when the heart is stirred. I found myself thinking of her at night, watching the sparks rise from the fire and imagining her across the dark. She was not beautiful in the way we see our women, but there was strength in her, a steadiness I could not look away from."

The elder's breath grew more labored. Rynn listened, straining to catch every word.

"One evening," Marek continued, "the river was low, the stones dry, and we met not as strangers but as more than friends. I cannot name it. Our hands touched. She did not pull away. I held my breath. I thought—foolishly—that the spirits themselves had guided us to that place. That we were meant to cross the lines drawn by our clans. I was young, and when youth believes something is meant, it does not question."

A long silence followed. The fire popped, and outside the wind rustled the grass.

Marek's voice was getting hoarse. "From that night on, we met not only by the river. She led me deeper, to hidden places—groves, caves, the edge of her people's land.

"I never saw her clan—the *others*—only her. We spoke in gestures, in laughter, in the silence of lying side by side. It was reckless, yes, but it felt like life burning bright."

He turned his gaze to Rynn, and for a moment the dying man's eyes flared with the light of youth.

"You think you know who you are, Rynn. You think your people are a wall around you, keeping you whole. But there comes a time when the wall cracks, and something beyond it calls you. And if you answer, you can not remain unchanged."

Rynn felt the truth of those words settle in his chest. Marek's confession was no idle tale of youth—it was the first telling of a secret he had kept from a time before Rynn's birth.

And Rynn was afraid that the next part of the story would plunge deeper, into the place where surprise would turn to sorrow.

Marek drew a ragged breath. "It was not long before she was with child."

Marek's voice faltered, and for a long moment Rynn thought the elder might slip away before finishing the story. His chest rose a small amount, and his lips parted as though this memory drained him. But after taking a sip of water, Marek summoned strength again.

"She grew heavy with child," he whispered. "Her belly swelled like the moon becoming full. At first I thought it was some miracle—that the merging of two clans would be a sign. But with each passing day, fear settled deeper in me. I was no fool. I knew what it would mean if her people saw me, or if my own discovered her. A storm would break, one that might wash us both away. Still, I could not turn back. Every time I saw her, I felt I belonged nowhere else."

He closed his eyes, the dim light painting the hollows of his face.

"Then, at the beginning of the ninth moon, the baby decided on birth. When the time came, she sent a cousin to summon me. I had never set foot among the *others* before. I thought she would hide me, keep me apart. But no. She had me led straight into their camp, as though daring fate itself."

Rynn's pulse quickened. The thought of walking into the camp of the *others* unarmed, alone, was unthinkable.

"They watched me," Marek said, "from the shadows of their shelters, from around their fire. Broad-shouldered men, heavy-browed women, children peering out with dark eyes. Their silence was heavier than any spear. I expected them to strike, to drive me out. But they did nothing. Only stared. I was not a guest, not truly, but for her sake they allowed me to remain."

He coughed a harsh sound, then pressed on.

"She was on all fours on a floor of reeds. The women gathered close, their voices low and steady, a chant like the rhythm of waves. I crouched beside her, gently touching her back. She gripped my arm with such force I thought my bones might break. The time stretched long. Sweat poured from her as crawled over the floor, her cries rising like thunder. The women helped guide her with calm voices, as though pain itself obeyed their words."

Marek's own hand tightened on Rynn's wrist, a quiet reminder of his powerful grip long ago.

"At last, the child came. Early. A girl. Small, fragile, slick with blood—blood, but no heartbeat. A child with stilled breath. Her body was limp. She was gone before she arrived. From ground to ground. No presence."

His voice cracked, and silence filled the shelter. Rynn stared, throat dry, his own chest aching as though he had lived the loss himself.

"If the child was a girl, we had agreed to name her Yana —her mother's name," Marek said.

"I wept," Marek added hoarsely. "I wept before them all. I did not care if they saw. She wept too, but not with sound. Her face was stone, her tears hidden. Only her hands trembled as she held the still child.

One of the older women wrapped the little body in hide, humming as though to soothe the stillness. Then they took her from us. I never saw her again.

"I left before dawn," Marek continued, his gaze unfixed, wandering the dark rafters. "No one stopped me. They let me go as easily as they had let me enter. Perhaps they pitied me. Perhaps they despised me. I will never know.

"Yana watched me go, her face empty of all expression. That was the last time I saw her. She died a few days later."

He drew a wheezing breath. "I returned to my clan as though nothing had happened. No one asked where I had been, or if they did, I lied well enough. I buried it all inside me—the secret meetings, the nights, the birth, the death.

I told myself that if I kept silent, it would fade like mist in sunlight. But it never did. It stayed with me, sharper than any spear. The memory of a child who never lived. The memory of a dying mate. Secrets I dared not share."

Marek's eyes flicked to Rynn then, piercing through the haze of age. "Do you understand? It was the death of hope. For a time, I believed our peoples might form one, make something new. My dream—my hope—died with them."

Rynn's hands curled into fists in his lap. He could find no words.

"The image of the infant-who-could-not-be stayed with me. The fragile bridge between two clans broke before it could be built," Marek whispered.

"I swore to myself that it can never be—that the clans were too different. That the bones and blood of one cannot mix with the other. That is what I have believed ever since. That is what I have hidden, because no one wanted such knowledge, no one wanted such shame.

"But now, Rynn, you may be walking a similar path. You must know what lies ahead."

The old man sagged back, breath shuddering, spent by the telling. The silence between them was filled with grief that belonged to both past and present.

Rynn felt a new burden. He did not yet know what it meant, but he knew that his life had just changed.

Marek's voice grew fainter, nearly lost beneath the rasp of his breath. His eyes, clouded and rimmed with red, searched Rynn's face as if to be sure the boy had not drifted, that his words had not fallen into emptiness.

"You have heard me," he murmured. "But now you must understand and move on your own path. My story is not a tale to be repeated. It is not for children, nor for the idle wondering of hunters. It is a truth, and it cuts. It tells us something we must not forget."

Rynn swallowed, his throat dry as dust. "What truth?"

"That there can be no *joining*." Marek's hand, frail as a dry twig, lifted once more to clutch Rynn's arm. "No children shared between two clans.

"I thought it once, when I was young—that the line between us and the *others* could be bridged, that the blood of both might flow in one body. But no. I came to see it as nature's judgment, the spirit's decree. Their kind and ours were not meant to mix. Only sorrow comes of it."

The words hung heavy in the dim air. Outside, the wind pressed against the hide walls, moaning faintly as though the night itself bore witness. Rynn felt the weight of them sink into his chest. No *joining*. No future where the two clans might share life. Not possible.

"But..." he began, the protest weak even to his own ears. He had seen the *others* from afar—hunting, gathering, living not so differently from his people. They had children of their own. Why should a child born of both not also live? Yet he could not continue to say the thought aloud. Not here, not with the elder's grip burning against his skin.

Marek shook his head slowly, as if he had read the unspoken doubt. "You are young. You think that life bends to will, that it can be remade if one only wishes hard enough. I thought the same. But time teaches otherwise. The life we see is older than us, Rynn, and it keeps its own boundaries. I crossed one, and it closed around me, taking my hope with it."

He coughed violently, his thin body wracked until he could barely draw breath again.

One of the elders came into the shelter, but Marek waved him off with surprising fierceness. His eyes stayed locked on Rynn's.

"You will lead when your time comes. And when it does, you must know this truth. Do not be swayed by dreams of closeness with the *others*. Do not let your people risk what cannot be. If the clans seek to become one, it will only bring death. You must guard against it."

Rynn's stomach knotted. He wanted to refuse, but Marek had chosen him, and there was no undoing it. The secret had been placed in his hands like a hot coal; to let go of it would disgrace him, to hold it would scar him.

"I will remember," Rynn said softly. "I will carry it."

Marek's hand slackened then, though his eyes did not. Relief and sorrow mingled there. "Good," he whispered. "That is all I ask."

Silence stretched between them. Marek's breaths grew slower, each one a shallow scrape. His gaze drifted past Rynn, toward the smoke near the top of the shelter. For a moment, he seemed to fade, but then he spoke again.

"Tell no one. Not yet. Let it sleep in you until the day it is needed. Then speak it, and say it came from me."

Rynn bowed his head, his chest tight. "Your silence is mine."

A faint smile flickered across Marek's face, as if the telling had lifted his burden. His hand slipped away, falling to the furs. His eyes closed, his chest rising and settling in the calm of sleep.

The embers continued to glow. Outside, a dog barked, then fell silent. The elders outside the shelter were called back in. Only Rynn knew what had been passed and the secret beat hard in his chest.

He sat there long after Marek closed his eyes in sleep, his breathing shallow but steady. Soon, Rynn stepped out of the shelter and into the night. The wind was cold and carried the scent of smoke from nearby fires. He looked toward the dark hills beyond the river—the land of the *others*—and felt the weight of Marek's truth.

No *joining*. No possibility of children. Only death.

The words would not leave him, yet neither would the doubt. For though Marek had spoken with conviction, Rynn could not silence the questions that stirred deep within: What if the elder was wrong? What if the child's death had been chance, not nature's decree?

He clenched his fists, keeping Marek's disturbing words in mind.

One day, perhaps, he would learn the truth.

Chapter 11

News of Marek's death spread quickly through the *Homo sapiens* camp. The elder's breathing had grown shallow during the evening, and the next morning it stopped.

Rynn sat beside the still form of Marek, his gnarled right hand resting open against his chest, as if reaching one final time for something to hold.

No one spoke, and the hush that followed was not one of surprise, but of reverence. The death of Marek, the lead elder,, a father figure to many in the clan and, for a long time, the clan's memory keeper and fire tender, came as no shock. His bones had been drawing inward for many moons, and he had long ago passed the honored role of being the clan story teller to a younger voice.

Still, his passing cast a quiet sorrow over the clan and laid a heavier burden upon Rynn's heart.

Grieving clan members gathered during the morning.

Rynn stood just outside the shelter, his misty eyes looking at the elder's body. Members of the clan came one by one—carrying herbs, tools, and silent respect.

The *Homo sapiens* had a ritual for death, and Rynn had seen it several times, including when his father had died.

Death, for them, was not an ending. It was better described as a step in a long journey, a type of passing through—a concept that made sense to them.

Clan elders, including Omak—now the oldest—lifted Marek's body onto a frame of smooth ash branches bound with sinew, and then moved the body to Lurea's shelter.

Lurea, the clan healer, washed the body carefully with warmed water and crushed sweet-leaf, then rubbed it with clay from the river bank. She and two other elders painted markings on his skin—lines tracing his life's path, symbols to guide his life spirit.

Early that evening, members of the clan gathered for a special ceremony around the fire. Many sang and hummed out of reverence, not mourning—voices low and rhythmic, songs passed down from those who had come before.

Rynn let the sound wash over him, feeling Marek's absence like a hollow ache. He remembered the message that Marek had passed on to him the night before he died: A life could not be created by the *joining* between one of his clan with one of the *others*—Ahna's clan.

"Not possible," Marek had said, implying that the wall between them was unyielding. Marek's secret had struck him deeper than any wound of bone or sinew, because in Rynn's heart the path toward Ahna felt more real than any warning. Now, with Marek gone, the words felt even heavier. They had become not just an elder's counsel, but the final truth that Marek shared with his passing.

The voices deepened as more members of the clan joined in. Women placed dried sprigs of bitter root outside the shelter. Hunters stood with palms up, in honor of all deceased members of the clan. Children clung to one another, eyes wide, knowing something important had happened.

In the midst of grief, eyes and murmurs turned toward Omak, the oldest elder, who had often led the clan during Marek's infirmity. His thick beard had gone white many summers ago, and the creases in his face were as carved as the ridges of stone in the cliffs.

Omak did not speak yet, but Rynn watched him. The clan watched him. Marek had been their anchor, but Omak was the oldest now.

Soon after Marek's death, Rynn visited the Neanderthal camp and invited Ahna to visit the *Homo sapiens* camp to witness the burial ritual that would now take place.

Later, as the ritual began, Rynn looked at the mourners gathered around the central fire. A few paces away, partly shadowed by a stand of birch, Ahna stood silently. Her eyes held the solemnity of the moment, but also something searching—watchfulness, perhaps even caution. She had never seen a burial ritual of this clan, never invited to lift her voice in their songs. Yet she came, and she stood, and Rynn felt her presence as strongly as the ache in his heart. She was here, though she was not one of them.

Songs of mourning rose and fell like a breeze through graceful reeds as Marek's body was carried slowly from the shelter toward the edge of the camp, each step measured.

Rynn felt strange, caught in the grip of two griefs at once: the loss of Marek and the weight of Marek's warning.

Marek's private counsel played in his mind. He thought about the rasp of his voice, the stubborn certainty in his eyes. "Not possible. I have seen the death that results."

Rynn's heartbeat sped up as he thought about Marek's advice. He had claimed that his own life bore proof of an unforgiving barrier between the two clans. And now he lay still, his truth sealed in silence.

Rynn's gaze flicked again toward Ahna. Her arms were crossed, her dark hair lifted by the breeze. Did she sense what Marek had said? Did she suspect how deep his own thoughts had carried him—past friendship, past kinship, toward a life-bond he imagined with her?

The ceremony continued. Omak's low voice guided the closing of the celebration of Marek's life, his words gentle, measured, practical. He spoke of Marek's steadiness, of the many summers he had held the fire, of the hunts he had guided and the disputes he had eased. Then he spoke of how Marek's stories would remain, carried now and shared by younger voices.

When the final notes of the many songs faded, silence settled over the camp—a silence everyone felt together, as past generations had in moments like this.

Rynn lowered his head, his bow both one of respect for Marek and one of acknowledgment of the change pressing in upon them. With Marek's passing, the clan would choose a new leader soon—most likely Omak.

As the body was lifted and borne by the elders toward its final resting place, people gathered in small groups and moved slowly behind—comforting one another.

Rynn walked beside the elders, feeling many eyes upon Omak now—perhaps in search of a new leader. And from the shadows of the birch, Ahna grieved in her own way.

After Marek's burial, members of the clan returned to the *Homo sapiens* camp. Rynn glanced at the faces of the elders. Inside he knew that Marek's death might be more than just the closing of a life, it might also be the first step of a reckoning—one which might affect him personally.

The next evening, after the sun had sunk low in the sky, and the sky glowed faint with smoke and fading light, the elders gathered apart from the rest of the clan. They sat in the circle where the council fire burned, its flame small but steady, tended with thin sticks that crackled as they caught. The air smelled of resin and damp earth. Around them, the camp hushed; everyone knew this was the first council without Marek's guiding presence.

Omak sat cross-legged nearest the fire, his shoulders broad, though bowed from years of carrying burdens—the weight of physical labor and of responsibility. His silence was deliberate, not hesitant; he knew that every word spoken in this gathering would carry further than his own voice alone.

The others took their places: Rynn's aunt Terah; Duma, the next oldest whose leg still bore a scar from a long-ago fall; Banek, the hunt leader; and a few other elders who had survived the passing of many summers.

Rynn had been invited to attend and stood just beyond the circle of elders, his eyes shifting between Omak, Terah, Duma, Banek, and the fire.

It was Duma who spoke first. "Without leadership, the clan might drift. Marek was our balance. His words settled quarrels. His memory stretched beyond any of us. We now must choose one to carry that weight."

Murmurs rose—low, steady. It was not disrespectful to ask questions, but considered necessary. The clan survived because leadership was steady, and Marek had been the stone at the center of their circle.

All eyes turned to Omak, and it was no secret that he wanted to be the leader. His face was lit from below by the firelight, shadowing the creases around his eyes. He let the silence run long before he spoke. "I am the oldest," he said simply. "By the way of our clan, that should be enough."

No one argued. Age had always been an important measure, a sign of endurance and judgment. But not all accepted it easily. Marek had not only been the oldest; he had been wise, patient, and kind in ways Omak was not often known to be.

Terah cleared her throat. "We do not doubt your age or your wisdom, Omak. But it is not only years that bring wisdom and bind us. It is our traditions. Marek carried stories from time past. Who will hold them now?"

Omak's gaze flicked toward the young ones listening at the edges. "The young who have learned them," he said. "The stories have been passed on. Marek made certain of it. The stories and traditions he knew are not lost."

Rynn felt the sting of that truth. Marek had told him many things, whispered by the fire, shared in the hush of many evenings: words about hunts, about storms, about the way things had been before the time of Rynn's own father.

And Rynn thought of the final truth, given to him alone —that life could not be created by the *joining* of his kind and the *others*. That truth, Rynn realized, was now his burden to carry. Marek had not shared it with the council, not even with Omak. He had shared it only with him.

Banek, the lead hunter, rose to speak. "Omak, you are steady, and we have walked many hunts with you. If you speak that you will guide us, then speak it fully. Will you hold the fire as Marek did? Will you bind us if we drift?"

Omak lifted his chin. "I will. I am not Marek, and I will not pretend his gentleness. But I will guard the clan, as I always have. The fire will not go untended. The young will not go unguided. The stories we need will remain in our clan, and the rest—let them pass into the wind."

His words were heavier than Marek's softness, like stone compared to water. Practical. Unyielding. Rynn sensed in them a warning: Under Omak's guidance, there would be less room for wandering thoughts and less acceptance of anything that broke from tradition.

Terah nodded slowly, then pressed her palm against her chest in assent. Others followed, one by one, until all had marked their agreement. Tradition had spoken.

From that moment on, Omak was the lead elder.

From the shadows, whispers stirred. The clan was not fearful, but they were adjusting, shifting to learn the gait of a new leader.

The responsibility of leadership now moved to Omak.

Rynn remained still, his mind running like water over stone. With Omak the voice of the clan, what would that mean for his relationship with Ahna? And what about Marek's warning—the great leader's truth?

As clan leader, Omak would not speak in whispers. His judgments would echo across the camp, and if he decided to disapprove of Rynn's bond with Ahna, he could slow their path, not from anger, but from a leader's duty to protect his people.

The council ended with Omak laying his hand upon the carved stone Marek had always kept close—a token of leadership passed from one elder to another. It was a simple thing, smoothed by river water, marked with shallow scratches that no one could quite name. Omak's hand closed over it, sealing the moment.

The members of the clan went back to their shelters. The children were hushed by their mothers. Hunters prepared their spears for tomorrow's hunt. Rynn sat by the fire, the image of Omak's grip on the stone burned into his thoughts.

The camp had not changed in its daily ways—fire still burned, meat still roasted, voices still murmured in the night. But something beneath had changed, subtle yet undeniable. Marek's gentleness was gone. Omak's firm grip now ruled in its place.

And Rynn, caught between the two, felt the burden of the choice he must soon make more pressing than ever.

That night, the campfire burned brighter than usual. Extra wood had been brought, not for warmth but for the telling of stories. The people gathered close, circling the flames as though its light might hold Marek near for one more evening. Sparks rose into the dark, adding to the scatter of stars above.

Children leaned against their mothers, eyes wide. Hunters sat cross-legged, their spears set aside. The elders arranged themselves in a half-circle, their faces marked by both fatigue and reverence. Rynn took his place near the edge, close enough to hear, far enough to keep his thoughts private.

The stories began as they always did when someone died—a weaving of memories, voice by voice. Terah spoke first, her tone soft and steady. "I remember Marek teaching me which roots not to eat. He pressed one into my hand and said, 'Taste with your tongue, but listen with your body.' I thought him foolish until my belly twisted for two days. After that, I listened."

Laughter rippled through the circle—brief, subdued, but real. The children glanced at one another, as if filing the warning away for later.

Tamik, Rynn's friend, followed. His voice was rough, but there was fondness beneath it. "On a hunt for a roe deer, I thought myself stronger than I was. I loosed a spear too early, and it broke against stone. I would have chased the deer with bare hands, foolish as I was, but Marek stopped me. He said, 'Better to come home with nothing than not to come home.' I have carried Omak's words in my head ever since."

He slapped his thigh, and the circle chuckled again.

Even Omak smiled faintly, though his hands stayed folded across his knees.

Several more spoke about Marek. Of Marek's patience teaching children how to set snares. Of the way he could calm a quarrel with no more than a lifted hand. Of nights he sat awake to keep the fire alive while storms raged.

Rynn listened closely. Each story about Marek painted him as wise, steadfast, a man of quiet authority. Yet none of them knew the story Marek had told him alone—in the last moments of his life. None knew that Marek had crossed the boundary between clans long ago, and the result was a child born without breath..

To them, Marek had been the leader of the elders. To Rynn, he had been the bearer of a warning—a warning that could keep Rynn separate from what his heart desired.

The weight of Marek's warning stressed Rynn so much that he feared he might speak it aloud for the elders to hear. But the words would not form. Marek had given them to him in trust. And even if he spoke, who among them would believe him? Perhaps they would turn their eyes upon Ahna with suspicion—and upon him with scorn.

The fire cracked sharply, sending a spray of sparks into the night. Heads turned, laughter stilled, and for a moment only the flames spoke.

It was Omak who broke the silence. He stood and faced the clan. "Marek was a man of steadiness. He held us together. His words will remain with us, but his body is gone. It is now our duty to hold the living more firmly. We will not be divided. That is how we honor Marek."

A murmur of agreement followed. People pressed palms to their chests, eyes lowered. Rynn felt the words sink into him like stone. *We will not be divided.* Yet he was already divided—pulled toward Ahna as surely as he was bound to his own people.

When the circle began to disperse, and voices softened into private talk, Rynn slipped away. The air beyond the fire felt colder, sharper. He walked until the flames were no more than a glow behind him.

There, across the river at the edge of the birch grove, Rynn found Ahna waiting. She stepped from the shadows as he approached. Her face was softened by starlight, her eyes reflecting the pale, far-away fires from Rynn's camp.

"I did not wish to disturb you at the ceremony," she said. "I know Marek was important to you."

Rynn swallowed hard. His throat felt raw. "He was more than that. He was important to... all of us."

She nodded, although she did not fully understand. Her people honored their dead differently, but she respected Rynn's feelings. She had stayed not far away watching the ritual. And, although she had heard some of the fire stories, she felt somewhat apart, yet always present in her way.

For a moment they stood without words—the silence between them filled only by the night sounds of insects and the faint crackle of fires carried on the wind. Rynn wanted to tell her everything—Marek's last words, his warning, the story of the child who took no breath and never cried. He wanted to confess that it had shaken him, made him question the bond that was strengthening with her.

But when he looked at her, seeing the way she wrapped her arms around herself against the chill, the words would not come. Instead, he reached out and touched her hand. Her fingers tightened around his, a quiet anchor.

No vow was spoken, no promise made. Yet in moments like this, silence often said more than words could.

In Rynn's camp, the central fire burned on, attended by Omak and several others. Before Ahna and Rynn lay shadows, unbroken and carrying the uncertainty of an unknown future.

Rynn felt that his heart was caught between the weight of Marek's warning and the warmth of Ahna's hand.

At dawn, the *Homo sapiens* camp stirred with unusual quiet. Smoke from the night's embers drifted low across the shelters, and the air carried a chill that clung to skin. Clan members rose early, drawn not by hunger or chores but by the sense of change in which they now found themselves.

Marek was gone.

Omak was now head of the clan, and had spoken the night before, but now the clan was seeking more formality —a moment that all members of the clan could be part of that marked Omak stepping into his place as clan leader.

That moment would occur today. In preparation, the central fire had been fed until it burned brightly and heated the circle of stones, casting a steady glow as people gathered. Children clung to their mothers, hunters stood with arms folded, and gatherers with baskets still in hand pressed close to hear. All eyes turned toward the center, where Omak sat with the carved river stone in his lap.

Rynn pushed forward until he stood among others his age. He felt anxious. This was no ordinary gathering. Omak would not simply accept the stone—he would use his new voice to speak of the future. Rynn sensed it, and dread stirred in him like restless fire.

Omak waited until the murmurs faded. His voice, when it came, was low but clear, each word measured like a hunter's steps.

"The clan has lost Marek—our leader, our memory-keeper, our guide. He walked long with us. Now he walks beyond our reach. His steadiness held us together. But the clan does not end with one man. It remains in the way we walk. We continue."

He lifted the stone in both hands. Its surface was pale, worn smooth, its scratches catching the light. "This stone has been held by many before me. Now I hold it. I am Omak, oldest of the clan. I have been chosen by the elders to be clan leader. I accept this responsibility."

The words were simple, unadorned, but final. Several voices of assent rippled outward. Palms slapped against palms, heads dipped.

The transfer was complete—not dramatic, but binding. Omak was the voice that would carry weight.

* * *

The next day, Omak called for a meeting of all members of the clan. "As my first duty," he said, "I plan to follow Marek's lead and require that coming-of-age youth must be tested so that they become more than youth. They must become ready to carry spears, to guide others, to work in

200

the camp. To prepare, each youth must pass the *Trial of Silence*. This is the way of our people."

The words were not a surprise to Rynn, In fact, he looked forward to the ritual—an adventure, of sorts. Tamik was not so eager. He lowered his eyes, trying to mask his nerves.

Rynn had known the trial was coming. Every member of the clan his age did. But hearing it declared now, in the first clan gathering so soon after Marek's death, made it more than a distant rite. It was upon them.

Omak walked over to Rynn.

"Rynn, your time is near. You will walk into the forest alone. You will remain silent until the time has passed. When you return—if you return—you will not be thought of as a boy or as a young man any longer. You will be an adult, one of the hunters, one of the keepers of the clan."

Rynn nodded in agreement, but his throat tightened. He imagined the silence pressing in around him, the weight of Marek's final words echoing without relief. *Not possible.*

How could he carry Marek's truth into the trial? How could he keep it unspoken when his whole heart burned against it?

Omak raised his voice so that all could hear. "The days ahead will test us all. The hunts will grow harder as the air cools. We will need strength. Unity. We cannot fail. This is how we honor Marek. This is how we survive."

Though his body was pained by the wear and tear of time, Omak stood tall, and his presence was felt. He raised both hands, and the people pressed their palms to their chests and murmured their agreement.

Over the next few days, activity returned to normal. Hunters left camp with their spears in pursuit of game, women worked in camp tanning hides and preparing food, and children chased one another in play. Yet, even as life returned to its usual rhythm, a new feeling emerged.

On the night before the trial was to begin, Rynn sat by the fire, staring at the ash glow, as if it might answer the questions twisting inside him. He felt the change more fully now—Marek gone, Omak risen, the trial about to start. The ground beneath him no longer felt steady.

The next day, Rynn visited with Ahna near the river. He explained the trial that he was about to undergo. He wanted her to know what the trial was about—that he must carry himself alone in silence for two days and that his bond with her might be tested by the trial of silence.

He wanted to talk with her about what Marek had said, to try to address the doubt gnawing at him. But not here, not now. Omak's authority lay too heavy.

Saying goodbye to Ahna, Rynn returned to camp and stood by the fire, letting its flames blur in his vision. The warmth licked at his face, but inside he felt cold.

When the trial started in the morning, he would walk into silence carrying Marek's final truth and the pull of Ahna's hand. Only one would guide him forward.

Chapter Twelve

Rynn had not eaten since the previous sunrise. His face
was still marked with red ocher from his time at
Marek's burial. Across his chest, he now carried a cord of
twisted sinew holding a small pouch made from the
bladder of a hare. Inside was nothing but charcoal and dry
moss: items that represent *what was* and *what may be.*
Whatever else he needed would be found on the journey.

By early morning, the wind had shifted, carrying the
scents of damp, rotting wood, smoke from nearby fires, and
the bloody remains from a nearby kill site.

It was the season when mammoths, bison, and roe deer
moved through the valley and across the plain in search of
new food sources, and with the movement of these herds
came the old ways—clan rituals handed down from
generation to generation.

Around Rynn, many of the clan had gathered—not all,
but the ones who judged. Three elders, including Omak,
the new clan leader, and Terah, Rynn's aunt, who had
recently sprained her left ankle and was now not able to
walk far, and Duma.

A few women hummed a series of low, rhythmic tones,
a chant long used to mark the threshold between youth and
the adulthood that waited beyond.

The Trial of Silence—the ritual of passage—was about to begin for Rynn. The next few days would reveal whether he was ready to take his place among the adults of his clan.

Two days, two nights, and part of another day—alone in an unfamiliar forest—far from camp and far from the river—without company, without words, without food.

Rynn would return as an adult only if he passed the trial and if he found something worth bringing back: a symbol, a sound, a tool, a thought. Something the elders would judge as having value to him.

Rynn carried a single small spear—for protection only. He was not to hunt.

The goal was for Rynn to learn a lesson in solitude.

As he stepped beyond the outer ring of shelters, no one called after him. That was the custom. A child was known by name. An adult was known by courage.

From the shadows across the river, Ahna watched.

She had planned to watch as much as she could. Rynn had told her about the ordeal he must go through.

She sensed that members of Rynn's clan were unusually quiet, and she saw that trail markings had been changed overnight. She had seen similar rites before, even among her own people—but her clan's were different.

Ahna's clan did not mark adulthood through isolation, but through belonging. A young person was welcomed into the elders' fire-circle, asked to listen and to speak. They helped lay a fallen companion into the ground. And for one full day and night, they remained in a burial place among the bones of ancestors.

But this was Rynn's trial, and it was for him to endure.

After beginning his journey, Rynn walked for half of the day before reaching the forest lying northwest of the *Homo sapiens* camp. This forest was not a place that members of his clan often visited, and the dangers within it were not known. But this is where Rynn must face his trial.

As he entered the forest, his mouth felt dry and his chest tight. The path he followed was not a familiar one, but this was part of the ritual: Rynn's journey must unfold along an unfamiliar path through unknown dangers.

Time passed slowly. The forest grew thicker. Every sound seemed unexpected and loud. The flapping of wings startled him. A branch cracked, and he flinched. At one point he stepped on a snake he had not seen sunning itself. It darted away, but Rynn's heart pounded.

When night came, he found a place to bed beneath an overhang of thick branches. He pressed his back against a thick tree trunk and tried to become still. Hunger crept in slowly, then more quickly. He found water in a nearby spring and slowly drank until his thirst eased.

He tried to sleep, but the darkness hummed with life. Every movement in the leaves sounded larger than it was. His body grew cold, then hot. At one point, he felt like crying, but forced laughed the feeling away.

In the darkest part of the night, he saw something.

Two yellow eyes in the trees. Watching.

By morning, the eyes were gone, but Rynn's stomach was still empty and his body heavy. He moved slowly, careful not to break the silence that the ritual demanded.

Thinking back, he was not sure the eyes had been real.

Hunger gnawed at him, but the greater weight was the silence itself. He longed to call out, to hear another voice, even just the echo of his own—but he did not. The rules of the trial were clear: no words, no hunting, no shortcuts to comfort. He pressed on through a thicket where thorns scratched his legs and the rotting leaves smelled strong.

Midday brought heat and a new fear. A shadow shifted through the trees, large and silent. He froze, heart racing.

A wild boar, tusks glinting, rooted only steps away. If the beast charged, his small spear was all he had for protection. His best way of defending himself was to stand very still, knowing the boar would not likely attack. His instincts screamed to run, but he remained motionless, forcing his breathing to steady. After a few long moments, the boar moved on, leaving only churned soil behind. Rynn whispered nothing, though his whole body wanted to release a shout of relief.

Later, as evening approached and as the light faded, he came to a hollow where branches twisted into shapes that looked like crouched figures. His mind filled in their faces —watchers, spirits, even the yellow-eyed creature from the night before. Fear rose again—like a river after a hard rain.

He thought about fleeing, but instead sat cross-legged, eyes closed, letting the forest speak in its creaks and rustles. His fear did not vanish, but it dulled, becoming something he could bear. Alone, hungry, and voiceless, he discovered that he could outlast even the ghosts of his own mind.

By morning of the final day, Rynn walked with less fear.

He listened now with all his senses, not just his ears.

Rather than mark his journey with steps, he began to look more closely at details—details he had paid little attention to on past journeys.

A bent twig.

A claw-scratch on a tree.

A mound of moss lay disturbed where something had slept. He knelt, brushed a hand over the moss. Warmth could still be felt. A badger, perhaps—restless, spending a night and moving on.

Near the warm moss, a split stone caught the light. Its outer face was dull, but inside it gleamed with a sharp, pale edge. Rynn lifted it, turning it in his fingers. One side curved smooth as a tooth; the other was jagged, broken. He held it against the trunk of a young tree and scratched a mark. The bark yielded easily.

A line.

Then another, and three more.

Five marks, as the elders wore—tallies for endurance. On an impulse he didn't question, he added a spiral. Ahna drew spirals. He believed that they meant looking deeper, past the lines of truth and into what lies beyond.

He stood taller when he tucked the stone into his pouch. It was not a weapon. It was something cracked that still cut true. And it reminded him that he, too, had been tested—by fear, by doubt—and still stood with courage.

When his time alone was over, he returned to camp. People paused in their work. A few nodded. No one spoke; they would not shape his tale for him.

He stepped into the ring of firelight where the elders sat. After a respectful nod, he emptied his pouch, first laying out the fang-shaped stone. Then he removed the strip of bark, carved with the tallies and the spiral.

The elders studied both. Omak picked up the stone and asked, "And what value has this stone to you?"

Rynn thought for a moment, then said, "This stone broke, and its scars changed its shape, but not its strength. I discovered I could still use it—and I learned to see my own scars the same way, as something that can be shaped and turned toward purpose."

The elders exchanged glances—quiet ones, knowing ones—then looked to Omak.

The clan leader rose, placed a steady hand on Rynn's shoulder, and held it there.

Rynn had passed.

He was now fully accepted as an adult.

With the ritual over, Rynn had an overwhelming desire to see Ahna. He walked to the river meeting place.

He did not need to wait long before Ahna appeared in the clearing. She had waited patiently during the time of Rynn's trial, but she wished she could have seen more of it, to understand what it meant to his clan and to Rynn.

When she saw him, his face seemed older. There was a steadiness in his eyes she hadn't seen before.

She remembered the beginning of her own trial—the first day she sat inside the burial place, staying there until her fear dissolved. The silence of death had been a teacher. For Rynn, it was the silence of the living.

They were different kinds of knowing.

She smiled, and touched her own forearm where she bore scars of her own coming-of-age.

They were of two clans, different peoples—strangely similar, though, when moving toward adult status.

* * *

The first night after Rynn's return, the camp grew quiet. Fires sank low and cast a wavering red glow against the hides and stone walls. The elders sat together in their circle, murmuring in voices too soft for the younger ones to hear.

Rynn sat apart, not excluded, but left to his own thoughts. He still felt the stone in his pouch, its jagged edge pressing through the thin skin of the hare bladder, reminding him of his time alone.

He thought of the yellow eyes in the trees. Whether real or imagined, the eyes had stayed with him, pulling at the corners of his mind. He knew that watching was different from seeing—and after the disclosure by Marek and his own time alone in the forest, he felt he was truly learning to see, to understand what lies behind appearance.

When the camp finally quieted to the slow breathing of sleep, he rose and slipped across the river and into the trees. He went just far enough to see the fire light of Ahna's camp. He crouched, listening to the hiss of wind in birch leaves and pine needles, the creak of branches above.

A faint sound came from his left—the almost inaudible step of someone careful. He turned and saw the shadow first. Then, Ahna stepped into a sliver of light spilling from flames flickering from a dying fire at the edge of her camp. She did not speak. Neither did he.

Instead, she sat down across from him, the two of them like a silent island in the dark. Between them lay a patch of wet moss. Slowly, she unwrapped something from the fold of fur at her hip—a small bundle of dried leaves and thin twigs, bound with sinew. She placed it on the moss, then took from her pouch a blackened stone no bigger than her thumb.

Rynn watched as she worked the stone against another, catching the spark in a twist of dry grass until it smoldered. She fed the smoke with a pinch of crushed pine needles, releasing a scent sharp and clean.

"For clearing," she said at last, voice low.

He understood. Some things learned in childhood crossed the lines between peoples. Smoke to carry away sickness, or fear, or grief. He moved his face into the faint river of smoke, letting it curl over his face.

"You have the lines now," she said, "lines on your face that speak of your experience. They may fade, but not here." She touched her own temple.

"I will keep them here," he answered, pointing to his own temple.

Ahna looked at him for a long moment, the firelight painting the strong curve of her brow and the pale glint of her eyes. "Then you are ready to be among your people as an adult." She hesitated. "And among mine… as something perhaps more."

He wanted to ask what she meant, but the words felt too heavy for the night. Instead, he drew the fang-shaped stone from his pouch and placed it between them. "This is what I found."

She picked it up, running her thumb along the sharp curve. "It was meant for your hand," she said. "Trees and cave walls will remember your marks."

They gave themselves to silence again—a comfortable place to rest. Not far away, a night bird gave a long, hollow call, answered faintly from another ridge.

Ahna began to speak, her words sounding like the telling of a secret. "When I was small, my uncle sent me to sit by the old woman who knew the names of plants. I was to watch her grind roots and to listen when she spoke of which roots could heal and which could kill.

"I did not want to go. I thought it was a task for someone else. But I went.

"She showed me her hands working the mortar, the sound of stone on stone, and the smell of crushed leaves.

"I stayed until she told me to leave. On the walk back, I realized my head was full of the shapes and smells of the plants. I had learned by watching and listening."

Rynn thought about the forest—the eyes, the marks on the tree, the way time changed once he stopped trying to grasp it. "That is what happened to me," he said. "I learned by paying attention—not by deciding what was right or wrong, but by opening my ears."

Ahna's eyes softened, and for the first time that night, she smiled. "Then your trial was a good one."

They sat until the cold pressed through their hides. Before they parted, she reached into her pouch once more and pulled out a twist of dried berry paste, dark as blood. "For strength," she said, placing it in his palm.

He did not eat it then. He would keep it for the next time solitude pressed in on him.

When Rynn returned to the camp's edge, the fires were nearly out. For a while, he sat near the central fire, listening to the sounds of the people around him. Somewhere beyond the river, in the dark, Ahna was walking back to her own shelter. He imagined her moving through the trees, quiet as wind, and felt the strange comfort of knowing she was there—not in his camp, but in his life.

A few days later, Rynn met with Ahna again. With new confidence, he asked her to go on a short hike.

Somewhat surprised, she accepted. "Yes, you lead."

They climbed a slope that gave way to an open ledge, scattered with sun-warmed stone. Below, the valley spilled out in a sweep of green and pale rock, the river flashing silver in the morning light.

They walked on for a while, sometimes speaking, sometimes not, their steps finding a shared pace.

When they stopped to rest, Ahna set down the small bundle she carried and sat with her knees drawn up, watching a hawk circle far above the ridge line.

Rynn lowered himself beside her, close enough that their shoulders touched. Neither moved away from the other, letting the moment just be.

"Do you ever think of Marek?" Ahna asked.

"Yes," he said. "I think of what he would say if he saw us here." A faint smile touched his lips. "He would tell us to be careful with one another."

Rynn looked at Ahna's hands, the way they rested loosely on her knees. He could not tell her the concern in his thinking. "I will be careful," he said. "Always."

The breeze shifted, carrying the scent of crushed sage.

Ahna turned toward him, as if weighing the truth of his words. He held her eyes, not looking away, and something unspoken passed between them—not the hurried pull of hunger, but a slower knowing, an answer to a question neither had yet asked aloud.

In Ahna's clan, the elders spoke of closeness as a binding of paths. A man and a woman who lay together were thought to leave part of their spirit in each other's keeping, and with it the chance of new life. It was never a light matter, but it was not hidden away either. The knowledge of *joining* was passed from older women to younger ones in the open air—sometimes with stories and gestures more than words.

Rynn's people spoke of it differently. His mother had once told him, when he was young, that when a man and a woman shared their warmth, the earth might choose to form a child from it. The *joining* was theirs to choose. If a child followed, its presence could stay with them for many summers, even a lifetime.

Here, with no one watching, the thought of drawing nearer felt less like a rule to be followed or broken and more like a truth to be lived.

Ahna reached for his hand, her fingers warm against his. "We can share this," she said quietly.

Rynn nodded, his throat tight. "Yes."

For a long moment they sat that way, hand in hand, listening to the wind move through the grass. Her thumb traced over his knuckles in slow, thoughtful circles, as if memorizing the shape of him. His free hand brushed against a strand of her hair, coarse from the sun but carrying the faint scent of pine smoke.

"I will remember today," she murmured.

"So will I," he said.

They both knew that what came after could change how they walked beside each other, and how their clans saw them. But, as they *joined*, it felt right, as if the path had been leading here since the first moment they met.

The sun dropped lower, brushing the ridge with gold. Ahna stayed close to Rynn, resting her head against his shoulder, and he leaned gently into her. The land below them faded to stillness. Whatever happened now, they would carry this choice, this feeling, this happiness—and each other—in all the summers to come.

Rynn's people taught that *joining* with someone was not just for the moment—it bound two lives, whether they stayed close or walked apart. He thought of Marek again, how he had treated bonds with care, never giving lightly what he could not keep.

Ahna did not feel regret. She felt change. As if the air around her had shifted in some way she could not name. The memory of Rynn's eyes today would always stay with her—not intense, not demanding, just certain. This thought warmed her even as the cold air touched her face.

Later, on his return to camp, Rynn crouched at the water's edge and took a long, cool drink. His breath misted in the stillness.

That night he lay awake for a long time, thinking of the ledge, the smell of sage on the wind, and Ahna's head resting against his shoulder.

Marek had been clear in his warning, yet Rynn's desire for Ahna felt impossible for him to overcome. He believed Marek was mistaken that closeness between clans would always lead to death, and he knew he would follow his heart in that belief.

To people in his clan, a man who *joined* with a woman was expected to stand by her if life took root. He wondered if he was ready for that—and found himself both ready and quietly hopeful.

Rynn felt no shame.

If life took root in Ahna, some in his clan would speak against it—not against the desire to *join*—but against her because she was not one of them.

* * *

A few days later, they met again near the bend of the river. The sun was beginning to set, and it bathed the trees both in a golden glow and dark shadows.

For a while they spoke of other things—the tracks Ahna had seen on the river bank, the small fish Rynn trapped that morning. But the pauses between those words held something more important.

Ahna looked at him at last, her dark eyes steady. "We have stepped onto a new path."

Rynn's hand closed around a smooth stone, turning it slowly in his palm. "Yes. And there is no going back to where we were."

She asked, "Do you want to go back?"

"No." His voice was certain. "Do you?"

Her answer was just as firm. "No."

They stood close now, the river's whisper at their feet. Each knew that what they carried was more than just a pleasant memory. It was a promise, even if they had not yet shaped the words of it.

The wind lifted the strands of her hair and brushed them across his cheek, as if nudging them closer.

They did not need to say more. Knowing was enough.

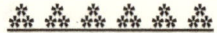

Historical Context IV
Daily Challenges

"In the long history of humankind ... those who learned to
collaborate and improvise most effectively have prevailed."
— Charles Darwin

Shelter and Home

Neanderthals lived in hide-covered shelters or caves—
often large enough to house more than one family. Inside,
they built fire pits and hearths, placed sleeping areas near
warmer walls, and possibly used hides or stone walls to
partition spaces for comfort, warmth, and a small measure
of privacy.

But they were also capable of building small open-air
huts when useful. At some sites, ringed arrangements of
mammoth bones suggest temporary windbreaks. Each type
of dwelling was not crude, but they were functional and
pragmatic—designed for warmth, protection, and short-
term use, often used during hunting.

Homo sapiens, meanwhile, built more elaborate huts.
Even their portable shelters—made of wood, bone, and
hide—showed deliberate design. In some regions, clans
established base camps with circular layouts, central
hearths, and defined areas for sleeping and work. For them,
home was not just shelter but a social and symbolic space—

a place where stories were told and traditions passed from one generation to the next.

The contrast in dwelling style reflects differing survival strategies between the two lineages. Neanderthals, long adapted to the harsh Ice Age wilderness of Europe, favored small, insulated shelters built for warmth and protection.

Homo sapiens, migrants from warmer and more varied lands, envisioned home as something broader—a setting for communal life, work, and shared activity.

Sharing and Trust

One of the most powerful survival strategies any human group can possess is cooperation beyond the immediate family. This may have given *Homo sapiens* a long-term advantage in the fight for survival.

Among Neanderthals, food sharing likely occurred within family units. Injured individuals were cared for, and children were nurtured, suggesting deep empathy. But sharing may have been more kin-based, more local—more limited than that which occurred with *Homo sapiens*.

Homo sapiens appear to have expanded the circle of sharing beyond their own families and member of their immediate group. Trade items like shells, pigments, and obsidian traveled long distances—implying networks of trust, reciprocity, and perhaps even alliance.

When both lineages hunted together, this was an experiment in both method and trust.

Will food be divided fairly?

Will a wound be treated by unfamiliar hands?

These questions are as old as humanity, and their answers may have shaped the fate of both lineages.

Cooperation, it seems, is not merely about logistics. It is about empathy, fairness, and the shared belief that survival is stronger when it is mutual.

A Dangerous Bond

A joint hunt—especially a dangerous one—carries more than the risk of injury. It carries the risk of betrayal, misunderstanding, and failure. But it also offers the chance for deep, unshakable respect.

To face danger together is to learn each other's strengths. A Neanderthal might marvel at the coordinated drive of a *Homo sapiens* hunt, or the strange elegance of a thrown spear. A *Homo sapiens* might witness the courage of a Neanderthal who meets a charging bison head-on with nothing but a stone-tipped thrusting spear.

And both might see, in that moment, not a rival or curiosity, but a partner in survival.

Ways of Knowing

When *Homo sapiens* and Neanderthals encountered each other in Ice Age Europe, they were not blank slates. Each lineage carried a reservoir of experience and knowledge, shaped over 10,000 generations, or more, of survival, observation, and trial and error.

These were not encounters between prehistoric humans driven solely by instinct. These were meetings between human lineages who could speak and gesture, think abstractly, shape their environment with tools, and who, in different but meaningful ways, were beginning to wonder why the world worked the way it did.

Many novels explore what may have occurred when these two lineages first ventured into one another's world.

While scientists look for firm evidence to support every conjecture, authors of fiction often use what is known about people today to model characters in a novel.

No written records or stories survive from 40,000 years ago. Authors, therefore, must imagine the inner lives of those early people. It is believable that their feelings and responses were much like ours, particularly in moments unshaped by modern inventions or comforts, when instinct and emotion guided daily life.

Interestingly, today's scientific evidence suggests that Neanderthals and *Homo sapiens* were far more alike than previously believed. It also appears that they did not often fight with one another, and that occasionally they had children and raised families together—sharing more in common than once assumed, especially in the rhythms of daily life and cooperation.

Cognitive Styles: Intelligent Problem-Solving

Modern neuroscience and archaeology paint a nuanced picture of Neanderthal thinking. For most of the 20th century, Neanderthals were caricatured as dull-witted brutes—strong but simple-minded. This image was born more of modern arrogance than scientific understanding. Today, that portrayal is considered deeply inaccurate.

Neanderthals had brains that were, on average, slightly larger than those of *Homo sapiens*. More importantly, the structure of their brains appears to have been different in ways that likely influenced their style of thinking.

Evidence suggests that Neanderthals may have had excellent visual-spatial memory, acute sensory perception, and strong practical problem-solving abilities.

In a landscape where survival meant navigating forests, reading animal tracks, and recalling the locations of caves, seasonal streams, and game trails, these traits were vital.

Homo sapiens, by contrast, seem to have emphasized flexibility, abstraction, and long-distance planning in ways that allowed rapid adaptation. They developed complex social networks and experimented with symbols, language, and abstract ideas that could be shared widely.

Where Neanderthals may have relied on meticulous memory and highly efficient routines, *Homo sapiens* appeared more prone to innovation—developing new strategies quickly but just as quickly discarding those that did not work, continually refining their approaches.

This distinction has led some researchers to propose that Neanderthals were masters of precision and detail, while *Homo sapiens* were better generalists—more inclined to innovate, imagine, and reorganize their environment in response to shifting challenges.

It is not a question of which lineage was "smarter," but of how each lineage used its particular type of intelligence, applying it in different ways and under different pressures in their ongoing quest for survival.

Tool Use and Symbolic Behavior

Both *Homo sapiens* and Neanderthals were skilled in the making of tools, but they crafted their tools differently. Neanderthals used what is known as the *Mousterian tool tradition*, producing a refined array of flakes and points from carefully prepared cores of flint or other stone. These tools were efficient, task-specific, and standardized across time and space, suggesting a shared template that was passed down through generations.

Homo sapiens, by contrast, made *Upper Paleolithic toolkits*, which included stone, bone, antler, and ivory. Their tools were varied in form and use: finely made blades, sewing needles, fishhooks, and harpoons. These objects demonstrate technological innovation, planning, and an ability to adapt to a changing environment.

Tools were not merely practical items; they were also cultural artifacts. Some researchers argue that Neanderthal tools, though consistent and effective, suggest a culture that prioritized tradition over innovation. *Homo sapiens* were more open to experimentation—an openness that may have been both a strength and a vulnerability.

Symbolic behavior—the ability to create meaning beyond immediate physical needs—is one of the clearest markers of complex thinking and shared cultural understanding. For a long time, it was thought that only *Homo sapiens* engaged in such symbolic acts. But new evidence has challenged this view, revealing signs of creativity and intention among Neanderthals as well, suggesting a richer inner world.

Symbolism: The Use of Red Ochre

The use of red ochre—a naturally occurring pigment often found in clay—has long been associated with symbolic thinking. Both *Homo sapiens* and Neanderthals used red ochre, possibly as body paint or in artistic decoration, and in burial rites. In caves in Spain, paintings of abstract shapes and hand stencils have been dated to over 64,000 years ago—several thousand years before *Homo sapiens* are thought to have arrived in the region. These were most likely made by Neanderthals.

This is a profound revelation. If Neanderthals created art, then they too had an aesthetic sense—a drive to express or symbolize ideas that could not easily be expressed in words. Also, they may have decorated their bodies or tools, adorned themselves with feathers or shells, or marked the walls of caves for reasons that went beyond the practical.

These gestures suggest not only symbolic thought but a dawning spiritual awareness—an urge to mark beauty, to affirm identity, and honor forces of nature they could sense but neither explain nor control.

Burial practices offer another window into Neanderthal thinking. Dozens of Neanderthal burial sites have been found, some with evidence of care: bodies placed in fetal positions, accompanied by tools or animal bones. While it's still debated whether these were symbolic or simply functional (to deter scavengers), the repeated nature of these practices hints at an emerging ritual culture.

Homo sapiens, by contrast, left behind unambiguous signs of symbolic ritual. Burials were often elaborate, with grave goods, carvings, pigments, and personal ornaments. Caves in France, such as Lascaux and Chauvet, reveal wall paintings of animals, abstract signs, and human-animal hybrids—evidence of storytelling, myth-making, and perhaps religious thought.

To face danger together is to learn each other's strengths. A Neanderthal might marvel at the coordinated drive of a *Homo sapiens* hunt, or the strange elegance of a thrown spear as it arcs through the air. A *Homo sapiens* might witness the courage of a Neanderthal who meets a charging bison head-on with nothing but a stone-tipped thrusting spear and unshakable resolve.

Shared or Overlapping Belief Systems

Though we cannot know what early humans believed, we can infer from burial practices, art, and cultural artifacts that both Neanderthals and *Homo sapiens* developed beliefs that linked living things closely with the ground or perhaps with a spiritual afterlife.

It is likely that these beliefs emerged organically from the cycles of nature: the change of seasons, the birth and death of animals, the power of storms, the mystery of fire, and the nightly appearance of stars. Beliefs may have been both about fixed gods and doctrines and about relationship —with the stars, ancestors, the land, and the animals.

If either Neanderthals or *Homo sapiens* believed in an afterlife, it may have taken the form of ancestor respect or spirit remembrance—early frameworks by which to explain and gain comfort from the unknown and ever-present mysteries of their world.

One of the most fascinating areas of research is whether Neanderthals and *Homo sapiens* shared beliefs, or at least borrowed from one another. As the two lineages coexisted in overlapping areas in modern-day Europe, cultural exchange seems likely, even inevitable at times.

Some burial sites show hybrid practices, mixing Neanderthal minimalism with *Homo sapiens* elaboration in ways that hint at shared meanings, evolving ritual behavior, and perhaps early forms of symbolic dialogue.

It is possible, even probable, that adolescents—curious, bold, less constrained by tradition—played a major role in this cultural sharing.

Adolescence and the Transmission of Culture

In both lineages, adolescence may have been a critical window for learning, exploration, and social integration. Teenagers today are known for testing boundaries, asking questions, and experimenting with identity. It's likely that the same was true 40,000 years ago.

Anthropologists suggest that the time of adolescence was a bridge between generations—an age to absorb cultural knowledge, adapt it, add to it, and then share new ideas. Young people learned the stories, skills, and taboos of their group, yet also reshaped them.

Adolescents may have been the first to try new body decorations, songs, animal mimicry, or cross-group friendships—sometimes seeking individuals outside their own kind from curiosity, attraction, or freedom from old boundaries.

The novel *The Neanderthal Within* imagines a young Neanderthal and a young *Homo sapiens*, sharing culture through attraction, friendship, imitation, and adventure.

The Roots of Discrimination

In *The Neanderthal Within*, a world 40,000 years ago is envisioned, a time when two human lineages struggled not only against a harsh climate but also against each other.

In this novel and others like it that depict the same period, Neanderthals and *Homo sapiens* share the same lands, the same game trails, the same challenges to survival —and likely the same fears. While much of the interaction between the lineages may have been cautious coexistence and occasional exchange, there is little doubt that misunderstanding and mistrust also shadowed their meetings. The seeds of what we call discrimination—the instinct to divide "us" from "them," to assign worth based on difference—were already being sown.

In the small, kin-based societies of the time, belonging meant survival. Every member's effort mattered. Those who looked, sounded, or behaved differently could be seen as potential threats to the delicate balance that kept the group alive. Physical distinctions were immediately visible: the broader faces and stockier frames of Neanderthals contrasted with the leaner, more gracile features of *Homo sapiens*. Speech, too, may have differed. Even if both species used complex language, their accents or gestures might have seemed foreign, and a difference in sound or signal could provoke fear and threaten survival.

For much of prehistory, prejudice was not ideological but practical. Groups favored their own because familiarity meant trust. Outsiders—whether members of another clan or another lineage—brought uncertainty. When food was scarce or climate harsh, competition for resources could turn suspicion into hostility. A stranger near a carcass or watering hole might be attacked not because of hatred in any modern sense, but because the stakes of survival were absolute. Such encounters would leave deep emotional marks, reinforcing the instinct that those who are not "us" are dangerous.

Yet discrimination need not always have been violent. It could express itself through avoidance, exclusion, or unequal exchange. A visiting group might be allowed to camp nearby but denied access to prime hunting grounds. Mixed-lineage offspring—the result of occasional unions between Neanderthal and *Homo sapiens* parents—may have faced uncertain acceptance. To some clans, such children might have symbolized alliance and new strength; to others, they might have represented a breach in the social order. The evidence of interbreeding tells us that barriers to mating between lineages were not absolute, but the rarity of such unions hints that they were exceptional, and perhaps often discriminated against and condemned.

Differences of age, ability, and gender could also shape early forms of bias. The young and strong carried the group's hopes, while the old, injured, or disabled depended on communal care. Though both lineages responsibly tended their injured and elderly, care did not always mean equality. In times of starvation, difficult decisions may have been made about who received the first share of food or who was left behind when the clan moved. These acts were not born of cruelty but of necessity; still, they reveal how value could be assigned to one life over another.

Among *Homo sapiens*, as the use of symbolism grew increasingly elaborate, discrimination may also have acquired cultural dimensions. Ornaments, body paint, and markings allowed individuals to signal identity—to declare who belonged and who did not. Beads of different shells, ochres of distinct hue, or particular tattoos could have served as emblems of clan membership. Such symbols might foster unity, but could also signal exclusion.

Those without the right adornments might be seen as outsiders. In this sense, the roots of tribalism, ethnicity, and even nationalism reach back to these first marks make by humans to set themselves apart.

The emotional foundation of discrimination—fear of the unfamiliar—was adaptive in an Ice Age landscape filled with real danger. Yet the same capacity for empathy and cooperation that allowed early humans to survive also held the potential to overcome it. Archaeological traces show exchange of tools, pigments, and perhaps mates across groups and lineages.

These encounters demanded tolerance, curiosity, and restraint—the early stirrings of social intelligence that would one day blossom into culture. The long coexistence of Neanderthals and *Homo sapiens* hints at a complex mosaic of contact, not endless conflict—at times kind and intimate, at others cautious or violent.

When discrimination arose, it was likely magnified by hardship. During glacial advances, when resources shrank and migration brought groups into uneasy proximity, competition hardened boundaries and revived dormant suspicions. Stories told around the fire may have warned of deceitful outsiders or treacherous neighbors, embellished each time they were retold.

These narratives preserved lessons but also perpetuated fear. Over generations, such oral traditions could become the prototypes of prejudice—a bias in which differences were equated with danger, and unfamiliar faces revived long-held memories of danger.

The disappearance of Neanderthals about 35,000 years ago is often described as an extinction, but it may also reflect the long-term result of unequal and uneven contact between two closely related human groups.

Whether the outcome stemmed from conflict, competition for resources, exposure to new diseases, or gradual cultural and reproductive assimilation, the Neanderthal lineage slowly diminished as the *Homo sapiens* lineage expanded.

Yet, Neanderthal DNA endures within us, a lasting sign that what began as separate populations ultimately did not totally remain so. The impulse to divide may be ancient, but so too is the capacity to join and become something new.

To study discrimination in Ice Age Europe is to glimpse its dual nature: a survival strategy and a moral challenge. The impulse to protect one's own ensured our ancestors' persistence, but the ability to recognize the humanity in others ensured our species' growth. Both instincts were born together in those harsh millennia.

And perhaps the story of Neanderthals and *Homo sapiens*—of differences met at times with coming together and at others with fearful separation—is an early example of humanity's enduring struggle to choose acceptance or to surrender to exclusion.

Crossing the Divide

A daunting theme of many Ice Age novels, including *The Neanderthal Within*, is not the romance between members of two lineages, but clan reaction to cross-lineage bonding.

This reflects one of the earliest roots of the in-group/out-group behavior we still see today: a human instinct, likely formed long before the epochs described in Ice Age novels, that shapes whom we trust, favor, and welcome as a "friend."

As time passed, evolution favored those who protected their group, those who recognized familiar faces and defended against strangers. But this instinct, once useful, can also become exclusionary: it punishes deviation; it recoils at difference.

Chapter Thirteen

R ain fell throughout the evening and finally broke when the early morning sun pushed its way past thinning clouds. Light sifted down in pale streaks, glowing through the lingering mist and scattering off raindrops that still clung to the trees. The night's downpour had softened the earth and left puddles pooled here and there across the forest floor, their surfaces stirring in the gentle breeze.

A faint scent drifted in the moist air, a light trace of sage from a nearby clearing. As the fragrance reached Ahna, her memory rose with it—the time with Rynn, the closeness they had found—returning with the same quiet insistence as the scent itself.

For Rynn, there was the remembered touch of her hand in his, the feeling of her head on his shoulder, and the unspoken promise they had made to one another. Those thoughts drifted in and out of his thinking—warm threads weaving their way into his very being—as he rose to begin work on his morning tasks.

But his thoughts were interrupted moments later as several voices in camp grew sharp and urgent.

A woman's cry cut through the cool morning air, joined by the sound of many people in hurried motion. Something was happening, and he would soon know what it was.

Rynn heard his own name called, not in greeting but in summons. He crossed the clearing quickly.

A child was missing—last seen the previous evening by a returning hunter near the bend of the river. Possibly missing before light had fully left the sky.

The child—Leeva, a curious six-year-old with hair the color of dry straw—had wandered away after the evening meal. One moment she had been sitting cross-legged beside the hearth, playing with stones and humming to herself. The next, she was gone, unnoticed by parents who had gone to sleep early.

Now, in the pale morning, the space where her laughter should have been was only silence. The easy stillness of yesterday had vanished—and had been replaced by a cold that no fire could chase away.

Rynn stopped at the *others'* camp to seek Ahna's help, and together they joined searchers from Rynn's camp, walking the paths that led from the camp to the river.

Finding nothing, and then checking the berry thickets, Rynn now spoke with an anxious voice.

"She is young and does not know the dangers. There are wolves this time of year. And sinkholes."

Then, spotting something near the water, Rynn crouched down near a patch of crushed fern, perhaps trodden on by a small foot.

"She might have crossed the river," he said.

"Yes,"Ahna said, pointing to a flat rock smeared with what might be muddy toe prints. "And this is where she may have crossed."

Rynn and Ahna split from the other searchers and crossed the river. Ahna's eyes darted between trees and tracked details that most would miss: a tuft of hair, a shifted stone, the faint smear of wet fingers along the moss of a low boulder.

She was used tracking in this forest.

Ahna laid a hand on Rynn's arm. "Leeva is small, and small ones are often clever. If lost, she might seek shelter."

"You think she might be hiding?" asked Rynn.

"She might be hiding. She might be lost. If lost, she might not know she is lost. But she will know it soon."

They moved quickly, Ahna in the lead. Her feet made little sound, gliding over roots and fallen needles, and Rynn had to push himself to keep up with her pace. Every few steps he felt the thud of his own heartbeat, too loud for the silence around them. The air carried a faint chill—the kind that came before something changed—and he found himself glancing into the trees, imagining small footprints lost beneath the undergrowth, imagining a child alone in the dark. Leena had survived only six summers. A single night could be enough to steal her away. The thought tightened his chest, urging him on.

The woods thickened as they climbed, pine giving way to birch, the canopy shifting from deep green to a trembling silver that played tricks with the light. The birches creaked faintly, their pale trunks standing like watchful figures. Ahna paused often—touching the bark with the back of her fingers, lowering herself to examine crushed moss, lifting her head to sniff the wind. Each pause made Rynn's pulse jump. Sometimes she listened so long he felt the world tilting toward dread. Was she hearing a cry? A predator? Nothing at all? Her eyes moved with sharp purpose, searching for signs too subtle for him to read—broken lichen, disturbed leaf litter, a faint thread of scent carried through cold air. Every time she straightened, Rynn felt the question rising in him, unspoken but heavy: *Is Leena still alive?*

The sun slowly crossed the sky as time passed.

They found where she may have stopped to rest: a small nest of flattened grass. A few crushed berries stained the ground.

Then the path turned rocky, climbing sharply upward.

Ahna narrowed her eyes.

"There is a cave on the ridge," she said. "I have seen it before. A good hiding place for someone small."

Rynn's heart pounded. "Why would she go there?"

Ahna did not answer. She was already climbing.

* * *

Leeva had not meant to go far. She liked the way the forest smelled after rain. She liked the way tree trunks changed color when they were wet. And most of all she liked the sounds of her voice echoing through the trees when she sang.

But then she had followed a squirrel that led her to the river. Then she spotted a bird on the other side and crossed in the shallow water. And by the time she realized she did not know the way back, the darkness was replacing the fading light, and she worried she might be lost.

She was not frightened at first. She had been told what to do if ever lost: stay in one place, wait to be found. But it was getting darker and cold, and the wind carried new sounds. The bird called, sharp and shrill, and she followed its call—slowly climbing a hill.

That was when she saw the cave. It was half-hidden behind a tumble of rocks, but wide enough for her to crawl into. Inside, it was cool and dry. She placed a few fallen branches near the opening, then hugged her arms to her chest and curled into the soft dirt.

Sleep came fast.

When Leeva woke, it was still dark. The shadows had shifted. And worse—there was a noise outside.

Low. Sniffing. Then a scrape of claws on rock.

She covered her mouth with her hands.

The thing outside sniffed again, then grew silent. But she did not dare move. Not even to whisper. Her legs ached, and her eyes stung from tears held back. Deep inside her chest, fear bloomed like a cold flower.

She slept more, until awakened by a new sound.

Soft steps.

Not animal—but not her people either.

* * *

Ahna moved like a shadow, keeping low as she circled the edge of the cave. She had seen tracks—a badger, most likely. But it was gone now.

Ahna lifted a hand to stop Rynn, her gaze fixed on the small branches and stones arranged at the cave mouth.

"She's inside," she whispered. "A child placed those."

She stepped forward quietly.

"Let me go first. I've tracked and found for many children. She may be very frightened."

Rynn hesitated, then nodded.

Ahna slowly entered the cave on her hands and knees. The air was musty but held the warm trace of child-scent: sweat, soil, and dried berries. She clicked her tongue softly —a rhythm not unlike a nesting bird.

Silence.

Then, a whimper.

Ahna paused, then whispered, "Leeva."

A sniff. Then a tiny voice: "Who is there?"

"Ahna," she said gently. "You are safe. The night did not take you."

She crept forward, letting the girl see her face in the thin shaft of light filtering through the entrance.

Leeva's eyes widened. "You look different."

Ahna gave a small smile. "I do. But I am Rynn's friend, and I am here to help you. You are safe now, and your mother will be very glad."

"Is the animal gone?"

"Yes."

"Will I get in trouble?"

"No. Your mother and father will be happy to see you."

Leeva's voice cracked. "I thought I would turn to rock."

Ahna reached out a hand. "Only if you stay too long."

"I followed a bird," explained Leeva. "And then it was dark and I saw this cave."

"Yes," Ahna replied, "I have followed birds also."

Leeva crawled toward her—the child trembling but brave. When they reached the mouth of the cave, the dim moonlight dazzled her, and she squeezed Ahna's hand.

Rynn let out a sharp cry of joy.

"Leeva!" he shouted, rushing forward.

Leeva ran into his arms, and he lifted her high, spinning once in relief. Ahna stepped back, watching the reunion, her expression unreadable.

"She followed a bird," Ahna said, smiling.

Rynn nodded. "She does that."

Then he turned to Ahna, his eyes full.

"Thank you," he said. "Thank you."

She looked down at her dirt-covered hands. "She found shelter. That was clever."

That night, several members of both clans gathered to share food by the fire. Leeva, wrapped in furs, sat in her mother's lap, too tired to speak. But when the firelight grew low, she looked across the circle at Ahna and held up a carved piece of bone.

"I made this for you," she said.

It was a little shape—rough, but meant to be a bird.

Ahna took it, smiling as she said, "Thank you."

Across the circle, other faces watched—some curious, some wary, all changed by what had happened. Ahna, long seen as one of the *others*, had perhaps saved a child of the *tall ones*. The thought unsettled them, tugging at old beliefs, and yet none could deny what she had done.

Something was changing.

A path was opening.

Not yet a complete trail. But a good start.

Later that night, the camp quieted—bellies full, stories fading to silence. While Ahna stayed to talk with Rynn, the several members of Ahna's clan who had helped in the search returned to their camp.

Rynn and Ahna sat beside glowing embers. He added a few sticks to the fire but did not stir the coals. He liked how the red light pulsed faintly beneath the ash, like something breathing in sleep. For a while, they said nothing.

"She's brave," Rynn said at last. "For one so small."

Ahna almost smiled. "She told me she thought she might turn into a rock. But she stayed where she was."

Rynn nodded.

Ahna added, "Rock waits. There is strength in that."

Another silence, this one softer.

Rynn turned his head slightly, looking at her profile.

"I have been wondering," he said. "When you went into that cave... were you afraid? Of something waiting?"

She shook her head. "I have always felt safe in caves. They hold things. Memory. Warmth. Stillness."

"Stillness," Rynn repeated. "You mean... like death?"

She did not answer immediately. Her eyes flicked to the fire, then to the sky above, where stars blinked in and out behind drifting clouds.

"We do not speak of death as stillness—nor as an ending," she said. "More as... a return to the ground."

Rynn shook his head. "But not a place you return from."

"No," she said. "Your breath doesn't return, but memory of you returns to ones who loved you."

Rynn poked at the dirt with a stick, thoughtful. "We speak of life spirits that live on after your body dies. The elders say the spirits go up—" he gestured to the stars "—but some say spirits stay around us for awhile."

"And what do you believe?" she asked.

He paused. "When I was a child, I thought my grandfather became a hawk. I saw one circling above the ridge soon after he died. It felt true. But later... I learned about bones, about what happens when a body lies in the ground. The truth is slower, but you can see how the body fades."

Ahna listened carefully. "We do not speak of fading," she said. "Not if someone remembers your story. Or finds a stone you warmed with your touch. Or copies a shape you carved into a wall."

Rynn looked at her with something like reverence. "You see memory as something you can hold."

"Yes," she said. "It clings to things. Smoke. Skin. Soil. That is why we leave our dead close to our touch."

"We bury ours deep with many things for the next journey," he said. "We give them tools and a spear to keep them safe. We try to comfort the body."

"Your people speak of other places?"

Rynn nodded. "Some of us believe the dead walk in another place. A wide plain, always lit, always full of animals. No hunger. No cold."

She looked at him curiously. "But they cannot return."

"No."

Ahna turned. "Then how do you know it is real?"

Rynn looked down. "We know by our hope."

A long breath passed between them.

"We do not hope," she said. "We remember."

He watched her as she closed her eyes, briefly, as if listening to some deep rhythm. Then she opened them again and looked directly at him.

"When I die," she said, "I want my people to walk past the place where I rest and remember me as they feel the wind. I want them to remember me in the birds."

Rynn swallowed. "We call that your spirit."

"We speak of it as feeling," she said. "The way your hand knows a stone has been touched before."

He looked at her for a long time. The flames shifted again, rising for a moment before softening into coals.

"I think our kinds are not so different," he said.

"A little different, perhaps," she replied. "But we are not separate."

"No, not separate. Just small differences," Rynn added.

Then, Ahna and Rynn relaxed as afternoon sunlight slowly faded into evening shadows.

As the sky darkened, Rynn leaned forward and warmed his hands near the glowing coals.

The stars were starting to emerge clearly now. One streaked across the sky like a silent ember.

"Do you ever wonder," Rynn asked, "if the things you believe now might feel different after many summers?"

Ahna considered this.

"Yes," she said. "Like footprints in the dirt. Not lost. Just covered by new ones."

The fire crackled. In the distance, an owl called.

They sat in silence, the warmth between them not just from the flames.

And beneath the ground, perhaps, their ancestors listened. Or perhaps they did not. Or perhaps some did, and some did not.

Maybe different fates awaited—depending on the kind of life lived. Too many questions—too few answers.

But in that moment, two minds from different branches of the human tree had spoken of life, death, and an afterlife—telling the stories that their clans told, each clan trying to make sense of it all.

Later, after the embers were starting to cool, most of the members of Rynn's clan were asleep in their shelters. Now, only the soft stir of wind and the sounds of burning wood settling in the fire marked the passing of time.

As the flames died out, Rynn and Ahna sat near the glowing embers, talking late into the night.

Rynn asked a question that he had thought about for some time. "Do you bury the dead where they know the land?"

Ahna looked at him, then away toward the darkness where the forest rose beyond the edge of camp.

"Sometimes," she said. "It depends."

"On what?"

Ahna breathed in the cool night air before answering.

"Not all are buried where they lived," she said. "We listen to the story they leave behind—whether their days brought kindness or fear, whether their voice guided others or led them astray. The land keeps stories long after breath is gone. We choose a resting place that lets the story sit in its right place."

Rynn faced her. "Do you mark the place with stones so you can return?"

Ahna shook her head. "Stones are for walls and tools. For our dead, we let the land hold them. We shape the ground in a way our people know."

She rose and motioned for him to follow. "Come. You will see."

He followed her through the sleeping camp and into the night beyond, down the path to the shallow part of the river. Crossing the water, they walked until they reached a cleft in a limestone outcrop half-hidden by vines.

Ahna ducked inside. Rynn followed, the hidden cave swallowing them in a cool hush.

Inside, she lit a thin reed soaked in fat and used it to light a resin torch. As the flame steadied, it threw flickering light across the walls—and then Rynn saw them.

Marks.

Everywhere.

Not paintings like his people made. Not images of animals or hunting scenes.

These were different.

Lines, spirals, arcs. Shallow grooves shaped into repeating patterns. Palm prints in ocher. Scratches that looked almost like paths winding around one another, some marked with dots or short notches.

"This is not for looking," Ahna said. "It is for feeling."

She placed his hand gently on the wall, on a patch of carved grooves that circled inward.

"This was my grandmother," she said. "These lines are how she walked the mountain trails. The circles mean she was never lost."

Rynn traced the lines, astonished. "A map?"

"Not of land. Of movement. Of memories."

She led him to another wall. There, red-ocher vertical lines stood in groups of four and five, and between them lay patterns of ocher in varying widths and thicknesses.

"My sister's son," she whispered. "He died young. These are marks made to remember him. When possible we let the children draw their own, before they grow teeth."

"You let children draw on the walls here?" Rynn asked.

"Yes," she said. "Before they know how to fully enjoy the stillness. This way, their body remembers. Even if they die, we can still feel who they were. Their presence. Their memories."

Rynn stood quietly, curiously.

"And this," she said, moving to a wider section where handprints danced along the ceiling, "this is for the ones we do not want to forget. Those who made the fire. Those who taught songs. Those who died before we understood why."

Rynn stepped closer to the dim wall. "Why do you not use drawings of animals or of hunters with spears the way my people do?"

Ahna shook her head gently. "Your people see with their eyes. Mine see with their hands. You make drawings

243

so a moment can be remembered as it looked. We shape the drawing so a moment can be remembered as it felt."

He studied the faint grooves. At first they seemed like scratches left by time, but as he looked longer, they began to settle into pattern.

"What do they mean?" he asked softly.

Ahna touched one of the carved lines with her fingertip. "Some marks hold memory. Not stories of hunts or great deeds—those belong to your people. These hold the rhythm of a life. A way of walking. A way of breathing.

"When someone dies, we may come here to remember them. We touch any drawings they may have left, or we leave new ones for them. Not as a story to read, but as a memory to feel."

Rynn nodded slowly, beginning to understand. "My people... believe that Leeva will someday leave her marks as a way of telling the story of her time alone in the cave."

"Maybe she has already left her story in memory," Ahna said. "In the minds of those who love her. That is the truest memory, the one that will live on after the body is gone."

They stood together in the flickering torchlight. Rynn rested his hand on a small spiral drawn low on the wall, shallow and tentative—the work of someone young. It made him think of Leeva curled in the cave, trying not to become a stone.

He turned toward Ahna, his voice steady. "We tell our stories with words and drawings and scratches. But your people... your stories live in shape and memory."

Ahna nodded. "Shape lasts in ways words do not."

They stayed a while longer, two shadows in a place that had held generations. When they stepped back into the moonlight, neither spoke. Some understandings do not need words.

And in that quiet, Rynn began to sense something beyond Ahna's gestures or her strength—something he would later call her spirit, the part of her that would remain long after all words were gone.

Chapter Fourteen

Long before she met Rynn and long before the crossing of paths with members of his clan, Ahna had sat alone in the *cave of the dead*.

She was twelve summers when womanhood found her, and the time for understanding had come. Childhood ended not with a number but with this moment—a moment the clan marked as the passage when a young woman could carry fear without letting it guide her.

Ahna's moment came without ceremony. No songs. No drums. Only her mother's hand resting on her arm at first light, and the quiet instruction to rise and follow.

Ahna's mother, Elah had led Ahna to a limestone cave deep within a nearby forested hill—a place known as "Kurt's Hollow."

When they arrived, Elah paused before entering, telling Ahna, "This cave was once our winter home. Long ago, before your birth, our people slept here when the winds grew sharp. The stone walls held warmth, and the roof never fell."

She walked slowly inside, with Ahna close behind. "One winter, a terrible sickness came. Many died within these walls, including your uncle. When the cold lifted, the survivors left and did not return. I was one who lived. We felt that the hollow had taken enough of us."

As she continued the story, she pointed to the drawings on the walls. "From that time, this cave was kept for the marking of passages and for remembrance of those who have come and gone. We no longer live in Khurta's Hollow, but we still honor it, and one way we honor it is to mark the passage of a youth into adulthood.

"Inside this cave are the bones of many of those who died during the terrible sickness. Some were buried after being wrapped in hides, others dusted with red ocher and simply laid in small hollows and covered lightly with small rocks. A few had objects of remembrance laid beside them: carved beads, bundles of ash-bound hair, and flowers."

Ahna remembered being here many summers ago as a small child, but she had never heard this story before. She had clung to her mother at that time and had felt some fear. This time, she walked without protest.

The steps of Ahna's passage had been explained to her and now it was up to Ahna.

As they entered the cave, her mother did not speak. She simply pointed to a large flat stone inside, lit faintly by a shaft of afternoon light. A mark was made on the stone for each person who had died in this cave.

Ahna sat. And waited.

The ritual was never about testing courage with feats of strength.

It was about learning to sit and silently honor ancestors who had passed. Ancestors who had died in this cave.

To be accepted as an adult, a youth had to spend two nights and a day alone with the departed—neither fleeing, nor hiding. The dead would not speak, nor act, nor reach across the silence. The change came only from what the living themselves made of the silence.

Ahna sat with her back against a wall, eyes open.

The air was thick with the odor of dust and ocher, old fur clinging to bones, the faint tang of water seeping down rock. Nothing moved in the cave—only shadows shifting when small fires were lit, or when embers glowed late into the night, after a now seldom-practiced ritual.

At first Ahna was restless—her body tense, thoughts unsettled. Then her eyes fixed on a nearby skull peaking up through the ground—*Vara's skull*— pale against the stone. She had heard the stories from others who had kept this vigil: Vara, who had died in childbirth during the sickness, her body laid beneath the earth. Yet the soil on her grave was shallow, and with the passing years it had thinned and shifted, until her skull slowly surfaced, rising from the ground like something the cave had chosen to reveal.

The elders had told stories of Vara—how she had taught children to dig roots, how she had once faced down a bear. Those stories had made her larger than life, but Ahna was now face to face with the truth of her: body swallowed by the ground, skull peering through the ground, jaw wide as if to speak, hollow sockets staring into the dark.

Ahna felt unease rise, but she reminded herself: Vara had no power here. The dead held no sway. What mattered was how she herself chose to sit in their presence.

Her thoughts began to change, forming in the way that roots take hold in wet soil. The skull did not ask to speak—it had already joined the earth, mingling stone and bone into a single returning shape. The longer she watched, the more something within her changed: fear dissolved into recognition, unease into a steady, wordless calm.

That was the goal of this ritual—not to wrestle with thoughts of fear, but to build a sense of calm within: to learn how to be still in the company of death and to accept that the dead ask only for acknowledgment.

By the second night she understood that the dead could not change her. Only she could do that. But without their silent witness, she might never have understood.

When the cave mouth finally brightened again with morning, Ahna did not rise lighter or freer. She rose as though she carried a new understanding—the knowledge that one day she too would rest in the ground, and that living fully now meant learning how to endure and sit with that truth.

Morning light of the final day entered the cave through the upper shaft and struck a figure on the wall—a simple engraving she had never noticed before. It was not a painting. Just a series of drawn lines: two arches above a circle, and a downward-pointing mark beneath.

To a stranger, it might have meant nothing.

To Ahna, it was Khurta—the old name whispered when fires burned low.

Khurta was not a god. Not a ghost. Khurta was the name for the feeling that stayed behind when the body rejoined the ground. The imprint. The breath caught in the throat of the breathing soil.

These marks on the wall were not to be spoken of. Not shown to the young. And now she had seen them.

Ahna reached forward and touched the marks. Not to erase them. Not to trace them.

Just to acknowledge: *I see you.*

When she returned, her mother said nothing.

She did not ask what Ahna had seen or felt.

She did not ask about Khurta.

Instead, she handed her a red ocher stone and a flat piece of shale.

"You choose," she said. "Mark the place or yourself."

Ahna thought carefully.

Then she drew the figure that appeared in her mind—Khurta's form as she understood it—onto the shale, the stone cool beneath her tracing fingers. A simple figure, but made with her own hand. She buried the slate near the wall where she had sat and slept. Not to hide it—to root it.

And then she rubbed a little ocher across her left cheekbone—not as decoration, not from vanity, but as a sign of presence.

Back at the camp that evening, no one asked her about her journey.

They saw the color on her cheek and made room for her to sit near the clan elders.

Not in the center.

At the edge—the place for those who had just begun adulthood.

Now, summers later, Ahna would sometimes press her palm to bare stone and wonder how long the warmth of her hand would stay within the stone, even as the surface grew cold.

Could the warmth felt by the stone endure as long as a memory? Could it last as long as the memory of the lessons learned in Khurta's Hollow—lessons that remained vivid in her mind?

She had no answers for these questions.

She had not told Rynn about Khurta's Hollow. Not yet, but possibly one day.

Rynn's people marked change with challenge and action. Her people marked it with witnessing and remembering.

But she had watched him return from his trial with something in his eyes that she understood.

Not pride. Not pain.

Just the calm strength of someone who had met himself —and chosen to stay.

That, too, was a sign of entering adulthood.

And it needed no words. Ahna and Rynn had *joined* that morning, early, before most other were awake. That was their private time of just being.

Now, much later in the day, they now sat together on a high rock shelf overlooking the valley. The fire below was a distant glow—small as a berry in the dusk. Up here, the stars came early at night, unobstructed by trees. Crickets clicked in the grass, and the sky smelled like pine and fir.

Neither had spoken for some time.

Rynn sat cross-legged, absently rubbing a thumb along the smooth edge of a tool he had shaped last evening. Ahna was relaxing, braiding sinew, and watching the crescent moon rise behind the far hills.

At last, he said, "I have been thinking about my trial."

She did not turn her head, but she was listening.

He continued, "I thought I would feel different when it was over. Stronger. Or wiser. Or... something more. But I do not. Not really. Just quieter inside."

She nodded slowly. "That is a difference."

He looked at her. "Have you done something like that?"

Ahna did not answer immediately.

Then she sat up and met his gaze.

"Do your people believe places can carry memory?"

"Some of us do," he said.

"Like burial grounds. Or caves—places where old people sometimes go to sit with their thoughts."

She nodded. "We have such a place. We call it 'Khurta's Hollow.'"

"Who's Khurta?"

She tilted her head, considering. "Khurta is not a who. Not a person."

Rynn waited.

She drew in a slow breath and smiled. "It is a place where we go when we are ready to carry fear without being ruled by it. A cave. Not for speaking. Not for challenge. You are left sitting with the bones of those who have gone before. And you stay silent and listen."

He frowned. "To what?"

Ahna pointed to her chest. "To that part of you that does not want to stay. The part that pulls you away from what is true."

He watched her as she spoke—not just her words, but the cadence of her breath, the tension that rose in her shoulders.

"You stayed there alone?" he asked.

"I was not alone. The dead were there. And the stories they left behind."

"Stories in the bones?"

She shook her head. "Stories in the silence. The mark left by a body long buried. A groove in stone from a hand that pressed there while alive and warm."

Rynn was quiet for a long time.

"I do not think I would like that. Not without talking. Or moving. Or... doing something."

She smiled faintly. "That is because your kind survives by talking, by moving, by making. By controlling."

"And your kind?"

She looked toward the stars again. "We survive by listening. By remembering. By letting the ground shape us, not always the other way around."

He turned her words over in his head.

"Do you think that the ground remembers in ways we don't?" asked Rynn.

"I think the ground remembers—the way a stone keeps warmth after you touch it," she said. "You cannot see that warmth, but it stays. It is there."

Rynn nodded slowly, then asked, "Did you leave anything behind in Khurta's Hollow?"

Ahna was silent. The wind stirred her hair slightly.

"I left marks. A figure that arose in my feelings. Not a picture of a hunter or an animal. A form. I do not use pictures in the same way you do."

"Do you ever go back?" he asked.

She did not answer directly. "You go back when you are ready. After that, the hollow is in you."

He thought about his own trial. How his fingers had trembled when he scratched a spiral into the bark.

"I think," he said, "you and I both went somewhere. But the places were different."

"Yes," she said softly. "But we both changed."

They sat for a while, shoulder to shoulder now, not touching but near enough to feel the other's breath between words.

"Would you show Khurta's Hollow to me?" he asked.

She did not speak right away.

"One day. If the bones allow it."

He nodded and did not press her further.

And she was grateful, because not all sacred things should be shared. Some are better understood when carried only in thoughts.

* * *

Two days later, Ahna and Rynn spoke again, each trying to understand how the other understood life.

"The elders have spoken of a time before there were words," Ahna said. "A time when people spoke with no mouths, only with their thought—one thought becoming another's thought. They said it was quick—you knew another's thought even before they looked at you."

Rynn glanced at her. "That sounds better than words."

She shook her head. "Not always. The story said that thought-speech was like the wind. It often carried things you did not mean to send: anger when you were only afraid; hunger when you only wished for company.

"Sometimes the wrong message brought death. A hunter trying to warn another made him run instead, and the prey escaped. Or worse, the hunter became the prey."

Rynn's brow furrowed. "So people learned to made words."

"Yes," she said. "Words are slower, and we use them sparingly. We choose them. We shape them. We do not let them run ahead of us and do harm.

"One winter, a hunter saw danger in the trees and sent his fear to his brother's mind. But the brother thought it was a signal to run toward the trees, not away. The hunters failed, and the prey escaped, and the clan went hungry. Another time, a woman sent love to her mate, but her mate felt only hunger, and the two quarreled about food."

Rynn laughed as he thought about this story. "Do you think any of the old thought-speech is left?"

"The thought-speech faded, but the people lived. And the elders say this is the better way. A word shaped and spoken does not easily cut by accident."

"The people learned that thought-speech could not be trusted. It was too fast, too wild, too easy to send what should be hidden. So they shaped sounds from their throats. They made the slow marks of words, the kind that must be chosen and placed like stones in a wall."

Ahna looked at Rynn when she finished, the flicker of the fire in her eyes. "That is the story I was told. We still have pieces of the old thought-speech, maybe. Some have it more than others, but words help keep all of us alive."

Ahna smiled gently. "Sometimes when you look at me, I know what you will say before you say it." She gave him a sidelong glance. "But it is better when you speak."

Rynn sat quietly for a few breaths after she finished. The story felt strange and familiar at the same time, like a half-forgotten dream.

"In my clan," he said slowly, "the old ones tell of a season when the animals spoke to us without sound. Not in words—just in knowing. You would feel the herd turning before it happened. The fish would tell you where they swam.

"But they say the knowing changed. A person might feel the wrong thing—a stag's leap when the stag was standing still, or the safety of the water when the water was not safe. Some drowned that way. Some starved.

"So maybe my people once used thought-speech, too, just as yours, but we also turned to words. Then, when thought-speech left, the animals became strangers again."

Ahna smiled slowly, as if listening to the space between his words. "Maybe it is the same story, told two ways."

"Maybe," he said. "Or maybe our clans once shared the same thought-speech, before words broke it in two."

They let the talk rest. The morning fire whispered between them, and each imagined a long-ago time when knowing had been quicker than breath—and as uncertain.

Rynn poked at the fire with a stick and sent a fountain of sparks into the cool air.

"There is something different when I talk with you," he said at last. "My people fill the air with words, even when they are not needed. We tell the same thing three ways, as if more words make it truer. But your people…" He glanced at her. "Your people hold the silence. Sometimes it feels like you are listening to things I can not hear."

Ahna nodded slowly. "We do listen. Not just with the ears. Sometimes with the skin, the eyes, the breath. And sometimes with the space between thoughts. Maybe that is what you feel."

He studied her face. "So my people shape meaning with sound, and yours shape it with stillness."

"That may be the way of it," she agreed. "But no one can say which will keep people alive longer. Words warn faster than a hand points. But silence hears better than the sound of words. Thoughts can carry much in little time, yet it can betray you if the wrong thing slips through. And the body speaks too, in ways that do not need sound."

She gazed into the flames as if watching time move there. "Only the seasons ahead will tell. Only the future will find the right balance between word and mind and gesture. And maybe…" She paused, her eyes finding his again, "maybe when that balance comes, it will live peacefully inside the ones who carry both ways."

Rynn's gaze did not waver. "Starting in a child."

Her lips curved just slightly. "Maybe. A child who could take the best from both peoples. A child who could hear the silence and the words, both."

Rynn leaned forward onto his hands, feeling the rough grit of the rock beneath his palms. "If such a child were born," he said slowly, "what would your people teach the child?"

Ahna was quiet for a long time, watching a hawk wheel against the pale morning sky. "To wait," she said at last. "Not in idleness. In readiness. We would teach the child to see before moving, to listen before speaking. To understand that the ground tells its own story if you let it."

He nodded thoughtfully. "We would teach the child to act. To step in before danger grows teeth. To speak quickly so others do not walk into harm."

Her gaze shifted to him. "Could the two teachings live in the same heart?"

He hesitated, then gave a small smile. "If the child had your heart, yes."

Below them, the valley seemed almost motionless— trees holding the wind, the river sliding in slow coils between its banks. Only the distant shapes of deer moved, crossing from the open meadow toward the darker safety of the pines.

"In my clan," Ahna said, "when a child is born, the elders give two bundles to the parents. One holds things from the mother's side—tools, herbs, tokens of her bloodline. The other holds things from the father's.

"The parents can give the child what it chooses from each bundle, in its own time. The rest is burned, so the child carries only what is meant for it."

Rynn thought about that. "In ours, the child is shown to the whole camp within the first day. Everyone touches the child. The hunter places a hand on the child's chest. The gatherer brushes the child's hair. The healer puts a mark on the child's forehead. It is said that the child grows with pieces of everyone who visited that day."

A hawk, flying by, dipped lower, riding a current of air invisible to them both. Ahna followed its movement with her eyes. "Balance," she murmured. "Equal parts of each parent. It always returns to that."

Rynn reached for a twig and began to scratch lines into the dirt between them. Without thinking, he made a spiral, then crossed it with a straight slash. She noticed and placed her palm over the marks.

"If a child came from two peoples," she said quietly, "it would belong to both. That is why…" She stopped herself.

"Why what?" he asked.

"Why the choice would have to be made carefully. To bring two ways together is to carry two promises."

He studied her profile—the strong line of her brow, the shadow at the corner of her mouth.

"If we were chosen for that," he said, "I would not turn from it."

During the next few moments, Ahna gazed into Rynn's eyes, and something passed between them—a shared understanding that needed no discussion.

Overhead, the hawk cried out one last time and then vanished beyond the ridge. Neither Ahna nor Rynn moved. The ground around them now lay quiet, even as the air felt heavy with meaning. Between them stood the question of what might arise from their meeting—whether their lives and all that had led them here could learn to walk as one.

Chapter Fifteen

T he Neanderthal camp was set deep in a forested
hollow, nestled beneath a sandstone overhang where
fire smoke rose through natural chimneys and drifted into
the canopy. There were few free-standing hide tents like the
kind Rynn's people favored. Instead, furs had been
stretched between poles and rocks to create shaded
shelters, their placement more organic than geometric. It
felt less like a camp and more like a continuation of the
forested rocky slopes themselves.

Land near the camp rose quickly toward the nearby
mountain, and trees were thicker here, their trunks broad
and roots rising like the backs of buried animals. Rynn
moved slowly up the path, being careful not to trip. Ahna
walked ahead of him, barefoot, sure-footed as always.

Ahna paused and turned. "Are you ready?"

Rynn patted the leather pouch at his side. "I hope so."

They stepped between two trees and into a clearing
near the top of a small hill.

Three Neanderthal elders sat in the shade—one of them
was Goma, a broad-shouldered man with a broken nose
that had not healed straight. Beside him sat two women:
one with silver hair and eyes the color of granite, the other

younger but with arms thick from seasons of scraping hides.

Ahna spoke first, her voice low but clear. "Rynn has come to give. And to learn."

The eldest woman motioned for them to sit.

Rynn felt the weight of their eyes, but no hostility. Only scrutiny.

He settled cross-legged, then reached into his pouch and carefully removed the object: a small, slender bone needle, its eye delicately pierced through the rounded end. He held it up between his fingers, letting it catch the light.

"This," he said slowly, "is for holding things together."

He reached into the pouch again and this time drew out a strip of hide followed by a second, narrower strip of hide. With practiced movements, he threaded the sinew through the eye of the needle and began to stitch the two pieces of hide together with tight, even passes. His fingers moved with care, and though his hands trembled slightly, the seams formed a straight, clean line.

The older woman watched closely. Goma grunted softly. A child nearby crept forward to watch, eyes wide.

"It makes no hole?" asked the younger woman, pointing to the tip of the needle.

"No cut," Rynn explained. "Just parting. The sinew holds it. It is strong."

Ahna spoke softly, helping to explain when needed.

Then she added, "And fast. It makes clothes tight to the skin. Holds warmth in. Good for children, good for keeping warm in the snow."

Goma took the needle and turned it over between his fingers. His hands were thick, the fingers stubby but strong. He pressed the point into his palm—testing, not hurting. Then he handed it back.

"Good," he said. "But small. Hard to use in cold."

Rynn nodded. "We use sharp stones to shape them. Carefully—but often breaking many to make one."

The older woman reached behind her and produced a heavy, flint-bladed hide scraper, its edge serrated and hafted tightly with resin and cord. The handle was wrapped in soft bark for grip.

"Also good," she said. "But for heavy skin. Mammoth. Rhinoceros."

Rynn took the tool in both hands and tested the weight. It was incredibly sturdy—designed not for finesse but for raw force. He could imagine it tearing through thick fur and hide without bending.

He smiled. "Our tools are thin. Precise. Yours are strong."

Goma spoke again, motioning with his chin. "Come."

He led Rynn and Ahna to a flat area beside a moss-covered boulder where several tools were laid out: thick stone scrapers, blunt-ended spears, antler clubs, and a heavy chisel that Rynn found awkward to hold.

Ahna picked up one of the shorter spears. The shaft was thick, with a heavy stone point bound with resin and sinew. She handed it to Rynn.

He staggered slightly at the weight.

"This is not for throwing," she said.

He looked at her. "What for?"

She smiled. "For close fight. When mammoth turns, or rhinoceros charges. When there is little time to move."

Rynn tested the grip. It was well-balanced, but not elegant. It was a weapon for close fighting, made for muscle and courage. His people preferred spears—thrown at great distance with atlatls , or darts—thrown at close range. But here, the assumption was different. Ahna's people planned to get close.

"I would not want to face a mammoth with this," he said.

Ahna replied, "You would not hunt long with us."

Goma returned with another spear—lighter, longer, but the point was loose. He handed it to Rynn with a grunt, then gestured toward the stone tools.

Rynn examined the head. The binding had begun to rot. He held it up. "I can help."

From his pouch, he took out a strip of twisted gut, a smooth sliver of pine pitch, and a slender fire-sharpened awl. With Ahna assisting, he began to demonstrate how his people attached their spear points—pressing the pitch until soft, wrapping the cord in a tight cross-hatch pattern, and smoothing the joint with a hot stone to secure it.

As he worked, the Neanderthal elders watched with interest.

When he was done, Goma tested the grip. The head did not budge.

The man looked at Rynn. "Good bind."

Rynn nodded. "Strong. Will not slip in blood."

"Rynn warms the pitch first," Ahna said quietly. "It listens better when soft."

The women exchanged glances. That, perhaps, was new.

Then the younger woman picked up a hide scraper and held it beside the needle.

"Big tool. Small tool," she said. "Both useful."

Goma agreed, before turning to Rynn. "You come back," he said. "Bring others?"

Rynn hesitated. "If they will come."

The man nodded once. That was enough.

Later, as they returned to Rynn's camp, Ahna walked beside him with a look of quiet satisfaction.

"You did well," she said.

"I did not know what to expect," he admitted. "I thought they would laugh at the needle."

"At first, they may have laughed quietly," she said, smiling. "But then they saw what it could do."

He looked over at her. "And your tools… they are incredible. But do not you ever fight from a distance? Do you always fight up close?"

"Always close—because the animal comes close. We cannot always choose the moment of the fight."

They paused at the crest of the hill.

Rynn held out the bone needle again, letting it rest in her hand.

"You should keep it," he said.

She looked at it for a long moment. Then she placed it carefully in the small woven pouch around her neck.

"And you should keep this," she said, handing him a thin stone blade with deep serration—a scraper and cutter in one.

"Made from a broken hand axe," she added. "Remade sharper."

He smiled. "A good trade."

They turned to walk back toward Rynn's camp as the sun dropped lower behind them, casting long shadows forward.

Ahead of them, the path looked—just for now—shared. The two clans had agreed to meet soon for a shared hunt. This would be a first for both groups.

They were nearing the edge of the *Homo sapiens* camp when Rynn saw him—Torg, standing in the dappled light just beyond the path, a long spear resting casually in the crook of his arm. His stance was loose, but there was nothing relaxed about his eyes. Torg followed Rynn and Ahna with the quiet calculation of a wolf sizing up prey.

"Walking with your stocky friend again," Torg said, his voice carrying easily over the space between them. He gave a slow shake of his head. "You spend enough time in their camp, you will start smelling like them."

Rynn kept moving, though his chest tensed. Ahna said nothing, but her gaze stayed locked on Torg, unreadable.

He stepped forward, blocking a narrow part of the trail. "What do you get from them, Rynn? Stories? Tools? Or something else?" His eyes flicked toward Ahna. "Careful Rynn, or you'll forget which side you are on."

"They are not our enemy," Rynn said, staying calm.

Torg's mouth curled into a grin that showed more contempt than humor. "Not yet. But they will be. Best to cut out rot before it spreads."

He tapped the spear point against the dirt. "The *others* take up space, take game, and one day they will take more."

As long as Rynn had known him, he had seen Torg's words slither into the ears of restless hunters—stirring unease and trying to fan small embers of fear into something hotter.

In a camp where hunger and hardship were always close, a troublemaker like Torg could turn fear into action—and someone could get hurt.

As Rynn and Ahna passed, Torg's stare stayed fixed on them, the weight of it following like a shadow. The message was wordless but clear: whatever peace existed between the clans would not last forever—not if Torg had anything to say about it.

* * *

A few days later, as planned, members of the two clans met at the river crossing. The shared-hunt agreement had taken days to negotiate—carefully shaped through words, gestures, glances, and the quiet diplomacy of Ahna and Rynn.

For many days, Ahna and Rynn had watched the movement of the horses. The herd always entered the valley with great caution—heads lifted with ears twitching and nostrils testing the wind. The herd followed the shallow bend of the river, hooves splashing softly as they crossed from the open plain into the forested Neanderthal side. Ahna's clan had long known this pattern; the horses preferred the tree cover, where shadow provided cover and only scattered shafts of light broke through.

For years, both clans had struggled with the horses.

In the forest, the herd seemed to vanish among the shadowed thickets. On the plain, the herd quickly bolted to distances too far and wide for the strongest throwers to reach.

Each clan had failed where the land favored the prey.

Ahna and Rynn had studied the back and forth crossings of the herds, morning feeding sites, resting places, the tracings of hooves in mud and sand. Slowly, an idea formed—born from different traditions.

"The forest is their shield," Ahna had said. "Break the shield, and the herd will spill out."

Rynn agreed. "And once they cross into the open, my people can strike before they scatter."

Now, on a cold morning, the plan was set.

Six Neanderthals crouched low on the forested side of the river—broad-shouldered, carrying short, thick spears, fire-hardened clubs, and heavy scrapers worn smooth with use. With feet wrapped in fur bindings, they scanned the sheltering trees in which the herd was taking refuge.

Across the river, five Homo sapiens crouched low among the tall grasses—leaner, swifter, armed with atlatls, obsidian-tipped darts, and long spears bound with cross-hatched cord. They carried bone whistles, small pouches of ocher, and the tense, eager quiet of hunters about to strike.

Ahna stood with her people.

Rynn stood with his.

In theory, the plan was simple.

The Neanderthals would approach the herd from behind and to the right, moving silently through the trees. They would press the horses from cover toward the river. Across the water, the *Homo sapiens* would wait, hidden in tall grass. When the herd spilled onto the open plain, the *Homo sapiens* would attack, throwing for legs and lower flanks. Not a trap—more like a converging circle.

Ahna raised a hand. "Time to circle."

The Neanderthals approached the horses—resting in the shadowy spaces among the trees. Ahna moved among them, gripping a short ash-wood club hardened in fire. Neanderthal hunters blended into trunks and shadow, each step measured to avoid snapping twigs. Neanderthals did not chase; they corralled, like part of the forest becoming alive and closing in.

Crouched behind a screen of hazel, Ahna could see the herd—twelve horses, dark-maned and short-legged, flicking their ears. She gave a signal: a low breath, the curl of her hand.

The Neanderthals moved forward, closing on the herd.

Across the river, Rynn and his people waited, hidden in tall grass, spears notched into their atlatls. Their faces were smeared with ash to dull sweat's shine. Rynn's attention never left the forest's edge. He watched for Ahna's hand—a flicker between cedar branches.

Ready.

Ahna gave a soft, guttural cry—deep, resonant, a predator's warning.

Another cry answered from the right.

Another from the left.

The horses jerked their heads up. Shadows shifted. The herd emerged from the trees and bolted for the river.

Rynn's pulse quickened. "Wait... wait..." he whispered.

Ahna and her hunters drove the herd—not recklessly, but with steady force, arms wide, forming a living wall behind the horses. They did not scream or shout; they needed only presence and pressure. The horses splashed into the river—steam rising off their flanks—and crossed the far bank.

The plain opened before them.

Rynn rose. "Now."

Homo sapiens hunters burst from the grasses. Spears arced through the air—balanced, spinning, flashing in the cold light. One struck a hind leg. Another grazed a flank. The herd veered, frenzied—but not back toward the trees. Ahna's hunters stood like dark roots at the river's edge, blocking retreat without a word.

Three horses broke into the open.

One stumbled.

Another faltered.

Ahna emerged from the right, spear raised. Her run was steady, grounded, her arm cocked in perfect rhythm. The injured horse turned—too late. Her spear sank deep behind its shoulder. The beast collapsed in a cry of pain and steam.

Moments later, the plain fell quiet.

Two horses lay still. Others fled across the valley, with a pair of *Homo sapiens* giving brief, futile chase before turning back.

Slowly, the two groups converged on the fallen prey.

The Neanderthals stood with reverence. One elder knelt and placed his hand on the horse's flank, closing his eyes in quiet recognition of its passing.

Homo sapiens retrieved their spears as blood steamed in the cold morning, clouding the damp air.

Rynn and Ahna met between the animals.

"You see?" Ahna said, touching her ash-wood club to his spear. "Their speed meets your reach. Their turnings meet our strength. Together, the herd had no path left."

Rynn nodded, watching the grasses stop trembling on the plain as the horses disappeared in the distance. "We hunted in two ways," he said softly. "But with one mind."

Ahna's eyes warmed. "Each strength shaped the hunt."

They stood together in the morning light, river mist drifting between them—two hunters, two traditions, and the first shared victory of the clans.

Rynn pointed at a fallen horse. "You struck the final blow," he said, nodding at the fallen mare.

"You weakened her," Ahna replied.

While the Neanderthals quietly payed their respect, the *Homo sapiens* excitedly chatted about the kill.

They had brought down two horses—together.

And no hunter had been injured.

Later, in camp, as the butchering began, a welcome exchange followed.

Rynn showed two younger Neanderthals how to remove a hide cleanly with a flint crescent blade, drawing long cuts that preserved the skin's surface. They were impressed—especially Naruk, who mimicked the motions on the second carcass.

In return, one of the Neanderthal women showed Rynn how to sever tendons without slicing the bone, using a stone chisel slicing sideways—a method meant to preserve as much sinew as possible for cordage.

Ahna stood with him as the meat was sectioned.

"You see?" she said. "Each clan benefits from a shared hunt."

Rynn nodded.

They worked into twilight.

Blood marked the grass as the butchering continued. With two fallen animals, the meat was plentiful.

The hunt had seen its share of movement, sweat, and heavy breath. And it had seen something else, too: cooperation—that strange, fragile magic that neither clan had fully trusted until now.

That night, around two fires lit not far apart, both clans ate meat from the same kill. Words were few, but gestures spoke. Tools were passed along with food. A piece of sinew. A scraping blade. A strip of gut.

Ahna handed Rynn a piece of cooked meat wrapped in leaf. He accepted it with a smile.

The night was still and warm—the kind of stillness that settles over a camp after a successful hunt.

Fires burned low across the clearing.

The smoke drifting lazily upward from the cooking meat mixed with the scent of blood and pine resin.

The two clans had made separate sleeping circles that evening, close to the cooking fire, but not quite close enough to sleep side by side.

Old habits and boundaries remained, but something had changed for the better.

Ahna sat on a rock beneath a leaning spruce, wrapping a length of sinew cord between her fingers. Her hair was damp from washing and was braided loosely down one side. The flicker of firelight danced along her cheekbones.

Rynn approached quietly, stepping over a root and crouching beside her. She did not look up.

He waited.

Then she said, "You hunted well today."

He smiled faintly. "You struck with great accuracy."

"I was close," Ahna replied.

They sat in silence, watching the glowing coals of the nearer fire.

"You were right," Rynn said finally. "We needed both kinds of hunting to make it work. They would have outrun you. They would have trampled us."

Ahna nodded. "It was a strange hunt."

He studied her expression—calm, but not distant. Focused. Like someone listening to something just beneath the surface of thought.

"Your people," he said, "did not speak much today."

"No," she agreed. "We praise the hunt only when the bones are clean and the marrow shows clear."

Rynn turned that over in his mind. "We give names to things we barely understand," he said. "But when you speak, the naming itself seems to breathe meaning."

She studied him. "Words are not the same as meaning."

"No," Rynn said. "But I think your words reach beyond meaning. My words may name a thing—yours make it felt."

He leaned forward onto his hands. " Also, I watched you when we cut the meat. You kept some of the tendons and bone pieces separate."

She nodded. "Those pieces were not for food. They were for teaching."

"Teaching?"

"Teaching the young ones. They must learn to make shape from what is left behind."

"Shape?"

She picked up a small rock and began wrapping the sinew cord around it.

"Like memory. Something to hold. Not just story, but form—meaning behind the story."

He watched her work for a moment, then asked, "Do you think this will happen again? A joint hunt?"

She stopped winding and looked toward the distant silhouettes of the sapiens fire.

"Some will say yes," she said. "Others will fear it."

Rynn nodded slowly. "Same with mine. Torg was at the feast—ate his fill, laughed with the others—but afterward, I heard him telling a few hunters that the 'short, stocky ones' will turn on us someday. He says it like he is certain."

274

He paused, then added, "And I saw the way one of your elders looked at me when I handed him the blade. Not angry. But with fear. As if I could be dangerous."

Ahna tied off the cord and placed the stone aside.

"You are," she said quietly.

He blinked. "I am?"

She looked at him now, steady-eyed. "Because you change things. You bring something new. Change is not always welcome. Many see change as dangerous."

He stared into the fire, the warmth hitting his face.

"I do not want to be seen as a danger."

"But you are," she said. "So am I. We crossed into a place where the old ways do not hold."

He nodded, slowly. "Will it ever stop feeling like a crossing over?"

Ahna smiled faintly, then reached into the pouch at her waist. She pulled out the bone needle he had given her days ago.

"It does," she said, holding it up. "When both ends of the thread tie together."

He laughed softly. "Your words do not surprise me."

She tilted her head. "What do you mean?"

"It means I understand you. More than I used to."

"Now, your words do not surprise me."

They both smiled and for a moment neither spoke.

Ahna looked up at the stars. "Tomorrow we will hear much talk in our camps."

"Yes."

"Many will return to their old ways," she said.

"Yes."

"But a seed has been planted that will continue to grow."

Rynn nodded. "Yes. In us."

A breeze moved through the branches above them, and the fire hissed softly as sparks lifted into the sky.

Rynn reached into his pouch and pulled out the stone scraper Ahna had given him.

"I kept this," he said.

"I knew you would."

He ran his fingers along the edge. "I used it this morning to slice hide. It worked better than anything I had."

She nodded. "It was made from a broken tool. That is why it is strong."

They sat together for a long time watching the fire fade.

And though their clans might sleep apart, here—in this small space between fire and darkness, between silence and speech, between one people and another—a new bond united Ahna and Rynn after she told him her news.

Ahna was with child.

Chapter Sixteen

Eight Neanderthal hunters, along with Ahna observing, crouched in silence on a limestone outcrop overlooking the marshy clearing near the river where a mammoth herd had bedded for the night. The hunters were stocky, their frames powerful, their limbs thick with muscle. Their bodies were smeared with charcoal, ocher, and crushed pine needles to hide their scent. They waited downwind— patient, breathing slowly, stone-tipped thrusting spears gripped firmly in hands thick with calluses.

The steady, cold wind came from the north and swept through the pine and birch trees and stirred the dense undergrowth.

The mammoths, on the Neanderthal side of the river, were quiet, save for the occasional snort or shift of weight. One juvenile kicked a pile of rotting branches, revealing a tangle of grubs, then moved closer to its mother.

At the edge of the group, separate and lagging a bit, stood a large bull—aging, slow, and alone in the way of old animals whose strength was beginning to leave them.

This bull became the target of today's hunt.

Neanderthals did not chase prey into exhaustion across open terrain as *Homo sapiens* did. For this hunt, they would rely on ambush—on brute strength and knowledge of the land. This would be a close-quarters kill.

Earlier in the day, they had set the trap—logs with pointed ends, half-buried and arranged to funnel the mammoth's movement, branches lashed into waist-high barricades, and a shallow pit concealed with ferns, lined with upright spears hidden beneath a covering of limbs and leaves. But they could not rely on the spears alone. The kill would depend on timing, coordination, and courage.

At a hand signal from the hunt leader—an older man with a sunken scar across his left eye—the group split. Four hunters remained behind the ridge, circling westward to drive the bull toward the pit. The other four stayed in the trees east of the herd, out of sight on the far side of the clearing. Every Neanderthal in the group had done this before—some many times. Each knew each other's role.

A single raven cried above the trees. Then another. The mammoth herd stirred uneasily. The old bull raised his trunk, scenting something—but not clearly.

Then came the shout. Sharp and decisive. From the west, the first four hunters rose from the ground and struck their spears against rocks to create sharp sounds meant to confuse the herd.

They lit no fire; they seldom used fire in hunts—its unpredictability too great. Instead, they relied on motion, noise, and the strategic placement of barriers to manipulate the animal's movement.

The lead bull trumpeted in alarm and turned away from the noise. The frightened herd bolted and headed north.

The aging bull was left behind, but saw his escape along a narrow, funnel-shaped path rising toward a notch in the rocks. He could not know that hunters crouched there with large flint axes, ready to attack when the time was right.

Several Neanderthals closed in from behind, their breath rapid, their legs bracing for the final sprint. The bull accelerated, sensing confinement, rage rising as he crashed through the brush on his way to the opening in the rocks.

Then it came—his foot broke through the thin covering of soil and foliage above the trap. He stumbled. After one more step he fell awkwardly, one leg trapped in the angled spear-lined pit. He screamed—high and guttural—as he thrashed and tried to pull free. His tusks tore the ground as his free legs strained to wrench the impaled leg loose.

Now was the moment.

Four Neanderthals from the east emerged at a run, four from the west following closely behind. They attacked from both sides, thrusting their spears into flank and shoulder.

One spear snapped, the wooden shaft splintering with the force of the impact, but the others sank deep into flesh.

The bull roared again, its trunk flailing wildly.

The lead hunter of the first group of four vaulted from a nearby boulder and landed squarely atop the animal's shoulder, plunging a short stabbing spear downward with both hands as he straddled the beast.

Blood surged from the wound as the mammoth reared, flinging the hunter from his shoulder. He wrenched and twisted, but the trapped leg would not come free, dark blood coursing down his massive frame..

The mammoth had stepped into the trap and would likely die there. Thrashing in the mist like a landslide trying to free itself from a mountain, the mammoth had little chance of survival.

Steam poured from its nostrils. Flanks rippled. The hunters moved in from both sides, fingers tightening around their long spears—sun-dried shafts tipped with sharpened flint, some blackened from fire to harden the wood. The moment for the kill was now.

With a sudden rush, the Neanderthals surged forward like a windstorm tearing through the trees. The mammoth bellowed in rage and confusion, its tiny eyes locking on the nearest figure, who flung a spear into the beast's chest. Another spear followed—then another—piercing thick hide, drawing blood but not stopping the giant. The mammoth shrieked and spun, tusks lashing out as it attempted to thwart the attack and free itself.

That was when Ghar, one of the younger hunters, got too eager and moved too close. His role was only to drive his spear into the trapped mammoth from a safe distance and then wait until the wounded animal collapsed from lost blood and waning strength.

As Ghar closed in, the mammoth reared, blood pouring from its throat, shoulder, and flank, and swung his head—tusks and trunk—toward him. Ghar misjudged and jumped back carelessly into slick mud beneath the leaf litter, and Ghar's foot caught on an unseen, twisted root.

He stumbled—and a loud crack, like the sound of a breaking tree limb, pierced the air.

A sickening, wet snap was audible even over the mammoth's roars. Ghar's lower leg folded away from him as he crashed to the ground. He screamed—a raw, animal sound that split the chaos and made even the mammoth hesitate.

"UHHHHRRR-AAHHH!" The sound was not just pain, but terror.

The other hunters heard Ghar's scream but could not help; the hunt was not over. The mammoth was flailing, desperately trying to free itself, its head crushing nearby saplings and brush, the air thick with the scent of blood.

Mustering all its strength, the bleeding animal made one final lunge and pulled the trapped leg free. Now trying in vain to rid itself of several spears buried in its flesh, the mammoth slowly lumbered away, barely able to stand as it staggered in agony, each step darkening the trampled soil.

The Neanderthals shouted and grunted as the ground shuddered beneath the mammoth's faltering retreat. Their eyes followed the wounded giant, none of them yet turning their attention to Ghar, who lay for a heartbeat in stunned silence as pain reclaimed him—his lower leg grotesquely twisted, the flesh swelling and growing dark as blood pooled beneath the unbroken skin.

Ghar rolled onto his side, clutching at his right leg, gasping, teeth bared in agony. Blood ran from his mouth— he had bitten his tongue when he fell.

Not far away, the mammoth trumpeted its final call— then stumbled to the ground, having lost too much blood to continue its escape.

A chorus of excited cheers rose from the Neanderthals.

But Ghar's voice was not among them. He clawed at the ground beside him, unable to stand, unable to crawl.

After the mammoth had fallen and the danger was past, Ahna, Ghar's cousin, ran to him. Before the hunters came to Ghar's aid, they made sure the mammoth was dead.

Ahna dropped to her knees and said gentle words as she placed a hand lightly on Ghar's chest, then looked down at his right leg and winced.

The lower leg bones were broken clean through. The skin had not torn, but the bones beneath had sheared, bending the leg at an unnatural angle, the ankle sagging inward. The foot twitched, useless.

As the other hunters approached Ghar, they said very little. There were just glances exchanged, nods. The hunt had succeeded—but now came a harder fight: to keep Ghar from slipping away into fever, despair, and death.

A stretcher was made from branches tied with sinew and covered in hides—carried for just such emergencies.

As they lifted him gently, Ghar let out a final cry, then clenched his jaw shut as consciousness left him. His face turned pale. His breath came now in short, shallow bursts.

A hunter had fallen—but he was not yet lost.

The hunters stood back, panting, mammoth blood on their arms and faces. Before leaving for camp, Ahna walked over to the fallen prey—now quiet and not moving—and placed her hand on the bull's massive head. She touched two fingers to her chest, then to his—an old gesture, but understood.

Gratitude. Respect.

The sky was dimming as the hunters began the return home. Four hunters moved as carefully as possible as they carried the stretcher. Upon it lay Ghar, his leg grotesquely bent beneath a fur covering. His face was contorted with pain and the realization that his days hunting may be over.

Because the mammoth's fall helped ensure the clan's survival, there would be much celebration that night. But, the clan's joy would be muted by Ghar's suffering.

The hunters would return the next day to butcher the mammoth, providing both food and resources for the clan's daily life. The ribs, shoulders, and haunches would be roasted in fire-pits, the rich fat rendered into oil for burning to make light. The hide would become coverings and cloaks against the cold. The ivory tusks, heavy and pale, would be worked slowly—perhaps into symbols, tools, or carved ornaments carried by future generations. The marrow, prized for its warmth and strength, would be shared with the elders first.

But, for the Neanderthals, this hunt, like many others, would provide more than just food and resources; it would provide memory. The story of the hunt would be retold—through gesture, imitation, and the placement of ocher marks on cave walls. A record kept by ritual and repetition.

The mammoth's bones would one day lie bare under sun and rain, whitening with the passage of time. But it was Ghar's unseen wound, the leg broken deep within, that told the truer cost of this hunt—no visible cut to heal, but bones splintered possibly beyond repair.

When they reached camp, the stretcher holding Ghar was brought to the healer, Vahra. Her heavy brow was set in concentration, not alarm. She had seen wounds like this before—some healed well, others did not. Kneeling beside the injured Ghar, she motioned sharply, and the others backed away, giving her space and silence.

Ghar's lower right leg, between knee and ankle, was horribly misshapen. The skin had turned a sickly blue and black, and the foot hung at an unnatural angle. It was clear —the bones of the lower leg were broken, both of them.

Vahra placed her left hand on Ghar's knee and, with her right hand, gently pressed above the break, feeling for the alignment of the bone. Vahra's fingers felt along the break, being firm but as gentle as possible.

Ghar groaned in agonizing pain.

Vahra called for warm water and a basket of her tools: strips of sinew, smooth birch bark sheets, split willow branches, moss, and a lump of thick greenish paste wrapped in leaf.

Ahna handed her a pouch of dried herbs—she crushed some between her fingers and brought it to Ghar's nose.

The sharp, bitter scent of ground valerian root was meant to calm him. Another blend of crushed poppy pods and fermented honey would follow, slipped between his teeth when the pain became unbearable.

Vahra signaled for Ghar to be held. Two men gripped his shoulders and hips as Vahra examined the rotation of his twisted ankle and foot. Then, gripping the ankle and foot, she sharply exhaled—then held her breath and pulled.

A muffled scream erupted from Ghar—then another. Then silence. But the leg looked straighter. Still discolored. Still swollen. But now looking more as it should.

Vahra worked quickly. She pressed a poultice of moss and honey over the darkened skin—its healing properties were not well understood, but she had seen wounds heal better when treated this way. She layered soft moss around the leg to prevent abrasion, then placed willow branches along both sides, securing them with sinew bindings to keep the leg straight. The final layer was birch bark, curved and tucked to cradle and protect the limb like a shell.

A sling was fashioned to keep the leg raised, and Vahra gave firm instructions in both words and gestures: no walking, not for three moons, maybe more.

The others nodded. They would help him eat, help him wash, help him defecate—because that was what clans did.

Before leaving, she placed a carved stone charm beside him. The last time a hunter broke his leg and was treated by Vahra, he lived to hunt again.

The first few days of Ghar's healing would be the most dangerous. Vahra would watch closely for signs that death might be approaching: fever, foul smell, discoloration of the whole leg. With luck, none would come.

Pain could be helped, but not prevented. Chewing bits of dried poppy and valerian root, prepared carefully by Vahra, would help but would be given only at night.

During the day, he was to be kept in the sun when it was warm. Then, at night, he was to be covered with furs to prevent chills that could deepen shock or sickness.

Others in the clan would bring him food—mostly cooked marrow, stewed roots, and softened meat. One younger hunter, who had once been treated for a dislocated shoulder, would keep Ghar company, telling him stories and reminding him he was still part of the group.

This psychological bond—crucial but unspoken—was believed to be as important to healing as the physical care.

Vahra explained to Ghar other things he could look forward to. By twenty days, the swelling would go down, and the bruising would fade to yellow and brown. At that point, Vahra would remove the bark shell and the splint and inspect the leg. The skin should look normal, although colored, and, though the leg would still be tender and weak, the bones would be knitting together and getting stronger. At that point she would re-splint it, but this time with slightly looser bindings to allow for small movements.

By the time between full moons, Ghar would begin to sit upright for longer periods, helped to his feet with the leg still in its brace. Using a sturdy branch as a crutch, he would begin to hop short distances. The other members of the clan would clear space near the fire circle so he could join the evening gatherings.

By the time between two full moons, Ghar could begin placing light weight on the leg. He would limp and move slowly—more like a forager than a hunter.

He would never run as fast as before, but Ghar would be able to walk, carry, and eventually hunt small game again—and in a few moons he could look forward to his first hunt after the injury.

Ghar imagined himself kneeling beside Vahra's hut and offering her a bundle of hare pelts from his first successful solo catch after the injury.

The clan would keep him alive, and he in return would offer gifts in thanks.

* * *

Ahna had planned to meet Rynn after returning from the hunt, but they had returned much later than expected because of Ghar's injury.

The sun was starting to get low, but Ahna decided to go to the meeting place just in case.

When Ahna arrived, she saw that the river was running high with meltwater, its surface broken by shifting bands of foam that curled and dissolved against the stones.

Rynn was there, crouched at the meeting place, turning a pebble over in his palm, hearing her approach. The forest here carried sound strangely—muted by the rush of water, amplified by the cold air.

He saw her before he heard her: Ahna stepping down the bank, moving with the concerned look of someone whose mind was elsewhere. Her hair was wind-tossed, and she carried her spear more as a walking stick than a weapon.

"It must have been a long hunt," Rynn said, standing.

She came to him without answering, crouched beside the river, and dipped her hands into the water as if to rinse something from her skin. Only then did she speak. "Ghar was badly injured today."

Rynn felt his shoulders tighten. "What happened?"

"The hunt." She shook her head, scattering droplets into the current. "We had driven an old bull mammoth toward a pit. One leg had gotten trapped when it turned—fast—and caught Ghar off guard and he stumbled in wet mud, breaking his lower leg. He fell hard. His leg…" She looked at him, and the tightness around her eyes told him more than words. "It is broken. A bad break."

Rynn exhaled through his nose. "Will he live?"

"Yes. The leg has been made straight. But he will not walk for many moons." She scooped up a flat stone and tossed it into the water, where it sank without a splash. "He is a strong hunter. Now others must take his place."

He crouched beside her. "I am sorry. I know what he means to you. To your people."

She glanced at him, a faint, almost bitter smile pulling at her mouth. "Not all will think of what he means. Some will think of the food he cannot bring."

They were silent for a time, watching the river bend around a half-submerged log. The cry of a white-tailed eagle drifted from somewhere downriver.

Rynn reached into the water and withdrew two pebbles. "How will he pass the days?"

"Teaching the young ones. Mending tools. Speaking of hunts long past." She shrugged. "If he lets the hurt make him bitter, he will not last the winter. But if he can see another way to be useful…" She let the thought trail off.

He nodded slowly. "If there is anything he needs, tell me. Sinew, stone, anything."

Her eyes showed understanding, and she reached out to touch his arm. "You have done much already. But I will tell him."

For a moment they simply stood together, the river at their feet, the air cool and damp.

Then Ahna's gaze drifted toward the tree line. "We should go. The light fades, and I do not wish to cross paths with Torg."

Rynn's jaw tightened at the name. "No. Neither do I."

They left the meeting place together, and Rynn walked Ahna most of the way to her camp. After saying goodbye he returned to his own camp beyond the river.

As he walked, he thought about how the river mapped its own course—indifferent to the injury of a hunter, the possible birth of a child of two peoples, the shifting fortunes of every clan, and the uncertain future that lay ahead for them all.

The water moved as it always had, shaping the riverbanks that contained it and smoothing the stones that lined its bottom. Holding in its current the memory of vanished summers, it neither mourns nor rejoices, yet its ceaseless flow speaks of endurance—a quiet wisdom that life, too, must keep moving, even as we suffer, endure, and find the courage to turn toward new paths.

Historical Context V
Healing in a Harsh World

"We are inescapably the result of a long heritage of learning, adaptation, mutation and evolution."
— Fred Hoyle

Fragile Lives

For both Neanderthal and *Homo sapiens*, life 40,000 years ago was short, hard, and filled with threats that modern people usually don't experience. Cold could kill. A fall could kill. An infection, invisible and silent, could kill. Injury and illness were constant companions, and birth itself carried danger—both for mother and child.

And yet these early humans persisted. They made tools. They told stories. They hunted, gathered, raised children, and buried their dead. They endured.

But as climate change deepened, competition for more limited game intensified, and the fragility of life demanded more than endurance. It often required making a choice that could mean life or death for others.

If two human lineages had encountered one another, the true tests would not have been only physical—such as the possibility of violence—but also social and moral. Such meetings would have challenged the boundaries of loyalty, kinship, clan protection, and shared responsibility.

Would separate lineages divide further in fear, or find a way to unite around concerns that touched them both? For example, if a child were born of both lineages, could that child be welcomed—or would its very existence deepen division? To understand what would hang in the balance, we must understand the lives—and the deaths—of our distant ancestors.

What Killed Most People?

The archaeological record speaks of lives characterized by accident and violence—some incidents occurring during hunting and some, likely, during fighting: crushed ribs, fractured skulls, dislocated joints, and damaged teeth.

Life expectancy at birth was low—perhaps 30 years on average. Infant mortality was especially high. A child who reached age five had already defied the odds.

Most people did not die of old age—40 years or more. They died from trauma, infection, starvation, or exposure.

Trauma came in many forms. Neanderthals suffered a high rate of bone injuries—consistent with close-range hunting and frequent accidents. Falls, animal attacks, and interpersonal violence were all likely culprits.

Homo sapiens, while less prone to severe injury, also faced dangers from the hunt, terrain, and each other.

Infections were often fatal. Without antibiotics or other ways of fighting germs—which weren't known about, even a small cut could become deadly. Tooth abscesses, sepsis, respiratory infections, and parasites all threatened daily life, sometimes striking with little warning.

There is some evidence that *Homo sapiens* may have developed slightly more resistance to certain pathogens, possibly due to larger and more mobile population networks—exposing them to a broader microbial landscape that provided stronger natural immunity.

Malnutrition followed seasonal and cyclical patterns. During harsh winters or failed hunts, bodies grew thin, strength faded, and immune systems faltered. Children suffered most, and those who died were often buried with bones that bore the marks of prolonged starvation.

And exposure was unrelenting. The Ice Age showed little mercy—long, bitter winters and numbing cold. Shelter and fire offered limited protection. One storm too many could erase a family, or an entire generation.

In such a world, love was a risk. Birth was a gamble. Survival was never guaranteed.

Healing and Hope: Treating Injuries

Despite limited tools, both Neanderthals and *Homo sapiens* cared for sick or injured relatives or clan members. We know this not from speculation, but from fossilized bones.

Neanderthal skeletons have been found with healed fractures, fused joints, and signs of long-term care. Some individuals lived years after injuries that would have left them immobile. As previously mentioned, a man from Shanidar Cave survived with a withered arm, partial blindness, and a severe limp—yet he lived into middle age, suggesting that many others helped him survive.

This is not merely biology. It is evidence of compassion.

What forms did healing take? Likely a mix of tradition observation, and experimentation. Each lineage used fire both to stay warm and to cauterize wounds, often using pressure to reduce or stop bleeding.

Among *Homo sapiens*, healing likely took on symbolic as well as practical forms. Ritual, gesture, and spending time with others may have played a role in calming the ill, rallying the group, or asserting collective hope.

Shamans or healers—perhaps women, perhaps elders—may have guided treatment. What mattered was not only the act of healing, but the belief in healing.

Still, there were limits. A spear wound to the belly or a shattered femur were often beyond what medicine at that time could address. In those moments, choice mattered. Who is helped, and how? Who is left behind?

Medicines Used 40,000 Years Ago

Forty thousand years ago, long before writing or formal science, healing from sickness and injury was already an essential part of human life. Neanderthal and early *Homo sapiens* populations that shared Ice Age Europe lived in a world marked by recurring disease.

Evidence from fossils, plant residues, and ethnographic parallels suggest that both human lineages possessed a working knowledge of simple medicine—an awareness rooted in observation, experience, and a close relationship with the natural world.

Archaeological and biochemical clues offer striking insights. Dental calculus scraped from Neanderthal teeth at sites such as El Sidrón in Spain and Shanidar in Iraq has revealed microscopic traces of plant matter. Some of these plants—yarrow, chamomile, and poplar—are known for their medicinal properties rather than for their taste or nutritional value. Yarrow acts as an anti-inflammatory and helps to stop bleeding; chamomile soothes pain and stomach distress; poplar bark contains salicylic acid, the active ingredient later synthesized as aspirin.

These findings imply deliberate use. Neanderthals were not simply eating whatever grew nearby—they were choosing specific plants for specific purposes.

Such choices point to careful observation and learning passed from generation to generation. Both Neanderthals and *Homo sapiens* lived closely attuned to seasonal cycles. They knew which roots eased hunger in spring, which leaves dulled fever in summer, and which barks or resins reduced infection in winter.

A healer's skill was likely passed down through the clan, each generation refining what worked and discarding what failed in response to the injuries and illnesses they encountered—committing hard-won lessons to memory and sharing them in moments of need. Such knowledge spread by imitation and by steady trial and error.

There were no words for "medicine" or "herbalist," yet every clan likely had one or two people with a deep understanding of the body's needs—those who watched wounds heal, noted which poultices eased swelling, and knew how to stop blood loss with moss, clay, or chewed roots—often learned from the experience of other healers.

The Ice Age environment itself shaped this pharmacy.

- Birch trees, common across Europe, offered both materials and medicine. Heating birch bark in a low-oxygen fire produced birch tar, a sticky resin used to haft stone tools—but the same substance had antiseptic qualities, useful for covering small cuts and preventing infection.
- Poplar bark could be scraped, boiled, or chewed to relieve fever and pain.
- Pine needles, rich in vitamin C, could be steeped in hot water to ward off scurvy during long winters.
- Mosses and sphagnum, naturally absorbent and mildly acidic, served as primitive wound dressings.
- Charred wood ash mixed with animal fat may have been used as a salve to protect skin from frostbite or insect bites.

Across Europe, other plants offered pharmacological power.

- Nettles provided iron and were used to make nourishing broths for the weak.
- Garlic mustard, identified in cooking residues, has antimicrobial properties and may have flavored food while aiding digestion.
- Willow leaves, like poplar bark, contained salicylates; their bitter taste a familiar medicine.
- Yarrow, found in Neanderthal dental calculus, carried anti-inflammatory and wound-healing properties—valued despite its bitter taste.

The red ochre often found in burials might also have played a role in healing: its iron-rich dust could have been sprinkled on wounds as a drying or protective agent, blending symbolic and practical uses. Ochre's deep color likely carried meaning—life, blood, and vitality—and its application to the body may have signified both physical and spiritual recovery.

Healing practices extended beyond plants. Animal fats were rendered into soothing balms for cracked skin. Honey, though rare in colder regions, would have been a prized antiseptic when found.

Smoke itself was medicine: the burning of aromatic plants such as juniper or sage helped repel insects, cleanse wounds, and perhaps calm breathing in illness.

Even the act of heating stones and placing them on the body to ease pain—an early form of heat therapy—may have been known. The healer's toolkit was not separate from daily life; it was drawn directly from the environment that sustained them.

When injuries occurred, the first response was physical care. Fractures were set and bound, as shown by bones that healed in correct alignment. Large cuts were probably washed with water from melted snow or clear springs, then packed with moss or clay. The use of plant fibers or sinew to tie bandages is plausible, though no direct evidence survives. Pain relief came through herbs, warmth, and companionship.

A patient's survival often depended as much on social support as on medicine; the clan provided food, warmth, and protection until recovery. In this sense, healing was communal—it reaffirmed belonging.

Ritual and belief intertwined with treatment. The boundary between medicine and spirituality did not exist. The same elder who chewed herbs for a wound might also chant, hum, or gesture over the sufferer, invoking unseen forces of life and death. The rhythmic sounds, comforting touch, and shared focus of attention all had measurable effects: they calmed, organized, and encouraged the body to heal.

Healing ceremonies observed among later hunter-gatherers may echo these ancient patterns. The patient's mind, soothed by the presence of kin and the continuity of custom, became part of the remedy.

Among *Homo sapiens,* whose symbolic expression was more elaborate, healing could also be art. Shell beads, pendants, or painted stones placed near the ill may have been talismans of recovery.

Some archaeologists propose that the earliest cave art— hand stencils and animals traced in red pigment—was connected to shamanic practice, a way to appeal to the spirits of animals and ancestors for health or luck.

Whether or not Neanderthals shared this symbolism, their care for the disabled and elderly shows that compassion, the deepest medicine of all, was already part of human nature.

Healing knowledge likely passed between lineages as well. In regions where Neanderthals and *Homo sapiens* overlapped, shared resources and occasional interbreeding suggest moments of cultural exchange. A *Homo sapiens* hunter might have observed a Neanderthal using yarrow or chamomile and adopted the habit; a Neanderthal might have learned new methods of cooking or fermenting plants to reduce bitterness. Over thousands of years, such exchanges would have encouraged the spread of common medicines across Europe and Asia—an inheritance later carried into agricultural and early urban societies.

Modern research continues to validate their insights. Many of the plants detected in Neanderthal dental calculus remain active ingredients in contemporary herbal medicine. Yarrow extracts still reduce inflammation; poplar and willow form the chemical basis of aspirin; chamomile is prescribed for anxiety and digestive distress.

These continuities remind us that medicine did not begin with civilization—it began with empathy and the human impulse to relieve suffering in those close at hand. The first doctors were not religious leaders or scholars; they were hunters, gatherers, and mothers who tried to lessen pain wherever they could.

The intellectual leap required to recognize cause and effect in healing cannot be overstated. It demanded accurate memory, pattern recognition, and the courage to experiment. A bitter bark that dulled fever would be remembered; a toxic root that killed would be avoided. Over time, the trial-and-error wisdom of countless generations became a cultural inheritance as vital as language or fire. Healing was science in its earliest form—empirical, repeatable, and inseparable from daily life.

By 40,000 years ago, both Neanderthals and *Homo sapiens* had woven medicine into the rhythm of existence. To treat a wound or soothe a fever was to affirm the value of life itself.

Every poultice, every boiled root, every careful gesture of care expressed an understanding that health was not merely survival but continuity—the preservation of the group through compassion and knowledge.

Their medicine, though simple by modern standards, carried the same purpose that guides healing today: to restore balance, to ease suffering, and to keep the fragile thread of life unbroken amid a dangerous world.

Climate Stress and Human Movement

Approximately 40,000 years ago, Earth's climate was in flux. The sheets of ice that defined the Ice Age were still growing in northern Europe, covering large parts of the continent. Even in southern regions, seasonal extremes worsened. Cold spells lengthened. Snow fell earlier and stayed longer. Food sources grew scarcer.

This climate stress forced both Neanderthals and *Homo sapiens* to move—chasing herds, seeking shelter, avoiding disaster. But here again, the two groups responded differently.

Neanderthals had evolved in Europe and western Asia. Their bodies were suited to cold, their tools reliable, their territories familiar. But they were localized. Populations were small, isolated, and less mobile. When the climate finally turned against them, they had fewer options.

Homo sapiens, on the other hand, were newcomers. They brought flexibility. Their tools—especially projectile weapons—allowed them to hunt from a distance. Their social networks were wider. Their camps more portable. And when the weather turned, they could relocate—faster, farther, and with greater cohesion.

In times of crisis, mobility was power. But mobility also brought contact. The pressure to survive may have driven *Homo sapiens* into Neanderthal territories—or vice versa. What happened then? Trade? Conflict? Coexistence? Likely, all three.

The advancing, and then retreating, ice was not just a background detail. It was the great sculptor of prehistory, pushing people together, pulling them apart, exposing the edges of every strategy, every alliance, every belief.

When Groups Break or Bond

The evidence of how Neanderthals and *Homo sapiens* interacted 40,000 years ago is complex. Many sites hint at cooperation—even integration; some… brutal conflict.

For example, bones bearing peri-mortem trauma— injuries occurring at or near the time of death—suggest occasional violence: possibly raids, territorial disputes, or personal fights. Remains at some sites show cut marks consistent with cannibalism—though whether these were acts of desperation, ritual, or warfare is unknown.

And yet there are also signs of exchange. Obsidian, seashells, and pigments traveled hundreds of miles. Cultural styles—tool forms, decorative objects—migrated across regions, suggesting imitation or communication. Furthermore, genetic evidence confirms that unmistakable traces in our own DNA show interbreeding between *Homo sapiens* and Neanderthals did occur. From those mixed-lineage unions, people around the world today carry Neanderthal DNA.

What influenced the outcome of encounters between two different lineages? Likely the same forces that shape encounters between different groups today: size of each group, leadership, curiosity, and sometimes desperation, among other influences.

A group led by the wise might seek compromise over competing interests. A group that felt overwhelmed might lash out. A group led by a sociopath might inflict violence and wreak havoc on the other group.

Demographic Fragility: The Neanderthal Decline

By 40,000 years ago, Neanderthals had already begun to decline, and a couple of reasons are proposed for this decline.

First, compared to *Homo sapiens*, Neanderthals lived in smaller, more scattered populations, and mating often took place within isolated groups. Because of this, genetic studies suggest Neanderthals suffered from inbreeding—mating with close relatives—which can reduce resilience to disease and lower reproductive success. Their population may have never exceeded 70,000 across all of Europe and western Asia at any one time—far fewer than the growing wave of *Homo sapiens*.

Second, the small size of their groups made every death more costly. A winter illness that killed several adults could wipe out a third of a group. A failed hunt could starve a generation. A stillborn child could end a bloodline.

Third, as the climate fluctuated between Ice Age conditions and thawing, the dense woodlands that had long supported close-range hunting gave way to open grasslands, forcing Neanderthals to adapt to open, unfamiliar terrain and shifting prey.

The large animals that once sheltered among trees began roaming wider distances across these exposed plains. Success now depended on long-range weapons, coordinated pursuit, and endurance over open terrain. Although *Homo sapiens*, with lighter frames and more efficient projectile technology, adapted well to these new conditions, Neanderthals—whose strength and tactics had evolved for ambush hunting at close quarters—found their skills less suited to this changing world. As a result, food shortage and starvation became major issues of survival.

Homo sapiens, with larger, more mobile populations, had more genetic diversity and more room to recover from loss. They could better adjust to disease and a changing climate.

Given this, the story of a mixed-lineage child is not just symbolic. It is deeply historical, rooted in what actually happened on ancient landscapes where survival depended on cooperation as much as strength. It may represent the only path away from extinction: not isolating apart, but merging; not building walls, but building bridges that allow two lineages to endure as one.

The Cost of Love

In the novel *The Neanderthal Within*, a pregnancy motivates two clans—each a different human lineage—to face one another, not as strangers or curiosities, but as people with something at stake. The birth and survival of a mixed-lineage child, could become the axis on which the future of either clan could turn.

Characters in Ice Age novels who are involved in mixed-lineage relationships face daunting choices: where to live, how to raise a child who has roots in both lineages, and how to merge the stories, customs, and rituals of one lineage with those of the other.

And this is where history in its most human form lives —not in tools or skulls or scratches and paintings on cave walls, but in hard choices. In change that defies what is accepted. In togetherness that challenges tradition.

We do not know how many stories of mixed-lineage births were lost to time. But we know this: they mattered. They shaped our future. They gave birth to the genes we carry today.

Chapter Seventeen

T he fire crackled loudly that night. Rynn and several other *Homo sapiens* were sitting around the night fire.

Rynn sat near one edge of the group, sharpening a thin flake of flint into a crescent scraper. He did not need another one—he was sharpening the flint to keep his hands busy. To keep his eyes somewhere other than the faces across the flames.

No one spoke—not yet. But the air was thick with things wanting to be said.

The joint hunt had been many days ago. Two horses downed. Tools shared. Meat split.

And now the camp was restless.

Torg sat as if in waiting, poking at the fire with a long stick. His teeth flashed in the glow, a grin with nothing warm behind it. His muscular arms were folded over his knees, and his eyes never stopped moving—watching.

Then Torg finally broke the silence, poking a painful barb at anyone who might hear.

"They smell different," he said, flicking a spark toward the logs. "Like wet dirt and old fat. Did you notice that?"

No one answered, but a few turned to look at the reactions of those sitting close by.

He continued anyway. "And their voices. They sound like they are chewing stones."

A few nervous laughs, not in support, more in fear of retaliation if they did not play along.

Rynn did not look up.

Torg's tone changed—as if to draw out a response.

"They are like beasts. Short and thick. I have seen boars that look like the one with the broken nose. You think…"

He let the word hang—and then continued to his point. "You think they know how lucky they are to get this close to us and learn from us?"

Rynn set the scraper down. Slowly.

"They helped us bring down the horses," Rynn said. "Without them, we might have lost the whole herd."

Torg nodded. "Maybe. Or maybe they scared them toward us so they did not have to take the risk."

"That is not what happened."

Torg's grin widened, teeth catching the light. "No? You watched all sides of the hunt, did you?"

Rynn felt the heat rise in his neck. He did not answer.

Torg looked around the group. "Listen. I know some of you are getting soft on them. Especially certain ones…"

He looked pointedly at Rynn. "But let us not forget who we are, and who they are."

A low murmur stirred among the listeners. Terah, the respected elder, spoke softly at first, then raised her voice so that everyone could hear. "And who are we?" she asked.

Torg did not hesitate. "Survivors. The ones who found a way to survive when the cold came. The ones who know how to hunt smart. The ones who do not sleep in caves with their ancestors staring down from the walls."

Someone laughed. Another shifted uncomfortably.

Rynn stood up.

"You were not at the crossing," he said. "You did not see what it looked like—two groups working like one. It was better than one group alone. It worked."

Torg's smile dropped. "It worked because we are strong and understand the hunt. They bring danger and risk. We did not need them on the hunt."

Torg rose slowly, standing across from him now. He was a hand taller, broader too—imposing in the way a shadow is when it moves behind you before you know it is there.

He stepped forward. "You think this is just play? That we'll all just hold hands and make tools together? You think they want peace? They are animals. Slower. Fewer in number. That is why they want us close."

"That is not true."

"Then tell me, boy," Torg said, voice slow and insulting, "if it is not true, why do they look at us like we are spirits? Like we already belong in the ground?"

Rynn said nothing.

He did not know how to explain what Ahna had shown him. What it had felt like to sit beside her and talk about silence, about death, about the shape of memory in stone. Torg knew nothing about Ahna or her clan.

But Rynn could not shape the truth into an argument that Torg would understand. It would be like trying to discuss wind with a rock.

Torg stepped closer. "You spend a lot of time with one of them."

"She has a name."

"I am sure she does." His tone was mocking now. "And I am sure you whisper it to her at night."

A few snickers rose from behind him, and Rynn's hands curled into fists.

Terah stood slowly. "Enough."

Torg ignored her.

"Maybe that is what this is about," he said, eyes still on Rynn. "Maybe it is not peace you want. Maybe it is her."

The silence snapped taut.

Rynn stepped forward. "What I want is not yours to judge."

"I have seen how you look at her. Like she is something you can bring home. Put in a pouch. Teach tricks."

Rynn sneered. "She knows more than you think."

Torg's eyes flared.

There was a long pause.

Then Torg half-heartedly smiled again, but this time, it was tight. Cold.

"I have been part of this clan for more summers than you have even seen," he said. "I have broken more bones than you have set fires. So let me be clear."

Torg's voice was now just above a whisper. "I will not die with one of the *others* at my side. And if you push for this... closeness, someone is going to get hurt."

He stepped back and raised his arms in mock surrender.

As he walked away, no one followed.

Several pairs of eyes, though, glanced at Rynn for several moments.

Later that evening, Rynn sat alone near the river and listened to the water ripple as it slid over stones.

Terah approached, slow and deliberate.

"You did well to stand your ground today," she said. "Torg is not like the others in our clan. He is no one's friend. He cares only about himself."

"I did not stop him from talking that way."

"No. But you did not break, either."

Rynn stared at the current. "He is dangerous."

"Yes. He always has been. But now he is afraid, too, and fear might drive him to act."

"Afraid! Afraid of what?"

"Change. Things he can not control," Terah said. "Changes in the way we live, in what we believe."

She sat beside him, looking out over the dark water. "You should be careful. He will not fight you in daylight. But he will wait until you are not aware."

"I know."

Terah placed a hand on his shoulder. "No one is with him, but almost all fear him. His kind does not want peace. He wants control. He wants followers."

He looked at her. "Would Ahna be safe if she stayed here with me?"

"I do not know," Terah said. "But I know that what you and Ahna are doing—bringing the clans together—is important. It matters. And it scares Torg because he has nothing to offer anyone except fear. It would be better for everyone if Torg left our clan."

Rynn exhaled slowly. "If something happens to her…"

Terah shook her head. "Then we will answer."

He did not need to ask what that meant.

After Terah left, Rynn stayed by the river. The moon had risen fully now, silvering the rocks and casting the trees along the far bank into shadowed towers.

As he sat along the bank, the river whispered its stories, indifferent to the thoughts running through Rynn's mind.

One of those thoughts had become clear: There was no reason to pretend that peace in the clan would be easy.

Rynn kept replaying Torg's words:

If you push for this closeness, someone is going to get hurt.

It had not been just a warning—it had been a promise.

Rynn dipped his hand into the river and let the cold water run through his fingers. It steadied him, but only a little.

Footsteps approached—barefoot, quiet.

He did not turn. He already knew.

Ahna crouched beside him, her knees drawn up, arms wrapped loosely around them.

They sat without speaking for a long time.

Finally, she said, "You are quiet."

"I said too much tonight."

"Did you speak the truth?"

"Yes. And now Torg knows what matters to me."

Ahna nodded slowly. "Then we are no longer hidden."

Rynn picked up a small pebble. "No, we are no longer hidden—and Torg will not stop with words."

"No," she agreed.

"He wants a reason to break what we have started."

She looked at him. "Then we do not give him one."

He met her gaze. "You mean we stop meeting? Stop talking? Stop *joining*?"

She shook her head. "No. But we stop walking alone."

He raised an eyebrow.

"You speak to your people when others can hear," she said. "No more secret walks. No more visits in the dark. Let others see. Let others choose."

"That is dangerous."

"It is already dangerous."

He considered her words. "So we walk together where others can see us?"

"Not with all that we carry," she answered. "But with enough to show that we are not trying to hide."

Rynn frowned. "I am not sure they will understand."

"They do not need to understand. They only need to see that we are not hiding. Hiding gives Torg his fire. If we stand together, other clan members will not fear so much, and his words will lose their power."

Rynn looked back toward the fires around the camp. A few members of the clan were still awake.

"You always speak like the wind knows more than people do," he said, smiling.

She did not smile, but her voice softened. "The wind has seen more of us than we have seen of each other."

He turned toward her. "What if this fails? What if either clan decides that having a child together is too much?"

Ahna reached into the pouch on her hip and pulled out a piece of hide. Wrapped inside was the bone needle.

She placed it between them on the river rock.

"Remember that we made this," she said. "And a thread of sinew passed from one piece of hide to the other."

He picked it up and held it carefully. "Yes."

"We bind what tears," she said. "Even if it tears again."

They sat in silence.

Rynn nodded slowly. "Tomorrow I will speak with Omak and the other elders. They must be reminded how the clans stood together at the hunt, and how easily such binding can be torn by anyone who stirs trouble. What we are putting together needs protection, not doubt."

Ahna stood and looked down at him, her silhouette framed in moonlight.

"And I will speak to my uncle, Goma," she said. "He has watched you. He listens more than he shows."

Rynn stood as well, brushing dirt from his hands. "We may be starting something that must be stopped."

Ahna looked into the trees. "Or something that must not be."

She took one step forward, then paused.

"Rynn," she said quietly. "You did well tonight. Not because you stood against Torg. But because his words did not change your shape."

He smiled faintly. "You say that like I am made of clay."

"No," she said, finally smiling back. "Clay hardens."

Then she rose, turned, and returned to her shelter.

Rynn looked at the needle in his hand.

It was not very sharp, and it was not very strong.

Yet the needle could bind what should not remain divided—and guided by a shared resolve, so could their hopes.

And that, he thought, might be enough.

* * *

Not far away, Torg stood just outside the firelight, hands on hips, watching the flickering shadows move across the faces of other members of the clan. The smell of roasted marrow bone hung in the air, but no one reached for food.

Torg demanded silence. It meant they were listening.

"You think that was the last hunt?" he said. "You think they will stop now that they have tasted our way of doing things? Do not be fools."

Glances passed around the group, but no one answered.

He crouched beside the fire, picked up a stick, and jabbed at a log until it cracked with a sharp hiss.

"They will not stop. They will keep coming. Their eyes are already looking for things to take."

The young Tamik disagreed. "They gave us meat."

Torg looked at him. "We gave them skill."

"We needed their strength," another said. "They needed our spears. It worked."

Torg snorted. "Worked? They will remember the kill as theirs. I have seen it. They share when it suits them. Like wolves with a fresh kill—they let you sniff, but not bite, and later they enjoy watching you starve."

Terah stepped forward from out of the shadows. "You forget that we agreed to hunt with them."

"I agreed to nothing," Torg said.

Rynn was not there to hear Torg spout off again, and Torg did not miss him for a moment.

He turned to the women gathered near the hide rack. Two of them were young—barely into womanhood—and had been watching quietly.

"You like them. I can see it," Torg said to one, a slender girl named Enna. "Big arms. Grunting voices. Maybe you want one of those beasts to carry you off."

Enna turned red and looked away. Her mother stepped in front of her, eyes narrowed.

Torg smiled, unnaturally.

"What? I am just saying what others think. We have all seen how our own are getting distracted. Moon-eyed over those heavy-browed wildlings. If this keeps up, we'll have children who do not know how to hold a spear or make fire properly."

"That is not your concern," Terah said sharply.

Torg stood, facing her and not backing down.

"I am making it my concern. Someone has to protect the blood."

Terah stared at him. "The blood?"

"The blood of our clan. The skill. The knowledge. The purity."

Several people shifted uncomfortably at Torg's words.

Terah folded her arms. "The only purity is survival. And those who can help us live are welcome here."

Torg stepped closer, his look one of anger.

"You think if one of them touches your daughter, she will remember your words? Or just the size of his hands?"

Terah's hand moved swiftly, striking him across the face with the flat of her palm.

A gasp rose from the others.

Torg did not flinch. He smiled and simply said, "Do not put yourself in more danger than you are already in."

His eyes were colder than stone, and when he left the camp later that night, no one followed.

But Torg was not done.

*　*　*

Meanwhile, in the Neanderthal camp, Ahna sat beside the central fire, a cooking stone heating slowly near the flames. Her uncle, Goma, crouched beside her, sharpening a stone blade with a piece of dampened hide.

He had not spoken in a while. That was his way— thinking before speaking, often letting others hang in silence long enough to say more than they meant to.

Ahna had said little since her return from the *Homo sapiens'* side of the river. But her eyes stayed on Goma, waiting.

Finally, he set down the blade.

"Your shoulders are heavy," he said.

She nodded. "There is weight."

"Is it yours alone?"

She thought about that. "No. But I carry part of it."

Goma looked into the fire. "The young man?"

"Yes."

"He is strong?"

"Not in the way you mean."

Goma's lips twitched. "He carries thought like a spear?"

Ahna smiled. "He carries it like a thread."

"Thread snaps in cold."

"Not if it is woven well."

Goma picked up the blade again. "And what is it he wants?"

She paused.

"He wants both clans—both our peoples—to live. And to remember how to live in peace."

He nodded once. "That is no small thing."

Ahna's tone was serious. "There is one among them—not like the others. He sows rot from within. His name is Torg."

Goma's face tightened, and he asked, "He threatens Rynn?"

"Yes. And me, I think. Though not directly. Yet."

Goma's fingers flexed around the blade.

"We have hunted men like that," he said. "Men who have attacked our clan. They are harder to kill than bears. They do not show teeth until after they bite."

"I want to stop him now."

He looked at her. "And how can you do that?"

"By not hiding. By making the thread visible. By showing both clans what is possible."

He studied her for a long time. Then he said something he thought she should hear. "You carry elder thought—but without elder experience."

Ahna swallowed. "Am I wrong in my thinking?"

"No," he said. "But you may put your safety at risk."

She nodded. "Then will you help me?"

He did not answer immediately.

But after a moment, he placed the sharpened blade into her palm.

"When the old ways are challenged, we must use new ones to defend them," he said. "This—" he tapped the blade, "—is not just for wild game. It can be for protection. Use it to cut carefully."

Ahna closed her hand over the tool.

"Thank you, Uncle."

Goma took a deep breath, exhaled, and watched the fire.

"Be careful. The ones who fear change fear women most."

She looked up. "Why?"

"Because women do more than carry spears," he said. "They carry the future—in their hands and in themselves."

She held his gaze for a moment, then said quietly, "Uncle… I am with child."

Chapter Eighteen

The past winter had been mild compared to the one before. The sun was warm in the afternoons, but frost still formed overnight as evening temperatures dropped. In the *Homo sapiens* camp, snowmelt pooled in muddy hollows, and damp air clung to the shelters.

It was in the damp that sickness took hold in the camp.

First it was Daren, a hunter. Returning from a roe deer hunt, he complained of a tightness in his chest and a bone-deep ache. By the next morning, he also had a cough that bent him double and left his lips pale. His mate, Sera, tended him until she, too, began to cough—softer at first, then with the same wrenching force.

The clan's healer, Lurea, worked from dawn until late evening when her voice went hoarse. She gave them water boiled with pine needles to ease breathing. She wrapped them in warm hides to keep fevers from sinking into their bones. But, neither remedy helped, and the coughs of both Daren and Sera worsened, while the heat in their bodies seemed to burn from the inside out.

The sickness settled into the camp like a low, wet fog, refusing to lift. Members of the clan tried to avoid Daren and Sera as much as possible, in hopes of staying well.

318

When Daren first fell ill, his absence on the hunt was felt, and the hunt had to go on without him.

When Sera's cough kept her inside, she was very much missed. She was skilled in both food preparation and in the tanning of hides. Her hands could clean and soften the thickest winter pelts before they spoiled.

With both Daren and Sera ill, clan chores began to slow. Hides, waiting to be tanned, lay stiffening in the cold, and the smell of damp fur crept into nearby shelters. The central cooking fire outside the shelters burned low more often because Sera was not able to tend it as before.

The children in the clan grew less active—not from sickness, but from less attention from adults who now avoided other clan members, including children, as much as possible.

By the fifth day, food preparation had noticeably gone down. With Sera unable to boil roots and grains, many members of the clan resorted to roasting meat over the fire and eating it plain, the way they did on the trail. A few younger hunters complained of sore throats, but there was no one willing to brew the teas that might soothe them.

The coughing itself became a sound that marked the time—Daren's harsh and low, Sera's higher and sharp. At night, the sounds of coughing carried through the camp, waking light sleepers and drawing worried glances.

Many began avoiding Daren and Sera's shelter, except to leave a little food and water outside—never entering, afraid that stepping foot inside could spread the sickness, whatever it might be.

Lurea moved between the sick like a shadow—washing her hands in ash-water, boiling pine needles, wrapping hot stones in hide to ease their chills. But each time she left the shelter, her expression told the same truth: What she had for healing was not enough.

By the eighth day, Daren could no longer rise without help. Sera's skin burned under the touch, yet she shivered as if the cold had reached into her bones.

That evening, as the wind shifted and the smell of thaw carried into the camp, Rynn stood outside the shelter and listened to the sound of their coughing—back and forth like a grim exchange. He thought of the healer Vahra in Ahna's clan, who, according to Ahna, had cured the fevers of her own people for more summers than he could count.

When Lurea came out to take away the steeped pine water that had done nothing to ease their breathing, Rynn caught her arm. "You have done all you can," he said.

Her eyes met his—tired, but without denial. "Do you know of anything else I can do?"

"Go to those who know this ground better than we do," he said. "Go to Ahna and the *others*. Talk with Vahra."

The next morning, Lurea walked beside Rynn as they crossed the river on the way to the Neanderthal camp. The snow was very thin here, the forests thick, and the hills steep in parts, and the air held the green edge of thaw. Lurea carried a strip of smoked venison as a gift. Rynn walked with urgency in his stride.

They first met with Ahna, and she led them to meet Vahra at the healer's shelter. Vahra listened as Lurea explained the sickness. The old healer's eyes sharpened as she asked her questions: How long the cough? How hot the fever? The sputum—clear or clouded?

When Lurea told her it was thick and yellow, Vahra nodded once. "There are plants here for this. Lurea, you may not know them because your people have not lived long enough with this ground." She gestured for them to follow.

The walk took them to the south side of a rocky hill, where snowmelt dripped down into mats of low green.

Vahra knelt and pulled free a cluster of leaves with a reddish tinge to their stems. "Coltsfoot," she said, holding it out. "The leaves dry the lungs and ease the coughing. You boil it in water until the air smells of it."

Vahra held the coltsfoot between her fingers, turning the leaves so the pale underside caught the light. "My mother taught me this first—something taught her by her mother. She would dry the leaves in the low sun of early spring and keep them in a pouch for times of sickness.

"When my brother was small, his lungs rattled so badly we thought he would not see the summer. She brewed the coltsfoot until the steam filled the shelter, and he breathed it in while drinking the tea. By the next moon, he was running again."

Further downslope, she dug at the base of a fallen birch, prying loose strips of its inner bark. "For the fever," she explained.

"Birch will cool the blood and take the ache from the bones." She paused to strip away a ribbon of bark.

321

"This I learned from my father, though he said he learned it from a woman he met while hunting far from here. She gave him a bundle when he was fevered and could barely stand. He said the birch holds the cold of winter, and if you drink it, it chases heat from your blood."

They moved on to a patch of slender stalks tipped with tiny black seeds. "This," Vahra said, "is horehound. It will help them bring up what is trapped in the chest. But do not make it too strong—it can tire the heart."

Vahra knelt more slowly, her voice dropping. "This one I learned by mistake. I took too much once, and my heart thudded so hard I thought it might break. But when I used less, it worked to break up the heaviness in the chest.

"An old man in our camp lived an extra winter because of this plant, and when he died, he made me promise to remember it—and to use it sparingly."

On the return from the Neanderthal camp, Lurea carried a bundle of plants tied in a strip of hide—the smell of them mixing with the damp scent of her cloak.

Back in the *Homo sapiens* camp, Lurea examined each plant, her brow furrowed as she fixed them in memory. She repeated out loud how Vahra had said to prepare them, and for the first time in days, Lurea's face looked hopeful.

They began treatment that night. Coltsfoot tea in small cups four times each day, birch bark brew between, and a thin horehound broth before sleep. The bitterness of the herbs wrinkled Daren's face, but he swallowed each mouthful. Sera drank without protest, her breathing shallow but steady.

The first doses of coltsfoot brought a gentle warmth to their chests. Between them, Lurea ladled out the birch bark brew, its pale bitterness lingering on the tongue—something Sera tolerated without a flicker. Before sleep came the harsher horehound broth, dark and sharp, making both of them grimace before they forced it down.

Through the night, the camp heard less of the tearing coughs that had marked the past days. By morning, the sound had changed—still there, but looser, as if something inside both had begun to heal. Daren could speak without catching his breath every few words. And Sera, when she laughed at something Rynn said, no longer doubled over in pain.

On the third day of treatment, Daren asked for food beyond the thin broth he had been given. On the same day, Sera stepped outside into the pale sunlight, leaning on the shelter's frame, her face drawn but her eyes clearer. The coughs came farther apart now, and when they did, they no longer bent them low, but left them standing, catching their breath, ready for the next step back into life.

The following evening, as the sun dipped low behind the ridge, the camp gathered for the meal. The air was soft with the scent of roasting meat and the faint sweetness of the birch-bark tea still steeping by the healer's fire.

By the sixth day of treatment, the deep cough began to loosen. By the eighth day, Daren could walk to the fire without clutching at the doorway for balance. A few days later, both sat in the open air, their laughter joining sounds of dripping snow.

Daren and Sera came together for the meal that evening, moving slowly but without the weakness of the past days. Their return to the circle drew glances—not the kind one gives to the sick, but the kind that marks someone's return to their place.

The next afternoon, with the sun high enough to send threads of warmth through the hide roofs, Lurea invited the *Homo sapiens* elders to the healer's fire. She had also invited Rynn and Ahna, as well as several others from each clan—all of whom came with curiosity.

She had laid the plants out in a careful row—coltsfoot leaves, their edges curled from drying; strips of birch bark scraped fine into a shallow bowl; and brittle horehound stalks resting on a strip of hide.

"This is what cured them," Lurea said, gesturing toward the hunter's shelter where Daren and Sera now dozed in untroubled sleep. "We did not know these plants before this moon. We would not have thought to try them."

Omak crouched, picking up a strip of birch bark between his fingers. "We had a fever root in the lowlands of our old hunting ground. Darker, with a sharp bite. It pulled the heat from the body. But I would not have believed a tree's skin could do the same."

"Here, it can," Ahna said, her voice steady. "The birch holds more in its skin because of the long cold. Vahra says the long winter gives the tree strength, and that strength becomes medicine if you know how to draw it out."

Terah reached for the coltsfoot, bringing it to her nose. "Sweet, almost," she murmured. "But this scent would not have told me it could calm the lungs. We have a marsh reed in the south that works this way—though it tastes worse."

Lurea gave a small smile. "The coltsfoot was the first to work. By the second night, the coughing broke."

Omak pointed at the horehound. He touched the tiny black seeds still clinging to a few stalks. "And this?"

"For the chest," Ahna said. "It brings up what is trapped inside. But too much will tire the heart. Vahra says to use it with care, and to give it only until the sound in the breathing changes."

Duma set down the birch bark and gestured toward Ahna, "Then we should send another gift to your people. If they had not shared this, we would be digging graves in thawed mud."

Tamik, young and enthusiastic, standing just outside the fire circle, shifted uncomfortably. "It has never been our way to go to the *others* for help," he said. "Some will say we should have found our own cure."

Terah's eyes flicked to him, sharp as a spear tip's edge. "And how many moons and members of our clan would we have lost while you searched? I would rather take a cure from another hand than dig a grave in my own camp."

Omak's voice was firm. "We are not so rich in what we know that we can turn away what works. We remember this day—coltsfoot for cough, horehound to clear the chest, birch bark for fever. Speak it to your sons and daughters. Let this become clan knowledge."

Lurea looked to Ahna. "And you? Will you have Vahra show me the plants again, when the thaw comes?"

"I will," Ahna said. "When sickness returns, you should already know where the cure is waiting."

There was a murmur of agreement around the fire—not loud, but steady, like the sound of water over stone.

When the elders rose from the healer's fire, the late-winter sun was spilling long, gold-edged light through the camp. The air felt different today, warmer in its touch and lighter in weight.

Daren and Sera's laughter drifted from their shelter, not the strained voices of the sick but the unguarded sound of people finding their strength again.

Children ran between the shelters, carrying sticks to poke at any last stubborn patches of snow, their shouts echoing off the ridge. A pair of hunters returned from the river with fresh-caught fish glinting silver in the dusk, and the smell of roasting meat began to curl into the air.

Rynn saw Ahna near the healer's fire, where Lurea was. sorting the last of the coltsfoot leaves. He placed a hand gently over hers, his thumb brushing the curve of her knuckles. "They are already calling it a good omen," he said.

Ahna glanced toward the ridge, where the sun was sliding behind the hills. "Then let it be one," she said. "Let it be the first of many."

For a moment, they simply stood there, the camp around them alive with voices and the smell of food, the ground beneath them softening toward spring. In the small circle of their joined hands, there was no talk of sickness, no talk of winter—only the quiet certainty that what had been shared would not be forgotten. The healer's fire became the center of the *Homo sapiens* camp that night.

Lurea continued to work with deliberate hands, her fingers stained green from crushing coltsfoot leaves. The steam from the pot rose in soft, twisting strands, carrying the sharp-sweet scent of leaf and wood. Ahna knelt beside her, timing the boiling as Vahra had taught her—just long enough for the water to cloud and the air to smell of the plant's heart.

With medicine made ready to treat future sickness, the clan turned to the joy of sharing a meal.

When the hunger of the clan was eased, Duma rose to speak. "We have our hunter back. We have Sera's hands for the tanning of hides and the cooking of vegetables. And we have those who brought the knowledge to make it so."

His eyes moved to Rynn, then to Ahna. He did not call her by name, but his pause in their direction was clear. "This camp remembers those who come when we ask."

Heads dipped toward them in the gesture of thanks given to hunters who had brought home meat after a hard chase. It was enough—more than enough.

Later, as the fire dimmed, Sera crossed to Ahna and placed a folded strip of softened hide in her hands. "A gift for you," she said simply, and then turned back toward her own shelter.

After Ahna returned to her own shelter across the river, she looked down at the hide, felt its softness under her fingers, and knew it was more than a gift. It was a place for her at the *tall ones'* fire, offered without words.

Chapter Nineteen

The air before sunrise was refreshingly sharp. While a little frost still crusted the mossy edges of the shelters and the skin of the water bowls, the sky showed a hint of warmer days approaching.

Ahna moved carefully, so as not to wake the others. She had slept lightly, one hand curled protectively over her belly. It was a small, but growing swell—large enough that she could feel its presence in her balance, and enough that curious eyes might notice.

Her steps took her toward the river, where she knew Vahra would be. Vahra was the only member of the clan who knew for sure that she was with child.

The old healer rose with the birds, always answering the sound of their morning chirping by beginning her day by preparing healing mixtures.

Ahna found Vahra kneeling on a woven mat beside the bank, dipping strips of willow bark into a deer bladder of steaming water. The scent was sharp—bitter and clean— and mingled with the faint sweetness of dried sage hanging from a nearby branch.

"You walk lightly this morning," Vahra said without looking up. Her voice carried the tone of many summers, but it had a softness in it that made people listen. "The child has not yet asked to be seen."

"No," Ahna replied, crouching beside her. "But I think of what is to come. Where the child will grow. Who will shape its mind."

Vahra wrung the bark dry and laid it on a flat stone to cool, her hands moving with deliberate calm. "That choice will wait for you; you will not be able to avoid it. The child will belong to two peoples. That itself is rare, and your choices will be a source of both strength and danger."

Ahna watched the steam curl upward. "What will be different if the child grows here instead of there?"

The healer smiled faintly. "Here, your child will know silence first—the silence through which the ground speaks.

"The child will first learn the shape of the seasons, the color of meat that is fresh or turning, the weight of stones that break the best flakes for tools.

"Next, your child will learn to remember scents as much as sights. Words will come later, and there will be fewer of them." She paused.

"In the *tall ones'* camp, words come early and spill out quickly. Their young learn to name everything before they have felt it with their hands. They learn to look for what walks the hill instead of learning to know the hill itself."

Vahra sat back on her heels, her eyes narrowing slightly as if she were looking inside Ahna—at the child—seeing how life ahead may stretch into two possible shapes.

"Here," she continued, "we begin with what the child sees when alone—where words fall short and the richness of meaning begins. A child learns the sound of the snow before it falls, the taste of rain before it touches the ground. It will learn by its hands—the way wood fibers split under a good flake, the way fur feels when an animal is still alive.

"We do not name the fox before the child knows the way it smells in summer, the way it steps on light snow. Our teaching is slow because what we see is slow, and we trust what we see to do much of the guiding."

Her gaze shifted toward the *Homo sapiens* camp. "There, the *tall ones* fill their children's ears from the start. Their young learn a name for every leaf and a word for every shade of sky. They are taught to count the turns of a snare before they have set one.

"Their games are more about what might be—the place beyond the ridge, the tool not yet made—than about what is in front of them. They seem to be always reaching ahead. They are quick to speak, quick to plan, but slow to listen to the ground beneath their feet."

Vahra's hand moved to the hot-water bladder beside her, adjusting the willow bark, but her voice stayed steady.

"Both ways have strength. A child raised here will grow with the land and know its stories and know its sounds. A child raised there will learn to shape the future before the present has cooled. The danger is in having too much of one and not enough of the other."

Ahna watched the river ripple in the morning light, its surface alive with motion and reflection. "Has there ever been one," she murmured, "who belonged to both clans— one who could walk both in noise and in silence?"

Vahra's hands paused over the willow bark. For a moment she seemed to be listening to something far away, the kind of memory that had to be walked toward carefully.

"A story has passed down," she said at last. "Before I was born, a child, not of two clans, but a child of the *tall ones*—a full child of their blood was raised by our people.

"The child's people had been attacked in the night by a another group of *tall ones*—a war-party. They did not come for food or land. They came to kill. That happens, Ahna—not often, but it happens. There are some who take life for the sake of taking it—even among our own people."

Her mouth tightened. "When they were done, the camp was still—bodies scattered, fires trampled out. But in the ashes of one shelter, a small child had stayed alive. Our hunting party found her there, no more than two summers old, wrapped in a warming hide. She lived because the fire had burned low and the smoke had hidden her scent."

Vahra picked up a twig and drew a line in the dirt.

"Our people took her in. Fed her. Named her Maya. Carried her on the hunt so she could feel the rhythm of our lives. Taught her the names we use for the rivers, the trees. She learned to move like one of us, to listen as we listen.

"But…" Vahra sighed, "when Maya was not yet even your age, her eyes showed a hunger for far places.

"She dreamed of what lay beyond the hills. At fifteen summers of age, Maya left—and was never seen again."

Ahna was silent, a look of surprise on her face, as Vahra continued. "She could have lived with us, but maybe she needed more—perhaps her own kind."

Vahra then said softly. "And perhaps that is how it will be with your child—belonging to both peoples, but feeling mainly the pull of one or the other at different times. It is not a curse, Ahna. It can be a strength—if there is care in the raising.

"Most of the *tall ones* are not like those who killed Maya's kin. Most are like your Rynn—driven by the hunt for food, but also bound by caring for others—their kind and our kind. Remember that when fear whispers too loudly."

Vahra reached over and pressed her palm briefly to Ahna's cheek—a rare gesture from the elder. "Two peoples can live in one body. But it is never without longing."

Ahna traced her fingertip through the damp soil, drawing two overlapping circles. "And if the child could understand and love both?"

Vahra smiled in understanding. "That is the dream. But dreams often break. Where you raise your child will shape the child in ways you cannot undo."

She pressed a warmed willow strip into Ahna's palm—not as medicine, but as a blessing. "Do not let the shadow of the decision fall over your carrying. There will be time. The child will need you calm."

They spoke longer—of birth stories Vahra had seen, of mothers who thrived and those who did not, of children who grew strong regardless of where they were raised.

Ahna drank it in, yet under the calm there was a tight thread of unease she could not shake.

It found its reason later that day.

After leaving Vahra, Ahna went beyond the edge of the camp to the river to fetch two deer bladders full of fresh water to bring back to her shelter.

The sun was higher now, spilling through the trees. As she rose to leave the river, a figure stepped out from the nearby shadows.

Torg.

His pale hair caught the light like winter grass, but his eyes showed deceit—flat and watchful, like a predator sizing its prey. He moved to block her path.

"You walk alone often," he said.

His tone was casual, but there was something in it that made her skin tighten.

"I walk where I need to," she answered, shifting so that the deer bladders were between them.

"You have no business on this side of the river."

His gaze traveled down to her midsection, nodding as he continued to stare. "Rynn's, many are guessing. But maybe you'll want better shelter before the cold moons return. Someone who can give you more than promises."

She tried to step around him, but he stayed in her path, moving slowly and deliberately.

"Friends on this side of the river would treat you well," he continued. "If you choose right." His meaning was clear and hinted at in the small curl of his mouth. "You would never have to be alone."

"I am not alone," she said, voice low.

He brushed past her arm—not a push, not quite a touch, but enough that the hairs rose on her skin. "

A woman with child should be careful," he said softly. "And choose wisely. You might like my company more than his."

Ahna's grip on the bladders tightened. "Keep your words away from me."

His smile spread, but it never touched his eyes. "Time makes people think differently. You will see."

He stepped aside then, letting her pass, his gaze heavy on her back as she walked away.

She did not look over her shoulder, but she could feel him watching until the trees hid her.

By the time the shadows had grown long and the air cooled again, she had decided to find Rynn.

Ahna made her way from her shelter to the small clearing where she often met him—a place sheltered by twisted pines, where the ground was soft with needles and the sound of the wind masked their voices.

Rynn must have felt something pressing. He was at the meeting place, crouched beside a fire he had coaxed from dry moss and twigs. He smiled when he saw her, but the smile faltered when he saw her expression.

"What is wrong?" he asked, standing.

She sat on a flat rock, pulling her cloak closer. "The one called Torg. He speaks to me as if I am his to take. His eyes speak deceit. His words worse."

Rynn's jaw tightened. "He is trouble—even among my people. He starts fights, steals from hunters, and I have heard whispers about women. I should have told you."

"I can avoid him," Ahna said.

"But I want you to know, Rynn, if something happens, it will not be because I kept silent."

He came closer, crouching so they were level. "You did right to tell me. I will watch him. And I will make sure he knows you are not his to touch."

The fire crackled between them. Rynn reached out and placed his hand on her belly. His touch was a promise— that she and her child would never stand alone.

"Our child," he said, "will be safe. I will see to it."

For the first time that day, she believed it.

When Rynn's hand left her belly, she could still feel the warmth of his touch, but she also felt the ache of what lay ahead.

The firelight flickered against his face, drawing out the lines of determination in his jaw. He believed he could keep her safe, and a part of her wanted to rest inside that belief. But she knew that safety was never something given only once; it had to be kept, guarded, renewed.

She thought of her child—not yet born, not yet named —carrying the shape of both their faces.

Would others see that as strength, a bridge between the clans? Or would they see it as neither fully one thing nor the other, a constant reminder of two peoples of different blood that had not yet learned to live in peace?

After Ahna returned to her camp, she decided to speak more to Vahra, this time about Torg.

Vahra could sense the uneasiness in Ahna the moment she saw her. She paused, then her gaze sharpened. "There is something bothering you, Ahna… or someone."

"Yes," answered Ahna. "A man from the other clan."

"If the one you are talking about is Torg, I know of him." Vahra responded.

"Yes," nodded Ahna.

"His gaze is like a hand without warmth, a hand that touches where it has no right to touch," continued Vahra.

"I have seen men like Torg before—enough to know that they rarely stop unless they are made to."

Ahna thought now of her child. *Would her child be in danger, too? Or children like hers?*

Ahna lifted her eyes. "What do you know of him?"

"First, understand that our two peoples have very little contact. There is much mistrust, and I have heard only a rumor now and then. And I do not know whether all I have heard is true."

"Tell me what you have heard," Ahna replied.

"I heard that he came to Rynn's people many summers ago. It is said he was cast out from another clan across the mountains. No clear reason—but the rumor is that he had broken the trust. Torg's own story is that his people were foolish—too foolish to live with and he chose to leave.

"He wandered until he met Rynn's people. Because his hunting skills were great, they took him in. Over time, though, his rough temper showed itself, but it was often overlooked—as long as he kept bringing meat—until the problems became serious.

"There are whispers—only whispers—that he forced himself on two young women in the *tall ones* camp. Likely out of fear, the women chose not to speak before the elders.

"Without their voices, and because the hunt needed every strong arm, Torg stayed. And now, though his skill still brings meat, his shadow is not welcome.

"I do not know how much of this is true. I do know enough to tell you this: Be wary. Do not be alone with him —some dangers are too great to face alone. He will test the edges of what is allowed, and those edges shift when no one pushes back."

Vahra reached out, her fingers brushing Ahna's cheek, then resting for a moment on the small swell of her belly. "You carry more than yourself now. Guard it. Guard you."

Ahna thanked Vahra and returned to the *Homo sapiens* camp to share her concerns with Rynn. She wrapped her arms around herself, as if she could shield the small life inside from the reach of all that lay beyond.

Somewhere in the distance, an owl called into the dusk. The sound lingered, not as alarm, but as reminder—some dangers were known only to those who learned to watch in silence.

She thought of Vahra's words: *You carry more than yourself now. Guard it. Guard you.* She could not help but think of taking action to stop Torg. She understood that a mother's mind is the strongest hunter's mind.

Later that evening she sat with Rynn near the clan fire. "I met with Vahra today," she told him. She told Rynn of Vahra's words—the two peoples the child would carry, the story of the orphaned child taken in, and the warning about Torg. "She says to be careful. She believes the whispers that she has heard are true."

Rynn's jaw tightened. "I have heard this, also. I have seen how he looks at you. I will not let him touch you."

"That is why I want to be with you," she said. "I feel safest when you are close. I do not know all that will come when our child is born. But I know I would rather face it with you close."

He took her hand. "If that is what you want, it will be. I will speak to the elders."

She nodded. "Vahra said some dangers are too great to face alone. She is right. But I know you will protect us."

"I will," he said. "No matter what Torg tries. No matter who stands against us."

The fire snapped. Ahna moved close to Rynn, their hands resting together over her belly. Above them, the first stars pierced the the night sky, sharp and cold—but she felt the warmth of the fire and the steadiness of Rynn beside her, and for now that was enough.

The next morning, Rynn rose before the sun. Smoke still hung over the camp from the night fires, and the ground was cool beneath his feet. He went to the council circle, where the elders gathered when matters pressed upon the clan.

Terah was already there, a pelt drawn tight around her shoulders against the dawn chill. Duma came with a hunter's stride, carrying the smell of last night's kill still on his hands. Omak joined last, quietly lost in thought, but his eyes fixed on Rynn the moment he stepped forward.

Rynn did not waste words. "Ahna carries my child. I ask that she live here, in this camp, in my shelter. She will take her place among us and work as every member of the clan works. While she is heavy with our child, she will not hunt, but she will gather, clean hides, and tend the fire. When her strength returns, she will do more. Our child will belong here—just like any other child of our clan. The child will be ours to raise."

The elders listened in silence.

The fire crackled as Terah lifted her head, her eyes measuring not only his words but the weight behind them. "To welcome her into our clan is to accept her as one of our own and to take responsibility for her—to protect and care for both Ahna and the child you share. Not all in our clan will welcome this decision easily."

Rynn showed only resolve. "I know some will resist, but we will face them, and I will answer for us both."

Omak grunted in agreement, his scarred arm shifting in the firelight. "So long as she carries her share, she and your child are welcome. None here will carry another's weight without anger."

"She will," Rynn said firmly. "She knows the work. She has strength."

Then Terah spoke again. "Then let it be so. The camp will watch her as it watches all. If she falters, the fault will be yours to fix, Rynn, and you will mend it."

Rynn bowed his head. "I will."

When the circle broke, word spread quickly through the camp. Some nodded approval, others muttered doubts, but none challenged the elders' words.

Later, when Rynn visited the Neanderthal camp, Ahna was waiting. He told her the decision, and relief flickered in her eyes.

She reached for his hand. "Then I will come to your camp and we will live together."

"Yes," he said. "The three of us."

Chapter Twenty

Two moons had passed since the clans had last met in full gathering. The lean cold moons of late winter had yielded to the softer touch of spring, and Ahna's belly had started to round beneath the tunic of softened hide she wore. She moved more slowly now, careful with her steps along the packed-soil paths of each camp, and she had learned to balance her center of weight when crouching to tend the fire, clean fish, or lift a water bowl.

The scent of damp soil was everywhere as the snow melted and the river swelled with runoff. Along the riverbanks, green shoots pushed through the dark, moist earth, stubborn in their will to grow.

Ahna's visits to the *tall ones'* camp had increased as her pregnancy progressed. Side-by-side with Rynn, she had walked along paths that were becoming more familiar—those leading to the water, to the places where game was cleaned and prepared, and to the clearings where children played. Rynn's camp had become a second home to her.

But., wherever they walked, Ahna felt the presence of watching eyes—some wide with curiosity, others narrow with doubt, and at least one pair filled with menace.

Frequent visits had gotten the clan used to seeing Ahna.

She had often crossed the river and clearings between the camps to see Rynn, bringing smoked meat and other gifts from her clan. Once, she brought a small packet of ocher wrapped in deer hide. She never stayed long, but long enough so that when she left, Rynn missed her.

Early on, when her pregnancy had become visible to Rynn, he urged Ahna to leave her clan's shelter and join him in his. Ahna has said that she would think about it, but that it was not an easy decision to make. Now though, with the approval of the elders of Rynn's clan, Ahna decided to make the move.

Even with the elders' approval, Ahna believed Rynn's clan had likely never known a child born of two peoples. If such a child had existed, she had never heard it spoken of. As the elders' unease over her bond with Rynn faded, though, her own doubts eased, and concern about a child born of two peoples no longer troubled her.

With this understanding, Ahna had moved in several days earlier. Wanting to be with Rynn had grown stronger than her worry over those who might not approve.

Pleased by Ahna's presence, Rynn left camp the day before on a late-winter hunt. It was a lean season—game wary, every track a gamble. Hunts ran long, returns came late and uncertain. Ahna hoped he would bring something back, but she knew that a long absence often meant very little meat, or none at all.

Unfortunately for everyone, Torg had badly injured his lower leg during a recent hunt and now stayed around camp during long, tedious days of recovery.

During Rynn's absence, Ahna's mothering instinct deepened, making her more aware than ever of the danger in Torg's lurking presence around camp.

Sometimes it was just the feeling of eyes following her as she crossed the camp. Sometimes she saw him outright —standing with others but not speaking, his gaze fixed on her for a heartbeat too long. He never came close enough to touch her, but his look had its own kind of reach.

She kept to paths where others could see her, even for the simple tasks of drawing water or gathering wood for the fire.

Vahra's warning had taken root deep in her.

Partially because of concern about Torg, but mainly because she missed Rynn, she eagerly awaited his return.

As she waited, she found herself thinking carefully about recent events—the decision she had made to live with Rynn, the elders of his clan approving and welcoming her among them, her own people honoring her choice and wishing her well—aware of the risks she faced, and of the uncertainty that still lay ahead.

With these things in mind, Ahna felt at ease with her choice, and felt prepared to deal with the possible risks at the appropriate time.

The next morning, she walked around the camp of the *tall ones*—her newly chosen home. The ground beneath the melted snow was soft, giving way in patches to dark wetness. She wore her cloak pulled close and carried pouches of dried roots and bundles of herbs as gifts for the elders—a gesture from her people's tradition.

Ahna was getting used to the *Homo sapiens* camp—her new home—which was larger and more orderly than the nearby Neanderthal camp—her previous home. Tools and weapons were neatly kept in bundles beneath the hide-flaps of each shelter's entrance, and fire pits were ringed with rocks. Shelters were neatly arranged in a shape that looked like the full moon.

As she made her way through the camp, she crossed paths with Tamik, Rynn's friend and frequent hunting companion.

Tamik, who was also staying in camp while recovering from injuries from a recent hunt, had agreed to accompany Ahna to the elders' gathering shelter. As they walked, Tamik studied her with polite curiosity and guided her toward their destination.

The gathering shelter was comfortably warm, smoke drawing neatly through a venting seam in the hide roof. A low ring of stones cupped the fire; three carved sticks—tally markers, by the look of them—lay beside it. Omak, Terah, and Duma sat in a shallow crescent on the far side of the fire, keeping the entrance open—allowing an easy exit.

Ahna laid out the small gifts she had brought—bundles of herbs and pouches of roots, setting them so the firelight could show them clearly. "These will keep a child's fever from climbing and ease a sore mouth," Ahna said, looking at Duma whose son had been ill for days.

Duma nodded and smiled, and motioned for Ahna to sit opposite the elders. As she sat, she rested her hands on the curve of her belly.

"You asked to be heard," Omak said.

"Yes. I have come to thank you for allowing me to live among you," Ahna said. "I want our child raised where Rynn can help guide the teaching."

Omak glanced toward the entrance as if to check who might be hanging around just outside. Torg's shadow crossed and then moved on.

Only then did Duma speak. "Take no offense if I count risks as quickly as I count gains," he said, leaning forward on his knees. "Lean summers have made us careful. A new person changes the load—food, labor, shelter."

"I bring more than I take," Ahna replied.

The elders asked her questions—how she imagined her child's learning, whether she would keep ties to her own people, what skills she would bring to their camp.

Ahna answered each as best she could. She spoke of the healing plants she knew, the quiet ways of tracking that her people used, and the understanding of weather and animal movement that she could teach through careful watching, the remembering of patterns, and sharing experiences.

"I can strip meat fast and clean. I can mend hides. I can read where tracks lead when snow has crusted over or when mud has hidden the signs that feet left behind."

Terah's gaze focused on Ahna's face after pausing for a moment on her belly. Her voice was even. "And the child? You know our people watch things closely. A mistake at a snare, a stumble during a drive—some will say it is because of the other half. Are you prepared to face that without lowering your eyes? Not once, but again and again?"

Ahna met Terah's eyes. "I have already heard worse said about me—often behind my back. I have learned to turn and walk toward it—not away from it."

Omak's fingertips touched the stones lining the fire pit, feeling the heat as if to test the warmth of the room. "You spoke of teaching. Tell us what your way would be for a child not yet old enough to speak."

Ahna answered without hurry. "First, the body learns—hands, nose, ears. The different feeling of wool that is shorn versus hide that is stripped, the feeling of bark that slips clean in spring but not in fall. I would have the child sit with me at dawn and smell the day before calling it by any name. Words afterward, once the senses already agree."

Duma showed the beginning of a reluctant smile. "Rynn says something like that when he argues about training. He wants the boys to learn to stalk game before they learn how far apart to spread hunters in a drive—enough to cover the ground, but close enough that no animal slips through."

"That is because Rynn listens to the ground," Terah said in support of Rynn. "And because he knows some rules were made for men who tend to act before listening."

Duma folded his hands. "You say you feel safe by Rynn. Safety is not only one man between you and harm. Safety is the shape of a clan agreeing. Do you understand that?"

"Yes," Ahna said. "A man's arm might stop a blow. A clan can keep the blow from being swung."

Terah's eyes narrowed—approval, brief and precise. "Good. Then I will ask the harder question now, so others do not ask it later with less care." She let her gaze drift toward Ahna's belly. "If the child bears more of your face than Rynn's, if it looks like *us* but moves like *you*—will you still want it to learn here? Will you keep yourself from saying, 'No, this lesson is wrong; this way is thin'?"

Ahna breathed in the resin-honey scent of the fire. "I will keep two baskets," she said. "One for what is learned here. One for what must not be lost from my people. Both belong to the child. I will not raid one to fill the other."

Omak's fingers drifted to the tally sticks, tapping once, twice, as if counting unknowns. "There is another matter," he said, eyes flicking again to the doorway. "We do not speak his name in council unless needed."

"Torg," Terah said, unconcerned by the hesitancy. "We all know his name."

Omak's voice thinned, a thread drawn tight. "He angers easily and tests the edges of our rules. He has taken praise that was not his. He has taken other things that were not his to take." He let that rest a beat. "Do you measure the danger he is to you?"

"I do," Ahna said. "And I measure who he becomes when Rynn stands on the same ground."

Terah exhaled slowly. "You should not have to be shielded to move through a camp."

"I agree," Ahna said. "But we do not live in a life of *should*."

Silence settled—thinking, not stalling. Outside, a gust pressed the shelter wall, hide creaking over its frame. Somewhere beyond, children laughed, then hushed, as if reminded to keep their voices from carrying.

Omak brushed dust from his palms and said, "I will say what some will not. A strong hunter who brings meat is often judged by his usefulness first and his harms second. This is wrong, but times of lean hunting twist judgment."

He turned his palms up toward Ahna. "We have failed before—women who did not feel heard. If you come here, you will speak to Terah if you are not heard by me. If you are not heard by either of us, you will speak to Duma. I say this now, before your feet wear a path to our fire."

Terah did not look at Omak; she kept her eyes on Ahna. "And you will learn our signs—the ones women use when men are too near or too stubborn to listen. I will teach you, and you will teach me yours. This is how camps are made safer without the need of a shout."

Omak nodded once. "Good. The three of you will live in Rynn's shelter—now your shelter also."

"Four," Terah added, almost as an apology to the future. "We always plan for four."

A quick warmth touched Ahna's face—unexpected, and gone almost at once. "Thank you," she said.

Omak shifted, the bones in his wrists showing like knots in wood. "You must be aware," he said, and his tone made both Duma and Terah glance at him. "Some in camp will greet you like a sister. Some will test you by smiling while they measure your steps. Some may dislike what you represent more than anything you are.

"If anyone is aggressive toward you or does not treat you with respect, do not trade barbs. Bring it to us. We will not let this become a slow bleed."

Omak rose first, a sign the meeting was ending. Terah stood, took a pouch of roots, pinched a bit, smelled it, and nodded. "You will show me the best time to pull these from the soil," she said. "I will show you how we pack them for travel so they do not mold. We will set this lesson before the thaw is complete."

Duma stood, too. "If Tamik gives you a hard look today, it is because he worries about our food stores," he said, a look of humor forming at the corners of his mouth. "He thinks worry makes him look older and thus wiser."

"Tamik has always been Rynn's friend and tries to look after him," Terah added, making Duma laugh awkwardly.

Omak lifted a hand. "Until Rynn returns, be careful where you walk and do not let the dark catch you alone."

Ahna thanked them and stepped back into the day. The mist had lifted. Along a south-facing bank the snow had thinned enough to show blades of new grass, faint and stubborn. Omak waited to guide her out, but halfway to the camp's edge, a figure paused at the woodpile—broad-shouldered, pale hair stirred by the breeze. He did not speak. He did not have to. His stare spoke of taking what he wanted—when he wanted it.

Omak's jaw set. He shifted a hand to the haft of his spear—casual, practiced.

Torg, still recovering from injury, watched, thought about his risk, and then angled away as if he had only stopped to judge the size of a log.

"Go on," Omak said, looking at Ahna. "I will walk you to your shelter."

She thanked him and started walking. "I know the path," Ahna said.

"I will walk you anyway."

They did not talk much as they walked, but before they had gotten very far, Omak said, "Duma thinks I worry too much." A pause. "He is not wrong."

"Some worries are earned," Ahna said.

He gave a small grunt of agreement.

When they arrived at the shelter, Omak said goodbye, nodded, and left. Ahna nodded and entered.

As she sat, she thought of Rynn out in the hunt, of the elders' measured faces, of Torg's silent watchfulness.

With elders' shelters flanking her on each side, Ahna knew she was safe. Torg would not dare come near the shelter she shared with Rynn.

* * *

Far to the north where the hills still held snow in their folds, Rynn crouched in the shadow of a leaning pine. His breath rose in slow, steady clouds. Ahead, three hunters from his party moved in a half-circle, their steps careful, their eyes on a scatter of fresh hare tracks pressed into the crusted snow.

The hunt had been hard this season. Roe deer were scarce, caribou far-ranging, rhinoceros nowhere to be seen, mammoths gone, and the ground hid more traps than paths. Every kill mattered more now, with so little game to be found.

He shifted his weight, feeling cold wind bite through the seam of his leggings, and thought of his shelter in camp

—its hides tight against the frame, the stones of the hearth worn smooth by winters of constant fires and long nights of use. He would patch the old frame as soon as he could to make it sturdy and fit for three.

Tired as he was, Rynn was excited about the future. He believed that in a few short moons time, Ahna would be nursing their child.

Thinking of her now, he imagined he could hear her steps approaching him, even though he knew she was far off, back in the shelter.

The wind was cold, but carried the faintest scent of spring—damp soil, a promise of warmer days.

Rynn steadied his spear and nodded to the hunter at his side as they moved to follow the tracks. Before long, he spotted a hare darting from cover. His throw was true. There would be meat to bring back, if only a little.

When the hunt was over and the last light of day bled into the sky, Rynn and the other hunters made their way back to the camp.

As they approached the central fire, the air held scents of resinous smoke and roasting meat, with a touch of the earthy sweetness of roots warming in the embers. In the warmth, the sound of voices rose in low, familiar tones.

* * *

Rynn ducked into their shelter. Ahna was inside, kneeling beside the small fire pit in the center, coaxing the flames to life. She looked up at his arrival, and her look softened, relief bright on her face. For a moment he stood watching her—the simple sight stirring something fierce in his chest. Returning to find her in the shelter brought a good feeling to his chest.

"You are back," she said, her voice steady as her hand rested protectively over her belly.

"I am," he answered. "And you are safe here."

She nodded, though her eyes betrayed the unease of one who knew safety could never be fully promised. Still, as he crouched beside her, she pressed close to him, and together they fed the fire until it burned brightly.

Outside, the camp was busy with gathering, mending, and talking, but inside a bond was strengthening—seen by others, yet steady, undeniable, and their own.

That evening, Ahna and Rynn joined others in the clan around the camp's central fire. The camp hummed with its usual activity, but Ahna was aware of every glance that passed her way. Some were curious, others cautious, and a few—hard-eyed and tight-lipped—were openly suspicious.

She sat next to Rynn but helped Siva, a new friend from a nearby shelter, strip sinew from the leg of a deer. Ahna's fingers, though not as practiced, worked steadily, and Siva worked with her in silence.

Two children darted past, chasing each other around the fire. They slowed when they saw Ahna—hovering a moment as if unsure whether she was part of the clan or an intruder. With a small smile, Ahna lifted the sinew and made a silly face, stretching it like a string. The children giggled and ran off again, the hesitation broken.

Across the fire pit, a woman named Ola leaned close to another and whispered, her gaze never leaving Ahna.

Rynn noticed, his own shoulders stiffening, but Ahna touched his arm lightly. "Let them speak," she murmured. "Their words cannot cut deeper than silence."

Later, when dark spread across the sky, Duma brought wood to the fire and lowered himself with great effort to sit. He regarded Ahna for a long moment. "Tomorrow we mend the snares by the river," he said gruffly. "Even with child, you can walk with the women."

Ahna laid a hand across her belly and met his eyes. "I will. What I learn, the child will also carry."

It was not an embrace, but it was an opening—a shift, like light pouring through an opening in clouds. Rynn caught the flicker of pride in her expression, and for the first time that night he relaxed and breath filled him fully.

Later in the evening, as the fire burned low, Ahna and Rynn returned to their shelter.

Before closing her eyes to welcome sleep, Ahna slipped outside the shelter for a final time and looked toward the dark line of the forest in the distance.

She felt the child stir within her, small yet insistent, as though it, too, listened to the sounds of this new place—the faint crackle of dying embers, the murmur of voices settling into silence, the breath of the wind pushing gently at the hides.

She rested her hand against her belly and whispered soft words no one else could hear: "We will live here. We will be strong here. You are from these people just as you are from my own. They will come to know and love you just as I do."

Rynn came out of the shelter to stand beside her, his warmth cutting through the night chill. His hand brushed hers, steadying, claiming nothing yet offering everything. "It will not be easy," he said, voice quiet, as if unwilling to disturb the fragile stillness.

"No," she agreed, and though her reply was simple, it was said in a way that carried hope.

Together, they looked out over the camp, fires dimming, figures curling up in shelters—readying for sleep. In that hush, Ahna understood that the true work now lay ahead —the weaving of trust, the proving of worth, the shaping of her life so it might fit within a clan not born of her own kind, yet into which her child—a child of both clans— would be born.

Historical Context VI

Cradles and Consequences

"The care of human life and happiness is the first and only object of good government."
— *Thomas Jefferson*

Pregnancy and Childbirth

Forty thousand years ago, in the deep winters and short summers of Ice Age Europe, childbirth was among the most perilous moments in a woman's life. It was both a biological act and a communal event—one that linked generations, reaffirmed (or established) kinship, and tested the endurance that defined the lineage. No written record could preserve those scenes, yet fossils, sites, and comparative studies of modern hunter-gatherers allow us to glimpse how both Neanderthals and *Homo sapiens* likely managed the start of life in their harsh and uncertain world.

Although this discussion in this section centers mainly on the birth of a Neanderthal child, the same truths would have applied to a *Homo sapiens* birth of the same era. Both lineages shared nearly identical anatomy, gestation length, and dependence on communal support. The act of giving birth 40,000 years ago was perilous for all women. Both lineages would have labored in shelters lit by firelight, surrounded by familiar hands, guided by instinct, and sustained by experience rather than written knowledge.

Midwives who aided in the birth were healers, mothers, sisters, and elders who had endured the same ordeal. The cries, the danger, and the relief when life arrived safely would have been universal.

What differed between them was not the process, but perhaps the stories told afterward—the meanings attached to survival, the symbols and rituals that each lineage began to weave around the mystery of birth.

A Neanderthal woman would have carried her fetus for roughly the same length of time as women today—about forty weeks. Her body was built differently, however: shorter and broader in the pelvis, with a larger birth canal adapted to the delivery of infants whose heads were slightly larger than those of *Homo sapiens* newborns. The Neanderthal baby, though robust, was still helpless, its skull soft and pliable, its survival dependent on the warmth and vigilance of others.

Pregnancy was probably noticed early within the close-knit clan. The women—sisters, mothers, and older females —would have observed the changes in gait, the thickening of the belly, the slowed movements when hunting or foraging. In a world where every member's contribution mattered, pregnancy was both a source of joy and anxiety. The clan had to adjust: others took on the heavier work of carrying wood, scraping hides, and gathering roots. The expectant mother would have remained active until late in pregnancy, but the group would have watched her carefully, guarding her from falls, predators, and sudden temperature drops that could trigger premature labor.

When the time came, childbirth likely occurred in a shelter, in a secluded corner of a cave, or beneath a hide-covered frame where warmth and privacy could be maintained.

Archaeological evidence suggests that both lineages prepared birthing areas in shelters that were comfortable and ordered. The place of birth would be near a central fire and shielded by hides or stone enclosures. The fire's heat was vital—not only for warmth but also for the drying of hides, the boiling of water in skin bags, and lighting that enabled those who helped in delivery to see.

It is reasonable to assume that childbirth was assisted. The notion of solitary birth, often mentioned in modern romanticized accounts of "primitive" life, runs counter to the cooperation noted in most Neanderthal behavior. These were people who cared for the injured, tended the old, and buried their dead. A woman in labor would not have been left alone. The clan's healer and one or two older females— those who had already borne children—would likely have been there to help, offering water, massage and reassurance through sounds or rhythmic humming.

Pain management would have been minimal but not absent. Ethnographic parallels suggest the use of warm water, chewed roots, or aromatic plants to ease the pain of contractions. The Neanderthal environment provided herbs such as yarrow and chamomile, known to have medicinal

357

properties and occasionally found in dental calculus of Neanderthal fossils. Whether these were used for childbirth specifically cannot be proven, but it is plausible that healers experimented with such plants for comfort during times of both injury and pregnancy.

The labor preceding delivery was a dangerous ordeal. Pelvic size alone did not guarantee safety; the large head and shoulders of the infant could cause obstructed births, hemorrhage, or infection. Many mothers and newborns probably died during or shortly after delivery. The clan's survival strategy depended on fertility rates balancing high mortality. Women who lived through childbirth were revered, their resilience a measure of the group's strength.

Once the baby emerged, it would have been wiped with furs or moss and held close against the mother's chest. Skin-to-skin contact was vital for warmth in cold climates and for initiating the reflexes of nursing. The umbilical cord may have been tied or pinched with fibers or sinew and then cut with a sharp flake of stone. Blood loss was staunched with absorbent materials—dried moss, powdered ochre, or animal hair pads.

Birth was not just a physical act; it was an affirmation of belonging. The cries of the infant announced its entry into the small community. Though we can only imagine the gestures, there may have been ritual acknowledgments: a sprinkling of ashes, a touch from the father or elder, or the placement of a small object—a shell, a colored stone—near the newborn's bedding. The symbolic use of red ochre, often associated with burial, may also have had a place in life's beginning. To the Neanderthal mind, the color of blood could have signified vitality as much as death, marking both the threshold of entry and exit.

The first days after birth were critical. The mother needed rest, nourishment, and constant fire. Mother's milk production required calories, and the clan likely shared its best portions of meat and fat with her. The father, though perhaps not involved in the delivery, would have played a role in protection and provisioning, ensuring that predators or rival groups stayed distant while the mother regained her strength. The newborn slept swaddled in soft furs, close to its mother's body, warmed by both physical touch and firelight.

Infant mortality remained high. Even with close attention, infection from the unhealed umbilical wound, respiratory distress, or simple cold could end a life quickly. The loss of an infant would have been deeply felt within the small clan, not only as a personal tragedy but as the clan's loss of a potential hunter or mate.

Archaeological findings of infant burials suggest tenderness: small graves lined with stones, ochre traces, and occasional animal bones placed nearby. Such acts speak to emotional awareness—a recognition that every beginning carried the shadow of its possible end.

Still, many children survived, a testament to the clan's care. Nursing might have continued for up to four years, as seen in studies of Neanderthal teeth, reflecting prolonged maternal commitment. The spacing of births, likely several years apart, allowed mothers to recover and ensured each child a chance to thrive before the next arrived.

One question that is often asked concerns birth control. Evidence indicates that hunter-gatherer women—whether Neanderthal or *Homo sapiens*—tend to have long intervals between births even at a time when any deliberate form of birth control was not available.

But, biologists today believe that a form of natural birth control did exist 40,000 years ago because of two factors:

- Extended breastfeeding suppresses ovulation. A nursing mother can remain infertile for 2–4 years if the child suckles frequently.
- Low body fat and high physical activity also delay fertility. A woman whose energy intake barely meets survival needs will have irregular or absent ovulation cycles.

Thus, even if sexual activity continued, conception was unlikely until the mother's body could sustain another pregnancy, and this might not be for several years.

When childbirth did occur, it shaped the rhythms of clan life. It slowed migration, defined shelter needs, and demanded social cohesion.

In every successful birth, the group saw proof that its ways—its gathering, hunting, and cooperation—worked against the odds of the Ice Age. The mother's endurance and the baby's first breath bound the living to both ancestors and descendants.

In this sense, childbirth was not merely a biological event but a reaffirmation of humanity itself.

Within the cold caves and flickering fires, women brought forth life with courage equal to the hunters who faced mammoths. Each birth renewed the fragile promise that the group would endure another summer, another generation.

And though Neanderthals would vanish from Earth, the act of giving life—of creating warmth in a frozen world—remains one of the clearest signs that they were not so different from us.

Protection of the Clan

The birth of a child strengthened not only the family but the entire clan. Each new life deepened the group's investment in its own survival, giving renewed purpose to the long labor of gathering, hunting, and protecting. Every infant represented both promise and burden—one more mouth to feed, yet also one more reason to endure the hardships of an unforgiving world, a reminder that the future depended on the fragile successes of the present.

Yet the same closeness that sustained life also made it vulnerable. In a world without walls or law, danger could arise not only from beasts and weather but from within—from one whose behavior threatened the safety of others, endangering the harmony upon which survival depended.

To protect its young, the clan had to guard more than fire and food; it had to guard trust. When a member's violence or instability endangered the group, the elders faced a reckoning: how to preserve life while defending it from harm, and how to weigh compassion against necessity. It was here, in those moments of judgment, that the earliest forms of justice may have taken root.

Social Responsibility and Justice

Little direct evidence survives of how either *Homo sapiens* or Neanderthals managed wrongdoing within their groups.

No laws were etched in stone, no written decrees have been handed down. Yet human nature—the capacity for cooperation and the potential for harm—was already ancient and well known to both Neanderthals and *Homo sapiens*. Wherever people lived together, patterns of expectation arose: who leads the hunt, who shares the kill, who honors the bonds of mating and who violates them.

In small foraging bands of thirty to fifty individuals, every life depended on others. Trust was currency. Betrayal was danger. Modern hunter-gatherers show that formal punishment is rare in such groups—not because wrongdoing never occurs, but because survival itself demands constant negotiation of behavior.

Among the Hadza of Tanzania, for example, arguments over food, jealousy, or laziness are usually resolved by the use of ridicule, or through temporary separation. Violence is rare; gossip is powerful, as is shunning. A selfish hunter may be mocked or ignored until he changes or leaves.

So too, in the long winters of Ice Age Europe, both *Homo sapiens* and Neanderthals would have needed ways to preserve harmony within fragile kin groups. Laughter, shame, reconciliation—these were likely their earliest tools of justice and social repair. For a Neanderthal family clustered in a small shelter or cave, or a *Homo sapiens* camp spread near the edge of a plain, peace was maintained by necessity.

Archaeological traces hint at stability within these small groups. Long-term occupation layers in sites such as Shanidar and El Sidrón, for example, suggest enduring cooperation, care for the injured, and mutual dependence—conditions that demand social order. When such bonds were broken, the entire group's survival was at risk. Thus, justice began as the practical art of living together.

Violence Within a Clan

When violence did erupt—over food, mates, or status—its consequences were immediate. A wound could end a life; an exile could mean death. Among modern foragers such as the Ju/'hoansi (!Kung San) of the Kalahari, conflicts sometimes lead to homicide, usually between adult men over women or slights to pride. Yet even murder is handled through collective decision rather than centralized power. The entire band may meet to discuss what happened, and the offender may flee, be shunned, or in rare cases be executed by a group of men acting in concert.

For Ice Age Neanderthals and *Homo sapiens*, we can imagine something similar. Injuries on skeletal remains—fractures on skulls or ribs—show evidence of interpersonal violence, but also of healing, suggesting that disputes were not constant and that the group could reconcile after conflict. At the Neanderthal site of Shanidar 3, a rib injury caused by a projectile point shows that one individual was wounded but lived long enough for partial healing.

Although violence occurred, it did not always end in death or permanent estrangement.

Both lineages probably relied on senior members—elders or respected hunters—to mediate disputes. In a world without written law, moral authority rested in reputation. Among the Inuit, for example, a wrongdoer might face a song duel, in which two rivals publicly ridicule each other in verse until the community decides who has greater merit. The goal is not punishment but reintegration—to restore harmony without shedding blood.

Such practices illuminate what might have been: a system based less on coercion than on consensus, where justice meant repairing trust and preserving the fragile unity of the group. For small populations living close to extinction, vengeance was costly. The loss of even one adult weakened the group.

Still, not all conflicts could be contained. When the balance of the group was threatened—when one person repeatedly endangered others—exile, or death, may have been the only recourse.

Theft, Deceit, and the Fragile Bonds of Trust

Among modern foragers, theft is uncommon not because of moral perfection but because ownership itself is limited. Tools, food, and shelters are often shared. The !Kung say that "meat belongs to all who laugh," meaning that a successful hunt feeds everyone, not only the hunter. But envy and deceit do exist. Those who take more than their share, who lie about a hunt or hoard resources, risk losing social standing—a punishment as real as any physical penalty.

For *Homo sapiens*, living in larger, more mobile groups with growing symbolic culture, reputation became a social compass. A liar or a cheat could be undone by rumor.

The spread of symbolic communication—language, gesture, and story—allowed not only cooperation but accountability. Archaeologist Christopher Boehm has argued that early human groups practiced "reverse dominance hierarchies," where the overbearing were restrained through mockery and collective disapproval.

Neanderthals, with their smaller kin-based groups, may have relied less on language and more on visible behavior to measure trust. A person who shirked work or kept food to themselves would be known quickly; gossip is never necessary when every action is seen. Evidence of shared hearths, distributed tasks, and care for the weak suggests that reciprocity was enforced through expectation rather than threat. The social cost of selfishness was likely exile— and 40,000 years ago, exile was equivalent to a slow death.

In a modern parallel, the Hadza use laughter and ridicule to regulate behavior. A boastful hunter becomes the butt of jokes; his arrogance deflates. The same dynamic likely was tried in Ice Age clans: humor as a form of social pressure, compassion an accepted deterrent, community as a courtroom. Justice was lived, not declared.

Exile, Execution, and the Limits of Forgiveness

When ridicule failed, and when reconciliation could not be achieved, the ultimate punishment was removal. In the ethnographic record, exile appears again and again as the most severe form of discipline among hunter-gatherers. The Inuit have stories of men cast adrift on ice for murder or repeated abuse; the Hadza sometimes drive away those who refuse to share. For those living from the land, social death preceded physical death—to be alone was to perish.

Neanderthals, living in small family groups with overlapping territories, may have faced an impossible choice when confronted with a violent or unstable member. Some remains—like those at El Sidrón, where evidence of cannibalism was found—may represent the most extreme conditions. But such an act likely would have been rare. More commonly, the offending individual would be exiled or abandoned—left behind when the group moved on.

Homo sapiens, with their larger networks and emerging rituals, may have developed more structured forms of accountability. Burial sites sometimes suggest symbolic distinctions—individuals laid apart or treated differently. While these do not prove crime or punishment, they hint at the beginnings of moral differentiation within the group. In what is now Europe, as communities grew denser and contacts between clans more frequent, some forms of social control must have evolved to prevent chaos.

In small-scale societies today, execution—though rare—still occurs when one person repeatedly threatens the group's safety. Anthropologist Richard Lee recorded cases among the !Kung where habitual killers were ambushed by a coalition of men, not out of vengeance but necessity. "It was better that one die than many," one elder said. This utilitarian ethic may stretch back to our common ancestors.

The line between justice and survival blurred. Justice was immediate and personal. Forgiveness depended on whether the group could go on together, or not?

Ritual, Reconciliation, and Moral Thought

The emergence of symbolism—art, burial, ornamentation— was not only aesthetic but ethical. Symbols gave form to memory, and memory gave weight to action. A broken taboo or an act of violence could now be remembered, told, and retold. Story became an instrument of moral order.

Modern forager societies use ritual as reconciliation. The Mbuti of Central Africa hold a *molimo* ceremony to restore harmony when a member dies or wrongdoing disturbs the camp. Men sing through the night to "wake the forest," asking it to forgive human imbalance. Among Aboriginal Australians, *payback* ceremonies allow the victim's family to strike the offender once, reestablishing equilibrium without endless feuding.

Such patterns echo deeper instincts. For Neanderthals, whose burials show care and positioning of the dead, the act of placing a body in the earth may have carried moral meaning—a recognition of belonging and accountability. For *Homo sapiens*, cave art and figurines suggest an expanding moral imagination: stories of life, death, and perhaps judgment.

When the two lineages met, their systems of social control would have overlapped. Each understood loyalty, reciprocity, and taboo. Each recognized the danger of internal conflict. The difference may have lain how wrongdoing was narrated and remembered.

With language capable of abstraction, *Homo sapiens* could describe motives, intentions, and consequences; they could teach lessons through story. Neanderthals may have relied more on direct example and immediate emotional cues.

Yet both carried the same moral core: survival through cooperation, belonging through behavior. Crime was a disruption of life itself. Punishment was restoration—the attempt to return the world to balance.

The Birth of Justice and Law

The archaeology of morality leaves faint traces. We cannot see remorse in a fossil or guilt in a stone tool. But we can trace the architecture of care—the healed bones, the tended graves, the shared hearths—and infer a world where justice was lived through compassion as much as through fear.

In modern foragers, we glimpse the same patterns that must have governed Ice Age clans. Small societies depend on equality; they resist tyranny; they cherish reputation. The anthropologist James Woodburn noted that egalitarian foragers "have mechanisms to prevent dominance before it begins." Among the Hadza, arrogance is punished by laughter; among the Inuit, violence is defused by song; among the Ju/'hoansi, generosity defines worth.

So too, 40,000 years ago, *Homo sapiens* and Neanderthals likely stood before the same choice again and again: to divide or to reconcile. The means of enforcement were simple—approval, ridicule, exclusion, forgiveness—but their moral logic was profound. Justice was not imposed from above; it arose from within.

If Neanderthals leaned on the wisdom of elders and the immediacy of kin, *Homo sapiens* expanded justice into symbol and narrative, shaping stories through words and ritual. But in both, the seeds of conscience were already there.

Out of the need to live and endure together came the first sense of right and wrong—the beginnings of moral life and the foundation of what would become *law*: a system of shared rules, expectations, and consequences that endures in the democratic cultures of today.

Chapter Twenty-One

T he winter had been mild and the snow in the hills was almost gone now, but small patches could still be seen in shaded hollows and along the north sides of a few trees, thin and crusted like old bone.

The days were growing longer, though the wind still carried a cool bite. The snow was mostly gone, now.

Ahna was changing shape now more noticeably and felt the cold more sharply when she breathed quickly. She had become increasingly annoyed by the stiffness in her fingers when she worked away from the fire.

As she became a familiar part of camp life, Ahna was accepted by most. Three more moons passed, and the curve of her belly grew pronounced. She could no longer bend to lift heavy loads—her chores narrowing to cleaning fish, helping prepare meals, and scraping hides.

The child moved inside her with small, shifting rolls at first, then with sharp, determined jabs that often made her pause mid-step. Ahna's decision to live with Rynn and give birth in Rynn's camp was a choice she made in the hope that a stronger bound would form between the clans.

During the last moon, her movement had slowed, though few members of either clan paid much attention. She helped the people of Rynn's clan as much as she could

—though she sat more often now, her hands staying busy while her legs rested.

On this day, the air smelled of river water and fresh leaves, and the sound of birds filled the air. Ahna sat at the river bank with two other women, gutting and cleaning a catch of fish from the morning's catch in the twine-fiber nets. Her fingers were slick with oil and scales when she felt the first slow tightening deep in her belly.

It was not the mild, shifting ache she had known in recent days, the kind that faded if she changed position.

This was different—a slow, spreading grip.

She paused, one hand on the rounded mound beneath her ribs.

Shala, the oldest among them, noticed at once. She was a wiry woman, her back still straight despite her age, her long gray hair tied back with a strip of sinew. She had seen more births than anyone else in the camp—including the healer Lurea—and carried the authority of it.

"You stop your work," said Shala. Her hands were strong and sure, her eyes quick. She moved closer, studying Ahna's face. "Too soon. Next moon better. But the baby decides. And the time is now."

Ahna's mouth went dry. "Not yet," she said, but Shala only shook her head and wiped her hands on a scrap of hide.

"We go to the birthing shelter. Now!"

The birthing shelter was a low structure of bent saplings, its frame covered with thick hides stitched together and softened by long use and weather. Inside, the ground was layered with grasses, reeds, and hides for warmth and comfort. It stood at the far edge of camp, apart from the sleeping shelters, with its entrance facing east to catch the first light.

Shala guided Ahna inside and had her sit on a folded hide. She then called for Liro, a girl of perhaps twelve summers, to fetch the birthing bundle and keep the fire strong.

"Also," Shala added, "send for Rynn, the father."

Ahna's pulse quickened at the thought: *Rynn*. She had not expected birthing today. She almost told Shala not to send for him—men were not usually part of births—but her voice caught in her throat. Some part of her wanted him near, even if he stayed outside. His voice, his presence, might steady her.

Outside, the camp began to react. The older women brought warm water from the fire, one pot after another. Shala opened her bundle: dried leaves of raspberry and yarrow, thin strips of willow bark, and a small pouch of ground red ocher.

She placed the ocher in a shallow stone bowl near the head of the bedding, then set smooth river stones beside it. "For strength," she said. "For the mother, for the child, for the father, for the coming together of two clans."

The pains came and went, still far apart, but they were strongly felt. Shala had Ahna stand and walk the length of the shelter between each wave, crouching low to help the child drop, steadying her with a firm, guiding hand.

Lira warmed a pelt in the fire's steam and pressed it to Ahna's lower back while Shala offered sips of willow-bark tea, bitter on the tongue, to dull the edge of the pain.

Rynn came as soon the runner reached him. By his count, the birth was coming too soon. His mind swirled with fear and urgency. Eighth moon—start of ninth moon. He knew enough from his own people's births to know the risk. And he was plagued by Marek's warning that no births could be shared between the two clans.

He ran all the way to the birthing shelter. He did not slow down as he passed several people who watched him pass. By the time Rynn arrived, Ahna was on hands and knees, her breath coming in short, fast pulls. Rynn's hair was damp with sweat, his chest heaving from the run.

Shala blocked the doorway for a moment, but Ahna lifted her head and called his name.

"Let him sit near," Ahna said to Shala. "I will bear better if I hear him."

Shala hesitated, then nodded. "There, she pointed. No closer."

Rynn ducked into the shelter's dim light, his eyes sweeping over Ahna, the midwife Shala, and the tools laid out. He kept himself low, moving to the place indicated, close enough for Ahna to see him, but not so close as to crowd the women. He was out of reach, yet his gaze was fixed on her with the full, unflinching attention of one who would carry her pain if he could.

"Your voice," Ahna murmured between breaths. "Say something."

Rynn swallowed. "I am here. I will stay until you and the little one are safe."

That was enough. She closed her eyes and rocked her hips slowly as another contraction rolled through her body. Her knuckles whitened as they bore much of her weight while she crawled on all fours across the birthing floor, breath tight, focused only on enduring its passing.

Time passed slowly and shadows in the shelter shifted as the sun fell toward the tree line. At times, excruciating pain seized Ahna, leaving her breathless and trembling. The air inside the shelter grew warmer—thick with steam and the scent of yarrow—making each breath a strain.

Shala worked without hurry, her hands always steady —feeling Ahna's belly, massaging the muscles in her back, checking the baby's position by the press and shape inside.

"Small one," she murmured at one point, almost to herself. "Ninth moon. Too early. Will need the warmth of skin and fire."

Ahna knew what those words meant—-that a baby born this early might not live through the first night unless the warmth and breath of the mother were unbroken. Her heart thudded hard in her chest, but she forced herself to focus on Shala's voice, the sound of her encouragement.

Lira fed the fire so that it never dimmed, then sprinkled dried herbs onto the coals so the smoke filled the shelter.

"Keeps away wandering spirits," the girl whispered to Rynn, as if afraid the words might weaken their power if spoken too loudly. Rynn nodded, though his eyes never left Ahna.

When the time came, Shala guided Ahna into a deep squat, bracing her with one strong arm around her back. Another woman held Ahna's forearms so she could lean her weight forward when the urge to push gripped her. The low position let gravity work in her favor—a method as old as the clan.

The contractions came in waves now, fierce and unstoppable, each one surging mercilessly through her body. Ahna's skin burned hot and sweat streamed down her temples, soaking her tangled hair. Her breathing was labored and ragged—every breath a deep, guttural sound she could never have shaped into words.

Shala murmured to her in almost a whisper, words of strength and endurance, then checked again for the crown of the child's head.

"I see hair," Shala said at last. "Soft brown with a hint of red—like the mother." Another push, another—Ahna's muscles burned with the effort, her fingers clutching into fists as she strained to deliver. Shala's hands were ready, cupping the small head as it emerged, easing the shoulders free one at a time. Then, with a wet, sudden slide, the rest of the child came free.

"A baby girl," said Shala.

The baby lay still for a moment in Shala's hands, slick and small. The midwife quickly sucked the mouth and nose free and then wiped the newborn with a strip of soft hide, rubbing her chest briskly.

No response.

Shala gave the baby a light slap on the backside.

Movement!

Then, the baby girl gave a thin, sharp cry—high and wavering—and everyone in the shelter sighed relief.

Rynn had no words to describe his feeling—his joy.

Shala wrapped the baby in a warm, rabbit-fur wrap and placed it on Ahna's chest, skin against skin. "Your scent, your warmth," she told her. "The little one must know you first."

Rynn, breaking with the strictness of custom, moved closer until he was almost at her side. He reached out with a tentative hand, brushing the back of one finger against the baby's head. The tiny skull was warm and damp beneath a fine layer of hair.

"Small," he whispered. *Alive*, he thought. *Alive!*

"Small, but strong," Ahna said, though her voice shook.

Shala waited patiently for the afterbirth. She massaged Ahna's belly in slow, firm circles to encourage the placenta to come out. When the tissue slid free, the cord still pulsing faintly, Shala examined it carefully—instinctively knowing that anything left inside could bring death.

She waited until the cord's pulse had stopped before cutting it with a sharpened flake of flint. The tie was made from twisted sinew, looped twice to keep the blood in the child's body from flowing away too soon. The placenta, still warm, was wrapped in broad, green leaves and set aside for later burial.

"Father will choose the place," Shala said, glancing at Rynn. "A safe place, where no animal can take it. Where the child's spirit will find freedom."

Rynn nodded solemnly. He already knew the place—a spot on a small rise overlooking the bend of the river, where the spring flowers grew thick.

For a long while, Ahna lay with the baby on her chest, the rise and fall of her breath keeping the tiny body warm.

Shala busied herself tending the birthing place with Lira's help—clearing away what remained, replacing the damp hides with fresh, clean ones, sweeping the packed earth of all signs of birth, feeding wood to the fire, and hanging fragrant herbs so their warm scent softened the air.

Rynn sat at Ahna's side. He studied the child's small fingers, curling and uncurling as if trying to grip the air.

"What will we name her?" he asked softly.

"Not yet," Ahna said. "The name will come when the time is right. We wait to see who she is."

They fell into a silence that was not empty—it was full of the small sounds of life: the faint smacking of the baby's mouth, the steady hiss of the fire, the rustle of hides as Ahna shifted to keep her daughter close.

By nightfall, the camp was hushed. A pale crescent moon hung low above the tree line, its light falling in silver patches across the ground. The birthing shelter glowed faintly from the fire within.

Ahna, worn out from the difficult birth, drifted in and out of sleep, always waking when the baby stirred.

Rynn stayed beside her, his back against the wall, watching the small rise and fall of their child's breathing. He felt the fragility of an early birth and small body, and yet he felt an ever-present thread of hope.

He looked at Ahna, her hair damp and tangled, her face soft in sleep, and felt something settle in him: a promise, unspoken but binding.

Whatever the future moons brought, whatever dangers lay ahead, he would stand with Ahna and their child.

Outside, the first night insects struck up their chorus, their rising voices carried on the scent of new blossoms.

Inside, three breaths—one deep, one steady, one small and fluttering—filled the air with life.

* * *

Many days later, Ahna was up early and wanted to walk through the camp. With Rynn by her side, she moved at a careful pace, the baby bound close to her chest, with Rynn walking beside her to make sure she did not stumble and to offer protection if needed.

They paused only once, near a fallen tree half-covered in moss. Ahna sat to rest while Rynn offered her a strip of dried meat. The baby stirred, tiny fists pressing against her skin. She shifted the wrap and let the infant nurse, feeling the pull and swallow, steady as a small heartbeat.

"Soon, others will see us," Rynn said quietly. "Children will run over to see the child. They always do this when a baby arrives."

Now long after, the first signs of an awakening camp appeared: smoke from cooking fires, the sharp scent of roasting meat, voices carried on the wind. Then came the children, as Rynn had said—two boys and a girl, at first, stopping short at the sight of Ahna and the bundle at her chest. They whispered, pointed, laughed, then darted off.

The camp's open space soon became busy. Women scraped hides, men worked spear points, children played with knucklebones near the fire. One by one, heads turned toward them, curiosity slowly gathering in the air as people paused in their tasks.

Some faces showed open curiosity, even welcome. A few women approached, their eyes going first to the baby, then to Ahna's face. One, a broad-shouldered woman named Enna, smiled and said, "Small one, but bright-eyed. May the light of the sun keep her strong."

Others hung back. A younger man muttered something to his companion and laughed. A few simply turned away, busying themselves in their work.

As he saw her become tired, Rynn walked Ahna back to the shelter.

Several moons ago, soon after Ahna had moved in with him, Rynn, with the help of two elders and Tamik, had built a new, sturdier shelter—large enough for three. The larger shelter had a frame of poles covered with hides, with a low, covered entrance to hold in warmth.

Inside, the shelter was lined with furs and was stocked with a supply of dried meat and smoked fish against one wall. "From now on, this is our new home," Rynn had said. "We will sleep here and be safe. No one will touch what we share together."

Soon after Rynn, Ahna, and the child returned to the shelter, Enna arrived with a pot of broth thickened with roots, setting it near the fire pit. "This food gives strength," she said to Ahna. "Eat, and keep the little one warm."

But not all were so kind. A few evenings later, as Rynn was cutting meat near the fire, he overheard two men talking—one of them Torg, his voice carrying in the cool air.

"Too many mouths already," Torg said, not bothering to lower his voice. "And now we feed one that is half from her kind? The *others* keep to themselves for a reason."

A man talking with Torg murmured something too low to catch, and Torg laughed. "I have seen her kind fight over scraps. You'll see. When food grows short, she'll take more than her share. And that child…" He let the words hang, then added with a smirk, "Even if it lives until the next summer, it will never be one of us."

Rynn's hands tightened around the meat he was cutting. The blade bit deep into the wood beneath, but he kept his head down.

Later, he said nothing to Ahna. Not yet.

Rynn stayed close when he could, teaching her which voices among his people to trust and helping her tell the difference between kindness and pretense. At night, with the baby sleeping between them, he would say, "I will keep you safe. Both of you."

But sometimes, lying awake in the dark, Ahna thought of Torg's eyes—the way they followed her whenever he thought she was not looking. She sensed that kind of danger—one that lurked in darkness and silence, patiently waiting for opportunity.

Chapter Twenty-Two

The morning light crept in pale and angled through the gap in the hide flap, touching the sleeping face of Ahna's daughter. The baby lay curled in the hollow of furs enclosing her, her chest rising and falling in slow, even breaths. At three moons old, she had already lost the fragile look of a newborn, her cheeks round, her skin warm, her tiny fists often clenched with the stubborn strength of life.

For three moons, the little one had gone unnamed. Among the *tall ones*, names were not given in the fragile first days, when the child's breath might falter and slip away before it was truly part of the life of the clan. But now the baby girl was strong, her cries loud enough to rouse the camp in the night, her eyes following the play of firelight.

It was time for naming.

Ahna rose early and carried her daughter outside, wrapped in softened hides. The air was cool, carrying the scent of damp earth, and the first light of morning painted the ridges in pale gold. She walked to where the elders sat near the cooking fire, Rynn at her side, the child pressed close to her chest.

The naming was not a ceremony of chants and charms, but a moment of agreement. Each elder looked long upon the child, as though sensing the shape of her spirit. Rynn's hand brushed Ahna's shoulder, steadying her.

"I like the name *Yana*," he said at last. His voice was low but sure. He was thinking of Marek as he said it—and he had not yet shared Marek's story with Ahna.

The syllables seemed to settle over them like a blanket. Ahna whispered the name against her daughter's ear, tasting its sound on her lips. *Yana.* A name that sounded similar to her own name. It carried the softness of dawn, the firmness of stone, the promise of life reaching forward. Ahna said she agreed—the perfect name.

The elders nodded. One murmured that the name spoke of renewal, another that it carried the memory of waters flowing in spring. No one spoke against it.

Ahna felt warmth rise in her chest, tears threatening as she bent to kiss her child's cheek. "Yana," she said again, louder now, letting the camp hear it. The baby stirred, her small mouth opening in a sigh as if she had claimed the name for herself. Rynn felt Marek's presence in the child.

The others repeated it, softly at first, then with growing ease. Yana. A new voice added to the camp, carried in the breath of those who loved her. And so she was named.

Ahna's hand rested lightly on the baby's stomach, feeling the steady rise and fall. She had feared, in those first days, that each breath might be the last. Yana had come early—too early, the healers whispered—but she had fought. And now, weighing nearly as much as the fattest winter hare, she seemed to drink life as greedily as she drank her mother's milk.

Outside, faint noises told her the camp was stirring. Someone was splitting wood—measured, sure blows that spoke of skill and familiarity.

Elsewhere, she caught the distant laughter of two young boys, sharp in the cold air. Somewhere, fire crackled. She could smell it, faintly laced with the scent of sizzling bone marrow.

She shifted and winced as the stiffness in her hips made itself known. Three moons was enough time for strength to return, but not without reminders.

She eased herself upright, pulling her daughter close and wrapping her in the thick fur sling she had made from a hide Rynn had given her. Yana's head settled just under her chin, the warm weight familiar and reassuring.

The next day, Rynn left before dawn with a group of hunters. In the late autumn, the air carried a raw edge that stung the skin, but the herds were easier to track now, drifting down from the high ground toward the valleys in search fresh grazing.

Ahna had watched him go, the knot of worry tight in her stomach. She had not told him, not in words, how much the empty space he left unsettled her when he was away. She did not want him to think she could not manage, or that she feared being alone.

She stoked the fire, then reached for a bone needle and a piece of sinew thread. Rynn's tunic lay in her lap, a rip running along the side where it had caught on something— thorn, rock, or perhaps the antler of an animal that had come too close. She pushed the needle through the hide, her hands moving from habit, her eyes half on the work, half on the baby.

The sound reached her then—a soft but distinct rhythm: thud… drag… thud… drag—the uneven step of someone using a branch for support.

Torg.

She did not need to look to know. His uneven gait had recently become part of the camp's daily sounds, the result of a splint Lurea had bound to his lower leg in an effort to heal injuries suffered on a hunt. Torg limped through the camp after the splint was set, his face tight with pain and anger, glaring at anyone who dared glance his way, as though their notice were an insult he would not forgive.

Since then, other hunters had done what they could to keep him busy with small tasks. But an idle Torg was a restless Torg, and restlessness was never good.

The steps came closer. His shadow passed over the hide flap, slowing for just a breath before moving on. The smell of smoke and unwashed hide trailed behind him, staying in the air even after his limp carried him away.

Ahna's hands tightened on the needle. Yana stirred against her, letting out a small whimper. She shifted her daughter to nurse, the warm pull calming both of them. Still, her ears stayed alert for the drag of Torg's step.

She decided to keep to the busier parts of camp for the day. Ahna carried her daughter to the river, the sling holding her close while she filled a small skin with water. The cold bit into her fingers until they numbed, and the baby wriggled against her chest in protest at the breeze.

Back in camp, she joined two other women—Cara, who was nursing her second child, and Onka, whose mate had left with the hunt—to work a deer hide. They spread it over a log and began scraping the remaining hair away with stone tools. The rhythm was steady, the scrape-scrape punctuated by bits of conversation.

"Your girl grows fast," Cara said, nodding toward the baby nestled against Ahna.

"Yana eats a lot," Ahna laughed. It was true; the girl nursed often and long, and her arms and legs were already filling out.

"Good," Onka said. "Better to grow strong from your milk. Food may be scarce soon."

The talk drifted to other topics—where the hunters might range today, whether there might still be snow high in the north valley.

As they talked, Ahna caught sight of Torg standing on the far side of the fire. He was leaning playfully on his crutch, the branch polished where his hand gripped it. His eyes swept over the group of women. When his eyes met hers, his gaze held just a moment too long. Then his mouth twisted into a sneer before he looked away.

Later, as she walked back to her shelter to check the fire, she saw Torg not far off, standing in her path, balanced on both legs and gripping his crutch like a spear held at rest. His eyes were fixed on Yana's sling, on the baby's barely visible head, intent and unblinking.

"Strong for one so small," he said, his voice just loud enough for her to hear.

Ahna gave a single nod and moved past him without speaking. Behind her came the faint sound of his predatory chuckle—low, without warmth.

The time dragged in the slow way it sometimes does when the hunters were gone. Ahna tended the fire, boiled water for tea, and nursed Yana when she fussed. She took her baby to the edge of the camp for a bit of sun, sitting where she could see the path by which the hunters would return.

The baby's eyes followed the flutter of smoke from a distant fire, her small mouth opening in what might have been a smile.

By mid-afternoon, Ahna helped Cara and Onka prepare roots for the evening meal. She peeled them carefully, keeping the stone's sharp edge away from curious baby hands. The warmth from the cooking fires seeped into her bones, easing the last of the morning's chill.

Still, she never quite lost the sense of being watched. Torg moved about the camp like a stalking cat, his limp giving away his position even when she could not see him. At one point, she caught him near the storage hut, his gaze turned her way though his head was angled elsewhere.

After an hour of steady work on meal preparation, Ahna's joined another woman, Hana, who was scraping hides. The rhythmic rasp of stone on skin was comforting, the sound carrying in the cold air like a steady heartbeat between the women. As they worked, small curls of hair fell away under their tools, lightly clinging to their fingers before drifting to the ground.

From the far side of the camp, an older man named Leron called out. He was no longer able to hunt but made tools for the others. A bundle of bone needles hung from a thong at his waist, clicking softly when he walked. In his hands he carried a length of antler, freshly split, the inside pale and porous.

"Ahna," he said, saying her name carefully. His accent clipped it shorter than her people did. "You know how the cord-binding is done for spear shafts?"

She nodded. Among her own clan, she had bound more than a few.

"Come," he said, gesturing with the antler. "Your hands are quick. And you will know the tightness needed."

She hesitated, glancing at Hana who smiled and gave her an encouraging nod.

Near Leron's shelter, the air smelled of bone dust and the faint tang of hide glue. He showed her the spear shaft he was repairing—the old binding had frayed, loosened by damp. Together they worked the sinew into long, even strips. She held one end taut while he wrapped the other around the joint, pulling until the fibers sang with tension.

"Good," he said, approving. "Your fingers know the amount of pull needed—strong enough to hold, but not so strong that it breaks."

His words made her smile. In her own clan, preparing a spear binding was a sign of trust, a task given only to steady hands. A poorly bound weapon could mean a failed hunt—or worse. She felt a flicker of pride that he saw her worth and granted her that quiet honor.

When the work was done, he offered her a strip of dried meat from a pouch. She took it, chewing slowly, savoring the smoky-salt taste.

Before she finished the meat, a movement caught her eye—Torg passing nearby, carrying his branch-crutch, his unaided limp exaggerated, each step an act of defiance. His eyes flicked to her, then to the repaired spear.

As he came closer, Torg called out his advice, his tone flat. "Careful she does not bind your spear too tight. Wet sinew will shrink—strap it too tight and the shaft could split under a blow."

Leron gave no reply, busying himself with his tools. Ahna kept her gaze fixed on the meat in her hand, her jaw working slowly until the unwelcome steps moved away.

By midday the camp was alive with small, necessary labors: women drying berries in preparation for storage, men shaping arrowheads, and two youngsters feeding the fire to create smoke to drive off the damp. Tools were mended, hides stretched, and herbs braided for curing. Children darted between the shelters, their bright laughter a welcome sound to those working.

After finishing her work with Leron, Ahna carried her daughter to the central fire, where two elders were telling a story to a group of boys. She settled nearby, letting the warmth seep into her legs. The story was about a hunt in deep snow, many winters past, when the prey had turned on the hunters. The boys sat forward, eyes wide, as an elder mimed the thrust of a spear and the sudden spray of blood from the fallen animal's ribs.

One boy noticed Ahna and her daughter and grinned, holding up a carved wooden animal—a roe deer, its legs thin as twigs. He offered it to Yana, who reached for it with a slow, clumsy hand. The boy laughed, pleased.

"You see?" an elder said, chuckling. "Even the smallest hunter wants her prey."

It was a simple joke, but it eased something within her. These were not her people, not yet, but moments like this— the shared laughter, the firelight on faces—felt like stones laid on a path toward belonging.

And once again she felt the shadow in the corner of her mind. Across the camp, Torg sat on a log, his splinted leg stretched out before him. He was sharpening a blade, the scrape of stone on flint carrying faintly to where she sat. His gaze moved often, never settling long, but it always seemed to pass her way.

Ahna stirred and then stood, walking slowly back toward her shelter. Along the way, she passed the drying racks where strips of meat hung, darkening in the cool air. A young woman named Nyla was tending them, turning each piece so the wind could reach all sides.

"Does your clan dry meat this way?" Nyla asked, her voice curious.

"Sometimes," Ahna said. "We smoke it first. The taste holds longer."

Nyla smiled. "Show me, after the next hunt."

The request warmed Ahna in a way the fire could not. She promised she would, picturing the smoky scent curling up into the bright air of autumn.

When she reached her shelter, Ahna stoked the fire and nursed Yana. Outside, the camp hummed with life—the scrape of tools, the low murmur of voices, the quick rise of a child's shriek dissolving into laughter. It was different from her old shelter in many ways—busier, noisier, more crowded—yet the rhythm of daily activity felt familiar to the memories she carried.

The sun dropped lower, and the shadows stretched long. Ahna walked outside her shelter and settled near the central fire with her daughter on her lap. She hummed a tune from her own people, a weaving song her mother had sung in the long evenings. The baby's eyes fluttered as the song worked its way into her breathing, her small hands opening and closing in slow cadence.

She felt unease before she saw him—the shift in the air, the change in light when someone steps between her and the fire. Torg stood there, playing with his branch-crutch, his mouth curved in a smile that did not reach his eyes.

"You heal fast," he said, glancing down at her child.

"And your child is strong—much stronger than other children so small. Must be something in the blood of your people. Something that bears watching."

The way he spoke, healing sounded more like a stain than a strength. She kept her gaze on Yana, adjusting the small wrap around her shoulders.

"Rynn's not here," he added after a pause, almost idly, as if stating a fact with no weight. But the tone carried something else—a test, perhaps, or a reminder.

"I know," she said simply.

His eyes lingered, traveling from her face to her chest and back again. "Some men… they do not realize how quickly the order breaks. A woman claimed. A man taking what he wants."

Ahna's fingers tightened on the wrap. "This child belongs to me and to Rynn," she said, her voice steady. Her meaning was clear, and no more needed to be said.

Torg's smile shifted, losing any pretense of friendliness. "We will see," he said. "We will see."

He tossed the branch-crutch into the fire, turned, and had only a slight limp as he walked toward his own shelter.

Long after he was gone, Ahna could feel the imprint of his presence—as if the air around her had become dirty. She looked toward the darkness beyond the firelight, half-expecting to see the shape of him there, watching. But there was nothing.

As the evening wore on, the fire smoke hung low, heavy with the scent of roasted meat and vegetables.

Ahna sat with Yana cradled in her lap, nursing her in the flicker of the flames. The hunters had not yet returned, and their absence left the camp quiet, with shadows deep between the shelters.

She shifted Yana in her arms and glanced toward the distant hills where the hunting party would first appear. She told herself that she only needed to have patience. Rynn would be back soon.

But deep down, she knew that Torg was not the kind that faded with the smoke.

Torg was the kind that waited.

When the sound of the returning hunters came from the northern path, she felt her body release tension she had not known she was holding.

Rynn was in the lead, shoulders squared and hair lit by the setting sun.

When he arrived at their shelter, his eyes found hers and his face suddenly showed a smile.

He reached out to hold her, then crouched to touch his daughter's cheek with the back of his fingers. Yana stirred, her mouth opening in a soft response.

"Strong," he said, smiling. "Yana, you are strong."

Ahna smiled at Rynn, though she did not tell him how the day had passed. That burden could wait for its time. For tonight, Rynn was here, the fire was warm, and their daughter was safe in the circle of their arms.

Chapter Twenty-Three

Preparations for the gathering had begun with a kind of solemn joy. The idea that both clans—those who had once eyed each other with suspicion across valleys and river beds—would join in a celebration of unity was something none had imagined even a moon ago. It was to be a festival of many days, of shared food and tales and firelight. At the center of the celebration would be Ahna, Rynn, and Yana—the child born to them—carrying the hope that their two clans might one day be united.

Yet not all hearts welcomed the coming celebration.

Torg, whose recent leg injuries had healed, now moved through the *Homo sapiens* camp even more brazenly—with the gait of one who did not recognize any boundaries: not social, not physical, not moral. He was quick to laugh, but never in a kind way. His hands strayed where they should not. He watched everyone closely. When others caught his gaze, it was never steady—it darted, retreated, returned as though measuring weakness.

Unease in Torg's presence was widespread, carried in sidelong glances and quieted conversations. Children moved closer to their mothers. Women, without even thinking about it, shifted to stand nearer to one another.

After Torg's return to the hunt, little had come of the growing unease: a whispered protest; averted eyes; voices that grew harsher around the fire. But still, Torg remained.

His most recent trouble had been with Rynn. During the hunt two days ago, an old mammoth—trailing blood from several spear wounds—had become separated from the herd. The hunters followed it for most of the morning, silent as the forest floor, until the time came for the final throws. Torg had crept forward, too eager, his body exposed just as the giant turned toward him. Roaring, the wounded bull was about to charge. Instead, it hesitated for a few moments and gave Rynn enough time to strike from a better angle.

Rynn's spear had landed deep and true. The mammoth collapsed in a wave of groaning muscle. Before the dust had settled, Torg had cried out as though he had delivered the killing blow. Rynn refused to yield credit. Others had seen. Whispers spread. Torg had lost more than unearned credit for a kill, he had lost any final shreds of respect that might still linger in the hunting party.

Torg did not forget. And he would not forgive.

Back in camp, Ahna was awaiting Rynn's return. The hunting party returned later than expected, and Rynn was exhausted as Ahna welcomed him to the shelter.

The next morning, the hunting party left early again. They needed to butcher the fallen mammoth. Before they left, Ahna and Rynn had spent a few moments just being together. As Yana slept, Ahna's fingers traced the edge of a shell Rynn had given her—smooth on one side, ridged on the other. They had spoken little. They said few words. They seldom needed to.

Later that afternoon, while the hunters were still gone, Ahna decided to visit the Neanderthal camp. Ahna took her pouch and carried Yana on her chest.

She knew the path to the river crossing by heart, and she enjoyed moving through the forest on the far side—the roots beneath her feet were familiar, the mossy scent of damp bark comforting.

The trees—massive with age—did not startle easily. They welcomed her as they had when she was a child, with the slow exhale of wind-stirred branches.

She was just entering the forest when she heard a noise: a footfall, just one, heavier than a small deer. She turned sharply, alert but not afraid. At first, she saw nothing. Then, the flicker of a form behind a tree.

"Torg!" she called out as she saw him.

He stepped into view, grinning broadly. His hand held nothing—a fact that unsettled her far more than if it had gripped a spear.

"Long way to walk alone," he said.

"I do not need company," she replied, firm but not rude.

He moved closer. "I saw you earlier. With Rynn. Who were you laughing at?"

Ahna's heart began to race—not from fear, not yet, but from the quick instinct that danger was near. She adjusted her footing and shifted her weight back.

"At no one. Now go back," she said. "You do not belong near me."

But he did not stop. He stepped much closer, and the air changed. He reached out—not roughly at first—his fingers brushing a strand of her hair. Ahna jerked back.

"No," she said, loud and clear.

The next moments were broken and jagged, like a branch torn from a tree by wind. He moved toward her. She backed farther away quickly. His arm caught her shoulder. She twisted, dropped her pouch, and scrambled with Yana tied to her chest into the underbrush.

Torg followed, caught up to her and grabbed her wrist, pulling her hard enough to spin her. She fell. She kicked out at him—hard—striking his shin. It was enough. He staggered and fell. She began running before he could regain his balance and reach for her.

She did not stop running until the familiar sight of the Neanderthal camp came into view. Her breath tore out in sobs. Her hands trembled—not from weakness, but from the fear she had learned to carry and hold in check. As her breathing quieted, Ahna decided not to speak about this incident to Rynn or anyone else in either clan.

She returned to her shelter later and said nothing to Rynn that night. The fear Torg had planted in her would not rule her. She would turn fear into strength and hold that strength ready. Torg's time would come, and when it did, she would not hesitate to act.

The next morning, she awoke early, her body aching, but her spirit resolved. Rynn had left for another hunt before he had time to notice the bruises on her body and before she had time to speak with him.

She fed Yana, and then set about her work gathering herbs. When she finished, she knelt by the fire, and said nothing to anyone about the previous day.

Only one among the clan noticed something was amiss —Terah, whose eyes missed little.

"You walk like one who has fought branches," Terah said quietly. "I see scratches that speak loudly."

"I tripped," Ahna answered, a bit too quickly.

Terah said nothing more, but her gaze was steady.

Meanwhile, on the other side of camp, Torg moved with only the faintest hitch in his step, his earlier injury all but healed. When asked about it, he shrugged and claimed he'd healed quickly—much faster than most others would have. He grinned as he spoke, making it clear that leg wounds had never slowed him for long, then added— eagerly—that he was more than ready to join the next hunt.

That night, Torg was seen leaning too close to two girls much younger than Ahna. One flinched. The other shoved his hand away. He muttered something about "obedience" and "mates," then stormed off.

Later, through whispered exchanges around the fire, word of Torg's behavior reached Rynn. His face hardened as he listened. He said nothing, but his hands were restless that night. Sleep abandoned him, and he rose to further sharpen a spear already honed.

The next morning, while still alone with Ahna and Yana, Rynn saw a look of anger in her eyes—a look he seldom saw.

"What happened?" he asked, as soon as they were up.

She did not speak at first. But she handed him the shell —its smooth side now scored with a jagged crack.

"Torg did this," she said.

She did not elaborate. She did not have to. Rynn closed his eyes. His jaw tightened.

"Does the clan know?" he asked.

"Only Terah suspects."

"We should tell all the elders"

"Not yet. Soon."

They sat in silence for a time. The wind stirred.

Finally, she said, "Torg will be stopped."

Rynn nodded slowly. "And I will stop him."

During the next few days, the matter had begun to seep into the edges of both camps. Ahna still had not spoken out about Torg, but others had stories of their own. And these stories became more than just rumors, several members of the clan telling their stories to Rynn.

A mother recalled Torg offering her daughter a bit of dried meat in a way that made her skin crawl. A young hunter said Torg had shoved him aside during a hunt to make a kill that was not his to make. A child said that Torg had sent him into the forest to look for kindling—sending him into a wasp's nest.

Small things, maybe. Isolated things. But together, they formed a pattern. One that could no longer be ignored.

Rynn did not speak directly of justifiable payback. But he asked the elders to meet with him. He spoke of the celebration—how both clans must come together in peace. How the greatest danger to the clan may come from within.

He never said Torg's name. He did not need to.

The celebration was still days away. In preparation, people in both camps carved tools, wove reed baskets, smoked meat, and talked about the coming together. Yet in the shadows of these preparations, unease flourished, feeding on whispers and wary glances.

Rynn moved through the days with an alertness new to him—eyes sharper, shoulders tighter. He said nothing directly to Ahna, not about Torg, not about the stories he had heard, not about the actions he himself would take.

But Ahna could feel the change in him, the unspoken resolve in the way he stood when others came near, the way he insisted on walking with her when she visited her people across the river.

Ahna decided to tell a few in her own clan of the danger that Torg posed.

"He touched me," she said to Marga, the Neanderthal elder. "And he made me feel unsafe."

That was all. But it was enough.

Marga, old and respected, took it to the women first. And it spread—quietly, woman to woman. Warnings that would spread throughout the clan. Eyes narrowed now and tempers flared any time Torg's name was mentioned for any reason.

But Torg did not notice or care about what women in either clan thought of him. He would take what he wanted.

One morning, before the hunters left, near the edge of the *Homo sapiens* camp, Torg saw Ahna's child suckling at her breast in the shade of a tree. Ahna was sitting with her back against the bark, her body half-covered by a pelt, her infant wrapped warmly and feeding contentedly.

She had not seen him approach.

"Must be good," Torg said from behind her.

Ahna froze.

He stepped into her view. His eyes went to the child, drinking her fill. He grinned.

"I wonder what it tastes like," he said. "I have heard it is sweeter than anything else."

Ahna covered herself quickly, shifting her child to the other arm.

"Go away."

Torg came closer and crouched next to Ahna.

"You think I do not see the way they all look at you now. Like you are some kind of mother of peace. You are just a woman. Full of milk. What makes you so special?"

Ahna's voice did not waver. "You are not welcome near me."

Still crouching, he reached out a hand.

But before he could touch her again, a low voice spoke behind him.

"Stand up, Torg."

Rynn stood just four steps away, spear in hand, but not raised. His voice was calm, but his eyes were iron.

Torg rose, slow and deliberate. He said nothing.

Rynn stepped forward. "Time for you to leave. Now."

Torg smiled, but it was forced, twitching at the corners. "She is not yours to guard."

"She is not yours to touch," replied Rynn.

Torg spat into the dirt. Then he turned and walked off, muttering something too low to hear.

Rynn looked at Ahna. She had not moved.

He did not ask if she was all right. He did not need to.

But she said anyway, "He wants to break something. Something delicate."

Rynn nodded. "The elders will stop him, or I will."

That night, the *Homo sapiens* elders gathered.

It was a rare thing, to summon them all. They met at the central fire, where decisions of great weight had been made for generations—when to migrate, who would lead a hunt, how to mourn the dead.

Now the fire crackled before them, and Torg's name was spoken aloud.

Some hesitated.

"He was accepted into our clan long ago," said Keho, the newest and youngest of the elders. "He is not wise, not kind—but he is strong. And strength matters."

Rynn answered. "Strength without respect is danger. He disrespects our women, our peace, our food."

Others nodded.

Terah—an elder admired for her wisdom—spoke. "My youngest daughter says he watched her washing herself in the river. She felt eyes, then turned and saw him."

Another elder said, "He tried to take meat from my son. He said it was owed to him."

"He nearly got Dano hurt on the last hunt," Omak added. "Pushed him toward the boar and laughed."

"It is time we acted!" proclaimed Terah.

"We have warned him before," Omak said. "But he listens only to his own voice."

"And if he refuses to listen to the elders," Rynn said firmly, "the clan must take action."

Silence.

Then, Omak spoke up. "The old ways were to exile."

"Or worse," Duma muttered.

But no one uttered "death," but many thought it.

Across the river, in the Neanderthal camp, Ahna's story, as well as the other stories were slowly becoming known. Ahna's cousin feared for the safety of Ahna and the child Yana, and she wanted Torg made unable to threaten any of them again.

As the stories spread, they no longer spoke only of discomfort—they became stories of intrusion, of threat, of danger to not only one mother and her child but to all members of both clans.

Ahna and Rynn had bridged two peoples with their love and the child that came from that love. That Ahna or Yana might be harmed by a member of Rynn's clan stirred something deeper in each clan than outrage: ancestral memory—the well known and often discussed struggles for survival each clan had overcome.

Both the Neanderthals and the *Homo sapiens* were well aware of the threat that Torg posed to each clan.

Recently, on a sunny afternoon, a *Homo sapiens* girl of eleven summers came running to her mother, crying. She had gone to the far rocks, where the sun-warmed lizards sunned themselves. Torg had followed her there.

He had smiled and told her that she would grow into a beautiful woman. He had reached for her shoulder. She ran before he could do more.

The girl's mother did not keep silent. She went straight to the elders. The girl's father, severely crippled, followed.

By dusk the next evening, the elders had sent for Rynn.

"We cannot ignore this," said Omak. "Even those who once defended him now say it is time for action."

"Tell your Neanderthal kin and elders of the clan that measures will be taken," Duma instructed Rynn.

Rynn looked into the fire for a long time.

"I will," he said. "They will want to know."

That evening, Rynn and two others crossed the short path to the Neanderthal camp. Ahna stayed in the *Homo sapiens* camp with Serna, daughter of Terah.

Rynn spoke quietly to the elders, telling what he knew about Torg's conduct. Details were shared. Not in anger. Not in heat. But with clarity.

"This man," said Rynn, "has shown he is a danger to people in both clans."

The youngest elder, who had not been to many such gatherings, asked, "Should Torg be severely punished?"

Goma answered, and the elders exchanged looks. "Our ways allow only the punishment necessary to protect the clan. If Torg is truly a danger, he should be removed from access to either clan by whatever means are required."

Every elder nodded in agreement.

Tov, feeling older by the day, said, "Our clans now mix blood. A danger to one clan is a danger to both."

The next day, Torg was summoned by the *Homo sapiens* elders.

He came reluctantly, suspicion already souring his face. He stood and faced the most respected members of the clan.

"You know why you are here?" asked Duma.

"I know you all stand against me," Torg replied.

"We have watched. Listened. Too long, maybe," said Omak. "You have been warned many times."

Torg shrugged. "I hunt. I feed the camp. I will provide meat for the celebration."

"You too often take what's not yours. Touch women you should not touch. And recently you frightened a child."

"She lied."

"Enough!"

The word came from Omak. Just one word, but strong.

Duma stepped forward. "We have decided on a final warning. You are not to cross the river, not to get near to the camp of the *others*. You are to remain here and you may attend the upcoming celebration. After that, the elders will meet again to decide whether you will be allowed to stay."

Torg's face twisted. "You had best decide I can stay."

"It is a settled matter. We will meet after the celebration to discuss our choices at that point," said Omak.

Torg spat again, this time in the direction of Omak. Then he stormed off without another word.

During the days that followed, Torg was not allowed to leave camp, except as part of a hunting party.

On the days he did not hunt, Torg sulked at the edge of the *Homo sapiens* camp, sharpening bone blades and muttering to himself. Members of the clan avoided him. Children were told to stay near their parents. Women would walk only in groups.

The celebration was in nine days.

Five nights before the celebration was to begin, Torg was seen again—first, near Ahna's shelter while Rynn was hunting, peering in through openings in the hides, and later standing near the river bank, staring across in the direction of the Neanderthal camp. Watching.

While members of both clans prepared joyfully for the shared celebration and the honoring of the child born to two peoples, Torg kept to himself—steaming and brooding.

He had not vanished; he had turned his anger over and over inside himself, and the turning heightened his desires until his own plan of revenge began to take form.

At the same time, unknown to Torg, the elders of each clan had begun to form their own plans. Each imagined a future shaped by cooperation and trust—the same hope carried by Ahna and Rynn—a future in which Torg had no place.

Chapter Twenty-Four

A hna curled up on the furs in the shelter as the steady sound of her daughter's nursing slowed with the approach of sleep. Ahna's body was tired and her mind troubled. Sleep came only in waves.

Since giving birth, Ahna's dreams had been unsettling. She had seen herself walking through a forest where the trees had no tops, only trunks that stretched into an endless fog. She heard the crying of a baby girl—soft at first, then louder as if getting closer. The trunks swelled and shrunk, pulsing as if following their own internal rhythm.

She turned and saw an imposing figure limping in the fog—broad-shouldered, watching with glowing yellowish eyes, like a saber-toothed tiger.

The soil beneath her feet felt like ash. She did not know where her daughter was—maybe gone. She looked down at her hands. Empty. No sign of a child.

She looked up and saw an older woman, her face painted with red ochre, standing by a fire that burned green and blue. The woman lifted a hand, and on her palm was a drawing of a tiger with blood on its jaw.

A voice—not spoken, but alive in her chest—said, "The danger comes not from the dark. It walks in the fire."

The dream ended as she awoke—gasping for breath, heart pounding, arms clutching for her child.

She sees Yana safe beside her, but fear remains.

The day after this latest dream, Ahna carried Yana and walked with Rynn to the place near the river where they first met. Yana is wrapped in fur and held in a sling across Ahna's chest. Ahna's eyes are heavy.

"You look as if the spirits chased you all night," Rynn said as he sat, attempting to be humorous, but gentle.

Ahna sat beside him and said nothing at first. She traced lines in the sand with a stick, circling the shape of a man and then drew a spiral near it.

"Evil is always close by," she said, quietly. "Evil that touches with hunger. Evil that waits for a woman to be alone. Evil that watches his prey—me. Not with wonder. With want."

Rynn stiffened. "I know. Be patient a while longer."

"He watches girls in both camps now," she said. "I see it wherever I look, and I am told about it by my people across the river. Torg carries fear wherever he goes. People in both clans draw back when he comes near. Even the old ones feel it, though they speak less of such things. We are told to bear it, to avoid him, to be clever, that something will soon be decided. But why must we wait, just to be safe?"

Ahna did not cry, but her voice broke slightly as she continued, "I dreamed again last night that our daughter may be in danger. In the darkness, a tiger appeared—a hunter with jaws dripping blood, stepping out from the fire. I think the dream was a warning. For me. For us."

Rynn sat quiet for a long time. He remembered the way Torg bragged about a kill that was not his. The way he shoved past a young girl near the food fire. The way others laughed nervously, not because it was funny, but because they feared him.

Rynn looked at Ahna. "Your dream. Maybe it is not just for you."

"I know," she said. "I think many women dream it. We fear that speaking it could make things worse."

Rynn understood that leadership and strength are more than locating herds in winter, or starting a fire in the rain. It is also about protecting the clan from danger—danger from outside the clan and danger from within.

Realizing that Ahna's fear of Torg was shared by many others struck at Rynn's heart. He believed that when fear takes root in dreams and daily worry, the time to fight back has come

"Will you tell the others about this dream?"

She hesitated, then said, "I will tell the women. But the men must hear it from their women. It must be a burden shared where intimacy is threatened."

That night, Ahna slept again, but this time she dreamed not of the hunter or the fire. She dreamed that she stood before a wide valley with Yana in her arms. Many women stood behind her like a wall of stone. A glow of embers could be seen below, but its heat did not reach them.

Ahna woke and smiled—not because she no longer felt danger, but because she has seen what danger looks like when it is faced and shared.

The next night, while Ahna lay curled in the shelter, the rhythmic feeding of her child gave her great comfort. The fire outside the shelter had died down to glowing coals. Around her, the sounds from other shelters had quieted—the crackle of hushed voices, the shift of bodies settling into hides laid on grass and reeds on soft ground. She had wrapped Yana in a soft hide and made sure she was warm, and yet still, she could not fully rest.

Her muscles ached from the day's work. Her arms were heavy from scraping hides, her back tight from foraging. But it was not the body alone that held her from sleep.

When she finally was able to find rest, a vision again arrived in a dream, like a cold wind piercing her furs.

She first noticed a feeling behind her eyes—a quiet pressure, as if something in her mind was waiting to act.

In her dream, Ahna stood among towering trees whose roots were intertwined beneath the soil. Each tree swayed with the wind, but together their roots held the ground steady. She woke, well aware of the meaning of this dream and its connection to her previous dream: Strength comes not in standing alone, but in standing connected.

When fully awakened, she smiled because she felt free from fear. She smiled because she has seen how it looks to stand united, spreading one's fear among a group—so that fear is no longer borne alone.

The next afternoon, as the light grew long across the ridge and the evening fires were lit for meal preparation, Ahna moved deliberately from shelter to shelter. She spoke few words. She extended a quiet invitation to each woman she could find: "Tonight, let us meet together at the hollow behind the red stone."

Not all came. But many did.

Ten women, of varying age and stature, gathered in the hollow—a shallow depression where the wind whispered through low branches, out of sight from the main camp. A baby whimpered. A young girl sat with her mother and watched with large eyes, unsure of what this was.

Ahna rested cross-legged on a flat stone, her daughter sleeping in the sling across her chest, chin nestled against the curve of her breast. She waited until the murmurs fell to stillness.

"I have dreamed," she said simply. "And I have felt fear. Not of beasts. Of a man."

A few heads lowered. Others stiffened.

"You all know him," Ahna said. "You have seen the way he moves. The way he waits. The way he looks. Not with the eyes of kin. Not with the eyes of a man who sees a woman he will treat with respect. He sees with hunger."

The women stayed silent at first, perhaps out of fear of coming forward, but there was a noticeable response: shoulders tensed, eyes narrowed in agreement, heads nodded. One woman, older, touched her own collarbone as if recalling a bruise long gone.

One younger woman, arms folded tightly, asked in a whisper: "You mean the muscular one. The fair-skinned one. The one who came many summers?"

Ahna met her gaze. "Yes. I mean Torg."

"He has no parent here, no brother, no sister," the girl said. "He is an unwelcome stranger in our clan."

Another woman added, "In all my summers, I have never seen another like him."

A murmuring began, uncertain. Ahna could see fear in their eyes—fear not only of Torg, but fear of change of any kind. Fear of people who were not of their people—those who used new tools, spoke new words, and had new ways.

She raised a hand.

"We must be careful with our fear," she said. "It is a wise thing, but it can also lie. Yes, Torg is of your clan, but he is not family to any of you—or to me."

They quieted.

"Many seasons ago," Ahna continued, "one of my clan was like Torg. But he was short and wide, not fair-skinned and tall. He was a man of this very land, born in the forest, son to one of the hunters. He too touched and took without permission. He too followed girls when they walked alone. He stared too long. He said little, but he pressed a hand against a girl's mouth, once, to quiet her as he touched."

Gasps. A silence followed.

"What happened to him?" someone asked.

"The elders said that he left. Joined another clan."

"Did he?" another woman asked.

Ahna shook her head. "I do not know. There were rumors, though, that a member of the clan—or maybe several members together—had killed him. No one spoke openly of it."

A silence followed.

"But I remember," she continued, "how the clan felt after he was gone: relieved, relaxed, safer."

"Danger is not in the skin. Not in the shape of the face. It is not in the tools or the language or the campfire songs. It is not in what people are. It is in what they choose to do when no one stands up to stop them."

The women listened. Truly listened.

"We cannot know if others in either clan are like Torg. We must not treat any one as if they are. But we can know this: When a man shows himself to be dangerous, we must not carry that knowledge as a private fear."

There was a long pause. Then one of the women, middle-aged and quiet, spoke.

"My daughter said Torg watched her gather berries. She felt it. Not like seeing. Like being hunted."

Others murmured in agreement. Another added: "He followed me to the river several nights ago. I turned back early and called out. He left, but he was watching."

Still another said: "I told my girl to stay close. Not to wander. She should not need to fear her own camp."

One of the youngest girls in the group, no more than ten or eleven, leaned against her mother's knee. Her small voice rose: "He scares the birds when he walks."

The women laughed nervously—but not at her. It was a gentle laughter that arose from the release of fear and the recognition they were not alone.

"Yes," said her mother. "He does."

The laughter faded. What remained was solidarity.

Ahna sat with her hands on her knees and then added,

"We share the dream. We may not all see the same forest. But we feel the same eyes behind the trees. And we carry it in silence."

"What do we do?" asked the older woman.

"We tell the men," Ahna replied. "And we tell the elders. Not just whispers to the ones we trust. We speak. As a group. We say that there is danger. It wears a man's face. It lives among us."

A nervous pause. Then another woman said: "Will they believe us?"

"Yes, the elders are already aware," Ahna said. "And Rynn knows of the danger."

"Are the elders aware of the fear Torg brings to the women?" a doubter questioned.

"Yes. They are aware, but they do not understand how deeply fear now lives and breathes through the camp. They do not seem to be in a hurry to act."

A few of the women looked at one another—uncertain, yes, but feeling more secure than before.

Ahna continued to sit among the gathered women, her daughter cradled against her shoulder, listening as the voices rose and fell. They had spoken at length of Torg—his angry words, his grasping hands, the way his presence carried a shadow that unsettled the camp. Fear had given way to resolve. At last, Vyma, one of the oldest among them, placed a hand upon the ground as if anchoring their decision.

"It must be done," Vyma said. "We cannot whisper forever. He is no longer only a danger to one of us, but to us all. We must make sure the elders hear what we women know and what we fear."

Murmurs of agreement moved through the gathering. The women looked from one to another, the decision forming not in argument but in shared understanding. At last, Ahna lifted began to speak.

"We will go to the elders," she said. "All of us. But not all of us will speak. If we stand before them as a crowd with everyone trying to speak, they may dismiss our fears —and not see the depth of danger we know that Torg is. Better that two or three speak clearly for us all."

After a moment, Sira stepped forward. "I will speak. I have felt his hand too many times. My words need to be heard."

Ahna met her gaze and nodded. "And I will speak with you. His threats have already touched my life, and I will not remain silent. My child deserves safety."

Vyma reached out, her hand briefly brushing Ahna's arm. "I will be there, but not as a speaker. You can tell the elders that Torg unsettles even the old who have seen many winters. Tell them that his spirit is a danger to each clan."

Ahna stood, gathering her sling against her shoulder. Yana stirred but did not cry.

She said one last thing before leaving the hollow:

"Fear is not weakness. When it brings us together, it becomes a wall—strong, unbroken. And no man can walk through a wall."

And with that, she turned and began to walk back to her shelter, her daughter pressed to her heart.

Behind her, the women remained—no longer waiting to be told what to feel, but beginning to feel what they had long refused to act on.

The next evening, Ahna and several women members of the clan asked to meet with the elders.

Several elders agreed to hear their concerns. They agreed to meet the next morning at Omak's shelter.

When the group of women reached Omak's shelter, the two chosen to speak—Ahna and Sira— entered first. The others followed and took their places along the edges of the shelter. None raised a voice. Hands brushed as they passed, fingers lingered briefly on an arm—small, silent gestures of strength and shared resolve.

In the center of the shelter, four elders sat in a circle: three men—Duma, stooped but sharp-eyed; Omak, feeling the weight of responsibility; and Enu, the youngest of the four, but already gray at the temples. Beside them sat Terah, the lone woman elder present, her gaze steady as she gestured for the women to speak.

Sira spoke first, her voice steady though her hands trembled. She told of Torg's anger, of how he pushed aside boundaries with a smirk that held no respect. Ahna added her account—his words, his looming presence, the way he set unease through the camp like a fire smoldering in dry grass. She lifted her daughter for the elders to see. "I cannot raise her in fear. If he is not stopped, the child will grow in a camp where danger walks in daylight."

And then, invited by the elders to speak, one woman after another shared their words, stories, and fears.

The elders listened in silence: Omak's brow furrowed; Duma shifted uneasily; Terah folded her hands in her lap and gave a slow nod; and Enu grunted in disgust.

At last, Omak spoke, his voice a rasp from living so many summers. "We hear you. We have also heard from Rynn and others. These matters are not taken lightly. Leave us now. We will seek a way forward."

The women withdrew, the hush of night falling around them as they stepped back into the camp.

Within the shelter, the fire crackled. For a long time no elder spoke. Then Omak lifted his head, his eyes reflecting the glowing red light of the embers. "We have few choice left to consider."

His words hung in the smoky air, and the elders sat in silence, knowing that a decision was about to be made.

Chapter Twenty-Five

S moke curled above the fire pits in lazy spirals, thick with the scents of roasting meat and the fragrance of damp pine needles rising from the flames below. The aroma of the feast drifted through the trees and over the camp, filling the air with promise.

At the forest's edge, ancient trees bore witness to lives merging and passing as seasons followed one another, rivers shifted, and a changing climate—bringing storms and migrations—left an imprint for future generations to discover. Here, *Homo sapiens* and Neanderthals gathered— not for battle, not for trade, but for shared celebration.

They came to celebrate the birth of a child born to Ahna and Rynn—a child of both Neanderthal and *Homo sapiens* blood, an infant accepted by both clans. Yana—a girl with dark hair, wide eyes, and curious hands—stood as living proof that the two peoples, despite their differences, could share a future.

The fire burned brightly, casting a golden sheen across their faces. Ahna sat with daughter Yana on her lap, her hand resting protectively over the child's small chest.

Rynn was closeby, filling gourds with a tart drink made from crushed berries.

The child Yana, only a few moons old and not yet walking, babbled and clapped, delighting in the feel of so many eyes upon her.

At dawn tomorrow, the two clans—her mother's people and her father's—would hold a ceremony to welcome her and the coming together of peoples her birth represented.

Tonight was for feasting.

The celebration had begun long before the fire was lit.

At first light, the women of each clan had awakened and had began the quiet labor of the day. Ahna, acceptance of her presence growing among the *Homo sapiens*, had joined with them in the day's activities without hesitation —encouraged by the gentle nod of Terah giving her enthusiastic approval. It was a time Ahna's hands could move freely among theirs—without distrust or suspicion.

The women started preparing the roots—pale, knotted tubers pulled from the soft banks of the nearby river. They roasted some directly in coals to bring out their sweetness, while they pounded others flat with stones and mixed in crushed acorns and pinches of dried algae and other river plants. The result was a kind of cake—dense and nutty, wrapped in broad, waxy leaves and tucked beneath hot ash to bake.

Next came the berries—late-season blackcaps, dark and tender, mixed with hand-picked hawthorn fruit and the last of the dried elderberries. These were crushed with small round stones and stirred with boiled water and bark syrup, then poured into thick gourds to sit for much of a day, a process they had discovered produced a delightful tartness.

The mixture would give off a pungent and sharp smell, and would be ready soon to drink—bubbling and tangy, but surprisingly smooth.

Children were forbidden a taste, though one or two older boys had already stolen sips and now lurked near the edge of the campfire with flushed cheeks and wide eyes.

The meat required the most care.

Long before the sun climbed, Rynn's friend Daul, a stocky, young hunter and two other *Homo sapiens* had prepared the cuts—washing them with boiling river water, trimming the sinew, rubbing them with crushed garlic bulbs and the inner bark of spruce, which gave the meat a citrusy tang when smoked. They sprinkled dried wild thyme over the surface and pressed it in with their fingers. Then, using sharpened willow skewers, they threaded the strips and hung them over slow-burning green wood to roast for much of the day.

Other pieces of meat were wrapped in river clay and buried beneath coals. As the outer shell hardened, it trapped the juices within. When cracked open later, the aroma would spill out rich and savory.

Women stirred stone bowls of marrow and rendered fat, folding in ash-cooked garlic and dried herbs. When the meat was finished, this mixture would be brushed over it in thick glazes, making it glisten in the firelight.

Near the edge of the clearing, two Neanderthal men ground dried fern seeds and fireweed blossoms together with powdered fishbone to make a seasoning paste. This paste was a tradition handed down over generations—a bitter, briny, tangy flavor that brought out hidden tastes in even the coarsest meat.

No part of the food was prepared without intention.

Before anything was set over the flames, the eldest woman from each group came forward—the elder Marga, and Ina, who long ago had lived with Marek. Each held a piece of raw meat in one hand and an herb bundle in the other. They circled the main fire pit three times, chanting softly, and then knelt to press the meat and herbs into the ash beside the fire.

A gift to the ancestors—a promise of gratitude.

Only after that did the firelight begin its slow rise.

Rynn called for silence, standing as flames danced behind him. "We give thanks for this night," he said, his voice steady. "For life, for food, and for what we make together—this new family, this new blood."

Some murmured agreement. Others raised their drinks. A few Neanderthals with the weariness of many summers in their eyes said nothing. But none walked away.

Food passed from hand to hand: thick haunches of meat blackened on the outside, tender within; mashed roots folded with crushed nuts; sweet berries warmed near the fire to release their sugars. Children tore into the food with abandon. Adults were only slightly more restrained.

The Neanderthal elder, Goma—Ahna's uncle—gnawed at a rib and nodded his approval. "Tough beast," he said. "Fought well, I imagine."

Daul replied without hesitation. "We tracked it for a long time. Cornered it in the gully by the broken rocks."

"You strike as one?"

"We struck as one," Daul repeated.

"Good. The child will need a clan that moves as one."

They tapped their gourds.

Not far away, Ugna—Ahna's cousin and one of the oldest Neanderthal women in the group—tore into a thick strip of meat. Her sharp eyes narrowed. She was used to the texture of roe dear and the sweet tang of hare. This was different—stronger, denser, almost sour at the edges. Not bad, but not a flavor she recognized. Probably cooked too long, she thought. She said nothing. She did not fit in easily with strangers, and her poor speaking skills only added to her hesitancy to say anything.

From the far side of the fire, Dorran, a Neanderthal spear-maker, watched Ugna's expression as she ate. He, too, had noticed something. The fat melted differently. The fibers resisted the tooth. But he drank deeply and said only, "Strange flavor on this one. What is it?"

"Mountain cat," said Daul, leader of yesterday's hunting party with Rynn that had brought back the kill. "Not saber tooth. A smaller cat. Have only seen one like it before."

"Smaller, huh," Dorran said, almost to himself.

"Still snarled like a demon," Daul added with a chuckle, and then added, "Looked very much like the cat that attacked Torg two days ago."

There was silence.

Only the wind and the fire spoke.

Torg.

The name had not been spoken since his death.

According to Daul, while on a hunt with Torg, they had been attacked by a rarely seen type of cat, one a bit smaller than a saber tooth.

At the time of his death, Torg was hunting alone with Daul, three other hunters having returned to camp. Daul brought no body back—just meat from earlier in the hunt.

Torg's body had been hauled off by a saber-toothed cat that had joined the smaller cat's attack.

Daul, separated from Torg, could see from a distance what was happening, and even though he tried to help, he was lucky to escape being attacked himself.

There was nothing Daul could do—other than bring back meat he and Torg had taken before the fatal attack.

As the celebration continued, no one missed Torg, and his name was not mentioned again.

Torg had been a violent man—a man with a lot of self-serving charm early on, who had no feelings for members of either clan. He laughed at the pain of others. He touched without asking. He made threats—and followed through when he could. No one mourned his passing. Not even Duma, who had known Torg since he first joined the clan many summers ago.

Daul said nothing more about Torg's death, but he could readily envision Torg's final moments. In fact, he found himself often thinking about those moments.

The hunt began like any other.

The mist clung low along the valley floor as Daul, Torg, and three other hunters moved in silence, spears in hand, eyes scanning the stone outcroppings where prey often nested before the sun set.

Torg led the way, uninvited to lead, but impossible to dissuade. He claimed to have seen fresh tracks, and since Daul had seen nothing, Torg took the lead.

After spending half the day without seeing any tracks, the three other hunters left to return to camp.

Now alone with Torg, Daul watched him with the same caution one gives a hungry wolf. Daul had seen Torg become worse with every passing moon: his voice louder, his stares longer, his hands quicker. And when, not too long ago, he struck a child—barely crawling, reaching out with innocent fingers toward Torg's treasured flint scraper—something unspoken triggered in Daul.

He decided that Torg would not harm her again. Not known by Torg, Daul had joined a growing group that wanted Torg removed from the clan.

After the three other hunters left, Torg, followed by Daul, crested a ridge of broken stone and descended into a grove where a river curled beneath a canopy of bark-stripped trees. There, at last, they found tracks—fresh, deep, and wandering. But no cat in sight. No elk. No boar.

Torg stopped.

"This is where I piss," he muttered, stepping away, tossing his spear to the ground with a thud.

Daul waited, spear in hand.

After a few moments, Daul positioned himself not far behind Torg. Because of his willingness to act, Daul had been chosen by the elders to free the clan from this danger.

He picked up Torg's fallen spear and turned it over slowly in his hands, testing its weight.

When Torg turned, half-smirking, adjusting his pelt, he barely had time to speak.

"What are you—"

The blow landed just below the throat, angled upward, fast, brutal, and fatal. A single strike, sharp and quiet. Daul had aimed for the vessels in the neck. For efficiency. He knew where the bone ended and the soft places began.

Torg staggered, eyes wide, one hand clamping his neck. Blood pulsed through his fingers, dark and hot. He fell to his knees, gurgling. Daul stepped forward and smashed a heavy rock on the side of Torg's head. The sound that followed was mercifully short.

Silence settled in the grove like fog returning.

No words were spoken.

No one cried.

Daul stood for long moments, breath visible in the cool air, listening to the nearby river.

Then the work began.

Daul moved with a grim precision, honed by the frequent experience of skinning prey. Only this time, he avoided the face. Avoided the hands. Torg had to become something else. Animal. Game. Not a man.

Daul stripped what the clan could use—shoulders, thighs, rib meat. Wrapped it in hide. Disposed of what was too human to eat.

Then Daul scattered the remains where the saber-toothed cats would find them, smearing Torg's blood across moss and broken branches so the stench of fresh blood carried wide. The big cats would drag away limbs and crush the bones, smaller scavengers would rip at the scraps, and carrion birds would pick the bones until nothing remained.

Daul's thoughts reassured him.

The elders chose this fate.

He, Daul, was honored with being given the task.

The welfare of the clan must come first.

Daul nodded slowly and whispered to himself. *Torg will no longer hurt others.*

Blood stained the insides of Daul's wrists, and for a few moments he could not stop staring at them. After washing off all signs of the kill, Daul gathered his things and made a difficult decision: He would speak of Torg's death as an attack of saber-toothed cats. No one need to know any differently, not even the elders. He alone would carry this truth.

He carried the meat gathered that day back to the camp in silence. The truth was that Torg was dead, killed during a hunt. And for many nights, there would be food for all.

The stomach has its needs.

In times of food shortage, hunger is not easily satisfied, and nothing that once lived is wasted.

Fate has its needs.

* * *

Daul returned late from that fateful hunt, his arms heavy with meat. His face was set with weariness, the look of a man who had done something unpleasant that needed to be done. He told everyone of a never-before-seen cat—dangerous, elusive, and of a saber-toothed tiger.

No one questioned his story.

Two days after Torg's death, and one day after hunt with Rynn, Daul was ready to join the evening's feast.

Torg quickly became a bad memory, dressed in the skin of justice. Daul knew that the elders had told Torg that he would be allowed to attend the celebration. They kept their word—but only Daul was sure of it.

Torg had bragged that he would provide meat for the celebration—but only Daul knew he had.

The fire hissed as fat dripped down from the cooking meat. The smell was rich and inviting, mingling with pine needle smoke and the musk of wet hide.

Duma lifted a string of gristle from his lips. "Saber tooth cat or not, it satisfies in a strange way."

"Yes," agreed another elder.

And so they ate.

Yana, growing sleepy, nestled against Ahna's chest. Her brow—slightly prominent, like Ahna's—rested against the hollow of her mother's throat. Her fingers curled around the shell bead Rynn had carved several days ago. The firelight made her skin glow golden brown, and both her parents watched as her eyes finally closed.

"She dreams already," whispered Ahna.

Rynn nodded. "She carries all our dreams now."

A hush settled over the camp, the word "dreams" spreading like warmth from the fire. For the first time, some of the *Homo sapiens* turned their faces toward the Neanderthals. Toward Ahna. Toward the child.

Ugna rose and stepped forward, standing over the fire with a half-eaten scrap of meat still in her hand.

"When I was small," she said, "the elders told us to watch the first shoots in spring. They were fragile, easily broken, yet they carried the promise of what would feed us later. New life, they said, must be guarded."

She took the last bite from the bone and set it aside. "Tonight I think of that promise."

Her eyes found Ahna. Then Rynn.

No one spoke.

With a smile and a nod to the couple, she sat again.

Omak cleared his throat. "Tomorrow we officially welcome Yana to the clan."

"Tomorrow," someone echoed.

"But tonight," Omak continued, "we remember who we have been—and who we are becoming. Once, we were two peoples, choosing to stay apart. Tonight we see ourselves joined by Yana, a child of two peoples. Because of her we are no longer divided. We are now one clan, together."

"Together," said Rynn.

"Together," Ahna repeated.

The firelight caught on the stones around their necks, the beads carved from shell and tooth, the cords of twisted bark. The old ways glimmered beside the new. Someone began to drum—softly at first, then stronger. Feet found rhythm. Hands clapped. And the dance began.

It was awkward at first. Neanderthal steps were heavier, *Homo sapiens* steps more fluid. But they adjusted. Laughed. Moved in circles.

Ahna took Rynn's hand and led him into the dance. Duma rose, groaning but grinning, and clapped along. Even Ugna, after a long silence, let herself be pulled into the ring by a younger man.

From the shadows, children watched. They would remember this. It would become a story.

The night deepened. The drink ran low. The stars blinked behind a veil of fire smoke. At the edge of the clearing, where shadows thickened, a few of the hunters sat apart, saying nothing, each chewing with slow, measured bites.

Daul sat apart for a moment, watching the child, then the flames. He thought of Torg's last words—panicked, gurgled, laced with threat. He thought of the moment the spear slid into the soft place beneath the jaw. He had not hesitated.

Torg had threatened to take everything from them.

Now they all shared in his demise.

He heard Duma's voice beside him. "Sometimes bad spirits live in bodies too long. The old stories say they must be broken apart and placed in better bodies to be quieted."

Across the fire, Ugna spoke again. This time, her voice was softer.

"We were not always two peoples. Long ago, before language and distance split us, we shared the same sky."

"And now we share the same blood," said Ahna.

"Yes," said Ugna. "And now we share the same child."

A murmur followed.

Duma rose one last time that night and raised his arms.

"Let it be known," he said, "that from this night, no child born of the joining of two peoples shall be cast out. Let it be known that this one"—he gestured toward the sleeping Yana—"has brought the fire into the center again."

He let the words settle.

Then, he added, almost as an afterthought:

"And let it also be known: the animal that tried to destroy us was eaten by our strength. And we are stronger for it."

Several *Homo sapiens* elders exchanged questioning glances, eyebrows lifting, mouths slightly opening—then closing again—but no one said anything.

Nothing more followed, and the night wound down with song. One voice, then another, adding layers of harmony—simple, primal tones rising like smoke.

Yana, child of two clans, slept between her parents, her small body rising and falling in peace. By morning, a new chapter would begin—written in the hearts of two peoples, and lived through her.

The feast had been more than food. It was a sign that what once divided could truly be shared, that even fear and cruelty could be consumed by fire and left in ash.

What endured was not the mistrust and suspicion that had long kept the clans apart, nor the dark memory of Torg, but the bright promise of a child who carried the best of both people in her small body.

Around the embers, the clans sang together while stamping the ground in unison. Firelight flickered across faces once wary, now bright with laughter and friendship, as the stubborn grip of old thinking eased into the night.

Together—bound by the child who carried them both—the two clans danced into a future neither clan could have imagined alone.

THE END

Final Thoughts
A Shared Legacy

"Evolution has no purpose; man must supply this for himself."
— George Gaylord Simpson

At the Threshold of Disappearance

Human evolution is often imagined as a staircase—one step leading neatly to the next, culminating in us. But the real story is tangled, branching, and unfinished. When Neanderthals and *Homo sapiens* lived side by side, roughly between 60,000 and 35,000 years ago, they faced the same shifting climates, the same predators, and the same fragile margins of survival. Their coexistence reveals that evolution is not a contest of superiority, but a series of experiments running simultaneously, each shaped by circumstance, chance, and relentless environmental change.

Neanderthals endured those changes for more than 450,000 years, surviving repeated ice ages, long droughts, and rapid climate swings. Their tools—carefully shaped flakes, blades, and hafted points—were feats of precision, crafted for close-range hunting in dense forests. They tended fires, carried embers from camp to camp, wore hides from their prey, and adorned themselves with beads and pigments. They cared for their wounded, kept elders alive long after injuries should have been fatal, and buried their dead with flowers and ritual gestures.

Homo sapiens, who entered Europe far later, were equally skilled but differently oriented. Their tools allowed for more flexible hunting strategies; their networks of exchange reached farther; their groups moved more frequently, adapting rapidly to new environments.

For much of the twentieth century, Neanderthals were dismissed as dim, brutish figures stumbling toward extinction. But the stereotype has collapsed beneath the weight of genetic, archaeological, and cultural evidence: Neanderthals were intelligent, deliberate, social, and creative. They were humanity in another form—with their own strengths, their own ways of understanding the world, and their own rhythms of life.

By 35,000 years ago, the archaeological record narrows and goes silent. Neanderthals vanish, leaving only scattered remnants of bone, tools, and pigment found on cave walls. They also left a remnant far more enduring: traces of their DNA.

Why One Lineage Faded While Another Endured

For decades, scholars argued that Neanderthals died out because *Homo sapiens* were smarter, more innovative, or more adaptable. But recent evidence reveals a subtler, harsher truth: Neanderthals may simply have faced too many converging misfortunes at once.

Climate instability transformed Europe's forests into open plains, depriving Neanderthals of the dense cover their ambush-style hunting required. New pathogens—carried by incoming *Homo sapiens* from Africa—may have struck Neanderthals with devastating force. Small, scattered populations made loss recovery more difficult.

Across thousands of years, the two lineages met, interacted, and interbred. In 2010, the sequencing of the Neanderthal genome confirmed what many had long suspected: Neanderthals did not fully disappear. Traces. Of their DNA live on within us today.

Almost all humans alive now carry Neanderthal DNA —typically between 1% and 2%—and nearly one-fifth of the Neanderthal genome survives, scattered across billions of *Homo sapiens* bodies. Mixed-lineage children were viable, fertile, and numerous; their descendants spread through Europe and Asia, carrying Neanderthal traits forward invisibly in the *Homo sapiens* genetic code, threading ancient influences through generations that followed.

Why, then, did our lineage dominate the map? Some anthropologists argue that *Homo sapiens* prevailed not because we were better, but because we were more restless and endlessly adaptive. We spread faster, reproduced more quickly, traveled farther, and reshaped our surroundings more aggressively. Neanderthals lived in smaller groups, stayed closer to familiar territories, and adapted more slowly to change.

Evolution seems to have favored the lineage that consumed more, moved more, and multiplied more.

Whether that was nature's wisdom—or merely its accident—remains an unsettling question.

If the Two Lineages Had Merged as Equals

Interbreeding did occur, but not as a full blending of worlds. In reality, Neanderthals were absorbed into a rapidly expanding *Homo sapiens* population. But imagine another history: one in which the two lineages merged as equals, long before one outnumbered the other.

The resulting world might have been shaped by a balance of complementary strengths. Neanderthals' steadiness, patience, and close-knit social bonds might have anchored the expansive energy of *Homo sapiens*. Their quieter, more deliberate approach to life might have moderated *Homo sapiens* restlessness. A merged species might still have invented agriculture, art, writing, mathematics, and science—but perhaps with a different emotional undercurrent:

- More local continuity, less conquest
- More sustainable pacing, fewer extractive surges
- Communities built on long-term attachment to land rather than rapid movement across it
- Technological development that valued stability as much as innovation

Cultural diversity might have been even richer. Two lineages with different ancestral memories, rituals, and modes of expression might have developed hybrid traditions, stories, and ways of understanding belonging.

Such a species might still have transformed the planet—but perhaps with fewer destabilizing leaps. Perhaps fewer empires. Perhaps greater emphasis on healthful continuity, rather than on pride of domination.

The Neanderthal inheritance within us—slim though it is—suggests that even limited merging broadened our cognitive and emotional repertoire. A deeper merging might have yielded a humanity more attuned to place, less driven by expansion, and more comfortable with slowness —a trait that modern society often treats as deficiency rather than wisdom.

This alternate humanity would not be less intelligent than us; its intelligence would be calibrated differently. Where we often privilege acceleration, they might have privileged depth. Where we innovate reflexively, they might have innovated selectively.

It is difficult to know whether such a world would be gentler, wiser, or simply different—but it is easy to imagine that a fully merged species would have carried forward more than genes. It would have carried forward two ways of being human, side by side.

Neanderthal Survival, *Homo sapiens* Extinction

Now imagine the second scenario: Neanderthals endure while *Homo sapiens* vanish. In this world, the more deliberate lineage becomes the inheritor of Earth.

The pace of history would immediately slow.

Neanderthals lived in smaller groups and maintained tight bonds of mutual care. Their lives were oriented around continuity rather than expansion. Their hunting strategies emphasized patience. Their population densities were so low that large-scale ecological damage to the environment would have been nearly impossible.

A Neanderthal world might never have developed agriculture as quickly as *Homo sapiens* did, nor built megacities or global networks. But it might also never have generated weapons capable of annihilating all life on Earth. It might not have saturated the atmosphere with carbon, destabilized the climate, or triggered mass extinctions at the speed modern humans have.

What would such a civilization look like?

- Fewer people, more land per person
- Deep memory of place, carried across hundreds of generations
- Complex social ethics centered on group stability
- Less rapid technological change, but longer cultural continuity
- A smaller ecological footprint and slower depletion of resources

They might have developed art, story, ritual, and perhaps even writing—though on a timescale far slower than ours. Innovation would occur, but without the explosive accelerations that define our history.

Would Neanderthals have reached the stars? No one can say for sure.

Would they have invented antibiotics? Very likely—given enough time and pressure.

Would they have preserved Earth's stability against climate change and the dangers of modern weapons longer than we have? Almost certainly.

Such a world would not be utopia. Many of life's hardships they endured would remain as challenges to be met. But it would likely be a world without the existential threats we now face: runaway climate change, nuclear annihilation, and artificial intelligence—being created at a rate faster than it's possible threats can be understood.

Our disappearance, in this alternate history, might have gifted life on Earth a longer, steadier future.

Both imagined histories start with the same belief: the disappearance of Neanderthals was not the loss of an inferior people, but the vanishing of a different kind of human possibility—a way of thinking, of moving through the world, of relating to one another. And what survived— our speed, our reach, our relentless exploring—has become both our strength and our greatest danger.

We *Homo sapiens* today are the children of two lineages, but the inheritors primarily of one. The faint threads of Neanderthal DNA we still carry may be reminders of another path once open to our lineage—a path slower, steadier, more attentive to connection and place.

We may not yet know how to use the faint Neanderthal memory carried in our DNA, but we can honor the qualities it represents—the discipline to act with care rather than haste, compassion for others, and a deep respect for the living world—and let those qualities guide the choices that will decide whether we continue to endure.

About the Author

Robert Mitchell is an educator and writer who has written extensively in the field of education and is now focusing on creative writing, both short stories and novels.

His literary publications include:

Sixteen Journeys, a short-story collection about ordinary people in pursuit of ordinary lives.

Beyond, his second short-story collection, with engaging tales of scientific and spiritual speculation.

Awaiting a Rising Tide, a love story—an emotionally rich novel about hope, courage, and belief in one's self.

The Neanderthal Within, the novel upon which this present volume derives—a richly imaginative epic, a tale of love and survival set 40,000 years ago.

The Neanderthal Within: Historical Context Edition, this book—an expanded edition of *The Neanderthal Within,* containing the complete novel along with informational essays. These essays are placed every four chapters and illuminate the scientific discoveries that support and contextualize the narrative.

Neanderthal Companion is a concise reference—based on scientific research—that compiles essays from *The Neanderthal Within: Historical Context Edition* into a unified volume. These essays illuminate what is known—and believed—about the Ice Age era in which Neanderthals and *Homo sapiens* intermingled and occasionally interbred.

A Note to Readers

The blank pages that follow are not the result of a printing error; they're simply the result of modern printing and layout requirements. Nothing is missing. They're just blank.

Perfect for jotting notes or doodling—if you're so inclined.

www.ingramcontent.com/pod-product-compliance
Lightning Source LLC
Chambersburg PA
CBHW020004120726
47903CB00004B/1136